Praise for y's Murdock ries

Murdock Tackles Taos (2013)

"Robert Ray is a gifted writer and the Matt Murdock series displays all his many talents. The prose is crisp, the characters vivid and the plot captivating. Read him now! Matt Murdock is part Jack Reacher, part Dave Robicheux. Fans of Lee Child and James Lee Burke will love *Murdock Tackles Taos*. A brilliant murder mystery with a splash of romance. The Matt Murdock series is one of my guilty pleasures!"
—Robert Dugoni, *New York Times* bestselling author

"I absolutely loved this book.... I give this a GIGANTIC 5 out of 5. Recommended for people who love the thrill of the chase, and the feeling of catching the bad guy in the act." Read more ...
—I Read a Book Once Blog

"What a mesmerizing read this turned out to be! Strong characters, thrilling adventure, psychological deviancy, (is that a word?), strong, well thought out plot and storyline ... an absolutely intriguing read!" Read more ...
—Beth Art from the Heart Blog

"Action and tension are high in a cleverly weaved 'whodunit' mystery. You actually know who did it very early on, but you read on for two reasons; one, the how do they get caught, and two, the why. I guarantee the why will knock your socks off."
—Joe Hempel, Top of the Heap Reviews

5 Stars: "A plot that is filled with action, mystery and suspense. This is the first book I have read in the 'A Matt Murdock Mystery Series' and was totally engrossed throughout the whole book. Between the author's strong, believable, and well developed characters, and the many twists and turns within the story line, I was kept at the edge of my seat wondering what will happen next. Highly recommended for all crime, murder mystery fans."
—Susan Peck, My Cozie Corner

"Murdock makes me smile. He's not a suave, sophisticated James Bond. He's not a disheveled, bumbling Colombo either. He's real. He's kind. He's somebody to share a good adventure with."
—Arleen Williams, author of The Thirty-Ninth Victim

"As with all of Ray's books, this one is so well written it's a pleasure just to say the words. When Ray brings Helene Steinbeck, his second sleuth, on stage he drags Murdock into the 21st Century with a bang .... In this book, the rich eat the poor. Steinbeck and Murdock set things right."
—Jack Remick, author of Blood, Gabriela and the Widow and The California Quartet series

"Robert J. Ray has succeeded in doing what Michael McGarrity excels at: developing characters that you want to take home."
—Marie Romero Cash, artist and author of the Jemimah Hodge Mystery series

"Game, set, match. Murdock Tackles Taos puts readers through their paces, serving up breakneck action, intrigue and murder in this winner-takes-all mystery thriller set in serene Taos, N.M. Can't wait for Murdock's next case!"
—L.M. Archer, freelance author and wine blogger

Murdock Cracks Ice (1992)

"Hard-nosed P.I. fare, with romance singeing the edges while our hero tries to toe the no-commitment line. Good reading, with frisky Chen and Hana definite scene-stealers."
—*Kirkus Reviews*

"The novel, crammed with action, moves rapidly on Ray's smooth prose and strong characterizations. Unlikely as it may be, Ray and Murdock make it believable."
—*San Antonio Express-News*

"For all the violence of the drug scene, the lean, rich characterizations provide a break from the grim realities that feels very much like life, in which love and the companionship of others bring relief and hope. Then, too, the plot moves briskly, with a kind of spare clarity that reflects Murdock's personality."
—*Cape Cod Times*, Hyannis, MA

"Robert Ray has woven a complex web of crime and intrigue that is sure to snare the reader and keep him hooked. And Murdock's chili recipe (page 8) is a good one, too!"
—*Mostly Murder*

"A welcome addition to the ever growing ranks of fine Seattle mysteries."
—*Seattle Times/Seattle Post-Intelligencer*

Merry Christmas Murdock (1989)

"*Merry Christmas Murdock* delivers a knockout punch. It comes wrapped in action and violence. But inside its rough exterior there is warmth and humor. Much like the hard-boiled detective whose story it tells."
—*The Clarion-Ledger*, Jackson, Mississippi

"Riveting. Private-eye Murdock is a sophisticated Mike Hammer, and Ray writes with the sardonic wit of a Mickey Spillane mixed with the insight of a Parker."
— *Tribune*, South Bend, Indiana

"It may be the best Murdock yet, representing a stylistic plateau for Ray .... the reading experience is immensely pleasurable. Ray has become the proverbial incurable romantic and some of the turns of phrase in *Merry Christmas* are irresistible, the kind one wants to read more than once."
— *The Register*, Orange County California

"It's nicer still when there's a decent yarn to spin, decently told, and this latest of the Matt Murdock capers is better than decent. .... This is an easy, unpretentious read. And Murdock is really awfully nice to be around."
— *The Drood Review of Mystery*

"It's a fast-moving, what-will-we-find-out-next story, with some likable characters and some you love to hate."
— *Chronicle*, Houston, Texas

"What a find author Robert J. Ray is .... Perhaps best of all, Mr. Ray has the rare ability to build tension bit by bit by bit and keep much of this throughout the last two-thirds of the book, almost without pause .... A crackerjack piece of plotting and writing and unhesitatingly recommended."
— *Mystery News*

"The style is punchy, the fast talk is zippy and the final shoot-out a honey."
— *Trenton Times*

"I liked the action-packed story line, the resiliency of the hero and the nifty, lucid prose."
— *Cape Cod Times*, Hyannis, MA

"Robert Ray's style is constant action leavened with antic laughter and surprising flashes of romance .... Murdock, a classic tough guy type, thrives in the land of gridlocked freeways and transplanted Midwesterners. He brashly confronts a host of foes, sorts through an avalanche of clues and finally prevails in a climatic shootout. Just another day for the irrepressible Murdock ...."
—*St. Louis Post-Dispatch*

"Fast-paced and easy to read, the adventure mystery won't be disappointing to the folks who like to get away from it all for a few hours by using someone else's imagination."
—*Press Register,* Mobile, AL

"Murdock is as hard-boiled as a 10-minute egg."
—*The Plain Dealer*

Dial "M" for Murdock (1988)

"Ray's well-wrought consideration of what can happen to those overtaken by 'greedy little-boy dreams' will leave readers eager for the next Murdock adventure."
—*Publisher's Weekly*

"Fast, accomplished and slick."
—*Kirkus Reviews*

Murdock For Hire (1988)

"The Robert Ray talent unfolds with every book and Matt Murdock becomes more and more likable and his friends more lovable."
—*Amarillo Sunday News-Globe*

"The central character is a rare find—tough, lonely, and incurably romantic."
—*Booklist*

"The writing is clear and direct, there is plenty of action, and even a romance."
—The *New York Times* Book Review

Bloody Murdock (1986)

"The Austin scenes are brief, but if you are a fan of the hard-boiled but sensitive private eyes of Raymond Chandler and John D. Macdonald, you will feel at home with Ray."
—*American-Statesman*, Austin, TX

"The story never stops and the lushly decadent southern California life was never more so."
—*Publishers Weekly*

MURDOCK ROCKS SEDONA

MURDOCK ROCKS SEDONA

A Matt Murdock
Murder Mystery

Robert J. Ray

CAMEL
PRESS

Seattle, WA

Camel Press
PO Box 70515
Seattle, WA 98127

For more information go to: www.camelpress.com
www.robertjrayauthor.com

Cover design by Sabrina Sun

Murdock Rocks Sedona
Copyright © 2016 by Robert J. Ray

ISBN: 978-1-60381-337-2 (Trade Paper)
ISBN: 978-1-60381-883-4 (eBook)

Library of Congress Control Number: 2015951906

Printed in the United States of America

This book is for Margot,

who took me to Sedona

to see the Red Rocks.

The nature of Infinity is this: That every thing has its Own Vortex; and when once a traveller thro' Eternity Has pass'd that Vortex, he perceives it roll backward behind His path, into a Globe itself enfolding, like a sun, Or like a moon, or like a universe of starry majesty, While he keeps onwards in his wondrous journey on the Earth, Or like a human form, a friend with whom he liv'd benevolent.

—William Blake

Turning and turning in the widening gyre, the falcon cannot hear the falconer.

—W.B. Yeats

Acknowledgments

JACK REMICK HELPED ME through every phase of this book, from the rough drafts at Louisa's to the cutting away of useless stuff, so I could focus on the spine. Catherine Treadgold taught me about villains and suspense. She is a terrific editor and a stalwart publisher. The writers at Louisa's Bakery and Bar listened to nine months of unborn, vestigial prose, while I struggled to give birth to this book which had been in my left brain for years. Thanks to my wife Margot, I can still work at this advanced age.

Prologue
Falling Man

The waitress with the black wig brought Walter a fresh drink, Martini on the rocks, aromatic Bombay gin, three olives, stabbed with a pink plastic spear. She flashed her smile, working on her tip.

"Do I know you?" he said.

There was a pause; she was selecting her answer. Three wives and multiple live-ins and beach-girls by the score, and Walter still didn't understand women. Her smile got brighter. She donated a bag of peanuts.

"You a gambler?" the waitress said. "I spent some time dealing cards in Vegas."

She did look familiar, no question. He did know her from somewhere. She was 40-something, tight hips, wise eyes, a girl who'd been around. Her face swam in his memory—sharp canines and a pouty mouth that could break your heart—but where had their paths crossed?

"What brings a girl like you to a place like Sedona?" he said.

"Guys like you," she said, and sauntered away. Walter knew that walk.

He turned back to the screen. It was Retro Film Night at

the Lemon Custard Bistro on Apple Avenue in Sedona. Six screens playing *The Big Lebowski*, smell of popcorn and weed.

A woman three tables away gave Walter the sign. A raised glass, a long look, a deliberate crossing of black leggings. The woman was blonde, tanned, inviting.

Walter walked over. She indicated the chair next to hers.

Her name was Doreen. She was traveling from L.A. to Miami, stopped off in Sedona to play tourist and waltz with a vortex. Up close, the blonde hair looked like a wig.

He felt her knee under the table. He finished his martini. The waitress appeared with a refill.

The second martini loosened him up.

Doreen sat closer. He smelled perfume.

He told her he was buying Sedona Landing, a historic hotel in picturesque Oak Creek Village, seven miles to the south.

Doreen was impressed.

The hotel was not all his. He was buying the ninth floor. Doreen was making sexual overtures. Had he ever waltzed in winter moonlight? For two hundred dollars, she could give him a taste of the vortex in the dark.

Doreen had Walter sweating. He was dressed for the outdoor life. A fast-dry T-shirt from ExOfficio. A wind-proof shirt from Abercrombie. A parka from North Face. The waitress came back. Doreen said "Hi, do I know you?" Walter watched the women shake hands. They did not seem like strangers. Two women wearing wigs—his lucky night.

DOREEN DROVE A LEXUS SUV.

She gave him the keys. Walter left his rental, a Cadillac Escalade, at the bistro.

They headed west, toward Cathedral Rock.

Walter had climbed it this morning; the trail was easy.

Doreen put her hand on his leg.

How come he wasn't married?

Walter was between wives.

He paid a ton in alimony, child support.

Her hand slid into his crotch.

The parking lot for Cathedral Rock was deserted.

Headlights from the Lexus bounced off reflective signs.

WELCOME TO CATHEDRAL ROCK.

Walter led the way up.

He'd been in Sedona for a week.

Had gotten lucky on Monday, a divorcée named Betty Sue something. Walter was 68, Betty Sue was early forties, with a knockout daughter. Betty's business was real estate. She lectured him—the plural of vortex was *vortexes*, and not *vortices*. Would he get lucky tonight?

Walter knew words. He had a BA from Princeton, an MBA from Wharton. An MFA from Rutgers. He knew proper singulars, proper plurals. The correct plural of vortex was *vortices*. The people in Sedona were dummies.

Close to the top, Walter felt the martinis.

A wave of dizziness.

"Are you okay?" Doreen asked.

"Gripped by the vortex," he said.

Doreen stood close. He liked her body heat. He liked her hand inside his pants. He heard a zipper being unzipped. His pants slithered to his knees. He saw a flash of light from the south. Some clown taking pictures in the moonlight.

The moon beamed down. Doreen went to her knees. Walter liked the way things were going. Every millionaire's dream—to get yourself undressed by a slave girl on her knees.

The boots were off.

The trousers were down. *Like shucking corn*, he thought.

Walter was waiting for an invitation. He believed in a woman's right to choose.

Women made you wait, consider, negotiate, get consensus, no worries.

Doreen got his trousers off, took his hands. Let's dance.

Out there to the south, Walter saw the tiny light winking.

Holding hands, they swung around, two lovers in moonlight.

A voice said, "Hello."

It was the waitress with the wig. She had exchanged her heels for hiking boots. She had a silver flask and three glasses. "Refills," she said. Walter was thinking, *Two is better than one.* His feet were cold. Doreen helped him with the boots.

The moon was bright now, cold yellow light, wind on his bare butt.

His wallet was in the trousers.

They had a drink.

Doreen stood next to Walter, her warm hip pressing.

You are not alone.

Doreen let go, the waitress gripped his hands. She wanted to dance. Walter was a baton, being passed from female to female. Where did he know her from?

She danced him in a circle; he was the vortex turning, churning.

She danced him close to the edge.

Did he remember her?

Inside his head, Walter flashed on a prairie town, red brick streets, elm trees in summer, Ackerman in shirtsleeves, a business housed in Quonset huts, a slim girl with red hair.

They whirled faster. He remembered her now. He whispered her name.

"You always had a good memory," she said.

And let him go.

Walter Findlay whirled in space.

He laughed. The tiny light was winking, closer now.

Before he hit the ground he saw the waitress.

On the edge.

Waving goodbye.

*****

THE LIGHT THAT WINKED in the dark came from a jazzy

camera belonging to Helene Steinbeck. The shooter was Matt Murdock, following orders. The camera was new. Helene wanted some pictures shot in the dark. "Get a shot of the moon," she said.

He'd asked her to come with him. She blocked him with excuses. Her feet still hurt, had he forgotten the rocks on Angel Mountain? She had to prepare for her writing workshop; the book was driving her crazy.

It wasn't just the book. They were having troubles with their relationship. Helene was avoiding him. She had stopped eating meat, was swimming twice a day. When Murdock asked was something wrong, Helene shook her head, gave him a bleak smile.

To keep busy, Murdock was helping at the hotel, spelling the desk guy, the security guy, the pool guy, giving Helene some space by running at night. His legs felt stronger. Maybe when he showed her the pictures, she'd give him a smile that said things were okay.

So he shot Cathedral Rock, using Helene's fancy new camera, a pricey megazoom. He shot the moon, hanging bright behind the mountain. He didn't know cameras or settings; he shot not caring what the camera would do. It was November, and Murdock was feeling the wind-chill. Time to head back to Sedona Landing.

Day One

I

A XEL ACKERMAN DREAMED OF falling.
He fell down the curved staircase at a fancy hotel.

He fell from a stepladder, changing a light bulb in a strange house.

He fell into a Dallas swimming pool, pushed by the woman who called him Pool Boy. He chased her through the kitchen, up the curved staircase, into the master bedroom. "Come on, Pool Boy, show me what you got." Her legs sprang open. Her red mouth mocked him. "Faster, Pool Boy. Sock it to me."

A flash from the doorway.

A fat kid firing a Kodak Instamatic.

His voice shrill in exaltation—"My Daddy's gonna kill you!"

"Should have aborted the fat one," the woman said.

Ackerman gave chase. The fat kid rode the banister with ease, grinning like a winner. Ackerman tripped on the landing, launched into a swan dive. The floor rose to meet him, and he heard laughter. "Now I got you, Pool Boy."

THE DREAM OF FALLING jerked Ackerman awake. He lay on the bed sweating, his heart loud, his calves cramping. He slept naked. He was 77 years old, skinny, too much pot belly. He had big hands and long arms, legs muscled from tennis, a twitchy prostate.

He sat up, feeling crazy, seeing the figure in the doorway—someone here to kill him. His feet were tangled in the sheets; his chrome-plated .45 was in the tennis bag, in the Executive Spa. A deep voice said, "Phone call, Master." The voice belonged to Bruno, his bodyguard, his brother-in-arms. The bedside clock said 5:10 a.m. Having to pee, he took the call sitting on the john.

The caller was Mrs. Walter Findlay, Walter's third ex-wife. What have you done with Walter? Are you boys crazy, buying an old run-down hotel? Walter was late with her alimony check, she said. Could Ackerman please send her ten grand, for old times' sake? He said okay. She hung up. The phone bristled with female frustration.

ACKERMAN DRESSED IN SWIM trunks, a bathrobe, Mexican sandals. He liked getting up early. He hated dreams about falling. Bruno walked beside him, looking bulky-burly in his white turtleneck. Bruno was black, born in Germany, an Army brat. He had a master's in art history. When he went to work for Ackerman twenty years ago, Bruno had been studying sculpture in Italy. They went through the security door, fresh carpet on the stairs, thanks to Ackerman's remodel.

Down on the ninth floor, Ackerman banged on Findlay's door, Suite 900. "Walter, you in there?" he called out. "Answer the goddamn door." There was no answer, so Ackerman tried his cell again. Goddamn the man. They had a meeting with Cypher at noon, the Vortex Bank. Findlay would cough up the cash, sign some papers—he was buying the ninth floor, he had wanted to buy Ackerman's penthouse. Today was Monday. The closing was a week away, and the owners were nervous.

They rode the elevator down to One—Lobby, Vestibule, Registration—where Giselle Roux met them with the contract, the book, and the cash envelope. Giselle looked tired. She had dressed for the day, jeans, a white shirt, a leather vest. The briefcase was a gift from Ackerman, a dozen years ago.

She had an MBA from Wharton, a year of architecture courses from The Design School in Tempe. She nodded at Bruno. They were like children taking care of a decrepit father, waiting for him to die. Ackerman okayed ten thousand for the ex-Mrs. Findlay. Trailed by Bruno, Ackerman and Giselle took the ramp past the Bell Rock Bistro to the pool where the woman was swimming her laps.

Ackerman swayed, tightened the belt of his robe. He was still feeling off-balance, blamed it on his dream of falling. Except for the woman, who was striking, he was wasting his time here, a fool's errand.

The woman's gear was piled on a chair. Rucksack, socks and Birkenstocks, her hotel robe. She swam with an easy crawl stroke, the product of early training—no visible effort, no wasted motion, smooth arms dripping, her shoulder muscles catching the light. She wore a white one-piece and a white swim cap.

The woman's name was Helene Steinbeck. She was here at Sedona Landing for a three-week writing workshop, engineered by Giselle Roux. Ackerman liked her pedigree—an ex-cop, a one-book writer, and two months ago she had killed a chief of police gone rogue, stopping his rampage, saving many lives by taking a single life in a crowded courthouse in Taos, New Mexico.

Ackerman was curious. He had never known a female killer.

2

HELENE STEINBECK LOVED SWIMMING.
She loved being alone in the hotel pool.

She loved slipping through the water, feeling sleek, wings of a dolphin.

She needed time to think through her relationship with Murdock. She kept retracing her time with him in Taos—their first meeting on Angel Mountain, their first kiss, their first time in bed, their first breakfast, the way they worked together on the case, the way Murdock looked at her, admiring, admitting she was smart, waiting for her to make a choice, that was so very big-time—when Giselle Roux arrived with Axel Ackerman, the billionaire who was buying Sedona Landing.

Why would anyone buy a hotel?

Helene was suspicious.

She had her mother's hair, skin, figure, love of art and literature.

She had her father's brain, his sharp eyes, his suspicious nose, his aversion to bullshit.

Rich men stepped on people on their way up the ladder. Who had this Ackerman guy stepped on lately?

The old man stood there watching her swim. His intense gaze stole her solitude, slaughtered her quiet, soft morning.

Helene was in her late thirties. Men still looked at her—they had been looking at her since she turned thirteen—but Ackerman's eyes did not hide their appraisal: *how much is this bitch worth?*

Helene made her turn, swam two more laps. When she climbed out, she saw the old man swimming, lane eight, along the wall, long arms, big bony hands to grab the water. Beside her clothes, Helene saw a table with coffee cups, a white pot, sugar, cream. Tea party at dawn.

Giselle was early forties, older than Helene. She had pretty blue eyes. There were silver threads in her red hair. Giselle had brought Helene to Sedona Landing for a writing workshop—Starting Your Mystery—three days a week, nine to noon. Giselle was the first writer to sign up. She wanted to be Helene's friend.

HELENE CHECKED THE BIG clock on the wall.

The time was 5:45. She had to shower, shave her legs, get dressed, eat, go over her notes, check with Murdock. He seemed ultra-restless in Sedona, nothing to do, no crimes to solve. The workshop started at 9 a.m. three hours from now—her first real job since resigning as Town Marshal on Drake Island.

"I wish I had time for coffee, but …."

Giselle handed over an envelope, 8x5, fattish-feeling. Inside, Helene found a thick wad of hundred dollar bills and a contract with simple terms: five thousand dollars for 24 hours of security work (body-guarding, detection), starting at signature time.

At the bottom of the page, Helene saw Ackerman's signature, then her name. Not Murdock's.

"Where's Murdock's name?"

"Axel wanted you."

"We're a team, Giselle."

"I'll speak to Axel."

"What are we detecting?" Helene said. "If we sign this thing."

"Someone's killing off his old friends, investors in this hotel. He says it's accidental. Old men die, Axel says."

"How many friends?"

"Two, so far. One in August, one in September."

"Where did they die?"

"The August death was on Fire Island," Giselle said. "The September death was in Palm Desert."

"We talking rich guys here?"

"Yes."

"How did they die?"

"They fell, both of them."

"Did you get police reports?" Helene said.

"Both deaths were ruled accidental."

"But you have this feeling, right?"

"More like an evil foreboding," Giselle said. "Something to do with this old hotel, its aura—like a shadow falling across your grave."

Helene saw movement.

Ackerman was out of the pool, being helped into his robe by a black man in a turtleneck sweater. The man wore a shoulder holster. His shaved head reflected the light. Giselle Roux identified him as Bruno Hoff.

Ackerman walked over, carrying a copy of Helene's book.

"Miss Steinbeck, your fame precedes you. I am reading your book. It would be an honor to own your autograph."

Up close, Axel Ackerman did not look so old, or so bony. His eyes were alive, filled with fire. The bald head was tanned and smooth and powerful. A man born to be king.

He had a beak nose and a winning smile that said he could buy and sell you before you knew what was happening. His teeth were yellow, his lips sensual.

"Is this for you?"

"Yes. To Axel, from Helene. And the date."

Helene signed his copy of her book. Her hand was jittery. This guy wanted her, this old person, bald and grinning, wanted to fuck her. She handed the book back. He read her words, nodded, held out his hand.

"Giselle was supposed to introduce us. I'm Axel Ackerman."

"I'm Helene Steinbeck."

His hand was big and warm, laced with power. He did not squeeze too hard. She was shaking hands with a billion dollars. She had met millionaires before, but Ackerman was her first billionaire. His hand let her go. She felt short of breath. He asked what she thought about the contract.

"Enough money to buy you for twenty-four hours?" he said.

"What about Murdock," Helene said. "We're a team. Where's his name?"

A shadow crossed Ackerman's eyes. He told Giselle to pencil Murdock in. She used a fancy fountain pen to add Murdock's name to the contract. Ackerman scribbled, turned to Helene.

"I heard your man was moonlighting, helping out our beleaguered hotel security boys."

"He likes to stay busy."

"But you did the Taos killings, right—no help from him?"

"Murdock was right there, backing me up," Helene said.

"Let's talk about the contract."

"Not much to discuss," Ackerman said. "I'm buying your combined skills—detection and protection—for twenty-four hours. I expect you to go through the motions, digging up dirt on my dead friends, but there's nothing there. Accidents happen."

"They both fell, right?"

"Will Tyler fell at twilight—highball time. Milt Coolidge fell because he had a trick knee. You got one drunk and one cripple, case solved."

Giselle Roux broke in, "Did you check with Walter?"

"I knocked on the goddamn door," Ackerman said. "No

answer. Probably got a floozie in there. Or maybe two."

"Who's Walter?" Helene said.

"One of our investors," Giselle said. "In the money pool. He's staying in 900, your floor, the suite at the other end."

"His name is Walt Findlay," Ackerman said. "Maybe you saw him around. He's tanned, fit, looks like a Beach Boy. Always on the prowl. His motto is love 'em and leave 'em."

"Walter thinks like a teenager," Giselle said. "He has three ex-wives ... that we know of."

"Let's have breakfast," Ackerman said. "You, me, Walt Findlay if we can rouse him, your Mr. Detective man. Eight-ish. You can guard my ancient body while in the midst of detecting, to satisfy Giselle. I'm halfway through your true-crime tome. I started at midpoint ... anything in the first half?"

"The author fell in love," Helene said.

"I love writers, the way they conjure."

Ackerman repeated his invitation to breakfast, eight o'clock, the Bell Rock Bistro, his personal table. The wait staff would know.

Helene watched him walk off, joined by Bruno, who carried a cellphone and a white sports bag with red markings.

Giselle handed over a purple binder. A label on the cover said: POLICE REPORTS, ETC. Giselle smiled, touched Helene's shoulder—the touch of a friend, or maybe not.

"Have fun at breakfast."

Helene Steinbeck wanted to say no.

She wanted to back off, no way, not me, not now, no security work, no bodyguarding a randy, skinny-legged old man.

Helene was here in the Sedona area for some R&R, a quiet place that was not Taos. A place in the sun where there was safety, peace, time with Murdock, time to work on their relationship. They had been here six days. Helene was feeling better. Her feet were healing, and she could walk a whole mile without pain.

Helene was shivering. Time for a shower. Time to face

Murdock. Things were edgy between them. How would Murdock react? *Hey, sweetie, I found a job for you, no killing, fill up your days so I can get some work done—okay?*

3

MURDOCK WAS UP, SHOWERED, wearing jeans and a khaki shirt, when Helene came back from her swim. Her face was lit with color; Murdock smelled a secret. He wanted a hug, a kiss, a sign that things were okay. She handed him a purple binder that said POLICE REPORT. She looked beautiful, determined.

He had eggs in a bowl, muffins from Red Rock Coffee, fruit from the kitchen, bacon sizzling in the pan. Helene's camera sat on the work table, next to her laptop, her notes for the workshop, her pile of manuscript. At the bathroom door, she told him they had a breakfast date.

"Who with?"

"Giselle Roux," she said, "and a billionaire remodeler, and someone named Findlay."

"The bacon is half done," he said.

"I need you on this," she said. "And I can't eat the bacon. Remember?"

She wore the robe into the bathroom. The door was ajar; he saw skin. The door closed, shutting Murdock out. He finished cooking the bacon, laid it out in strips on a paper towel. The shower turned off. He imagined her naked, water drops on skin. He sat at the table studying the purple binder.

Two police reports, two dead guys. William Tyler died on Fire Island when he fell off a deck. Horace Coolidge died in Palm Desert when he fell on a hiking trail. Tyler died in August, Coolidge in September. Both men were in their sixties. A computer print-out added three more names: Findlay, Delaplane, and Hawthorne—no dates of death.

Helene came out wearing the robe, running a comb through shiny black hair, holding a brown envelope. Her feet were bare, her curves shaping the robe to her naked body. Her eyes were still sad. They had not made love since Taos. The envelope contained a contract and five thousand dollars—51 hundred-dollar bills for 24 hours of security work. Two names were printed, Ackerman and Helene Steinbeck. Murdock's name was written in longhand, an afterthought.

"What do you think?"

"Good money," Murdock said. "Three-fifty a minute, two hundred eight an hour ... and change."

"I want us to sign it."

"What about the book, the workshop?"

"I was hoping we could share the load ... solve this thing before midnight."

"Two accidents in two fancy places?" Murdock said.

She was standing beside him, combing her hair. He felt her body heat through the robe. Her feet still had some tan. Her knee looked smooth. He wanted to show her the photo of Cathedral Rock in the dark. Wanted to know her thoughts. Wanted them to touch, on purpose.

"Is this Ackerman guy the billionaire remodeler?"

"Yes."

"What's he like?"

"Very down home," Helene said. "Mid-seventies, tough, still talks with a tiny Texas twang. He has yellow eyes."

"Could you feel the throb of big money?"

"If you Google him while I get dressed," Helene said, "we'll know more."

"These two dead guys, were they bankers?"

"How did you know that?"

"Investment banking?" Murdock said. "Private equity?"

"Something to ask at breakfast," Helene said.

She left him alone. He re-read the contract, felt the old tingle—a case to solve, a thread to follow. They had come to Sedona to escape Taos, to erase the memories of dead girls. They had come to Oak Creek Village, Sedona's bedroom community at the edge of Highway 179, lured by an invitation from Giselle Roux. Before they arrived in the village, Helene had researched the vortices of Sedona. Tourists came from all over the world to visit their favorite vortex. The testimonials sounded religious. Swirl in a vortex and get reborn. Get recharged, re-centered, released from your earth-bound servitude.

Helene loved the pool. Murdock killed time helping out at Sedona Landing, a hotel steeped in history. Helene's nightmares had stopped. She got busy with her new book. They had swapped serious kissing for brief hugs and the tentative pressing of cheeks. This fancy new job, security for a crazy billionaire, was one more activity to keep them in this limbo, together-apart.

Murdock ate a slice of bacon. It tasted flat, greasy, filled with unhealth. He chewed as he studied the contract, feeling the pull of big money. A gulf yawned between himself and this guy Ackerman. Murdock still needed Helene's take on the midnight photo. He dumped the bacon into the trash.

4

Axel Ackerman was bald and tanned, dressed like a tennis bum—a worn T-shirt, a beat-up cable knit sweater. His handshake was solid, like a straight-shooter's. Even bent by age, the guy still stood over six feet. Murdock was impressed, his first billionaire up close. Yellow eyes, a good laugh, a winner's smile. Ackerman introduced Bruno, a solid black dude in a white turtleneck, maybe sixty, packing a shoulder rig under a blue jacket, rolling a white canvas tennis bag, red and black stripes, with bulgy outside pockets.

Bruno welcomed Murdock aboard. His hand was warm, with that weight-room firmness that turns a fist into concrete. Bruno's smile was weary; you could tell he needed sleep. He yawned, asked to be excused, reminded Ackerman about grease and gas, and left for his nap.

At the breakfast bar, Ackerman loaded his plate with scrambled eggs, melon, a stack of Canadian bacon. Murdock had his travel breakfast—pancakes, eggs over easy, four links of the local sausage. Helene went meatless. Murdock craved more meat—and four slices of melon.

Ackerman had his own table in the Bell Rock Bistro, the

view window near the patio. He sat facing the entrance, like a gunfighter in a Western movie, giving Murdock the garden view, dusty crimson and autumn yellow.

On the wall to Murdock's right was a photo portrait of a young woman with her back to the camera, sitting on a yoga mat, holding her bare arms out in a pose of supplication. The time in the photo was early morning—you could tell from the long shadows. The girl was naked from the waist up, and her long hair cascaded down her back.

Miles away from the girl, Cathedral Rock rose from the desert floor like a red-orange monolith.

"I've been reading about your heroic exploits," Ackerman said. "You were a soldier, then a cop, then a private eye. You survived, you're here, you've landed yourself a beautiful woman. Congratulations."

"I tried reading about you," Murdock said. "No luck. I tried Google, Wikipedia, Ask.com—found a half dozen news clips, not a single photo. Your bio leaves no footprints, sir."

"You have questions, just say Open Sesame."

"Open Sesame," Murdock said.

"Ask away," Ackerman said.

"Where's your retinue?"

"You mean slaves, underlings?"

"Fawners and acolytes," Murdock said. "Footmen, ladies in waiting."

"I had a security cadre in New York and Paris, not when I came here. You're thinking of Warren Buffet in Omaha."

"So your only security is Bruno?"

"Bruno shoots Marksman level."

"What about you and weapons?"

"So glad you asked."

Ackerman worked a zipper on the racquet bag. Hauled out a chrome-plated .45, Colt, vintage 1911. The chrome winked in the morning light. People at other tables went on eating. Arizona was gun heaven. Ackerman handed the .45

to Murdock. Except for the shiny surface, it was identical to Murdock's personal weapon, brought back from the jungle, memories of Army days. Ackerman's safety was on, the pistol locked.

"Nice iron."

"It belonged to my father. He was the only Jew in the Texas National Guard."

"Can you shoot?"

"I put in my time on the range."

Murdock returned the pistol, pulled out the list of dead guys. Pointed to the name William Tyler.

"When did you see him last?"

"Are you working for me now?"

"Just sniffing the wind. How about Tyler, the last time you saw him?"

"Last summer."

"Where?"

"His place on Fire Island."

"How was he?"

"Healthy as an old horse."

"How long have you known him?"

"Decades," Ackerman said. "What's keeping Miss Steinbeck?"

"Doing her toilette. What about this guy, Findlay?"

"Walter will be along. He knows I have tennis at ten. I'm hoping you can decide before that—your signature, I mean. It's a mere twenty-four hours, after all."

"You want Helene, not me."

"She insisted, I added your name. Welcome aboard."

"You think it's bullshit—the contract, no security needed—so you're going through the motions."

"I'm enjoying our talk."

"You like jerking people around."

"I checked on you, Murdock. Your exploits, your kills. I'm curious about how you work. Are you asking for more money?"

Murdock was hungry.

He was having fun. He was here at this table sitting next to a billion dollars because Giselle Roux—she had hired Helene for the workshop—had seen police reports on two dead guys, buddies of Ackerman, and created a pattern that started in a *What If.* What if there was a third dead guy, a fourth, a fifth? What if they fell too? What if Ackerman was in danger? Murdock was here because Ackerman was a collector—he bought and sold people and called it contracting. Murdock was here because Ackerman wanted Helene—not a bad motive. The old guy had an eye for women.

Murdock built a forkful—chunk of pancake, then sausage, then egg. He had a rating scale for pancakes. These were number 8, on a scale of ten. He grinned at Ackerman, who grinned back, eyes gleaming, like a lion tamer with a whip.

"What's this guy Findlay like?" Murdock said.

"Temperamental," Ackerman said. "With the twitchiness that goes with being an artist. Walter is moody, sometimes bi-polar, a CPA who has very little grasp of numbers, so he makes sketches."

"What kind of sketches?"

"We go into a business that needed rescuing. The boys on the Crew do the regular stuff, interviews with management, the top labor reps. They study the books, measure the red ink, decamp to the nearest watering hole, make a battle plan. Not Walter. He's on the factory floor, sketching the machinery, the product, men and women at work. He sketches washrooms and delivery ramps. Walter works non-stop, two days, three nights, giving me magnificent three-D views of the business. Walter has talent. His sketches gave me the heart of the business. When he gets here, he can show you."

"How many on the Crew?" Murdock said.

"Four, sometimes five, maybe six."

"How close are you and Findlay?"

"We're business associates," Ackerman said. "Walter has a place in Vail, just up the road from my—"

"You have a place in Vail?"

"It's for sale. Five million-two hundred acres of glass. You interested? My broker is—"

"Is Findlay married?"

"Third time, contemplating a fourth. Walter has a weakness for the ladies."

Murdock watched Ackerman shovel food into his mouth. The guy had good footwork. Across the room, two people appeared in the doorway, a guy in a suit, and a woman in boots and khakis and a green jacket with a badge. With them was Giselle Roux, the concierge, looking all-business and very Arizona posh-resort-casual in designer jeans and a man's white shirt and showy sandals that matched her leather vest.

"Cops," Murdock said. "Coming this way."

"The male gendarme is named Slattery," Ackerman said. "A policeman from Sedona by way of Los Angeles and Phoenix. The female is a Coconino sheriff's deputy. We've never met."

"They share jurisdiction, right? He's city of Sedona, and she's county?"

"How did you know?"

"I was a cop, sir. It's all about turf."

Giselle Roux went away, talking on her cellphone. The two cops came down the stairs, looking serious. Murdock signed the contract, folded it, tucked it into his pocket. He was working for a billionaire.

Ackerman stood up to shake hands with a big welcome smile. His look was steady, not hurried, backed by millions of dollars in offshore accounts, a brigade of tax lawyers, and some tough experience in corporate boardrooms. Ackerman's manner was smooth, like a preacher welcoming parishioners, make them feel good before they opened their wallets. Murdock liked watching the guy maneuver, the handshake, the level look, the understated display of power. An easy five grand. How much could happen in 24 hours? Ackerman introduced Murdock.

Slattery's suit looked big-city expensive, with silver threads in his perfect blond hair. The suit did not conceal his shoulder rig. Connie Fremont, who wore a belt holster, beamed a smile at Murdock. The waitress brought coffee. Slattery ordered French toast. Connie ordered a poached egg on whole wheat toast, no butter, a lady watching her weight.

"What's going on, Steve?"

"A guest in the hotel, sir," Slattery said. "We're wondering if you know him."

"What guest?"

Slattery hauled out his cop's notebook, a gesture that pegged him as older generation—o spiffy electronic device. He exhaled, looked at Ackerman, who had stopped eating.

"His name is Walter Findlay."

"I know Walter, of course. Why do you ask?"

"When did you last see him, sir?"

"Tell me what's going on, Steve."

"A body was found this morning, identified as Walter J. Findlay, Colorado driver's license, residence in Vail, and—"

"Walt," Ackerman said, "are you sure?"

"So what time did you last see Mr. Findlay?"

"Jesus," Ackerman said, "five or five-thirty. Walter was feeling restless. He invited me for a drink in Sedona, I said no. Goddammit, Steve, I phoned him, left messages, Christ."

5

ACKERMAN'S FACE HAD GONE ashy white. When his mouth opened, no sound came out. He turned from Slattery to Murdock, his eyes begging. His big hands gripped the edge of the table, white knuckles under the tan.

Across the room, Murdock saw Helene Steinbeck framed in the doorway, dressed for her workshop, rucksack over her shoulder, looking beautiful. She was chatting with a college girl named Teri Breedlove, Ackerman's tennis partner. Teri was blonde, with showgirl legs and a Purity Ring on a chain around her neck.

Ackerman pushed himself away from the table. His chair fell over.

He tried to stand, stumbled, caught himself, one bony hand on Murdock's shoulder. Murdock gripped Ackerman's arm. Steady, easy, don't panic.

"Not Findlay," Ackerman said. "He can't …. We have a goddamn meeting. He's bringing earnest money. Murdock, goddammit, why don't you earn …."

Fremont took Ackerman's other arm.

Steve Slattery sat there, nothing in his face. No sadness,

no despair, just resignation. This is the way of the world. He nodded at Murdock.

Ackerman was too big to carry. Murdock hoped he would not faint. He could hear Connie Fremont murmuring, caring words to keep the old guy upright. Ackerman said, "Goddammit, not Walter too. The son-of-a-bitch hates meetings, better not leave me holding …."

He shook his head. There were tears in his eyes. Another name on Giselle Roux's list of soon-to-be dead guys. Who was next?

They met in the center of the room.

Helene asked what was wrong. Murdock told her that Findlay was dead. Ackerman stared at Helene, his eyes looked lost. The girl, Teri Breedlove, asked Ackerman were they still on for tennis. She needed to know, okay, because if they weren't, she could barista for extra hours at Red Rock Coffee. Teri was a Millennial—to her, *barista* was an okay verb. If her tennis partner cancelled, Teri would adjust her schedule. She just needed to verify, okay?

Helene's eyes flicked from Murdock to Connie. She took a deep breath, as if she was inhaling the situation. Ackerman said, "Goddamn police, goddamn Walter, goddamn fucking bad news."

Murdock saw Bruno coming down the stairs, looking worried.

"Bruno," Ackerman said. "Christ, did you know—"

"Come on," Bruno said. "I'm here. I've got you. Come on."

There were only three steps connecting the Bell Rock Bistro to the vestibule at Sedona Landing, but the journey of Bruno and Ackerman seemed to take forever. Two old men climbing the stairs. Life was short, a man only got a certain number of climbs, a finite number of stairs, then nothing. Murdock stood with Connie and Helene, watching Bruno use his keycard for the penthouse elevator. Teri Breedlove was on her cellphone, connecting about her schedule.

"I hated coming here this morning," Connie said.

"Where was the body?" Helene said.

"Below Cathedral Rock."

Murdock said, "Got a time of death?"

"Around midnight, an hour on each side, why?"

"I was out there," Murdock said. "I shot the moon around midnight, maybe a mile away and—"

"Why were you shooting Cathedral Rock in the middle of the night?" Connie said.

"Couldn't sleep," Murdock said. "A hotel security guy got sick, I volunteered to help out. It was a great night—no wind, that big moon."

"It's a new camera," Helene said. "Murdock was testing it for me."

"We've got a great forensics gal," Connie said. "Steve's going crazy, a death on his turf. Where's the camera?"

"In our room, ninth floor."

"Let's get it," Connie said.

"You two go for the camera," Helene said. "I've got that workshop. I need some food."

"Let's do it," Connie said.

*****

ACKERMAN RODE THE ELEVATOR leaning on Bruno, who said nothing. No de-briefing, no cross-examination. The walls closed in; his claustrophobia was back. His head was cold, felt steamy. He told Bruno to call Freddy Delaplane, then Georgie Hawthorne. Tell them not to come, Ackerman said.

The door opened on Ten, penthouse level, the smell of sheetrock mud drying. They were behind on the guest bathrooms, something wrong with a tile-setter. Down the hallway, he saw two workmen carrying plywood. They called out good morning. Findlay was dead from falling. The workers kept working.

Ackerman stumbled his way across the carpet to the black

door. He eyed the knocker, eight inches of black iron, curved like a scimitar. The knocker dated from the Middle Ages. Purchased from a shop in the Place des Vosges, from a woman in a tight white dress, a woman who took Ackerman's money, then invited him in for a drink.

A woman with a French nose, Parisian lips, slim wrists.

The woman in the white dress collected nudes. Slim boys, slender girls. The centerpiece was a copy of Donatello's David, the curls, the beribboned hat, the sword, the girlish buttocks, the hint of naughty Parisian sex.

She sat across from him, skirt rising up, presenting her crossed legs. His heart beat faster.

He remembered she took her time refilling his glass, a litany of moves, slow and precise, loaded with seductive intent. A brush of her thigh, a hand on his face, burning. A finger probing his ear. Ackerman remembered the bedroom, the narrow bed, the white dress draped on a chair near the window. The woman was smooth, like the statue of David, smirking in his cocked hat. "I like you, Monsieur American. How long can you stay?"

Ackerman had other business in Paris; he was buying a hotel. He left the woman, took the black door knocker. It traveled back with him to America, speaking for him —Ackerman's fist in the face of an uncaring universe.

I am old. I am alive. I am a man yet.

Now they were trying to kill him.

Bruno used the keycard to open the black door. Ackerman went inside, pushing death away. He lay on the bed, staring at the ceiling. Bruno brought tea. Ackerman thought about the old days, Walt Findlay sketching, a clipboard, a yellow legal pad, colored ink, another business to rescue. When the phone rang, Ackerman was crying. The caller was Dr. Tim, downstairs. Dr. Tim had Ackerman's pills. Permission to ascend?

*****

In the elevator, Connie Fremont asked questions. Oak

Creek Village was her beat. How did Murdock like it? How long had he been here? How had he met Helene Steinbeck? Connie was reading Helene's book. Could she get an autograph? The elevator stopped at Nine. Murdock led the way to Room 919, a corner suite. Findlay's room was down the hall, Room 900. Murdock remembered seeing him, two days ago, a medium-sized guy with a Caymans tan.

Murdock unlocked the door to 919, the complimentary suite, part of Helene's package for teaching the workshop. He was feeling edgy. Connie Fremont went in first. Helene's camera sat on the table, next to the manuscript. Connie asked to use the bathroom. Murdock pointed to the bedroom and said, "Through there." He checked the photos. Maybe the camera had a time-stamp. Blur, blur, blur, and then the camera caught the moon behind the rock, and a black something silhouetted.

The toilet flushed. Connie Fremont stood in the doorway, smiling. "I like what you've done with the place," she said. She stood next to him, checking out the photo, holding her deputy hat against her thigh. Her hair smelled like ripe wheat. Her head tilted down, Murdock had a close-up of her ear. She looked up at him, like an actress presenting her face for a kiss.

"So, if that's him we've got two people up there," she said. "A gal gets a guy's pants off, then gives him a shove. What's the motive?"

"Or we've got three people," Murdock said. "Two gals and a guy."

"It was down to twenty degrees last night," Connie said. "Even if he had the hots, why would he …. I guess we better wait for the labs."

"How did he get out there?" Murdock said. "Where was he before that?"

"We're checking for a rental vehicle now."

The elevator going down felt tight, like the walls were closing in. Murdock had sweat under his arms. Connie leaned against the wall, hands behind her, palms against the wall, like a slave in a dungeon. Her slack pose told him she was available. As the elevator doors opened, Connie touched his arm, "Thanks for showing me the view."

Murdock almost asked her where she lived. A little voice told him not to.

6

HELENE CHECKED HER WATCH.

Eight twenty-eight, not much time for breakfast. She hated to be late. At the table, Helene met Slattery, a cop with suspicious eyes. Was the blonde deputy with him?

Josefina the waitress took orders. Helene got a poached egg on whole wheat toast. Teri Breedlove ordered Danish and hot tea. Helene sipped her coffee. Things were happening fast at Sedona Landing, a new week, a new rhythm to her day, a new corpse.

Murdock came back to the table. Time for introductions. The blonde with the badge was Deputy Connie Fremont, a warm handshake for Helene but she had eyes for Murdock. How long did it take to fetch a camera, anyway? Slattery's cellphone rang, and he left the table.

Helene turned to Connie. "How does the body look," she said, "after a fall like that?"

"Not a pretty picture," Connie said. "Ribs crushed, his shoulder shattered, his cheek caved in. We're waiting for Olivera, the Crime Scene tech. She's out there now. The guy landed on his shoulder. One arm was twisted, the other was flung out, like he was trying to fly."

"Olivia Olivera?" Murdock said.

"You know her?" Connie said.

"We worked a couple cases in California."

Helene sipped her coffee. Another female rising up from Murdock's past, and this one a crime-scene person with an exotic name. Helene felt Connie hovering, waiting for the right moment, ready to pounce. Then Giselle Roux came down the steps, carrying her laptop and a yellow legal pad. Helene was jealous of Giselle's figure, long legs, tight tush, her red hair sleek and perfect. The waitress arrived with fresh coffee. Giselle sat next to Helene, her eyes grateful.

"Thank you both for helping us out on that contract," she said. "Axel is an old fool. His macho bullshit kept him from seeing reality. I liked Walter—he was so artistic, I hate that he is dead—but now we have turned a corner, no more denials. You've got to find out who's behind these killings."

"Did you say 'killings,' plural?" Connie said.

"Two bankers," Murdock said. "August and September, old business pals."

"So Findlay is number three?" Connie's voice was sharp. "Why wasn't I told?"

"I mentioned it," Giselle said.

"When? I don't remember."

"Early fall," Giselle said. "A man named Coolidge fell at his home in Palm Desert."

Slattery came back to the table. He leered at Giselle, some history buried there. He held up his cellphone.

"That was Olivera on the horn, people. She's on the way, with a warrant to search the victim's room. So we'll need a key, okay, Miss Roux? There was something else—what the fuck was it, oh yeah—seems Olivera is buddies with Sherlock Murdock, wants him with us when we check out the room. One more amateur to fuck up my case, just kidding and …. Where are you guys going?"

"Helene's teaching a workshop," Giselle said.

"Just what the world needs," Slattery said, "more amateurs writing about real cops. You want, I could be persuaded to give a guest lecture."

"Thank you, Lieutenant," Helene said.

"Call me Steve, okay?"

"I could turn this case over to Sherlock Murdock here," Slattery said. "Bring him out of retirement—the case of the falling banker."

"Steve," Connie said. "There's a serial possibility here. Findlay is corpse number three."

Teri Breedlove went pale. She stood up, muttered something about making a call, and walked away. Steve Slattery watched her go.

ıı ıı ıı ıı ıı

Helene checked the time, ten minutes to nine. The contract lay on the table, next to Ackerman's plate. While Helene watched, Murdock signed the contract. She gave him a smile. Across the table, Slattery and Connie were discussing the case—three dead, two to go, why hadn't they been alerted? Then Slattery told Connie she was ruining his breakfast. She excused herself, be right back. Slattery said to the table: "No killings here, not in my fucking backyard. Where the hell is Olivera?"

Helene stood up, nodded at Slattery, touched Murdock's shoulder. Giselle Roux left with Helene. Who was this Olivera person who wanted Murdock at the crime scene? Another old girlfriend?

As they approached the stairs, Giselle indicated the photo-portrait of the young woman staring across the desert floor at Cathedral Rock. Giselle said, "Do you recognize our own Teri Breedlove?"

"My God," Helene said. "How old was she?"

"It was a couple years ago. She was maybe sixteen."

"What's going on with her and Axel?"

"She flirts, he dreams of conquest," Giselle said. "She keeps him dancing, he pays for college."

"She's so young," Helene said. "So smart and polished, I remember being gawky at that age."

Giselle nodded, and a look of sadness crossed her face. She took Helene's arm, gave her a smile, and walked with her up the steps, a right turn to the Yavapai Room, for the first day of the mystery workshop.

7

OLIVIA OLIVERA LOOKED THE same—five-six, short black hair, that wide smile when a case went well. She gave Murdock a quick hug, good to see you, how long has it been, come with us while we check out the vic's room. They had not seen each other since that case in Newport Beach, six or seven years ago.

In the elevator Connie handed over Helene's Sure Shot camera. Olivera would hand it over to the lab guys. Slattery said he was sure the camera would solve the case, open and shut, and gave Murdock a look that said, *Beat it, Bud.*

Findlay had the 900 Suite, corner windows, with a view of highway 179. A lot of space in here—a sitting room, giant TV, master bedroom, king bed, giant TV number two, a big bathroom with a Jacuzzi tub, a bidet, a shower with two nozzles, a guest bedroom. Olivera handed out white latex gloves and blue booties that crinkled when you walked.

Walter Findlay had traveled light. One suitcase, one carry-on. His computer was an AirMac Pro. Olivera slid it into a padded envelope, labeled it, set it aside. In the closet, they found corduroy trousers, a tweed jacket, a button-down shirt and red necktie. A pair of Mephisto walking shoes that made Slattery whistle and say, "How the one percent lives."

"These puppies start at three-fifty," Olivera said.

The suitcase was Kenneth Cole, the carry-on was a Ferragamo, gray leather, exuding the sleek sexuality of money. Slattery hefted it, testing, then looked inside. From the way he handled the carry-on, Murdock could see envy working.

"Fuck," Slattery said. "Would you look at this?"

"I want one of those," Olivera said.

"You got people checking his back trail?" Murdock said.

"Hey, Sherlock, this is Sedona, not the big city. We are spread so thin that … okay, so what theory are you pushing?"

"What if Findlay had a date?" Murdock said. "What if he met some gals at a bar? What if they hauled him out to the Rock. What if they promised sex if he gave up his pants?"

"That is fucking crazy," Slattery said. "Enough with the *What-Ifs*. We got photos, Olivia?" Before he could ask more questions, Slattery's phone rang, taking him out of the room. It was not easy, being in charge.

Olivera opened the padded envelope and hauled out the fancy silver Macintosh. She raised her eyebrows when it booted with a soft beep. "God forgive me," she said. "I'm in love with a machine." Murdock watched over her shoulder. Connie stood close, smelling faintly of perfume.

In a document called Walt's Pix, Olivera found photos of a thin-faced guy she guessed was Walter Findlay. One grouping of photos portrayed him as a happy family man—a house in the hills, rocks and pine trees, a child on the porch, Findlay grinning into the camera, holding the hand of a second girl, a woman holding the other hand.

Olivera said: "Got a wife and mother here, two kids. You know where he lived?"

"Vail," Murdock said.

Slattery reentered, started tossing the bed. His movements were excessive, too much noise, a bull male in the forest.

Another set of photos showed Findlay with more tan, hoisting a dark bottle. He was sitting on a beached catamaran, barefoot, wearing baggy beach shorts and dark glasses, grinning at a girl wearing bikini bottoms, no top. The girl came back twice in the photo set, posing with Findlay and a second girl. There were 22 photos; 19 showed Findlay and two girls, some with bras, some bare-breasted.

"Hard to believe this old guy is wired for two-twenty," Slattery said.

"The pix support Murdock's theory," Connie said.

"What fucking theory?"

"Two Female Killers," Murdock said.

"Nothing in the goddamn bed," Slattery said. "Except maybe a whiff of old jism. Might as well have a theory."

"Can you get me a couple prints?" Murdock said.

Olivera nodded, shoved in a memory stick. The laptop made a silvery noise like a ghost whispering. Olivera said, "Done," and handed the stick to Murdock.

Slattery edged up, close to Murdock, while Olivera went through the photos. Slattery was short, his eyes were three inches below Murdock's, but he wore his bulldog face, the jaw thrust forward, and gave Murdock the steel-cop gaze.

"Okay," Slattery said. "You want into my case, find out where Findlay was last night. So flash some photos around, run the bars, report everything to me—and no cowboy bullshit. You got a weapon?"

"In my room."

"You're after intel, got that? We need more dope on this Findlay guy. I heard about your interrogation techniques. No bent fingers, no busted noses, okay?"

"Okay."

"And take Fremont with you ... for the badge."

"Happy to do that."

"Remember ... anything you say or even fucking think, Fremont will tell her boss, Sheriff Coconino. He's up for re-election, which is why he sent her over on this fucking Findlay thing. So keep your lip zipped, understood?"

"Shut up, Steve," Connie said.

They left Slattery and Olivera in Findlay's suite. Connie Fremont was quiet in the elevator, soft smile, a twinkle in her eyes. They stopped at the desk, where Raul printed six color photos from the memory stick. They took the side entrance, around the pool and past the tennis courts, where Ackerman was playing mixed doubles with Breedlove. She had good strokes. Her footwork showed experience. Her backhand, hit with two hands, was better than her forehand. Ackerman's old white tennis bag rested on the courtside bench, putting the chrome Colt .45 three seconds away.

The players changed sides. Ackerman broke away and walked over. The color was back in his face. He asked about the contract. Murdock nodded.

"Did Findlay say where he was going?"

"Hunting," Ackerman said. "Where he always went."

"Did he mention a local bar, maybe a restaurant?" Connie said.

"Not to me."

"If you think of anything," Murdock said. "Give us a call."

"Catch the turd who did this," Ackerman said.

Connie gave him a smile. "Mr. Ackerman, you're looking more like yourself, sir."

"Are you married, Deputy?" Ackerman said, grinning. "Are you open for dinner with a lonely old geezer?"

8

HELENE STEINBECK STOOD AT the door to the Yavapai Meeting Room, greeting her fledgling mystery writers. She welcomed them with a smile and a firm handshake, then passed them onto Giselle Roux, who gave them a hand-lettered name tag. Helene had 18 names on her roster.

She explained the rules of writing practice—keep the hand moving, don't cross out, spend it all—and then she wrote key words on the white board: *crime, victim, killer, discovery, reporting the crime.* Then she printed out the writing prompt:

My name is....

I am the killer.

My first kill was ....

Silence in the Yavapai Room, eighteen writers writing. Helene wrote a piece for her next book. She was trying to use writing to get a grip, to understand why she had almost died. She stared at her handwriting—it was barely legible. Her hand was cramping. *Terror in Taos.* When the timer went off, she asked for volunteers. The first reader was Giselle Roux, who wrote about female slaves trapped on a desert island ruled over by an aging potentate, probing her time with Axel Ackerman.

The last reader was Karla Kurtz, late twenties, black hair, a hard face, Indian blood. Karla stood straight, with the tight body of an athlete. Her voice started soft, then got stronger:

My name is Faith Marie Hunsaker. I am eleven years old and big with promise. My first kill is Uncle Lonnie Dove. He fathers my baby. Uncle Lonnie is Mama's younger brother. He's always after me, just one kiss. First I give in, then I fight him; he wants to fornicate with me. Fornication is a sin. I bloody his nose, he hurts my arm, pinches me to raise welts. One hot afternoon, Uncle Lonnie covers my head with a smelly pillow slip. He ropes my arms with a clothesline. Uncle Lonnie is a red-faced man, thirty years old. He smells like cat pee, laughs in my face, forces my legs apart, sticks it inside. I am real good with numbers. Ten weeks after he forces me I begin to show. Papa notices first. Papa is a man of God, a preacher in the church. Abortion is a sin. Papa tells Mama, she shakes me by the arm. You are going to Hell, she says. It was Uncle Lonnie, I say. Mama washes my mouth out with soap; it makes me throw up. She whips my legs with a belt. My daddy drives me to a rickety section of town. I lie down on a cold sheet in a cold room while a skinny man called Doc spreads my legs and takes my baby, a bloody mess. Seven weeks after they take my baby, Uncle Lonnie comes at me again. I'm down by the river. He smells of whisky; he chases me onto the footbridge. It is evening, the sun is low, I am dressed like Mama in a shirt-waist dress. Eleven years old and already a jezebel. He grabs my arm. I say okay, Lonnie, you get one kiss, give me five dollars. He laughs, pulls me close, holds me tight, I dance him to the edge, my knee gets between his legs. He says, You are all growed up, girl. I raise my knee, hurting his privates. He grunts and lets go my arm and I push him over and he falls with a whump into the water. He is my first bastard fornicator. He made me bleed something terrible and ....

When Karla finished reading, the class applauded, making her blush. Listening to Karla read, Helene was excited. This woman had talent. Her readings lit a fire under the other writers.

At the door, heading out, Helene stopped Karla Kurtz.

"Great storytelling, Karla. You had us on the edge of our seats."

"Thank you, Miss Steinbeck."

"Call me Helene, okay?"

"Gotta run, I'm late for work. See you Wednesday!"

HELENE PACKED HER RUCKSACK, feeling revved. With such a great start to her workshop, she was glowing, had forgotten about the three dead men. She had not forgotten about Connie Fremont. She walked with Giselle to the Bell Rock Bistro, where she was meeting Ackerman, for a walk to Vortex Bank, where he was meeting with his banker, who would open an account for Helene.

Helene asked Giselle about the guy who had fallen off Cathedral Rock.

"Did you know Walter Findlay?"

"Oh, yes. We met my first year with Axel."

"What was he like?"

"Like all of them," she said. "Walter hated getting old. He biked, he jogged, he did push-ups."

"Did he ask you out?"

"They all ask me out—"

"They?"

"To Axel's business brothers," Giselle said, "any female looks ready to lie down and be pillaged by Huns."

"So did you go out with Walter Findlay?"

"A long time ago, we had a drink. Walter was always between marriages. He knew nothing about a woman's needs. He tried to get me into bed. He was drunk, I remember, and not so charming."

"How did he get along with Ackerman?"

"They're men; they had an ongoing pissing contest," Giselle said. "Walter wanted the penthouse, but Axel got there first with a pricey remodel."

"He told me you were acting as general contractor."

"I love to build," Giselle said. "I managed a remodel for Axel's house in Vail. If I could get away from him, I'd plunge into architecture."

"What do you mean, 'if'?"

"Can't you tell? I love him. I wish I didn't. We think alike; he vibrates with power. Don't tell me you can't feel it?"

9

MURDOCK AND CONNIE FREMONT started with the pubs in Oak Creek Village—flashing the Walter Findlay beach photos in P.J.'s Pub and the Full Moon Saloon. No takers. No one remembered. Lots of old guys hunting in Sedona.

Then they drove north on Highway 179 in bright winter sunshine, seven miles to the center of Sedona, population 10,001, showing the photos in Mooney's, the Oak Creek Brewery, the Cowboy Club—almost a positive ID there, then a headshake, wrong guy, sorry. They visited the two Rs— Renee's and Relics. Nothing there. Connie moved aside, letting Murdock work. She smiled at him, nodded encouragement. She kept brushing him with her shoulder.

They wound up at the Lemon Custard Bistro, where the Sunday night customer magnet was Retro Film night from 9 p.m. to whenever. The film from last night was *The Big Lebowski*.

Connie said: "I came here once. My date was a film buff and they were showing *Blade Runner*, with Harrison Ford—be still my heart."

Murdock said, "Maybe Findlay was a closet film buff."

"Let's ask Mr. Ackerman."

"What do you think of Ackerman?"

"He undressed me," Connie said. "Stripped off my clothes right there at the table. I felt those old eyes measuring me. It was invasive, but certainly not surprising. He wanted me and he let me know it."

"Did you want to arrest him?"

"Hey! He's old, rich, but a girl always likes to choose … you know?"

She squeezed Murdock's arm. Gave him a little smile.

The day manager, a woman, led them past the giant wall-mounted TV screens to the back office, where the night manager was napping. The night manager was a chubby bald man in his late forties, a jowly hang-dog face, a pungent body odor smelling of dirt and sweat. He sat on the edge of the narrow bed, blinking at them and sipping coffee laced with brandy. He stared at the photos—Findlay on the beach—took a close look at the photo with the two women.

"Yeah," the manager said. "There was a guy who looked like that, all by himself—good tan, a little too old for the regular crowd. The next time I look up he's sitting with a blonde. A looker, sitting close."

"Remember who waited on him?"

"We had a waitress out with the flu. She sent along a friend to fill in."

"Remember the friend's name?"

"Something biblical," the manager said. "Faith or Hope or something. She was maybe my age, tight body, black hair, only it didn't look real."

"A wig, you mean?"

"We get a sprinkling of older ladies in here," he said. "It's like this reflex. The hair, I mean. A guy with no hair notices someone with fake hair, like that."

"What was he drinking?" Connie said.

"Martinis," the manager said, "with three olives."

"How were the women dressed?" Murdock said.

"Hiking togs," the manager said. "The blonde had a good-looking parka, maybe North Face. The brunette had a yellow parka and a long red scarf, good quality there too. Why all these questions?

"Our man has turned up missing," Connie said.

"You suspect foul play?" the manager said.

"How were they with each other?" Murdock said.

"How do you mean?"

"Did the two females know each other? Did they act like strangers? Were they competing for this guy's attention?"

"That's a tough one. You know broads; they got this thing where they build these instant relationships. They meet, they look each other in the eye, they start bonding. It's a foreign language. If you're a guy, you are shut out, totally. How the fuck should I know?"

"What time did they leave?" Murdock said.

"Sorry," he said. "I look up, they are out of here."

"Did they leave together?" Connie said.

"I think maybe the guy left with the blonde, which I would have. Man, this place was a circus."

"So the waitress did not leave with the other two?"

"Jesus," he said. "Has something happened to this guy? Something I gotta worry about? Jesus, do I need a lawyer?"

Connie Fremont left her card.

Outside, they stood in the sun. Murdock liked this temperature, warm in the daytime, cold at night. What was it like in the summer? Connie's cellphone rang. She said, "Hello, Steve," and walked away.

Using What-Ifs, Murdock replayed the scene in the Lemon Custard Bistro.

What if two women picked up Walter Findlay?

What if they were pros, a planned operation, a careful exit.

What if they motored him out to Cathedral Rock—he was juiced on martinis, got him on the trail, up the mountain. What if they got his boots off, his trousers, a real swinging dick in the moonlight.

So what if Findlay knew he was going to get lucky and played along? They shoved him off, or made him trip and fall. They did not report the fall. They were pros.

What if they wanted a corpse who fell?

What if they were motivated by hate—they wanted revenge on retired bankers?

What if they were motivated by money—someone paid them to do the dirty work?

Connie was off the phone, grinning at Murdock. He shut down the What-if machine.

"That was Steve," she said. "How about a date, just you and me ... and a crime scene?"

10

After lunch, Helene Walked to the bank with Ackerman. She kept thinking about the writing of Karla Kurtz, so powerful, so with it, all that intensity.

A man had died last night, someone Helene had never met, falling off Cathedral Rock. Helene took a deep breath. She was alive, she could feel the sun-heat. It was late Fall in Oak Creek Village. Every day gave her more distance from Taos.

The envelope of money, fifty fat hundred dollar bills, bulged in the flap pocket of her cargo shorts. Her first day's pay, working for Ackerman, a new joint account with Murdock, four thousand five hundred for the bank, $500 for pocket money.

For the walk, Helene wore a Tilley safari hat, light-tan color, new from REI. Her old hat was lost up there, somewhere on Angel Mountain.

In sneakers with white ankle socks, she matched strides with Axel Ackerman. Her Glock was in her shoulder bag. She was bodyguarding her first billionaire.

Ackerman's legs looked bony in his knee-length shorts. The shorts were khaki, and his windbreaker was pale blue, matching his eyes. The tennis cap was dark green, sporting the Nike logo. He swung an old wooden cane, in case his knee went out.

It was heavy and scarred, with a pistol grip handle crossed with black electrical tape.

"This historical stick belonged to my father," Ackerman said. "He was the premier men's tailor in Dallas. Papa inherited the cane from his father, when the family came over from Vienna. You want to know what happened to Papa's business?"

"Yes. What happened?"

"Hart Schaffner Marx—that's what—and Brooks Brothers ready-made suits and those washable suits from Haspel—God forgive me, when I went to work for Lehmann's, I had three Haspel's in my closet. Like a lot of old world artisans, Papa got sidelined by technology. His old customers died, the new customers bought business suits off the rack. They saved a couple bucks, but Papa spent his last years doing alterations for a department store ...."

"What was his name ... your father?"

"Israel Axel Ackerman. His big dream was going back to Europe, Vienna, Prague, even London, where they still cut their cloth using chalk outlines. There's the bank, perfect for a village like Baja Sedona."

The street curved toward a strip mall. Helene saw a dry cleaner, a used book store, and a bike shop. Vortex Bank was a two-story adobe with a red tile roof and big tinted windows in front. The entry was red pavers, a black-stone walkway, and a gurgling fountain. To reach the front door, you walked past a giant vortex made of Plexiglas and turning on a black pedestal. Ackerman told her the vortex was eighteen inches taller than the statue of David in Florence. As they passed the vortex, Helene shivered. She felt something tugging at her.

"This particular vortex is masculine," Ackerman said. "It turns clockwise, with the clock."

"I heard just the opposite," Helene said.

"About vortexes?" he said.

"You know men," she said. "Their lust for conquest. Two men in a room, they stage a pissing contest—the masculine vortex turns backward, against the flow of time. That's a perfect example of male arrogance, pushing against the clock. Do people really pronounce it like that? Vortexes?"

Ackerman said, "Ask Giselle Roux. One day I said *vortices*, she corrected me. How's she doing in your workshop?"

"You want to know what she's writing about?"

"Is she writing about me?"

"Sorry, workshop writing stays in the workshop."

The heavy glass door opened and Helene saw a woman in slacks and a short jacket. The woman smiled. Her name tag said MARTA, MANAGER, and she was nodding—yes, of course, anything I can do—flashing signals that acknowledged her awareness of Ackerman's wealth. Across the lobby, next to the walk-in vault, was a glassed-in office, where a good-looking man was talking on the phone.

"That's our Mr. Cypher," the manager said, "he's ready for you."

Inside the glass office, Helene shook hands.

The man called Cypher wore a khaki suit, great fit—it had to be tailored—and a striped tie. He wore brown Cordovans, a heavy sole, high polish. His handshake was firm, warm blood, level gaze, a hand kept strong with exercise, a keeper of the money under tight control. His haircut was short, almost military, and his eyes took her in. She felt a vibe of interest, boy-girl, welcome to my glass-walled office. On the corner of the desk were two books. One was *Murder on Drake Island*, the other was Homer's *Odyssey*. Cypher was a reader.

He printed words on a card. New Account, $4,500. Helene Steinbeck and Matt Murdock. He welcomed her to the bank, very formal, no ironic undertone.

She felt dusted off, the unwanted female in male territory.

He offered to see her out—he had business with Ackerman, this Findlay thing, how terrible.

"Findlay's dead," Ackerman said. "Can't change that. Steinbeck works for me; she stays."

"As you wish," Cypher said.

Cypher opened the lid of his laptop, turned it so Ackerman could see.

"Mr. Findlay's share was ten million and—"

"I'll cover it," Ackerman said. "I covered for Tyler and Coolidge."

Cypher sighed, shook his head.

Standing, he marched to the window that looked out onto the parking lot.

Two pickups were parked side-by-side, then a Chevrolet and a Land Rover and yellow bike with red leather panniers.

"All these dead men," he said. "It cannot be mere coincidence."

"That's why I hired Miss Steinbeck … to figure things out."

"I feel terrible," Cypher said, "as if it's my fault."

"Get over it," Ackerman said.

"I'm worried about your safety, sir," Cypher said. "As if there's something brewing out there, something we can't see, an evil someone. I feel so helpless. It's the Hindu Kush all over again, and—"

"The meeting is tomorrow," Ackerman said. "I spoke to Freddy Delaplane earlier. He'll be here. I hate what happened to Walt Findlay. We had a history, and he was a great guy, a friend. The cops are on it, Slattery and the deputy. That's their business. Your business, Cypher, is brokering my goddamn hotel deal."

Coming back to his desk, Cypher opened the top drawer, pulled out a legal-size folder, tan, businesslike. The tag on the folder said RAMSBANC REAL ESTATE, DALLAS. Helene remembered Ramsbanc from her time in Taos. She also remembered Gerry Ramsay, the tubby CEO, who had been part of that final manhunt. Ramsay was still not in jail, still connected, still walking around. The memory of Gerry Ramsay, his fat face, pissed Helene off.

"What the fuck?" Ackerman said.

"It's a surprise offer," Cypher said. "Seventy-two million for Sedona Landing. It arrived this morning by courier. I phoned my owners in Tucson, who were delighted. Are you familiar with Ramsbanc, Mr. Ackerman?"

"I know they're hurting for capital, assets frozen. Their CEO's getting a bad name in the business world. Is he the buyer?"

"No. Mr. Ramsay is the broker for an Arab consortium."

"Fucking Arabs! Are they here in town?"

"They're coming. I'm not sure when. They want to visit the property. My hands are tied, you see. I work for the owners."

Ackerman hauled out his cellphone, punched in some numbers, talked to a man named Julius. Helene heard him say "twenty mil, that's right, talk to Cypher, tell him the check is in the fucking mail." He passed the phone to Cypher. "Twenty covers Findlay's ante plus the Arab money."

Helene was impressed. Ackerman was like an armored vehicle, barrier blocking the road ahead—not a problem, lower your head, blast on through. She had just opened an account with forty-five hundred dollar bills, in cash. Ackerman had just delivered twenty million with a phone call. What was an Arab consortium doing in peaceful Oak Creek Village? Cypher pressed the Off button, handed the phone back.

Ackerman said, "They want a casino so they can launder their goddamn petro dollars."

"We can't be sure of that, sir."

"You know any Arabs?"

"Just a handful of Afghans, from the war."

Ackerman growled, then grunted as he stood up. He jerked his head at Helene, time to go. His eyes were angry. He liked full speed ahead—didn't like people who blocked his path. Helene stood up. Ackerman was grinning.

"Fucking Arabs," he said. "I don't like that purda shit—what's the word for that sack-dress they wear?"

"The word is *burqa*, sir. The veil is called a *yashmak*."

"Yeah, well, they did one smart thing, keeping their women from behind the wheel of a Bentley. I got three ex-wives. None of them could pilot a vehicle worth a good goddamn, and with every divorce, my auto insurance dropped by sixty percent. You ready, Steinbeck? I need some fresh air, untainted by Arab frankincense."

Helene thanked Cypher for opening her account. She told him Murdock would drop by to sign up for the new account. Cypher asked Helene to sign his copy of *Murder on Drake Island*. Cypher's first name was Jeremy. She was getting a vibe off him, something sexual—maybe AC/DC, she wasn't sure. The way he looked at her—not predatory male, but interested.

Outside, in the sun, Helene bopped Ackerman's shoulder.

"Easy there, Steinbeck."

"That crack about women drivers, Ack ... you're a real sexist."

"Man-talk," Ackerman said. "Male bonding with Cypher. And God's own truth about my exes—the proof is in how the insurance premiums dropped."

"Just don't do the macho sexist thing around me, okay?"

"Okay. What's your read on the banker man?"

"He's worried," Helene said. "Something happens to you, he'll get blamed."

"He was in the Army," Ackerman said. "Not sure where, but today, he seemed, I don't know, three steps beyond cautious."

Helene looked up, saw the tower at Sedona Landing, Ackerman's penthouse on top, unfinished, the never-ending remodel. As they headed up the hill, Helene briefed Ackerman on Gerry Ramsay, the manhunt on Angel Mountain, bleeding feet, Murdock's clever landslide, how Murdock had taken Ramsay's boots.

"Perfect," Ackerman said. "Taking another man's boots, making him walk in his socks. Goddamn that Murdock anyway. I see why you like him." Ackerman grinned, showing Helene his teeth. They were mottled, coffee-stained, old-man yellow. Not like the film-star teeth of Jeremy Cypher. How could anyone have teeth that white?

II

KARLA KURTZ WAS A runner and a biker. She stood five-eight and weighed 135. She was half German and half Peruvian. She wore black leggings against the morning chill. Over the leggings, she sported expensive Ex Officio hiking shorts from REI. A white blouse with two buttons undone showed the darkness, a hint of mystery, highlighted by a red neck scarf and a tight black vest, like a bartender's.

She was headed for the table of Mr. BMW, who watched her coming. His eyes stripped off her clothes. Karla was used to being stripped; that's what men did. It was in their DNA. They stripped you down and then you made them pay.

It was noontime at Red Rock Coffee and Karla was preparing herself for later, for the afternoon, the evening, the night, the money in an envelope. Her day had started at 4:30 with a quick bike ride through the golf course, nothing moving; the only light came from Mr. Cypher's place on Fox Hollow. No guest-car in the driveway, no rival female in his bed. Karla's heart sang. Then an easy bike ride to open the coffee place. Two hours wearing her barista mask, then a bike-ride to Sedona Landing, for the workshop with Helene Steinbeck.

The writing had been a surprise. Hiding in the point-of-view of Faith Marie Hunsaker, a fictional character, had been so fun. Karla surprised herself, the words flowing out of her, a river of words, reading aloud, feeling the heat, and then the sacred praise from the teacher. "Karla, that was so terrific!"

Karla loved living here in Oak Creek Village. The weather was great. She felt safe. She had this amazing job. If a girl had to work, Red Rock Coffee was terrific—friendly fellow-baristas, a good boss, great tips from the old geezers. Karla had worked here for six months. Like the Army, it was good cover.

She said 'Happy Monday' to Mr. BMW and he said, 'Call me Morrie, all my friends do,' and she said 'Happy Monday, Morrie,' alert to his age now, his coming incapacity, aware of the red-rimmed eyes, the way his old hands grasped the cup, holding onto something, wanting to grab on to Karla. He was a bachelor. She wouldn't mind being grabbed if the price was marriage. He invited her for dinner at Elote, a pricey eating place up the road in Sedona, and she said 'Let me check my calendar' and he said, 'Life is short; this could be my last meal,' and she said 'Sorry, Morrie, but I have a date already." She waited while he studied his smartphone, feeling the heat, the bald desire, naked male lust never-ending.

"How's tomorrow for you?" he said.

"What time?"

"Five-thirty," he said. "I'll pick you up."

"I'll meet you," she said, and named a place.

She walked away wondering if she could marry this one, live in a good house with good insulation, sleep late, not worry about paying the bills, losing her job. She had researched him already. Morrie Baskin owned three domiciles. One in Manhattan, one on Fire Island, and one here in Sedona. He was divorced, four kids, four grandchildren. Morrie Baskin had three bank accounts, a big investment account at Fidelity.

After her shift ended, Karla flew from Cottonwood to Santa Fe, the only passenger in a Lear Jet. She felt special as the plane lifted off from the Jim Bridger Airport. The weather report for Santa Fe said snow so she wore her black leggings under her new jeans. She wore the white shirt from work, the black vest, and a new down parka from North Face. Her black knee boots had cost $750. She loved not being poor.

A silver limo motored her to the hotel, El Condor, one block off the Santa Fe plaza. She registered, using the name Doreen Dorado, the name on her fake business cards. She took a soak bath, then a nap. The phone woke her. Charity Plum's voice.

"He's here. Big room on the Terrace level."

"Where are you, girl?"

"In the lobby," Charity said.

"Are you okay?"

"I always get edgy … just before," Charity said. "You want to go over the plan?"

"An accidental encounter at the bar," Karla said, "followed by some sweet talk, epic sexual stimulation, stairway, bell tower, over to you, right?"

"Costume?" Charity said.

"Black skirt, black knee boots, no stockings."

"Wear the stockings," Charity said. "He's a sucker for mystery."

"How about the sheer Gothic blacks?"

"Killer stockings," Charity said. "No underwear."

"Is this it?" Karla said. "This one, and we're done?"

"You're my bait, sweetie. Be present, mind on the job, okay?"

12

They drove in Connie's SUV—white, with Coconino Sheriff on the door—southwest, from the Lemon Custard Bistro, slipping along Highway 179 to the Back of Beyond Road. Like Helene, Connie was a good driver. Murdock could relax. She held her speed to a steady two miles over the limit, pushing the passenger vehicles out of the way, asserting her cop authority without flaunting it.

They waited for Slattery in the parking lot below Cathedral Rock. Murdock had seen it from a distance—the jagged peaks, the three hollows called "saddles," but now he was putting himself in Findlay's boots: if Cathedral Rock looked this rough in daylight, how would you feel climbing in the dark?

"He had to be drunk," Murdock said, "or stoned."

"Or maybe horny," Connie said. "One city guy, alone in the moonlight."

There were vehicles in the parking lot—cars, SUVs, pickups, two Jeeps, a small tour bus—and people in hiking clothes standing behind a temporary fence of yellow ribbons strung on bushes. A Sedona cop guarded the entrance. Connie showed her badge and vouched for Murdock.

When Slattery arrived with Olivia Olivera, Connie briefed them on Murdock's What-If theory. What if Findlay left the Lemon Custard Bistro with two women? Slattery sighed and said he had too many fucking What-Ifs already. What he needed was facts.

"Like I told you," he said, "I don't command the manpower to interrogate the local talent."

Slattery had changed from the sharp city-cop suit into a blue police jumpsuit, complemented by ankle boots, a walkie-talkie, and a baseball cap that said DODGERS. Armed with a hand-drawn map, Slattery led them through the underbrush to the trail, where a rectangle of yellow ribbons marked the place where Findlay had landed. There were more signs saying CRIME SCENE, DO NOT CROSS. As they approached, Murdock saw climbers up ahead, two guys and a girl, passing around a water bottle.

Slattery called out. "Hey, shithead, can't you read? Get the fuck out of there!"

The hikers stopped, heads turned toward the signs. Slattery repeated himself, held up his badge, SEDONA POLICE. The hikers said they were sorry, then climbed over the yellow ribbons, chatting. They were alive; Findlay was dead.

Murdock was behind Connie, who was behind Olivera, who was behind Slattery, who was shaking his head. "Fucking ghouls, visiting a crime scene. If I had time, I'd toss them into the pokey. What have we got, Olivia?"

They studied the map, Cathedral Rock and environs. An X pinpointed the landing spot. Murdock remembered falling off a ladder picking peaches at harvest time in California. He remembered a sudden blank place in his mind, the world tilting, then a split second of realization—you have wasted your life—then boom, into the soft dirt, hearing laughter from the other pickers. Murdock imagined the feeling of falling off Cathedral Rock, the wreckage of bone and muscle on impact. What did Findlay think of going down? When he fell, did he have time to hear the crunch of bone on rock?

The ground inside the yellow ribbons was a well-worn hiking trail. Rock and hard pan, packed by thousands of tourists wearing bright happy hiking gear. Olivera pointed at a place beside the X.

"Looks like he landed here," Olivera said.

"Jesus Christ," Slattery said. "Let's climb up there, see if there's anything left of the goddamn crime scene."

"Did they find his trousers?" Murdock said.

"In the lab," Slattery said.

The climb up Cathedral Rock was steep. Slattery took the lead. His feet kept sliding, the little rocks making skittery sounds. He was climbing too fast, the head man in the lead, sweating and cursing. Olivera, sounding like a worried mother, told him to take it easy. Connie was sweating, grunting when the grade steepened, and Murdock was feeling okay, glad he had spent the last week running, getting his body in shape after Taos. Halfway up the trail, Murdock broke a sweat. The wind came around a corner, a sharp November breeze. The sun was dropping fast—autumn in Arizona. They had maybe 90 minutes of light left.

Slattery ran up against a cul-de-sac. He said, "Fuck it," and gave the lead to Olivera, who followed the hand-drawn map around a rock wall, the trail narrow now, through an arbor formed by twisted desert trees, their trunks turned magical by wind, and adorned with a hand-painted sign that said "Vortex, I Am Here, Show me the Way." Through the twisted trees, they followed Olivera to a flat place looking south, where stakes and crime scene ribbons corralled an oval area.

"They think he went over here," Olivera said.

"What do the scuff marks tell us?" Murdock said.

"The techs found five different boot-sole types. One of them matched Findlay's boots. They're testing the dirt samples for DNA."

"So he died with boots and without his trousers?" Connie said.

"So he got thrown off?" Slattery said.

"What if they danced?" Murdock said.

"How you figure that?"

"Follow the swirls," Murdock said. "What if they started out a threesome, dancing in the dark, then what if one of them broke free, leaving a twosome?"

"And then they were one," Connie said. "One man falling."

"I don't fucking get it," Slattery said. "You want someone killed, why go to all this trouble? All this work—the bar, the drive, the climb, the sexy dancing? Why not just stab him and leave him down below?"

"They wanted a splash," Murdock said.

"*They*? You mean the two broads?"

"Or the person who hired them."

"What person? Where the fuck does this theoretical shit come from, Murdock? What splash?"

"Look out there," Murdock said.

Murdock pointed to the roads approaching Cathedral Rock, a line of vehicles coming this way.

"Christ," Slattery said. "You're saying they wanted this kind of publicity?"

"I think it's a *he*," Murdock said. "*He* wants the world to notice. And he's thinking big-time. And maybe even thinking acceleration."

"Thank you for that theoretical analysis, mister private eye," Slattery said. "That's very helpful, it really moves the investigation forward—your hypothetical *He*."

A beep from Olivera's smartphone. She pressed a button, listened, and said, "Send it to me, okay?" Then she said, "Okay, guys. It's Murdock's photo. Look at this."

She passed the smartphone to Slattery, who said, "So what?" and passed the phone to Connie.

"It's all blurry," Connie said, and passed the phone to Murdock.

The little screen showed a blow-up of one photo from last

night. At first, Murdock saw only the brightness of the moon and the darkness of the rock. Against the brightness, he saw what looked like an object bisecting the line where bright moonlight gave way to the dark. Could that be Findlay falling? To the left of the object, Murdock thought he saw a dimness that could have been one of the hypothetical killer females.

His fingers were tight on the phone, which he handed to Connie. She looked sad. Olivera looked sad. Slattery looked exasperated, wasting time here. Murdock felt wasted and useless.

Maybe he was getting too old for detective work. Maybe he should stop detecting and ask Giselle Roux for a job, working security at Sedona Landing, the graveyard shift. Unwind his last years checking doorknobs.

MURDOCK AND CONNIE WERE on Verde Valley School Road, on the way to Sedona Landing, when her cellphone beeped. Findlay's rental car had been found in the parking lot at the CRMC—the acronym for Cottonwood Regional Medical Center. Murdock had seen it from the road a couple days ago. As they approached the hotel parking lot, Connie asked how long he and Helene had been together.

*****

HELENE JOTTED NOTES ON her meeting with Cypher. A neat guy, precise, edgy about the dead guys. She jotted questions. How did Cypher stay in shape? How much was he worth? Where did he grow up? There was no gold wedding band. Had he been married? Was he really reading the *Odyssey*?

She typed the notes into her laptop. Drank coffee, edited pages in her manuscript. She kept writing, but nothing clicked, the words had no bite. She was behind on her schedule. She still had nightmares. She was worried about her relationship with Murdock. He was off with Connie Fremont, Little Miss Western Girl Deputy Person.

Helene paced the room, arms crossed, her mouth soured by too much coffee. Suite 919 looked down on the tennis courts, where she saw Javier Trujillo with a leaf blower. Helene grabbed a sweater and her racquet, took the stairs down.

Javier was a skinny kid, fifteen, with a big loop forehand and a two-fisted backhand. His job was court maintenance, hitting with guests for tips. On weekends, Javier played doubles with Ackerman and Teri Breedlove. Helene hit with Javier for an hour and felt better. The lights came on, and a chubby guest in tennis whites replaced Helene. She gave Javier a ten, and in perfect unaccented English, he said thanks. She looked around. No sign of Connie's white SUV.

THE WIND WAS CHILLY—TOO cold to sit outside—and Helene still had on her shorts and a sweater, so she took a window table in the Bell Rock Diner. The window looked east, onto the parking lot. From here she could see the sun flashing off vehicles on Highway 179. She could feel the buzz of coffee from an afternoon of trying to write, so she ordered Green Tea. She called Murdock on her cellphone. He was in Connie's SUV, heading for Sedona Landing. Helene asked what they had found, then listened as Murdock briefed her on Findlay leaving a bar with two women—shadow dancers at the crime scene—and the landing place, a hard end for Walter Findlay, a corpse with no pants.

Helene asked about Connie, who came onto the phone to comment on Murdock's marvelous detective intuition. The admiration in Connie's voice told Helene what she had suspected—Connie had eyes for Murdock. Helene caught the waitress, ordered a glass of Pinot Grigio.

Helene tried to jot notes—the book kept calling to her—but she was thinking about Murdock and Connie, the end of the day, night coming on, how your life could change in an instant.

HELENE'S WINE WAS GONE when the white sheriff's SUV pulled

into the parking lot. It sat there, like the jalopy at the curb just before midnight curfew in a sappy teenage romance, last-minute kissing before the girl runs inside, back to the family. Connie and Murdock were taking a long time to say goodbye.

Her cellphone buzzed. It was Ackerman. He wanted her and Murdock for dinner. His voice did not sound shaky. Where were they on the case?

Helene watched Murdock leave the white SUV. He did not close the door right away. They were still talking. Helene felt a rush of heat, jealousy, anger. Murdock closed the door. Connie drove off. Murdock turned toward the hotel—could he see Helene behind this window?—and raised his hand. Her heart took a leap. If there was so much love, why did she feel so empty?

13

FREDDY DELAPLANE CAME INTO the bar at the Inn of the Fathers Hotel and saw what he wanted. She sat at the bar between two guys.

She had black hair and a silky red neck scarf and a tight ass.

He wanted her in his bed with her legs open.

He wanted her to beg for it.

She turned, laughing, and grabbed the arm of the guy on her right. Her mouth was open. Freddy saw white teeth and a smooth throat. She was dark, Mexican or South American, with a hooked nose straight from ancient Rome. The guy on the left went away and Freddy took his seat.

He introduced himself. Her name was Doreen—a disappointment there, not classy enough. But the skirt was up above the knee, and the sheer black stockings sent his brain whirling, and when the other guy left, they took a table. Her card said Doreen Dorado, Dorado and Associates, Beverly Hills. Freddy knew his way in the business world. The word "associates" was code for a one-woman shop.

"Real estate?" he said.

"A lowly bean-counter," she said. "What about you?"

"I dabble," Freddy said. "Software, shipping and handling, my background was in banking. But enough about me. You live in L.A., which means I live just up the road from you, in Pebble Beach."

"A beautiful area," she said. "What brings you to Santa Fe in a snowstorm?"

"Trying to save the country."

"Save it from what?"

"Burning itself to a crisp," he said. "Running out of water—small stuff like that."

"Does saving the country include saving little old me?"

Her question got him going on politics. He was here in Santa Fe for a strategy session. His group was called LFA, Let's Fix America. There was a website, they needed members, was she interested? The job of LCA was putting the right people into office, fiscal conservatives. He got going on morality and religion, God was not dead, lecturing, aware of his own voice. He loved making speeches, he was on the right side, gotta do something with all that money. He was off to Paris for a conference on oil, but first a stop in Sedona, where he was buying a hotel.

Doreen Dorado stood up. Something in her face told him he had turned her off, all that political stuff. Freddy loved politics; he was good-looking, he was thinking about running for office. She walked away, stopped, then came back to him and held out her hand. He took it.

His heart thumped as she led him to a sofa. Pulled him down beside her. The skirt rose to mid-thigh. He saw bare skin, a dark exotic flash above the stocking-tops. He wondered if she was wearing underwear. He was the hunter, she was the prey. She didn't seem to mind. He wanted to kiss her. Better to let her make the first move. She wanted another drink. Her hip was tight against him. Her blouse was open; he felt invited. He looked down and saw darkness and wanted more of this one. He wanted to eat her up.

"I have to go," she said.

"No way."

"A business thing," she said. "Before I ran into you … gotta feed the old bank account."

He gave her a business card. She read it, taking her time. Then tucked it away into a black evening purse. He invited her to see his Pebble Beach place … if she was in the area.

"I love your take on the world," she said. "If I joined your group, maybe we could see each other again."

Her hand squeezed his leg. She had strong fingers. He felt the jangle, an erection starting. He turned to her; time for a kiss. She squeezed harder. But when he tried to kiss her, she said, "Not here."

"Where?"

"I should go," she said.

"Go where?"

"Like I said, I'm meeting someone."

"Cancel it. You're with me tonight."

"I've got some time tomorrow. We could—"

"I'm gone tomorrow, like I said. Sedona, then Paris."

"You're scaring me, Mr. Delaplane."

"I certainly don't intend to."

"Look," she said. "You're very rich, you don't hide it. I find that very attractive and you're very good-looking and I'm still trying to shake free from a sticky relationship and—"

"Tell me about that."

"Tell you about what, Mr. Delaplane?"

"Your sticky relationship. Because I myself am trying to get—"

"You're married, aren't you? A good-looking guy like you, you're so, I don't know …. I'd better go."

When she stood up this time, she lost her balance and grabbed onto his shoulder and the thighs were in his face, a split second of closeness. Her scent made him crazy, and she was saying, "So sorry, omigod, Frederick," and her hand was holding onto his collar, warm hand, and she smelled like musky perfume and he wanted her in his bed. He told her he was getting a divorce. He did not say it was divorce number three. She said, "Sorry," and edged away.

Freddy watched her go. Goodbye, Dorado. His night on the town was shot. A woman sat at the window, looking out at the snow. She had blonde hair, a Valentine face ... he knew her from somewhere. Freddy sipped his drink. The woman at the window was not Doreen Dorado. He was gearing up to try his luck when his phone beeped. It was Doreen. Her voice was breathless. She invited him to the Bell Tower.

"Take the elevator," she said. "Bring brandy, like you're a St. Bernard on a rescue mission."

Freddy bought a bottle. He was alone in the elevator, his brain dancing with flashes of male conquest, himself on top, thrusting deep. *Take that, hot bean-counter bitch.* The Bell Tower was outside in the weather and he needed to grab her and get her inside before they both froze. He planned to make this quick. Have a drink and a kiss and get her to his room and into his bed, strip off everything except the black stockings.

The elevator door opened into cold wind. She waited by the doorway that led to the stairs. She wore a black parka from North Face.

"Are you crazy? We'll freeze up here."

"This is a character test, Mr. D."

She did not ask for brandy. When they kissed, he felt her leg slide between his thighs. Then his hand was under the black skirt, feeling the raw heat, the hot lights of sexual conquest exploding in his head. Her tongue filled his mouth cavity, filled the universe. She had her teeth on his upper lip. One bite and he would bleed. Where had she come from? Who was she? She made him forget the cold.

The door to the stairway was open—he didn't know how—and they were turning in a slow circle. She said, "Let's get down, Frederick," and someone grabbed his collar from behind—the blonde from the bar, she looked familiar, pulling him away from sexy Doreen. His brain was on red alert as a pair of hands from nowhere whirled him down the narrow stairwell, bouncing him off a wall, slamming his shoulder, hip, elbow—he heard the bone crack. Then a pain in his head, *boom*, and stars rushing at him, a giant yellow asteroid, followed by a cold, merciless, uncaring dark.

14

TONIGHT, WATCHING FREDDY FALL, Charity Plum felt old.

She heard someone whispering and turned to see Karla, her face tight, her lips pursed.

"Come on, girl."

"What?" Charity said.

"Check the neck."

"You do it," Charity said.

"Not part of the deal," Karla said.

"Are you cold?" Charity said. "All that shivering?"

"Check the neck, Charity."

Charity sent Karla ahead—*you go first, girl*—straight onto San Francisco Street. Charity waited, two minutes, then three, before she headed for the exit to Cathedral Street, a thick door, heavy with age, a tradition reaching back to Spain. The smirky female bartender was in the entryway, lighting a cigarette. She blew smoke at Charity, invitation sent.

"Hey," she said.

"Hey, yourself," Charity said.

"I'm Ginger."

They shook, and Charity felt heat. This woman was coming

onto her. Through the glass panes, Charity saw snow falling straight down.

Ginger the bartender was not bad looking, younger than Charity. She wanted to buy Charity a drink. Sorry, she had a plane to catch, but Charity was tempted. There was suffocating loneliness after a kill, and Karla—the one Charity wanted— was so unavailable.

Then she saw Karla crossing the street, black on white, vulnerable in high heels. She made an excuse and headed into the falling snow.

In the hotel, Karla counted her money from the pay envelope. "You're short again, girl."

"I am not the paymaster," Charity said. "I only get half; you get half of that."

"What's Mr. X up to, Charity?"

"You don't need to know … ever."

"This is Job Four," Karla said. "You get the plan early; you tell me at the last minute. I hate that. You can prepare, get yourself psyched. I'm like walking onto a stage without a script. Then you short me and blame it on Mr. X."

"I keep my promises," Charity said. "We split everything fifty-fifty."

"You're fucking him, right?"

"What's gotten into you, girl?"

"I can tell because you get all gooey when you talk about him, this Mr. X guy. You know something I don't. You think it gives you power."

"You had a chance to know me," Charity said. "You shut me out."

"When we're done," Karla said, "you're gonna tell me why he wants these guys dead."

Charity watched Karla turn away, thinking how anger made her even more beautiful, like a dark goddess. She watched Karla close the zipper on her rucksack. Charity preferred a nice suitcase, a matching carry-on; she was not a rucksack person. Karla hefted the rucksack, walked to the door, not so pretty now. The anger in her face had shifted to regret. Karla was tough on the outside, soft down deep.

"What's up with you, girl?"

"I kind of liked this last guy. He was lonely, asked me to call him Freddy."

"Men are trouble and you're a fool."

"He invited me to visit him in Pebble Beach. With him I could have made it work."

"He was a man," Charity said. "Men are heartless bastards. You give, they take."

"Not this one," Karla said. "When we kissed, he was into me, like totally."

"You're losing your edge," Charity said.

CHARITY HEADED WEST ON Airport Boulevard.

Snowflakes snapped against the windshield

Karla sat in her seat, arms folded, fuming.

The tower at the Santa Fe airport was adobe, with slanted windows up top. Before she got out, Karla asked again about the money and Mr. X, showing her doggedness. Her voice had an edge. Her eyes glittered in the half-dark.

"It's need to know," Charity said. "Remember the rules."

"You were good tonight, with that guy."

"What do you mean, good?"

"Familiar," Karla said. "Like you knew him from way back."

"I never saw him before," Charity said.

"That's what you always say."

"If I got invited to your house," Charity said. "And if I got asked to stay over, then Pandora's Box might open—you'd know everything."

"Remember the rules," Karla said.

"What rules?"

"Rules by your Mr. X," Karla said. "Two girls, two different travel arrangements."

"He'll never know, hon."

"Now you're the one who's losing her edge."

The door opened, snowflakes flew in, sharp as knives. The door closed. Charity watched Karla walk toward the terminal. She hated watching her walk away. So beautiful, so strong, so hopeless, gone.

AT BERNALILLO, THE SNOW softened, stopped. The drive to Albuquerque was clear. Charity turned in the rental car, took a shuttle to her hotel, the Hawthorn Suites, where she used her Sharon Gold credit card. In the room, she checked her phone—no message from Joey. Charity soaked in the fancy bathtub.

She made the call from her bed, sipping a martini. "Santa Fe went down just fine," she said. "Where is the money?" Karla would have said, *Where is the Fucking money? Where is the Goddamn money?* But Charity was raised in the church, and Mama said that dirty talk came from a place of dirt and that was Hades.

She checked the time, after midnight. She was into Tuesday and she had money parked in The King George Bank in the Caymans, where she had a date for Saturday, an old Southern boy who wore suits by Palm Beach, sporting a planter's hat.

He was already talking marriage.

Day Two

15

HELENE'S PHONE HAD THIS little trill, a snatch from a Bach partita. She was awake when it rang, her mind working on her relationship problem with Murdock. The caller was Ackerman. He wanted them upstairs, and his voice sounded shaky.

"Are you okay?"

"Just get up here," Ackerman said.

"Axel," Helene said. "What is it?"

"Goddamn Freddy Delaplane," Ackerman said.

"What about him?"

"He's dead," Ackerman said. "Just get Murdock and get up here."

THE PENTHOUSE LEVEL WAS number ten. The elevator door opened, and Helene saw Bruno holding the big black entry door. He thanked them for coming. They asked about Ackerman. Bruno shook his head, "He hates to be wrong."

In the penthouse living room, Axel Ackerman was pacing the floor, gripping a coffee mug. The TV was on, a snow report from New Mexico. Santa Fe was icy—stay home if you can.

Helene gave Ackerman a hug. She beckoned to Murdock, and the three of them hugged like a family. Ackerman's face was pale, but not dead white like yesterday. He had a number on a notepad, and these words: "Calderon, State Cop, tell him I know the fucking governor."

Helene passed the phone to Murdock. "Tell Julio hello. He's my favorite cop."

She led Ackerman to the sofa.

*****

MURDOCK WANTED PRIVACY FOR the phone call, somewhere quiet where he could focus. He walked down the hallway to the executive spa, a combination weight-room and billionaire pleasure palace. It smelled of rubber and leather, sweat and steam and sweet massage oil.

Murdock sat on the massage table and called Julio Calderon. Julio was an orderly guy, a good cop with political ambitions and a captain in the New Mexico state police. In their last case, he had used the power of office to shield Murdock and Helene from the media. When Julio answered, his voice was calm, polite, and familiar. He was at the crime scene, the Inn of the Fathers, a four-star hotel in Santa Fe.

"Hey, *compadre*," Julio said. "How's life in peaceful Sedona?"

"We've got sun," Murdock said. "High today will be fifty-seven."

"Your boss," Julio said, "he's got some major political juice. I got called out of bed by the lieutenant governor. What are you doing for this guy Ackerman?"

"Bodyguarding," Murdock said. "Digging up the past."

"What past?"

Murdock briefed Julio on the men from Ackerman's Crew who had died from falling. Tyler, Coolidge, Findlay—and now Delaplane. He mentioned the hotel, the gathering of old pals, a reunion of investors, their last job together. Julio knew about private equity—he called it Vulture Capitalism, a leftover from the Romney election campaign. Julio had called Ackerman because Delaplane's PDA listed Ackerman's phone number.

Julio said, "They found the dead guy at the bottom of the stairs leading up to the Bell Tower. It's closed for the winter. They suspect alcohol in his blood stream. No sign of foul play; they're calling it accidental. How close was your guy to this guy?"

"Delaplane was a business partner," Murdock said. "Did see his room?"

"A suite," Julio said. "They dusted it, no extra prints."

"Any money on Delaplane?"

"No wallet, no cash."

"How old was he?"

"Mid-sixties," Julio said. "A little heavy, great-looking head of hair."

"What was he wearing?"

"Khakis, a fresh shirt, leather bomber jacket that could have cost two grand. Pricey ankle boots, maybe six hundred."

"What time did they find him?"

"Seven thirty. A door was banging in the wind; they sent a maid to check it out."

"Have they tracked his movements before he went to the Bell Tower?"

"He was in the bar. The bartender remembers him—he tipped good, paid for drinks for a broad, guys and gals, nothing out of the ordinary."

"The bartender, what's his name?"

"Ginger," Julio said. "He's a she. The reason I know is, we had a couple dates a while back."

"You do get around," Murdock said.

"Life is short," Julio said. "How's the lovely Helene?"

"Peachy," Murdock said. "You mind if I grill your barkeep?"

JULIO FOUND THE NUMBER for Ginger Rooney, the bartender at the Inn of the Fathers. Julio had to run—a thief was loose on the ski slopes, and that kind of rumor was bad for the tourist trade. After they hung up, Murdock stared at the wall. The executive spa had a sauna big enough for two and a hot tub with steam rising. The bathroom shower had two nozzles. A bidet sat next to a tall toilet. There was a closet with a brushed-chrome door.

He opened the door and saw a mini-kitchen—a fridge, a two-burner cook top, a microwave mounted on the wall. A coffee pot and an Italian espresso machine. Murdock used the pot. There was half-and-half in the fridge. Sugar substitutes in a little shot glass. While the coffee pot sputtered, Murdock yawned, shook his head. He was worried about Helene pulling away. How could he get her back?

16

FORTIFIED BY COFFEE, MURDOCK phoned the bartender, Ginger Rooney. After the phone rang three times, a woman answered. Murdock identified himself, used Julio's name. The bartender had a flat voice. Yeah, she remembered Delaplane—good-looking guy, good tipper too. She asked why Murdock was interested. He told her about Findlay, who fell in Sedona. Rooney put that together with Delaplane, who fell in Santa Fe. Murdock asked what she remembered about Delaplane.

"Yeah," she said. "He was in the bar. If you were female, you noticed. He was not bad to look at, and the leather jacket told you he had bucks. He was polite, this great smile. He had his eye on this woman at the bar, getting the rush from two different guys. She ran them off, made a place for your guy, like she was sorting out the suitors. Like she was still young enough to do that."

"Did they know each other?" Murdock said. "Maybe from before?"

"They shook hands like strangers," Rooney said. "He asked what she was drinking. She did not play hard to get."

"How old was she?"

"Late twenties, maybe thirty. In great shape, like she worked out. A very sharp black dress, shoes with medium heels."

"Was she a guest at the hotel?"

"When she came in, her coat was wet from the snow."

"Remember the coat?"

"A black parka," the bartender said. "You still hanging with that writer, Steinbeck?"

"Yes," Murdock said.

"I'm reading her book; she's quite a gal."

"Yes," Murdock said, "she is. And you are very observant."

"Helps pass the time. I need a siesta before my shift. Anything else?"

"Was the woman wearing a wig?"

"Nope. She had black hair, and it was real. Why?"

"Just a theory I'm working on," Murdock said. "How long did they stay at the bar?"

"One drink, then they moved to a sofa. She had him going by then. You know how guys look when they catch a whiff of sex."

"Tell me," Murdock said.

"They look poised and predatory," she said. "Ready to spring, eyes narrowed, neck tense, the whole bit. This guy was like that, poised on the edge. She was leaning into him, had her legs crossed. The dress was sexy, like she was asking to be pounced on. Then she gets this phone call and heads out and the air goes out of your guy, like he was a balloon, like she used her needle."

"Who else was in the bar?"

"Two couples," the bartender said. "One couple, they were celebrating a wedding anniversary—good tips to follow. The other couple, maybe a first date. Then there was a woman who sat alone; she wore a green dress and those tinted eyeglasses."

"Why did you notice her?"

"She was mid-forties, five years ahead of me. Plus, the dress did not go with the hair, if you catch my drift."

"Blonde hair?"

"Like I said."

"Could it have been a wig?"

"Is this your theory thing again?"

"The dress was wrong, you said."

"Yeah."

"So what color would the hair need to be, to go with the dress?"

"Red," the bartender said. "Is there a cash reward for this game?"

"A hundred," Murdock said. "You're doing great. Don't stop now."

"If she was wearing a wig, that would explain the dress."

"Keep going," Murdock said.

"I wore a wig once, to a party; it looked crazy. I didn't know why, but people kept staring, people who knew the real me. And then a girlfriend said the dress didn't go with my wig. What was that all about? So I take off the wig, check the mirror, and bingo, wrong combination, the dress goes with my real hair. Now is that worth two hundred, or what?"

*****

CHARITY WAS DREAMING ABOUT snuggling with Karla, like two turned-on lovers, when her phone rang. It was Joey, wanting a report.

"Where are you?"

"In bed. Where are you?"

"Any hitches?" Joey said.

"Not a single hitch, captain."

"How did he look?"

"Like always, captain. Strong, confident. He still has the teeth ... and that head of hair."

"The money will be yours tomorrow."

"Karla wanted hers last night."

"The money will come via FedEx, per usual."

"When?"

"Tomorrow, midday, or after. Get yourself some R&R, soldier. That's an order."

17

MURDOCK WROTE DOWN THE bartender's name, Ginger Rooney, and her address, a PO box in Santa Fe. He was addressing the envelope when Helene came into the room. She asked what he was writing. He showed her the address, told her about the money—a reward for information from the bartender. She asked what he was paying for, her voice was sharp, edgy. He told her about the woman with the wig. Eyes narrowed, she looked down her nose at him, skeptical.

"Is this the theory you cooked up with Connie Fremont?"

"It was my theory," Murdock said. "Connie saw the same photos."

"Photos of Walter Findlay, right?"

"Findlay and two females."

"How many photos?" Helene said.

"Seven," Murdock said. "Here's a sample."

He pulled a photo from his shirt pocket. Helene studied it, then handed it back.

"Where did you get this?"

"Findlay's room."

"When?"

"Yesterday morning."

"I saw yellow ribbons," Helene said. "That room is a crime scene."

"Technically speaking," Murdock said. "I took the photo before the yellow ribbons went up."

"Does Connie know you kept the photo?"

"I don't know what Connie knows."

"After spending the whole day with her, all that cozy togetherness? She looked at you and saw candy."

"We interviewed the bistro people; we checked out the crime scene. You were tied up in your workshop, then you went off with Ackerman, to meet the banker."

"Why do you sound so defensive?" Helene said.

"What's going on, Steinbeck?" Murdock said.

"I put Axel to bed," Helen said. "I'm going back to the room. I have a book to write, a contract, a deadline."

"Don't you want to know what I learned?"

"Is this the part about sending money to a pretty female bartender in beautiful Santa Fe because she supported your crazy theory about two female killers, a theory that comes from a photo of a playboy on a beach with two bikini babes that you cooked up with Connie? Am I missing something here?"

"I'm missing you," Murdock said.

"Don't change the subject," Helene said.

WHEN HELENE LEFT, THE room felt empty. Murdock's coffee was cold. When he went into the living room, he found Bruno on the sofa, arms crossed, eyes closed.

"Are we experiencing the occasional woman trouble?" Bruno said.

"How did you know?"

"Your woman is smart, strong, fit. She has killed. She will have moods."

"Is that why you're not married, the moods?"

"I was married," Bruno said. "She ran off with a man who claimed to be a duke."

"Where was this?"

"Florence," Bruno said. "I was studying art; I wanted to be a sculptor. She was an actress and a singer. So of course, we were doomed from the start."

"What's your theory on who's after Ackerman?"

"Someone from the past," Bruno said. "What about you?"

"Yeah," Murdock said. "But which past?"

"A past with a woman player, perhaps?"

MURDOCK TOOK THE STAIRS down to Nine and used his keycard to open Room 919. Helene was hunched over her laptop. Murdock was sweating; Helene's resistance was a wall. He was drowning, calling for help, where's the lifesaver?

She looked up, frowning. "Let me finish this sentence."

Murdock drank a glass of water. His head buzzed—too much coffee. His brain felt hot. He was on to something—he didn't know what. He needed Helene's intuition.

"Okay," Helene said. "What is it?"

"I need your help," he said.

"Can it wait? I'm in the middle of a hot paragraph—like this prose is smokin.'"

"You took notes on Ackerman, while he was rambling on about his Crew. Giselle was there. We were at the table in the Bell Rock Bistro, yesterday evening."

"You want my notes?"

"If I read them out loud, can you type them up?"

"I am not your secretary."

"I feel something there, something we missed."

"Do I hear the clanking sounds of another massive Murdock hunch?"

"They're working up to Ackerman," Murdock said. "The killer wants us to notice."

"We knew that yesterday."

"The answer is back there," Murdock said. "I need your brain on this, Steinbeck."

"If I do this," Helene said. "Will you give me two hours? This new book, it's … I just need to get this work done."

SHE GAVE HIM HER notebook, a yellow legal pad.

He read her notes, and she typed them into her laptop.

As Murdock read, he felt more connected to Ackerman's past. Ackerman had been in his early forties when he started his fledgling business. He had experience working for the big boys on Wall Street—Goldman, Sachs, J.P. Morgan—when he founded Arc-Angel Equity. His first years were make or break. Ackerman had one thing in common with the boys on the Crew—they were all hungry.

When they were done, Helene printed out her notes and Murdock went through them, boxing in names, circling places. He made a list; they would have to check with Ackerman. The list went back thirty years. Ackerman's Crew had visited six towns, had taken over six troubled businesses in the Midwest, dumped into bankruptcy by Arc-Angel Equity.

Wichita, Kansas—Bellknap's Farm Machinery
Topeka, Kansas—Redfearn's Building Materials
Lamar, Colorado—Hempstead's Bridles and Saddles
Amarillo, Texas—Wilson's Fine Furniture
Tulsa, Oklahoma—Howard's Grain Silos
Lubbock, Texas—Jerome Trucking, Inc.

18

THEY TOOK THE LIST to the penthouse.

Bruno let them in.

"If it's any help," Bruno said, "I vote for the TFKs—two female killer theory."

"Men," Helene said. "All of you are assholes."

They got three mugs of coffee from the kitchen, tapped on Ackerman's door, heard his voice and went in. Murdock nodded at Helene, who led the way.

Ackerman was lying in bed, propped up with pillows.

Helene handed him a mug of coffee.

He sipped the coffee, took a deep breath. "What?" he said.

"These five guys on your Crew," Helene said. "Were they all bankers and CPAs?"

"Odd question," Ackerman said. "No."

"What were they, what did they do?"

"Didn't I already cover that at breakfast?"

"You told me about Findlay," Murdock said. "Just when the cops came."

"Okay, well, Freddy Delaplane was a salesman. He would charm the managers, the top brass, the owner. He had an

MBA from somewhere in Missouri. Milt Coolidge was the CPA. He checked the books, could smell red ink from five miles away. Milt worked with Will Tyler on financing. Will was an investment banker with a degree from Michigan State, I think. Like I said, Walt Findlay had a degree from Cal-Tech, mechanical engineering. He was a loner, a dreamer. Walt made sketches of the business, not only the product, but the assembly line, the workers. His target was the process, what made each business unique. Georgie Hawthorne was our front man, an attorney. He did our agreements. I've been calling Georgie, to warn him, but he has not called back. How did I do?"

Murdock handed the list of towns to Helene. She showed the list to Ackerman. He studied it, glanced at Helene, then refocused on the list.

"Your list is out of order," Ackerman said.

"How so?"

"Amarillo was our last job out here, not Jerome Trucking. In Amarillo we rescued Wilson's Fine Furniture, family-owned, the last in the series. It became a turning point for Arc-Angel Equity."

"Why is that?" Murdock said.

"It was our last job," Ackerman said. "We made the owner rich. After Amarillo, the Crew dissolved. Will Tyler took a job back east. Hawthorne and Coolidge had family troubles that ended in divorce, cost them both a bundle. Walter Findlay took a job in Florida—Walt had a thing for beach-towns. Freddy Delaplane? I heard he went to work for an agricultural consortium. Those were golden days for me, nonstop travel, no rest—I flew, I drove, I rode the train—I was tireless, I was exhausted, I was exhilarated. We completed six jobs in five months."

"Were you married during this grand exhilaration?" Helene said.

"Divorced," Ackerman said. "I was between wives. Don't be snide, Helene."

"Who was the woman?" Helene said.

"What woman?"

"You were between wives," Helene said. "There had to be a woman."

Silence in the room. Murdock said nothing. This was what he needed—Helene at her best, going for the jugular. She moved closer, stood beside the bed. Ackerman rested his coffee mug on his chest.

"Her name," Ackerman said, "was Penny Diamond. A Southern girl, Charleston, somewhere like that. Miss Diamond was a prodigy—good with numbers, good with people. A one-woman PR department."

"Was she pretty?"

"She was nineteen," Ackerman said. "At that age, they are all lovely and fresh."

"Did you have a relationship?"

"None of your business," Ackerman said.

"This is your life we're trying to save, Axel."

"All right. She threw herself at me. We united in consensual sexual congress. Are you happy now?"

"Did she work on all six jobs?" Helene said.

"The last three," Ackerman said. "Tulsa, Lubbock, Amarillo. Didn't I already tell you that?"

"What happened to her?"

"She broke into my New York office," Ackerman said.

"Because you hurt her?"

"Why do women always use that word, *hurt*?"

"Because betrayal *hurts*," Helene said.

"Jesus Christ," Ackerman said. "A madwoman breaks in, smashes my office, steals funds ... and you call it betrayal?"

"How much money?" Helene said.

"Two hundred thousand," Ackerman said, "and change."

"In today's dollars?"

"Half a mil," he said.

*****

Helene stood there, staring down. Men were idiots. Ackerman had his cagey look—can't catch me, like a little kid playing tag on a school playground. She could feel Murdock off to the side, holding back his questions. As a couple, they were still out of sync. And that feeling of being tilted, off-balance, carried over to their sleuth work. Helene kept thinking about the TFK, Murdock's crazy theory about two women, working together, killing four guys, then thought of Penny Diamond from Ackerman's past—was she the key?

"Was Penny pregnant?" Helene asked.

"She claimed to be. I saw no external evidence."

"Was the baby yours?"

"She accused me," Ackerman said.

"How did you feel about being accused?"

"Women," Ackerman said. "They give a little, they take a lot."

"What happened to the baby?"

"What relevance does this have to—"

"Motive for revenge," Helene said. "Tell him, Murdock."

Murdock was sitting down, the chair next to the bedroom wall, looking half-asleep. His voice was speculative, he did his favorite tactic, What-Ifs.

"Okay," Murdock said. "What if you got Penny pregnant? What if she was on the run, living off the two-hundred grand? What if she gave up the baby for adoption? What if the baby died? What if she blamed you?"

"What if she's after you now?" Helene said.

"Enough," Ackerman said. "You have worn me out with your hypotheticals. Go away. And don't badger me at breakfast."

"We need to go there," Murdock said.

"Go where?"

"Amarillo," Murdock said. "Where it ended."

"Murdock likes to dig," Helene said.

"Not on my dime," Ackerman said.

19

THE PHONE RANG, SLICING into Karla's pregnancy dream. Her belly was big with promise, her hands were on the wheel, the stolen pickup rammed into the father of her child, Benny Kelwin—Karla caught him leaving his girlfriend's house, caught him with the deer-guard, sent him whirling, one hand clutching his favorite necktie, *take that you bastard*, watching him crash head and shoulders into the windshield of his gold-plated Cadillac.

The dream scene triggered a flashback, a Casino bar in Las Vegas, sitting across the table from Charity Plum, looking like a witch, pinch-faced and superior, tapping her fingers on the table while Karla stared at the words POLICE REPORT.

The subject of the report was Kelwin, Benjamin H. In the dream, Karla stared at the word HOMICIDE. Is this report real? Is it a fake? Charity's mouth opened, the words came from a loudspeaker with big amps. *You are wanted for questioning, honey-pie*, and then Karla said, I *am not going to fuck you, girl*, and Charity said, *Wanna make some easy money, honey?*

The call was from Mr. Ackerman. He was nervous, edgy, wanted a massage.

KARLA CHECKED THE STREET outside her condo, looking for cops.

They would come for her in the night, riot gear, storm-trooper boots.

Karla Kurtz, wanted for questioning.

She took a deep breath. No cop cars, no surveillance van.

She showered, shaved her legs. Was the hair growing faster? Was she getting old? She checked her body in the mirror, saw the roll of belly fat, thought of her mother growing stout, sighed. She uniformed up—leggings, shorts, blouse, vest. Ran a comb through her hair, grabbed her rucksack. The air was chilly. Ten minutes to Red Rock Coffee.

Karla's bike zoomed along, fresh air in her lungs. Her legs felt strong. She was 28 years old. She had money in the bank. Miss Steinbeck dug her writing. Maybe she had a future as a crime writer.

The bike tires whispered on the walkway that cut through the golf course. She saw a light burning at Mr. Cypher's house, Fourteen Fox Hollow, but no red Tahoe. Was he finished with the Breedlove person?

Karla imagined him in his kitchen—the valley rumor mill said he could really cook. Why wasn't he married? Her thoughts shifted from cooking to marriage. Would it ever happen for her? She pictured herself in a wedding gown, holding on to Mr. Cypher's hand, church steps in the sunshine, a shower of rice, the limo that said Just Married.

THE BIG ESCALADE ROARED out of nowhere. The village speed limit was 25; the Caddy was doing 55, 60. Driveway on her right, Karla turned in, felt the draft from the Caddy. She saw a Texas license plate, she saw a face in the passenger window, maybe a woman's. She hung in the shadows, shaking, the shock of almost dying, a hit-and-run, a puddle on the road, an echo of her dream. A second vehicle slid past, a Mercedes with D.C. diplomatic plates—KV, Saudi Arabia.

She phoned Ackerman from work. He answered with a growl; she was on a six-month contract. He thought he owned her forever. They made a date for later in the afternoon.

*****

HELENE WAS BACK AT her laptop, feeling edgy.

Murdock was making fresh coffee.

"Why Amarillo?"

"Clues," he said.

"What kind of clues?"

"Okay," he said. "It's a hunch."

"What hunch?" she said.

"Because Ackerman's hiding something."

"He's old," Helene said. "He forgets. Maybe he just can't remember."

"He's a Chinese puzzle box," Murdock said.

"If you get there, what's your first move?"

"Gotta go there to find out," he said.

She watched him fix her coffee, dash of cream, no sugar. She had two thoughts. One, she had known him forever; they were joined at the hip. Two, she didn't know him. He was a total stranger; she would never know him.

She took a first sip. She wanted to talk about what was going on between them—this wall, this eerie detached feeling where she felt trapped. It would take a while, the talking. Murdock was knee deep in the Ackerman job, doing her work, her thinking. She felt sad for him. She was also nervous about competition from Connie Fremont, the new female—and edgy about Olivia Olivera, the old flame. Helene had agreed to the Ackerman gig, hoping it would bind them close. Instead, it was pushing them apart. She needed time to think.

"Why don't you go," she said.

"Alone?" he said.

"I've got this workshop," she said. "I can keep an eye on Axel."

"We're a team," he said. "I need your intuition."

"It's only half a day," she said. "If you left this morning, you'd be back for dinner."

"You asking for one of those trial separation things?"

"I'm not feeling what you're feeling … about the case."

"What day is it?"

"Tuesday."

He was sitting on the bed, staring into space. Helene touched his arm. "Murdock, I really need to work."

He gave her a look. He said nothing. She watched him go out the door. Her heart was beating fast.

*****

WHEN HE GOT OFF the phone with Karla, Ackerman saw Death—a skull face, yellow teeth, a tattered gray garment. The bony hands held a scythe. Death came at him fast from the window, forcing him out of the black leather chair. He went to the kitchen, Death did not follow. He dumped his coffee into the sink, took a deep breath, sat down.

The kitchen had been remodeled first. They knocked out walls, installed more outlets, cabinets by Giselle Roux—it was her kitchen, and now he could feel her withdrawing. Thirteen years was enough. She hadn't told him, but this feeling of being abandoned had to come from somewhere. Who could replace Giselle? Twelve years of solidarity and balance, gone. Maybe he should have proposed.

He checked the time—7:40. He had tennis at ten, doubles with faithful Teri Breedlove. His legs were cramping, his brain felt dead, he feared death. He dressed in shorts, an old T-shirt, his battered cable knit sweater. Bruno was napping. Delaplane was dead. Time for breakfast. Ackerman took the stairs.

*****

ACKERMAN ENTERED THE BELL Rock Bistro. He felt the man pills working. Josefina got him seated, brought his coffee—he drank a blend of French roast and decaf. He ordered melon, bacon, a muffin. He opened the screen on the smartphone. Time for the test. "Smartphone," Ackerman said, "who killed Delaplane?"

He saw Death on horseback, riding at him. He pressed a button, Death faded away. Easy enough.

Why had Murdock locked on Amarillo? What went on inside the mind of a sleuth? Ackerman had dim memories of the little city, just another railroad town in the Texas Panhandle, a hub city for wheat and oil and cattle. His time there had been short, one afternoon, one night. He didn't remember having sex; Penny Diamond had been on a tear. Honest Joe Wilson was rich and depressed, nothing to do there. The Crew was eager to move on; there were jobs waiting.

There were so many small towns back then—Kansas, Oklahoma, Texas. Towns with elm trees, red brick streets, a church on every corner, lawns. They all lusted for growth, for the big-time. In every town, there were a dozen firms crying out to be saved—businesses that would not survive without the surgical expertise of Arc-Angel Equity.

Ackerman flashed on Honest Joe Wilson, the rumpled church-meeting suit, the strong hands, the solid handshake. Wilson was an artist—his furniture had style—but the fellow was a fool. He hired his friends, bought too much equipment, made payroll with borrowed funds. Ackerman remembered the plant—a gaggle of wind-battered Quonset huts on the edge of town. The makeshift showroom was an afterthought.

Inside Wilson's Fine Furniture there were lathes and wood-presses, that sawdust smell. Ackerman remembered the town banker, a jowly man in an ill-fitting suit. He had forgotten the banker's name.

Josefina delivered Ackerman's breakfast. He was stabbing a piece of melon when Murdock walked in and sat down without asking permission. Ackerman liked that in a man, just enough push.

Murdock leaned toward Ackerman, got right into Ackerman's

face. "How much time did you spend in Amarillo, total?"

"A night and a day. Why?"

"That's why I need your plane."

"Do you ever have doubts, Murdock?"

"What happened to Wilson?"

"He died."

"How did he die?"

"I don't know. Where are you going with these questions?"

"I want to know how Wilson died."

"When you're dead, you—"

"What if he died by falling?"

"Now you're talking crazy."

Ackerman turned his head. A flicker of movement in the doorway and Teri Breedlove was walking this way—tanned legs, hair in a ponytail. Teri was life; she drove Death away. Teri shook hands with Murdock. The time was quarter to ten, just enough for a bathroom stop and a warm-up hit.

Teri took the chair next to Ackerman, asked was he okay? He lied, told her he was fine, took another bite of melon. Murdock sat there, anger in his face.

"What's up, dudes?" Teri said.

"Murdock was just leaving."

"You okay, Axel?" Terry said.

"You already asked that."

"You look pale, partner, just like yesterday, did somebody else die or what?"

Ackerman stood up. He grabbed his tennis bag, headed for the doorway that led to the courts. His stomach did flip-flops. He felt queasy, he stumbled, caught himself. Behind him, Ackerman heard Murdock talking to Teri. He heard the words *airplane* and *Amarillo*. He heard *life* and *death*. He pushed through the door, leaving everything behind—Teri, Murdock, Findlay, Delaplane, Tyler, Coolidge, Death on a horse. Ackerman needed sun, tennis, sex … *something*.

20

ON HIS WAY TO Vortex Bank, Murdock made a reservation, Phoenix to Amarillo, tomorrow, ten o'clock. There was nothing earlier. He paid with his credit card, one aisle seat.

The wrought-iron statue of a vortex that guarded the entrance to the bank cast a heavy shadow across the patio. It was flared wide at the top, narrow at the base, rotating on a pedestal of black stone, counter-clockwise.

A woman wearing a name badge that said MARTA escorted Murdock to a glass-walled office. Cypher got up to shake hands. He fit Helene's description—medium size, short haircut, wearing a khaki suit and brown Cordovans.

Despite the handshake, despite the khaki suit, despite the invitation to sit, Murdock noted that Cypher was edgy. A man under pressure, brittle as glass, trapped in a glass-walled office. He sat down. Murdock sat down. Cypher coughed, hand over his mouth. Then he left his chair and stood at the giant window, his hands jammed into pockets. Cypher's shoulders were hunched, sharp blades inside the khaki jacket. Helene had mentioned his copy of the *Odyssey*. Today, it sat on the window shelf.

Outside in the parking lot, Murdock counted four vehicles—two pickups, one sedan, one SUV—and a bright yellow bicycle. Did Cypher bike to work? What kind of vehicle did he drive?

"I heard about the death in Santa Fe," Cypher said. "I met the fellow last year. I was hoping you'd tell Mr. Ackerman to call off the purchase."

"Won't your bank lose a chunk of money?"

"Money for human life," Cypher said. "It's a bad bargain. I hold myself partly to blame. Will you relay my message? Mr. Ackerman won't return my calls."

"Sure," Murdock said. "I thought it was your idea, buying the hotel."

Cypher sat down—his face was angles and planes—and picked up the red phone. There were two more on his desk, one black, one white, cables snaking into a hole in the desk. He dialed a number, said he did not want any interruptions, and jammed the phone back in its cradle.

"I Googled you—hope you don't mind. You were Army, right? First in Special Forces, then the MPs. Mind filling me in?"

"They sent me to Viet Nam after Saigon fell," Murdock said. "My team rescued guys from those MIA prison camps."

"That was not on Google," Cypher said. "Were you a captain then?"

"NCO," Murdock said. "We worked with the CIA. I was young and tireless ... I loved it."

"I served in the Hindu Kush," Cypher said, "where I lost a platoon."

"Ouch," Murdock said. "What happened?"

"It was my last tour of duty in Afghanistan. The platoon had a run of bad luck. When their CO got killed, I replaced him. Up to then, my record was spotless. I was on the way to bird-colonel. It was a night raid, a village elder, your basic ex-fil. One of my guys stumbled, made noise. We got ambushed. It was ugly."

"That's war," Murdock said. "Not your fault."

"That little night raid shredded my future," Cypher said. "Before that, I felt at home in the Army. I felt useful, like I was doing important work, saving the world from oblivion. I felt wanted. I saw myself as a career soldier. That all changed in thirty seconds. But enough about me. So, you said military police, right?"

"My CO said I had an instinct for homicide."

"May I ask a question?"

"Sure."

"Mr. Tyler and Mr. Coolidge—their deaths were ruled accidental. I haven't heard any official report on Mr. Findlay, but I was wondering about Santa Fe."

"It looked like a fall."

"You were there?"

"I know a guy in the New Mexico State Police."

"I envy you your contacts," Cypher said. "Mine are all financial, bankers, CPAs. I think I'm in the wrong business."

"What business would you rather be in?"

"College professor," Cypher said. "I always enjoyed school. I coveted the teacher's pet appellation. I have worked toward the PhD. Sorry, I'm rambling. I suppose it's because I'm enjoying our talk. Do you feel like we've met before?"

"Yeah," Murdock said, "I do."

"Like we had served together, in combat?"

"Yeah," Murdock said, "like that."

"Sorry for all the bleating," Cypher said. "This is a work day and you're here as the second holder on Miss Steinbeck's brand new account. There are forms to sign."

Murdock watched Cypher switch gears, from wistful soldier to helpful banker. His face changed; precise movements cloaked his emotion. With great care, he opened a desk drawer, extracted a folder of bank forms. He passed Murdock a fancy fountain pen, green with gold flecks. There were little yellow sticky tabs on the forms—sign here, initial here.

While Murdock signed the forms, Cypher explained the bank philosophy: "I came here to Vortex Bank because they were into customer service. In the age of smartphones and electronic cash, Vortex Bank has a heart. All the employees are expected to know the names of every bank customer."

Murdock returned the signed forms. Cypher made a call on the white phone. Marta the manager came through the glass door. Her smile was wistful; her body language said she was soft on Cypher. He didn't seem to notice. Marta left with the forms. When the door closed, Murdock turned to Cypher.

"Why do you blame yourself?"

"I knew these men," Cypher said. "They met in this very office. I shook their hands."

"Did you know Findlay?"

"Briefly. It was Saturday morning. He came for advice."

"What kind of advice?"

"He was interested in meeting women," Cypher said. "He asked me for tips."

"What did you tell him?"

"I sent him to Raul, at the desk, Sedona Landing. I'm not much of a night owl." Cypher checked his watch, calmer now. He said, "I could use some air, do you have time for coffee?"

"Sure do."

"Let's walk to the Red Rock. A lovely day, a new comrade. Let me find my sunglasses …. Oh dear, we've got company."

Murdock saw movement at the glass door.

A flash of teeth, pale lipstick, blonde hair like wheat.

The door opened, blocked by a woman brandishing papers. She was medium-sized, early forties, with crazy eyes. The teeth were straight out of a toothpaste whitening ad. Her dress was one size too small.

Her hand was out. Her voice was loud.

"Hi," she said. "I'm Betty Sue Breedlove, and you must be the famous detective."

Her hand was hot, the palm moist. The glass door opened

again. Teri Breedlove stood there, looking sheepish.

"Mom," she said. "Let go of Mr. Murdock. He's been spoken for."

The woman handed Murdock a business card. Betty Sue Breedlove, Valley Patio Homes. Her logo was a vortex. An arrow led from the vortex to a cute model home next to a pond.

Murdock waited outside with Teri, watching the action through the wall of glass. Teri was still dressed for tennis— shorts and T-shirt, a white sweater thrown across her shoulders.

They watched Betty Sue drop papers onto Cypher's desk. The papers were in sets, stapled.

"Loan apps," Teri said.

"Your mom looks possessive," Murdock said.

"They dated," Teri said. "Jeremy's real popular with the ladies. Mom's pretty, but she's a terrible cook. Not Jeremy. He digs good food, takes cooking classes. She made a big mistake, targeting his taste buds."

Through the glass wall, they saw Betty Sue drop an object onto the desk. It looked like a replica of a vortex. Teri explained: her mom led tourists on vortex tours to add to her customer base. The tiny vortex was an amulet, Teri said, with the power to get Jeremy back. Murdock asked how it worked.

"That little vortex is female," Teri said. "It spins counterclockwise. Jeremy is a male—guys spin clockwise. If he accepts the vortex, he'll go into reverse."

Inside the glass office, Betty Sue leaned across the table, her hand on the vortex statue. Cypher stood up, ending the meeting. He did not touch the vortex amulet. Betty Sue headed for the door. Mission failure.

"Does she think it will work?"

"A girl's gotta believe in something," Teri said. "Me, I've got my ring."

"Oh?"

Teri showed Murdock the Promise Ring. It hung from a silver neck chain. "Jesus is my guy," Teri said. "He saves my ass from whatever."

The glass door opened and Betty Sue whirled through, scowling. Her eyes were glazed, her shoulders slumped. She stood there for maybe 30 seconds, staring back through the glass wall, biting her lip. Cypher was on the telephone, heels on his desk, his back turned, facing the window that looked out onto the parking lot. The yellow bicycle caught Murdock's eye. The Village was perfect for bikers.

Betty Sue wrote on a business card, handed it to Murdock. She was having a party, she wanted Murdock to bring his writer friend, what's her name, Steinbeck. Everyone was talking about her book. The party was Friday. Betty Sue shook Murdock's hand. The body heat was less intense; her fierce eyes were cooling down.

Cypher waited for the women to leave; then he came out, looking furtive.

21

THEY WALKED TO RED Rock Coffee. Cypher was quiet. Murdock could feel him thinking. The sun was warm on Murdock's shoulders, great weather for November. Cypher was smaller, but he matched Murdock's stride—two soldiers marching. Murdock asked where Cypher lived, did he always bike to work? What kind of vehicle did best in rural Arizona?

"I drive a Subaru," Cypher said. "May I explain ... about that harpy?"

"Not necessary," Murdock said.

"After a couple of dates," Cypher said, "she invited me for dinner. The food was poisonous, an omen. She doesn't bike or play tennis. Sex is her exercise. She has this move, calls it her Vortical Swirl. She's an energetic woman, voracious even. I broke it off. She has a different agenda. I will never understand the female sex. Whatever you're having, it's my treat, banker to new customer—a new comrade-in-arms."

Inside Red Rock Coffee, they ordered two tall Americanos, double shots, room for cream. The barista was dark, slender, athletic. Her name tag said Karla. Her body language said she wanted attention from Cypher, who didn't seem to notice.

Murdock had seen her before, maybe at Sedona Landing.

Red Rock Coffee was crowded and noisy. They took their coffees outside; no wind here, no downhill breeze. "What were you chatting about with Teri Breedlove?"

"She was telling me about the vortexes," Murdock said. "The males whirl one way, females whirl the other."

"Teri's quite bright," Cypher said. "Latching onto Mr. Ackerman was a stroke of genius."

"He pays her, right?"

"Oh, yes. She keeps the cash in a box at our bank. Teri's a saver; the mother's a spender. Did she recruit you for her Friday soiree?"

"Yes. Will you be there?"

"I have other plans for Friday," Cypher said. "Did the girl regale you with her career plans? From a Criminal Justice degree to CSI, capped by law school?"

"She's a Millennial," Murdock said. "They know how to plan."

"She's sweet," Cypher said. "May she not follow the mother into harpy-dom."

Murdock laughed, switched subjects.

"How did you meet Ackerman?"

"Because of this hotel sale," Cypher said. "The owners, a brother and sister, wanted to sell. They came to me for advice."

"You put the deal together?"

"As I recall, Mr. William Tyler made the initial moves."

"You knew Tyler?"

"He was an avid biker. We met on the Chicken Point, a local bike trail. He had a flat tire; I helped him out."

"When did Tyler come up with the idea of buying the hotel?"

"He mentioned it to me over drinks. He was in town alone. We chatted about the nature of change; he had a philosopher's way about him. A very thoughtful man, a straight arrow ... and now he's gone."

"Why did the owners want to sell?"

"They were nervous about the cost of maintenance. Every

repair bill and they phoned to complain. Mr. Tyler gathered some old friends, Mr. Ackerman among them. But I still blame myself."

"So what happened first?" Murdock said. "The need to sell or the offer to buy?"

"From my purview," Cypher said, "events seemed wondrously fortuitous—the buyers, the sellers. It was charming, old friends getting together for one last venture, like a veritable Knights Templar brotherhood, old comrades home from the Crusades. I stood apart, a facilitator, a keeper of records. Now Mr. Tyler is dead, and the others, and I feel responsible."

"Like losing a platoon?"

"Exactly. How did you know?"

"These dead guys are not your fault," Murdock said.

"Thank you," Cypher said. "Coming from you, that helps."

Cypher's smartphone rang. He got up from the table, moved away. His voice was crisp, and the message was short. He was needed at the bank. Before he left, Cypher urged Murdock to speak to Ackerman about not buying Sedona Landing.

After Cypher left, Murdock pulled out the photo of Findlay and the two babes on the beach. How much money would it take to motivate two women to kill four old men?

22

THE MONEY FOR THE Delaplane kill reached Charity Plum on Tuesday morning. She was at the office, sipping cold coffee, snatching a moment to run photos of her baby. His name was Howard. He was married, one child, ran his own little business, landscape gardening, in Mt. Pleasant, east of Charleston. The TV was on, but there was no news from Santa Fe. Outside her window, tumbleweeds bounced in the wind. Hard to believe her baby Howard was 30 years old.

The money arrived in a FedEx envelope. Charity signed, made the driver wait. She packed Karla's half in a new envelope, pre-addressed to a Sedona mailbox. The driver asked her to dinner. His name was Fred. He was a man, he wanted to fornicate with her, his marriage was on the rocks.

Charity sent him away. No man thought fornication was a sin.

The FedEx money triggered a flashback, months ago, sitting in this same ugly office, when her computer bonged—email from Joey. He was in town. He wanted to see her, how about lunch? Charity had trouble breathing. How had Joey found her?

What did he want?

Minutes before noon, Joey appeared, all grown up now, in town for a banker's convention. He wore a sharp suit, that same serious look, *let me take you to lunch.*

He took her to Gillcy's, overlooking the Strip. Ordered her a double martini, how did he know?

Joey had a new face. Charity asked why.

My plastic visage, Joey had said. He was playing hero in Kabul when he ran into an IED. Joey had been a sniper. He brought out his cellphone, opened a screen. "Guess who?" he said.

Charity was shocked. She stared at shots of her only child, baby Howard, given up for adoption because she was on the run. "Flip through," Joey said. "Like this."

Photo One—there was Howard in his truck, Schumacher's Gardens.

Photo Two—there was Howard's little family—Howard, his wife, his baby.

Photo Three—there was Howard in an ambulance, getting his head bandaged, while a cop jotted notes. A caption read: *Driver At Fault.*

Photo Four—there was Howard's poor truck, its front end buried in a yellow school bus. A caption read: *Accidents Happen.*

Joey described how he had shot Howard's truck tire, making the truck skid into the school bus. Joey was crazy but cool. What was he doing with the photos?

Joey brought out the list. It had five names: Tyler, Coolidge, Findlay, Delaplane, Hawthorne. Joey wanted them dead. Did she remember how they had treated her?

Charity remembered them, no worries there. They were macho bastards, jazzed on testosterone. They had ruined her life. Beside each name was a number. $40K for Tyler, $45K for Coolidge, prices ratcheting up with each kill. Joey smiled. She smelled revenge. Joey's voice was calm, matter-of-fact.

Charity's child was 30 years old. If she wanted him to celebrate his 31st birthday, she better say yes to the kills.

She was seeing Joey's nasty streak: he was using the photos of Howard as part of a motivation package: money, revenge, blackmail.

She was too afraid to ask the question: did Joey know that Ackerman was Howard's daddy?

23

Gerry Ramsay's reputation was at stake.

He was broke.

His debts kept piling up.

The courts had his money tied in knots.

His oldest boy was in prison.

His youngest boy was in psychiatric counseling … after being brain-washed in Taos.

Gerry piled the Arabs into the Escalade.

His wife stood in the doorway of the vacation rental.

She was turning into a real bitch.

It had to be the money.

He drove the sinuous streets of the Village, then parked in the lot at Sedona Landing.

Gerry was getting paid 50 grand for babysitting four Arabs. The main Arab was Prince Kemal. He was mid-20s, the youngest son of an oil sheik. The prince wore a new Stetson, a fringed leather vest, and snakeskin boots, pale green. The uncle of the prince was Rashid, brother to the oil sheik, with a PhD in economics from some hot-shit school in London. He told Gerry to call him Uncle.

The two bodyguards were chunky. One was Hassan, one was Hussein. They had already knocked off one case of Red Bull. The Arabs piled out. The uncle came last, he was on the phone with Senator Hiram Fish. He spoke like a Brit, upper-class snotty.

Gerry made a phone of his thumb and little finger. He wanted a word with the senator. The uncle shook his head. The prince pointed to a girl on the tennis court. Blonde, tanned, athletic, smooth moves on the court. The prince pointed at her, did his John Wayne imitation.

"That one, Pilgrim. Connect me up."

Gerry nodded. No worries, Prince.

They took a curved sidewalk to the lobby.

Gerry spoke to the guy at the desk. They were here for the walk-through. The desk guy was not happy. His name badge said Raul. He got on the phone.

The security guys, Hassan and Hussein, stood at the view window that looked down on the pool, pointing and grunting.

A frosty redheaded woman introduced herself to Gerry.

Her name was Giselle Roux. She had instructions from the banker to give them a tour. The prince kissed her hand. His eyes lit up, his teeth gleamed. The prince walked beside her, jabbering in French.

She led them through the hotel.

Lobby, restaurant, Bell Rock Bistro, pool, tennis courts—the blonde had left—beauty parlor, the Member's Spa. There were three elevators—two for the hotel, one for the penthouse, worked on a keycard.

They took a regular elevator to One. She let them into Room 100, a two-bedroom suite. She led them up the stairs to Two. Uncle asked to see Five.

Gerry said, "This is a hotel, Uncle. Same all the way up."

"The senator wishes to have a report, eyes-on, as you Americans say."

"If the senator says jump," Gerry said, "you say how high. That right?"

"You Americans," Uncle said.

On Five, Uncle checked out all the rooms.

He muttered in Arabic. One guard took photos; the other one took notes. The uncle asked to see the penthouse. Giselle Roux pulled out her cell, turned her back for the call. Gerry heard her murmuring. She finished the call, told Uncle it was impossible.

Gerry asked for the number; he knew Ackerman from way back. Giselle made a second call, handed the phone to Gerry.

"Hey, Mr. Ackerman, this is Gerald Ramsay. I met you thirty years ago, you might not remember—I was a great admirer back then of Arc-Angel equity—and I'm here in your town with some Arab friends. I made a promise they could have a quick look at your—"

"Arabs?" Ackerman said.

"Arab friends," Gerry said.

"No fucking way," Ackerman said.

The phone went dead, Gerry hit redial, got a busy signal. They followed Giselle Roux to the ninth floor. At the end of the hallway, Gerry saw the yellow crime scene ribbons.

"What's this?" Uncle said.

"A guest died," she said.

"Foul play?" Uncle said. "Here in the hotel?"

"You'd better ask the police."

"Mr. Ramsay, please investigate. Thank you so much."

When the elevator door opened onto the lobby, Gerry saw the blonde from the tennis courts. She was coming out of the penthouse elevator. "That one," the prince said, and introduced himself, kissing her hand.

"Whoa," the blonde said.

Giselle Roux introduced the blonde. Her name was Teri something. The Prince invited her for a drink.

"Prince of what?" the blonde said.

The Prince said something in Arabic. He hauled out his wallet. The blonde giggled. He talked bullshit; she fucking liked it.

"Well, Mister Prince," the blonde said. "If you have some time later, I barista at Red Rock Coffee, so maybe you could drop by?"

"I will do it," he said. "The Red Rock Coffee."

She took her hand back.

Took her time walking away—long legs, tight ass, Arizona dream girl.

Beside Gerry, Yancey Latimer said, "Maybe the prince will bring her to Uncle's little party."

"You see the ring?"

"What fucking ring?"

"It's a Promise Ring," Gerry said. "My kid dated a babe who wore one. He never got to first base."

"Promise to who?" Latimer said.

"To Jesus," Gerry said. "And the correct pronoun would be *whom*."

"Christ, Ramsay" Latimer said. "If all the world was on fire, you'd bring out your fucking grammar book."

BACK AT TEN FOXGLOVE Lane, the uncle said, "You told me you were friends with the old Jew."

"I do fucking know him."

"Not well enough, it seems."

"Ease up, Uncle. Your nephew connected with a hot babe."

"You promised me a view of the penthouse."

"You saw what happened, Christ."

"I saw an ineffective plan," Uncle said. "Crafted by a banker without a bank. What time does the entertainment arrive?"

"When they get here," Gerry said.

"Then you have time to check with the police … about those yellow ribbons."

24

VORTEX BANK CLOSED AT five, but Cypher stayed in the office, catching up. It was still twilight when he locked the big outer door. A vehicle pulled into the lot—Teri Breedlove in her mother's Tahoe. A second vehicle rumbled from the street. Teri's voice sounded frightened.

"I need help, Jeremy."

"What's wrong?"

"The pickup behind me," she said. "It's Tito Trujillo."

"What does he want?"

"I was hitting some balls with his brother Javier—the kid could be good—when Tito invited me for a beer. I said no, he came on real strong. He followed me here."

Cypher didn't like it. He had a yen for this girl. She was luscious, the proverbial girl next door. He didn't want to confront Tito Trujillo; the fellow had a reputation. The Tahoe had a bike rack. Cypher stowed the yellow bike, climbed in next to Teri, and smelled marijuana smoke. A female at the wheel made him edgy.

She grabbed his wrist. "I could kiss you," she said.

It was a mile to Cypher's home on Fox Hollow. The pickup

left them after two blocks. Teri sighed, said, "Thank you so much, Jeremy, you're a sweetheart." On the drive to his house, she chattered on about tennis. They had lost their doubles today because Axel was off his game. Some guy fell down some stairs in Santa Fe, she didn't know who. She had met an Arab prince at the hotel. Babble-babble.

She took a corner going forty-five, and the big car tilted. She was going too fast for the Village streets. Cypher flashed on another big overpowered car, another teenage driver with golden hair, another female who drove too fast. Christmas, 30 years ago.

Images flickered in his memory: snow, Christmas Eve, no traffic on the icy brick streets of his small town.

Cypher had been fifteen. He sat in the death seat, knew he was going to die.

The girl next door was going to kill him.

Her name was Alyson Smith. She was going way over the speed limit, driving like a banshee. *Christmas Eve is so boring, let's get high!* She tucked his hand between her legs, and he felt the muscles squeezing. She was insane. He loved her.

Curve coming up, Alyson was braking, turning the wheel, the big car spinning, *touch me now!*

Two rotations. The car slowed, spun to a stop. She was panting, nodding. She dislodged his hand—and then an ambulance streaked past, lights flashing, and Alyson followed, more excitement on Christmas Eve.

The flashing lights stopped at Wolflin School.

A fire truck, a police car, men in white pushing a gurney toward something dark on the ground.

Cypher remembered his feet pounding on frozen playground dirt.

He remembered colored Christmas lights, cozy houses.

A voice said: "Your dad died from falling, son."

He telephoned Mother from the hospital.

She was attending a church party hosted by Brother O'Brien.

Mother adored parties; her voice turned sharp when Cypher stammered the news.

Father's death notice did not make Page One. LOCAL BUSINESSMAN DIES FROM FALLING, pushed way back to page fourteen.

25

THEY WERE SEATED AT Ackerman's window table in the Bell Rock Bistro when Helene saw Marina Ramsay, looking hesitant in a pale purple track suit. Murdock was eating. The soup was beef barley, aromatic. His face was weary; he was on his third glass of red wine. He saw Helene looking past him, so he turned around, a quick glance, and went back to his soup.

"Who is that beautiful woman?" Ackerman said. "Why is she looking this way?"

"Her name is Marina Ramsay," Helene said.

"You know her?"

"We met up with her in Taos," Murdock said.

"Ramsay?" Ackerman said. "Isn't that the name of the craphead banker who brought those goddamned Arabs?"

"She's here," Murdock said. "You can ask her yourself."

Marina Ramsay stood in the doorway, scanning the room, an actress waiting for her cue. Giselle Roux appeared, Marina nodded, and they walked down the steps into the Bell Rock Bistro. Marina had thinned down since Taos. Her face had the high color that came from recent exercise and her black hair was tousled. She looked restless, edgy, maybe even afraid.

As she came toward the table, people turned to watch. Marina had been a Miss Universe runner-up when she was eighteen. That was twenty years ago, but she still knew how to make an entrance.

Ackerman stood up. Murdock stayed seated. Helene stood up and held out her hand.

"Hello, Mrs. Ramsay."

"I'm sorry to interrupt," Marina said. "But I came to warn you …. Are you Mr. Ackerman?"

They shook hands. Ackerman held a chair for her. She gave him her watery-eyed, pleading look. Marina said thank you and ordered hot coffee and a splash of cognac. When the coffee arrived, she dumped in two packets of sweetener. When she stirred, her hand shook. Ackerman said, "Warn us about what?"

"So sorry to barge in," she said "My house is all Arabs and burnt meat. My husband is drinking—he had a loss of face today. He promised them a tour of the penthouse. When the tour was refused, my husband turned on me. It was my fault, he said, for not coming along. He was ready to sell me, he said. Auction me off to the Arabs. I ran away. The streets are so confusing, with their curves. I saw the lights, I came here."

"Where is your house, ma'am?"

"It's not mine," Marina said. "It's a rental, borrowed from some friends. Where is it? Off there in the dark somewhere on another curved street, called Something Fox or Fox Something. Your street names here sound so much alike. I can't go back. I came here, to this wonderful old hotel. I was feeling desperate when I saw Miss Steinbeck's name, the workshop. Giselle brought me here. While I'm confessing, I would like to apologize to you people for what happened in Taos. You must understand my position. I was a mother frightened for her children, and well, we are still feeling the aftershocks, and I still have two sons in dire jeopardy and—"

Ackerman stopped her, his hand on her arm. She thanked

him. Then, playing the white knight, he offered her a spare bedroom in his penthouse. She argued with him, but her words were a sham, flirty and ultra-feminine. Marina was the lost princess in need of sanctuary and her presence gave Ackerman a chance to play lord of the manor.

Helene looked at Murdock, who had gone back to his soup. Ackerman waved at the waitress; Marina ordered scrambled eggs and toast. Her coffee was gone, would she like some wine? Oh, yes. White or red? Whatever Ackerman was drinking was good enough for Marina. The waitress brought the wine.

"So," Ackerman said. "You're trapped in there with four Arabs, one husband. Anyone else?"

"Just a friend from Dallas. His name is Latimer."

"Benjamin Latimer?"

"Yancey," she said. "His son."

"Another goddamn banker?" Ackerman said.

"Yes. And having quite a run of bad luck. We all are."

"What I heard," Ackerman said. "The Arabs want to turn this old hotel into a casino?"

"The sheikh's son, Kemal, has this thing about the Old West, cowboys, gunfighters. He keeps watching old Western movies. His hero is Shane."

"Four Arabs and two Dallas bankers," Ackerman said. "How are they getting along?"

"The man called Uncle simmers with anger," she said.

"We can check on him for you," Ackerman said.

"Oh," Marina said. "I hate being a bother."

26

HELENE HEARD ACKERMAN USE the word, *We*. It was not an accident, a slip of the tongue. He looked at Helene, then he looked at Murdock, who was reaching for a hunk of bread. There was silence around the table. Murdock glanced at Helene.

She and Murdock were part of Ackerman's royal *We*, his hired help, his in-house detective-servants. They had started at five thousand for a single day. Delaplane's death in Santa Fe had landed them a two-day contract, at twenty thousand. From Ackerman's point of view, if they took the money, they were there to serve.

Murdock took his time spreading the butter. The bread was whole wheat, with pumpkin seeds. Helene watched Ackerman lift the wine bottle. Instead of topping of his own glass, he filled Marina's.

Her scrambled eggs arrived. She took one bite, exhaled, looked around the table, and said thank you. Helene saw big changes in this nasty wife of a nasty Dallas banker. When she first came in, Marina's eyes had been frightened. With each bite of food she looked better, a woman with real bounce-back.

Murdock finished his soup and stood up. He was still pinch-hitting for Manolo Quintana, doing hotel security.

"Where are you going?" Ackerman said.

"Gotta do my rounds," Murdock said. "Check those old doorknobs."

"I need you to check on that den of Arabs."

"When the hotel is secure," Murdock said. "Meanwhile, boss, stay off the stairs."

Ackerman grinned, shook his head. He liked Murdock, liked people who stood up to him. Ackerman asked Giselle for the keys to the Humvee. They were in her office.

"Okay," Ackerman said. "When Sherlock is done doing his rounds, you people take that Humvee for a test drive. Before you come back here, check on Mrs. Ramsay's husband."

Helene said okay. She liked cars. She'd been wanting to drive the Humvee, see how it handled. It was cold outside, and she needed her parka.

As she left the table, Helene heard Ackerman snapping orders at Giselle. He wanted her to replace Murdock on this silly hotel security substitution thing. He wanted a penthouse keycard for Marina Ramsay. He wanted Mrs. Ramsay to have guestroom four. Helene heard Giselle replying—she was busy, the maids were off duty, why didn't Ackerman make the bed himself? Then Helene heard Marina Ramsay saying, not a problem, she herself was capable of making up a bed.

HELENE LOVED DRIVING THE Humvee. She zoomed along Highway 179—no traffic at this hour—then hopped onto the interstate, roaring south down the freeway toward Phoenix. At 97 miles per hour, the Hummer gave a little shimmy, got worse at 100, gone at 110. She found a place to make a U-turn.

"Feel better now?"

"I want one."

"Couple weeks working for Ackerman, you can buy one of these with cash."

"He's treating you like a son, you know."

"He's one sad old dude," Murdock said. "Let's check the scene of the crime. Maybe catch your pal Gerry in bed with a hooker."

"Ackerman put Marina into guest room four," Helene said.

"She's got the instincts of an alley cat in heat."

"She was trying to be pleasant," Helene said.

"She's in a tight spot," Murdock said.

"Did you ask Cypher about the Arabs?" Helene said.

"I was about to when he took a phone call."

"Maybe when we check on Gerry Ramsay, we can ask him."

"I forgot my rubber hose," Murdock said.

"You can offer to give him back those boots."

"No way," Murdock said. "Those are good boots. I earned them."

"What's that street again?"

"Ten Foxglove Lane," Murdock said. "It's between Fox Hollow and Fox Glen."

"It's like Fairyland," Helene said. "Living in this village, these soft street names."

*****

MARINA RAMSAY YAWNED AS she tucked in the top sheet. She was in Guestroom Four, the inner circle, with Bruno, Ackerman's manservant. She felt safe here; she felt opportunity. She was fed up with Gerry.

"I hope I'm not running anyone out of bed."

"My room is off the kitchen," Bruno said. "Miss Roux has Guestroom One."

"Where does Mr. Ackerman sleep?"

"The Master Bedroom, madam."

27

TEN FOXGLOVE LANE—HASHISH SMOKE, laughter from the kitchen.

The doorbell rang, and Gerry went to answer.

But Uncle beat him to it, throwing open the door, *welcome to Sedona, ladies*. Framed in the doorway Gerry saw two hookers, one in red, one in black, ladies of the night straight from Phoenix.

The hooker in black was mid-30s, dirty-blonde hair, a wicked mouth, holding it together in a tough profession. "I'm Suzanne," she said.

Her friend in red was a Latina, maybe twenty, with mesh stockings and a sweet smile that she turned on Gerry.

"*Hola*," she said. "I am Rosita."

Gerry smelled perfume, soap, woman. Their vehicle, a big pickup, was parked in the driveway, behind Gerry's Escalade.

Rosita's warm handshake made Gerry want her, ten minutes, fifteen, man on top, real sex with a real woman who gave a shit. His wife had cut him off—what a bitch.

Then Uncle said, "This way, ladies."

They left Gerry standing in the hallway, pissed off. Uncle had the money, U.S. greenbacks in a green North Face backpack. In this transaction, Uncle was the Big Dog,

Gerry heard applause from the kitchen, loud Arab voices, laughter, have a drink, ladies. The blonde's voice carried: "Is the pool heated? I'd love a dip." Gerry turned his back on them, opened the front door, no wife in sight, no Marina Alessandro Vargas Ramsay. The bitch had been running in Dallas, morning and night, her quick feet taking her away from the marriage, toward divorce.

They were bunked down in Oak Creek Village, a dead little suburb south of Sedona, to buy an old hotel for Prince Kemal—his Saudi daddy was rich in petro-dollars—and turn it into a casino. Gerry was brokering the deal because he needed the job, because the fucking courts had frozen his equity—endless fallout from that fucked-up mess in Taos—and because his wife was cozying up to Hiram Fish, who was cozy with Arab oil.

Gerry flicked on the TV—football, football, football, golf. He had given up his membership at Brookhaven, because of Taos, that guy Murdock, who still had Gerry's boots. Uncle walked by, sweet-talking the blonde. She carried a bottle of Chivas. The Latina walked by, holding hands with Prince Kemal, son of a sheik, a fresh-faced boy, cigarette dangling, who looked at Gerry and said, "Okay, Pilgrim, who said this: 'Only the farmers won. We lost. We always lose.' "

"Yul Brynner in *The Magnificent Seven*," Gerry said. "He was talking to Steve McQueen."

"I'll get you yet, Pilgrim."

"Is he really a pilgrim?" the Latina said.

"A figure of speech, beautiful lady."

"In my language, that would be *El Peregrino*."

The Prince laughed, pointed at Gerry, and mouthed the word, *Peregrino*.

The Latina blew Gerry a kiss: *you're next*. He heard her high heels on the hallway pavers.

This house, Ten Foxglove Lane in Oak Creek Village, belonged to a friend back in Dallas. It had eight bedrooms, five baths. It was built like twin space pods, connected by a breezeway. The pool was Olympic size, with a covered patio. Then a low fence, an arroyo between the fence and the golf course. Where the fuck was Marina?

In the kitchen, the two Arab bodyguards were smoking—Gerry smelled hashish. There was an action flick on TV, Tom Cruise leaping across rooftops. Gerry poured himself a drink of Chivas and sat down next to Yancey Latimer, his friend from SMU, back in the day. The Arabs nodded as they left the room. Gerry lifted his glass. Fucking button men with shaved heads—no way to keep those names straight. Outside, on the patio, Gerry saw movement, a shadow gliding. When he looked again, it was gone.

Latimer talked about women. He was having wife-troubles too, fallout from Taos, the Angel mountain thing. Gerry heard noises from the bedroom wing. A whispery sound, then a thump, like furniture falling. The music was loud, coming from the TV.

"You hear that?" Latimer said.

"Hear what?"

"Sounded like a goat farting."

Gerry yawned. He needed sleep. The Chivas tasted bitter. Outside on the patio thin smoke rose from the barbecue. The lid was closed; Uncle was smoking half a sheep.

Gerry looked up. A man stood in the kitchen doorway. He wore black battle dress, a black baseball cap, no team name, and yellow shooting glasses. His eyes behind them were steel-blue. He shot Latimer with an automatic weapon, ammo in a curved banana clip. When the rounds hit home, Latimer was halfway out of his chair.

Latimer slumped, grabbing for the table.

Gerry was a hunter from Texas. He knew his guns. The guy in the doorway was armed with an MK17. The rounds were nine mil. The clip looked like a 30. The guy wore a balaclava that covered his mouth, but his eyes were smiling. He shot the two button men; one had a pistol out. Chairs crashed onto the kitchen floor. The gun swung to Gerry, and his right hand exploded.

Gerry felt faint. He slid off the chair, putting the table between himself and the shooter. Gerry's hand blazed, hot fire. He needed ice, *holy shit*.

Yancey Latimer was on his back, eyes staring at the ceiling. Gerry wished that his wife, snooty Marina, would walk in, right fucking now. Get a taste of this gunfire. Gerry tried to stand, but his legs were shaking. His head rang with klaxons from a European cop movie. He crawled to the doorway leading to the patio—*get away from this house, this fucking madman*. He was reaching for the doorknob when he felt a tap on his shoulder. It was the shooter. His eyes were smiling behind the yellow lenses. The balaclava had a slit for the mouth.

"Hey, Ramsay," the mouth said. "Remember me?"

Gerry shook his head. A voice from the past, tugging at him—*hey, Ramsay*. Gerry's brain did a back flip, diving into the past. His brain was a camera, the camera was airborne. It homed in on a dusty schoolyard, dusk of an autumn day, leaves blowing, sepia tones, like an old photo. A chain-link fence, steel poles for a volleyball net. The wind was fierce; it never stopped in that tiny town. Red leaves, yellow leaves, dead leaves, and this little nothing shit wanted to fight.

"We can work something out," Gerry said.

"Still the wheeler-dealer."

Gerry's hands were red with Latimer's blood. He clawed at the door. His belly was bloated; he felt a belch starting. Too much food, not enough gym-time. You had to push yourself to not be fat. The Chivas came back up, burned his throat.

Helpless, feeling the nearness of death, he watched the shooter advance. Felt the muzzle against his forehead. There was a soft pop, then nothing.

28

THE HUMVEE WAS ON Fox Hollow Road when Murdock told Helene to cut the lights. Helene glared at him, *who's the driver here*, then swung onto Foxglove Lane. It was a corner house, a three car garage, five bedrooms, maybe six. Lights were on. A barbecue sat on the patio, smoke rising. Murdock rolled down his window and the smell of burnt meat made Helene nauseous. Movement on the patio caught her attention. They were coasting now, easing down as the street sloped. A shadow broke the yellow light from the patio windows, moving fast.

"Goose it," Murdock said.

"I'm driving here."

"Sorry."

"I've got him."

Helene caught the man in the headlights once, a runner in a track suit, wearing shoes with no reflectors. The Hummer was closing the distance—sixty feet, fifty feet away—when the runner vanished. Helene saw a glint of metal. It was up the street, near the corner. When she turned the corner, there was no one.

"Maybe he had a bike waiting," Murdock said. "No noise. No reflectors, no lights."

"A black bike," Helene said. "Or we'd have seen something."

"Let's check the house."

Helene parked the Humvee up the street at the edge of the golf course.

She pulled latex gloves from her rucksack, handed a pair to Murdock.

Helene was a cop's daughter, *always be prepared*.

They checked their flashlights.

She followed Murdock across the drainage ditch, over the short adobe wall, on to the patio at Ten Foxglove Lane. The burnt meat smell came from a gas cooker on the patio. No sounds came from the house. Helene felt sick. She remembered Angel Mountain.

She stood with Murdock, looking through the kitchen window.

Broken glass, broken wine bottles, bullet holes in the walls, a guy in a shirt and jeans. And someone lying against the back door. She saw white tennis shoes, no socks, the pale yellow legs of a track suit.

The house was two pods connected by a corridor with skylights.

There was no water in the pool. They found an open window, a body on the floor, boxer shorts white in the flashlight beam. Murdock went in first. Helene kept watch outside. Eleven o'clock in Oak Creek Village and nothing was moving. Was this normal for a Tuesday?

Murdock called her inside. Helene climbed through the window, into a bedroom. The white shorts went with a dead guy on the floor—hairy legs, wearing a red tank top, his blood still wet and gleaming on the carpet. One of Ackerman's Arabs.

A woman in the hallway—blonde, blowsy, wearing a yellow teddy, and one shoe, red, with a spiked heel. Her eyes stared at nothing.

A second dead guy in the adjoining bedroom.

He was young, late twenties, his beard two days old, edged thin by a barber.

Three down, how many to go?

They worked their way down the corridor. The curtains were closed, blocking the view of the empty pool. In the third bedroom, they found a third dead Arab and a woman about Teri Breedlove's age, black hair, black panties, her face dotted by bullets. The guy was still dressed.

The fourth Arab lay face down, a pistol on the floor, where the connecting corridor exploded into the high-ceilinged living room, leather furniture and another fake fireplace where fake flames leaped.

They moved across the carpet, guns and flashlights, then on to the parquet floor of the dining room.

The kitchen was king-size, a curved countertop with bar chairs, a six-burner range, two ovens built into the wall, two microwaves, two dishwashers.

The man Helene had seen through the window was Yancey Latimer, a Dallas rich guy who had been part of the Ramsay gang in Taos.

The dead guy in the silky yellow track suit had his back to the patio door.

There was shattered glass around him, blood streaks on his hands, as if he had crawled through glass to the door. Congealing blood around a wound in his foot.

His chin rested on his chest. There was a bullet hole between his eyes. The dead man was Gerry Ramsay, banker from Dallas, wearing tennis shoes, no socks.

Helene thought of Gerry's wife, Marina Ramsay.

She was safe at Sedona Landing, under the protective wing of Axel Ackerman. Marina had missed getting killed by a couple of hours. Maybe she got a signal, her woman's intuition. Maybe she'd had a tip, *get out now*.

29

HELENE CHECKED HER WATCH. They had been inside six minutes; time to go. Before they left, they looked for surveillance cameras, recording devices. There was one surveillance camera, mounted above the wide front entrance. It was dead, riddled by bullets. They found no microphones.

Outside, the air was chilly, no breeze.

They stripped off their latex gloves, Helene tucked them back into her rucksack. She phoned Steve Slattery on his cell. She reported a dead man at Ten Foxglove Lane.

Slattery said, "Holy shit, did you tell Deputy Fremont?"

"We phoned you, Steve."

"Stay there, don't touch a goddamn thing. What's the address again?"

Slattery hung up. Helene phoned Connie Fremont.

They sat in the Humvee. The dashboard clock was digital; each minute took an hour.

Seven minutes after Helene's call, headlights lit the street.

A white SUV braked to a stop in the driveway at Ten Foxglove Lane, bumper nosed up close to the black Mercedes with diplomatic plates. Two Coconino deputies climbed out, one holding a shotgun.

Helene glanced at Murdock. Inside the house, they had been a pair, two ex-cops working together. Outside, Helene felt the wall slide between them.

She remembered her first crime scene, her first murder victim, a dead wife in the Bronx. Helene had been on patrol back then; the sergeant in command was a friend of her dad's. They wanted her to understand the job. That was before she killed anyone. Killing made you see things from a different angle. It hit you in the stomach.

The next arrival was a patrol car from Sedona. Then a Crown Vic, Slattery's ride.

Then Olivera's crime-scene van, doors opening, Olivera with her valise, an assistant behind her, a chubby guy hustling to keep up.

Another white SUV paused outside, backed up, turned the corner, and drove up the dark street, stopping beside the Humvee.

The window of the SUV was down, Connie Fremont at the wheel. She said, "I brought coffee for three."

Connie parked in front of the Humvee and appeared at the door with a sack from Red Rock Coffee. Climbing into the back, she closed the door and handed out the coffee.

"So we got corpses?" she said.

"We only saw one," Helene said.

"Where was that?"

"In the kitchen."

"You get inside yet?"

"No way," Helene said.

"The crime scene is sacrosanct," Murdock said. "Thanks for the coffee."

"Run it for me," Connie said. "What were you two kids doing out here in the dark?"

"A woman asked us to check on this house," Helene said.

"Her husband was alone with some Arabs, so she left the house, ran to Sedona Landing. We knew her from Taos. She had no money. Axel offered her a bedroom for the night. Before coming over here, I took the Humvee for a little speed test. The interstate was wide open."

"Ackerman wants to sell you his Humvee?" Connie said.

"He's shifting to hybrid everything," Helene said. "He gets first dibs on the new ULT they're building for the army."

What's that mean—ULT what?"

"Ultra Light Vehicle," Helene said.

"So what made you check the house?"

"We saw this guy, this shadow … he jumped the ditch right there. He was in our headlights for like two seconds, moving really fast; then he crossed the street and disappeared. We went around a couple blocks, found no sign of him."

"Might have had a bike," Murdock said.

"So then you rang the doorbell?" Connie said.

"We did not touch the doors. We did look in the kitchen, where we saw broken glass, bullet holes, a guy on the floor, backed up against the patio door. He was not moving. We phoned it in."

"You called Steve first," Connie said.

"He's got the rank," Helene said. "Standard procedure."

"Have you forgotten what it's like to be a female cop?"

"Sorry," Helene said.

Connie's voice sounded hurt. Helene felt bad for her. The Coconino sheriff had two female deputies, Connie was one. As a female, she bridled at working with Steve Slattery. Maybe they had dated, sometime in the past. Connie was attractive, she had a great smile, she worked out, she jogged, she kept herself in shape for the job. Connie needed a break, something to give her career a boost; maybe this case was it. Only now it looked like two cases—how did the Dead Bankers connect to the Dead Arabs? And how did Ramsay and Latimer fit in?

Murdock's cellphone rang. Maybe it was Ackerman, calling for a report on Gerry Ramsay, Marina's husband.

30

THE VOICE ON THE phone came from out of the past. The caller used Murdock's nickname from the jungle. The caller-window said Homeland Security.

"Foxy Murdock, this is your commandant calling. Are you in country? Over."

"Monty?" Murdock said. "What the hell?"

"You may address me as Agent-in-Charge, Soldier."

"Where the hell are you?"

"Coming up on your flank, Soldier. How about we reconnoiter on the lighted patio."

"Roger that," Murdock said.

The voice from the past went away. Murdock could feel Helene looking at him. Before she spoke, he knew what she was thinking.

"Don't tell me," she said. "It's another of your crazy friends from the jungle."

"Monty Featherstone," Murdock said. "He was the agent-in-charge, wore a shoulder-rig. His trousers always had a crease."

"Did he call you Foxy?" Helene said.

"Aye-aye, captain."

Connie spoke from the backseat. "Is Foxy some kind of secret macho-sexy code name?"

"Murdock knows his way around," Helene said. "Mountain, gully, desert, or swamp—so the guys in his unit nicknamed him Foxy, short for the Swamp Fox, a famous name from the Revolutionary War era, a soldier named Francis Marion."

"Francis Marion won the war, single-handed," Murdock said. "Without him, we'd still be speaking the King's English. As for me, I am honored to carry his sobriquet, passed down through time, from soldier to—"

"He's delirious," Connie said. Her voice had the undercurrent of admiration.

"This guy Monty," Helene said. "Tell me he's not as crazy as Sammy Savage."

"Savage …" Connie said. "Where do I know that name from?"

"Forget it," Helene said.

"I remember," Connie said. "Something about gun-play in a courtroom in Taos, right?"

"I'm trying to forget, okay?"

"Better leave your weapon in the vehicle, Steinbeck."

"No problem," Helene said. "If this old jungle buddy gets out of line, I'll let Connie shoot him."

"Let me get a look at him first," Connie said. "Is he single?"

THERE WAS NO BREEZE, and the smell of scorched meat hung over the patio. Monty Featherstone wore a leather jacket, dark pants, and horn-rimmed glasses. Monty was not as tall as Murdock remembered. He looked shrunken, stooped. What was he doing in Oak Creek Village?

Murdock introduced Connie first, then Helene. When he shook hands with Helene, Monty held on for two extra beats. Asked for a briefing, Helene repeated the story she had told Connie Fremont. Featherstone did not take notes. He nodded but he did not ask follow-up questions; instead, he asked to see the officer in charge. Connie went off to find Slattery.

Helene said, "You and Murdock are old jungle buddies?"

Featherstone said, "Foxy was in-country, where the fun was. I was at the firebase, sipping whiskey, smoking cigars, playing poker with retired generals, politicians who needed photo ops."

"When did you sign on with Homeland Security?" Murdock said.

Monty said, "It's a pre-retirement ploy. To lock in my pension, I get ferried around in black SUVs, keeps me on the payroll. How many Arabs are dead in there, anyway?"

"Beats me," Murdock said.

"You peeked in a window, then you called the authorities ... just like that?"

"There were bullet holes," Murdock said, "and broken glass, and spilled wine, and blood, and a guy lying there. It was a crime scene. We didn't see anyone moving, no calls for help, no reason to enter, so we left it for the pros."

"The pros have arrived. Your problems are over."

Connie Fremont came around the corner, talking to Steve Slattery. Murdock made the introductions. Slattery's handshake was brusque, his voice low, an animal growling. He spent some time staring at the federal ID, then he handed it back.

"So," Slattery said. "Homeland Security, you're here because we got four dead Arabs, right?"

"Correct," Monty said.

"I worked with Feds in L.A.," Slattery said, "and in Phoenix, where they fucked up my crime scene, mucked up my investigation. So how big a Fed footprint have I got to put up with here in peaceful little Oak Creek Village?"

"I have only two requests," Monty said.

"Oh, yeah ... what?"

"I'd like to see inside, verify the identities of our Saudi friends."

"How do you do verify?" Slattery said.

"Matching photos," Monty said. "Confirmed by DNA from your lab people."

"Okay," Slattery said. "You got it. What else?"

"I'd like a copy of your weapons inventory," Monty said. "We'll run it through our database."

Slattery's cellphone rang. He turned away, walked to the edge of the patio. When he rejoined the group, he said, "That was Olivera, our CSI tech. She's got a preliminary report. After that, I'll take you inside."

"Roger that," Monty said. "Is there coffee?"

Slattery yelled at a cop to bring six coffees.

Murdock had questions for Monty Featherstone. How did he get Murdock's phone number? How did he get here so fast? But Olivera came onto the patio, and before she could get going on her report, the cop arrived with six coffees. Monty wanted milk and sugar. The cop went away. Murdock did the introductions, and Olivera gave Monty a look that became a smile. Slattery asked her to get going.

They stood in a half-circle while Olivera checked her notes.

"This is preliminary," Olivera said. "We've got four dead Arabs and two dead females, probably out of Phoenix. We've got two dead Anglos. One is Yancey Latimer, Dallas. The other dead guy has been identified as Gerald Ramsay. He owns the Escalade in the driveway. He's a banker, also out of Dallas. Since you're on the scene, Agent, we could use Federal help identifying the Arabs. Okay, where was I? There. Ammo expended … we've located forty-seven rounds so far. My guess is the shooter used an automatic weapon with a thirty-round clip and reloaded once. Everyone except the Ramsay guy had multiple wounds. His hands are bleeding—looks like he crawled through glass—and there's a lesion on his head, but the thing that killed him was a single shot between the eyes."

Monty Featherstone said, "Any info yet on caliber sizes?"

"The thirty-round clip was probably a nine mil," Olivera said. "The single shot to the eyeball was small. I can't be sure until the autopsy and the lab work, but I'd bet the bullet was a twenty-two, and shot from a pistol. If we find powder burns, we could assume that the shooter was close—eyeball to eyeball with Ramsay—when the trigger got pulled."

Olivera offered to get Monty inside, professional courtesy. He grinned; his charm was working. The grin hid something. He shook hands with Helene, then Murdock, then walked off with Olivera. Slattery and Connie followed, talking jurisdiction.

Back in the Humvee, Helene said, "What is it with your old buddies? Sammy Savage was nuts; now here comes smooth Monty Featherstone, same era, same jungle. When did you give him your cellphone number?"

"I didn't, Murdock said.

31

IN THE PENTHOUSE ELEVATOR, Helene used the keycard. She felt sticky, crusted with the day's deaths. A shower would be nice.

The construction guys had left a narrow path marked by sawhorses. Helene smelled sawdust, paint thinner, and sheet rock. The security camera tracked their progress to the door. Helene was reaching for the big black doorknocker when the door swung open and she saw Giselle Roux, in jeans and a baggy sweatshirt. Giselle's hair needed washing. Her eyes showed her weariness.

They followed Giselle into the living room.

Ackerman sat in the black-leather armchair. The TV screen was on, playing a cop show rerun. Nothing on the massacre yet.

Marina Ramsay was not in the room.

Helene stayed quiet while Murdock briefed Ackerman on the Foxglove Lane crime scene. The lone shooter, the automatic weapon, the thirty-round clip. Ackerman kept his steely look. Giselle Roux said, "Oh no." Ackerman pushed himself out of his chair. His wine glass spilled, red wine sloshing the carpet.

He stared down at the wine. He jerked his head at Giselle. She left the room, headed down the wide hallway.

Bruno came in from the kitchen. He wore an apron and there was sweat on his bald head.

He went to his knee, pressed the tea towel onto the dark spot, the spilled wine.

Ackerman pointed a finger at Murdock. His hand was shaking. He sat down again.

"Dead?" he said. "Her husband is *dead*?"

Giselle Roux came back, arms linked with Marina Ramsay.

Marina's hair was ruffled from the bed. Worry lines marked her face. She asked about her husband.

"He's dead, Mrs. Ramsay," Ackerman said.

Her face collapsed, and she moaned, slumped onto the sofa. Ackerman sat beside her, put his arm around her. What would she like? Coffee? Tea? A glass of red wine? "Did you see him?" Marina asked.

Helene nodded. She had questions; she waited for an opening. Marina Ramsay was a survivor, and the bereaved widow pose was an act. Giselle Roux brought a blanket. Ackerman tucked it around Marina's legs. Bruno came back with a teapot on a tray. A tiny teacup, a tiny cream pitcher, a bowl of sugar cubes. As she drank the tea, Marina eased her face into fake sorrow mode. When she set the teacup down, it did not rattle the saucer. Lady in control.

Helene studied Marina on the sofa, sipping her tea. Her eyes watered. She kept asking if they were sure. Was her husband really dead?

Tired, Helene waited for an opening. Murdock was no help. He looked half-asleep—a better word would be *quiescent*—his eyes closed, his breathing steady. But under the quiet, she felt his brain working, chewing at the case. The room waited while Marina Ramsay sipped her tea.

32

HELENE WIGGLED HER TOES.
 Still there, reality check, ten toes, two feet.

She pulled off her right sock. The foot was less tender. Maybe she should call Karla Kurtz for a massage. She slid off the black leather sofa onto the floor. Murdock touched her shoulder, the fingers of a stranger.

What was going on with them?

Helene had no clue. There was this wall between them.

A wall, Helene thought, *what a shitty metaphor for separation.* More like the little lattice-work screen in the confession booth, the Catholic church, her mother's church; Helene's mother was a French Catholic girl who fell in love with a Jew named Steinbeck. Helene was 12 when her mother died. She went one last time to the church, the musty confession booth and spilled her sorrow into the half-dark. The priest murmured. His words stopped at the little scrollwork screen.

"I can't hear you, Father."

The words from the priest came again, mumbles, murmurs. God was so far away.

"Father," she said. "I cannot hear you."

"My child," he said. "You are…."

The words faded, died, leaving a silence worse than silence.

Helene looked at Murdock out of the corner of her eye. He looked back. He was baffled too. They had that in common, being baffled together.

The phone rang. Bruno picked up in the kitchen, then reported to Ackerman.

"The person from Homeland Security," Bruno said. "He wants an audience with Mrs. Ramsay."

"Fuck him," Ackerman said.

"Please," Marina said. "I will go down."

"No you won't," Ackerman said. "Tell him okay, Bruno."

"Yes, Master."

Helene smiled. Bruno and Ackerman were like brothers, one black, one white. They read each other's thoughts. The doorbell rang.

AGENT MONTY FEATHERSTONE WAS a good-looking man. An East Coast guy, he knew how to dress. Helene was from Brooklyn, a cop's daughter, and she knew the power of the upper classes.

If you were upper class East Coast, they taught you how to operate. How to play tennis, billiards, croquet at lawn parties. How to charm the teachers, get those grades. How to get into the top schools, join the top clubs, root for the right teams. How to get the top girl, a trophy female to stand by your side at the best parties.

If you were upper class, they prepped you to take the helm, to stabilize the status quo.

Featherstone's trousers had the knife-edge crease. Helene had not noticed at the crime scene. In this light, his leather jacket looked worn but expensive—that hand-me-down vintage heirloom look.

He wore the button-down shirt open at the throat—as if he had just this minute removed the stylish necktie. His black shoes gleamed in the flickering light from Ackerman's fake fireplace.

He shook hands with Ackerman.

He accepted a glass of wine from Bruno.

In a solemn voice, Featherstone expressed the perfect dollop of sympathy for Marina Ramsay's dead husband. He was stalling, feinting, posing—he had crossed the threshold into Ackerman's world. Why was he really here?

"You have questions for me?"

"Is this a good time?"

"If you don't have so many," she said. "I am so—"

"Is this a good place," Featherstone said. "Or would you prefer—"

"I am among friends here," she said. "Please."

"What time did you leave the residence at Foxglove Lane?"

"Around eight. I was afraid, I don't know."

"Mrs. Ramsay arrived here at 8:05," Ackerman said.

"What motivated you to leave?" Featherstone said.

"He sold me," Marina said, "to that beastly Arab person."

"Which Arab, ma'am?"

"The older one, the uncle. What a swine."

"Did you know him from before tonight?"

"He came to my home … in Dallas."

"Did he make any advances there?"

"Yes."

"Did you tell your husband?"

"Gerry told me to be a good hostess."

"When you left Foxglove Lane, what was happening then?"

"They were drinking. They were quite loud, bragging about their sexual prowess."

"Did you see the money change hands?"

"It's why I left."

"Was it an IOU? Cash?"

"It was cash" Marina said.

"There was no cash found—not that much, anyway—at the crime scene."

"I'm sorry," Marina said. "Was there a question?"

"I only have a couple more."

Ackerman said, "Don't cross-examine her, goddammit."

Featherstone turned to stare at Ackerman. His voice had an edge. He represented the power of the state.

"I'm with Homeland Security, sir. What we have here is the making of an international incident—I'm hoping to exclude you from the investigation."

"I made a couple phone calls," Ackerman said. "You work for Hiram Fish. You're his goddamn official fixer."

"The Senator sends his regards," Featherstone said. "He speaks warmly of you."

"These dead Arabs," Ackerman said. "Were they oil people?"

"Prince Kemal's father happens to be an oil sheik, yes."

"Four Arabs," Ackerman said. "Two gotta be security goons. So there was one more raghead hotshot. Who was he?"

"Jamal Rashid," Featherstone said. "Attached to the embassy, hence the diplomatic plates."

"There's something else," Ackerman said. "Or you wouldn't be here."

Helene felt the shift in the room, a change in the atmosphere. Featherstone was lying, Ackerman had caught him—something political, maybe. Murdock's old jungle Buddy was not here to interrogate Marina Ramsay.

Featherstone stood up, locked eyes with Ackerman for moment, then drained his wine glass. Bruno led him to the door.

As Featherstone left the room, Helene felt like a weight had been lifted. She got to her feet. An idea buzzed in her head. She turned to Marina Ramsay.

"Mrs. Ramsay," she said.

"Please call me Marina."

"Okay, Marina," Helene said. "Did the Arabs contact your husband ... or did he contact them?"

33

Silence in the room while Marina Ramsay sipped her tea. She looked at Ackerman, who gave her his best fatherly smile. Marina took a deep breath, Helene could hear the gears shifting.

"It was through Yancey Latimer," she said. "He knew someone in Washington."

"So was buying this old hotel Latimer's idea?"

"They were always cooking something up."

"Were they using a local bank?" Helene said.

"If they were, Gerry didn't tell me."

"Did your husband mention that he knew about Mr. Ackerman … that he was buying the hotel?"

"All I know is that Mr. Ackerman was some kind of hero to Gerry."

"Now I've heard everything," Ackerman said.

"What do you mean 'hero'?" Helene said.

"Gerry had this story about going to New York," Marina said. "He was right out of high school. He left messages at Mr. Ackerman's business. He tried to make appointments. They never made contact."

Helene turned to Ackerman. The old guy was twisted around in his chair, staring at Marina Ramsay. Maybe it was the brandy, but she seemed perkier, more color in her face, the pallor ebbing.

"When the hell was this?" Ackerman said.

"Gerry was just out of high school," Marina said.

"How did he know about me?"

"He worked on the high-school newspaper," Marina said. "He interviewed local businessmen."

"Where was the newspaper?" Helene said.

"I don't remember the town," Marina said. "They were talking about the old days, before Dallas. We were in the car, Yancey Latimer was driving. I was in the back seat, trying to sleep. They were talking about driving at night, escaping their small town. They compared the cars of today with their cars in high school. The high school memories got Gerry going. He wore glasses back then. They called him Clark Kent, boy reporter. He was bragging about interviewing Mr. Ackerman for the high school newspaper. This time, he said, he would get in to see him."

"Are you sure?" Ackerman said.

"It's not your average name," Marina said. "So this afternoon, Gerry and his friends were not allowed up here. He lost face. The Arabs turned rowdy. That awful man came after me. But if I had stayed…."

Marina stopped talking, her face pale. She turned her head, fixed her gaze on Ackerman.

He said, "You poor gal."

Silence filled the room. Helene nudged Murdock. His eyes opened; he observed Marina Ramsay. She was fidgeting with her tea-cup. Helene wondered how much of Marina's story was true. Bruno topped off her brandy and vanished into the kitchen.

"Mrs. Ramsay," Murdock said. "How well do you know Senator Fish?"

"Not well. Why do you ask?"

"What about your husband?"

"He supports the Senator … or did, when we had money."

"Murdock?" Ackerman said. "Where the hell is this coming from?"

"Just trying to fit the pieces together, Ack."

"What pieces?"

"Arabs and oil money," Murdock said. "Arizona real estate, competing bids for an old hotel. Senator Fish chairs the Senate committee on energy. He's also on the committee that oversees Homeland Security. Has the Senator been to your house often, Mrs. Ramsay?"

Marina Ramsay dropped her teacup. It hit the carpet and bounced, splashing tea laced with brandy. She stood up, put her face in her hands, and started crying. Ackerman gave Murdock a look of disapproval. He got to his feet, gripped Marina's shoulders, and turned her over to Giselle Roux. Marina and Giselle left the room.

Murdock was on his knees, sopping up the spilled tea, the perfect clean-up man. Bruno came out from the kitchen, tried to take over the mopping up, but Murdock waved him away, like a sinner doing penance.

"Was that really necessary?" Ackerman said. "The poor woman's just lost her husband."

"Tell us about this guy, Fish."

"Fat face Hiram Fish," Ackerman said. "He was seven years behind me in school. I knew him because I cleaned the family swimming pool. That smug prick would stand in the shade, order me around. Fish was too fat for sports—there's a story of him puking at football tryouts—so he chose politics, became senior class president. He scratched his way up—city government, county, state, the house, the senate."

"How do you guys get along?"

"He's a born-again right winger. I'm a liberal Jew. Why?"

"Working on our list," Murdock said. "People who hold a

grudge against Axel Ackerman. We'll add Fish."

"Fish is a coward," Ackerman said. "He's in bed with the Arabs, but he doesn't have the balls to engineer these kills. Speaking of kills, you two look dead. Something going on, something in Sleuth Loveland I should know about?"

*****

Ackerman was in bed, dreaming of Daphne Fish, mother of Hiram, when he heard the door opening. He saw a figure silhouetted in the hallway light. The door closed. Ackerman smelled perfume.

His visitor was Marina Ramsay. She didn't ask permission. She said, "I am freezing to death and very lonely" and climbed in beside him. Cold hands, steamy body. She wore pajama tops but not the bottoms. She pushed herself against him, and Ackerman felt the magic of Doctor Tim's man-pills as blood stiffened his dick. He liked this woman, this sumptuous widow from Texas via Argentina. She was warm and needy. She knew her way around men. Her hand was on him and she got him inside with an expert shimmy. She told him to go slow, *por favor*. Ackerman sank into her. How long since his last woman?

"What will happen to me?" she said.

"Don't talk," he said. "You're here. I'm here. You're not dead. I'm certainly feeling alive. Thank you for coming."

"You are a good man," she said. "May I show you something?"

Ackerman said yes. Her finger found his asshole. His prostate was ancient. But Marina's finger brought magic, flicking that dead old gland. His orgasm arrived with bright tears smarting and a happy, pulsing dick. Marina held onto him, letting him know she expected a fee for services rendered. Ackerman was a pay-as-you-go guy. He opened the drawer in his bedside table, felt the vial of man pills next to the money stack. He laid the money on the bed sheet. The woman smiled, and the smile turned into a low chuckle. There were no words. Just her hand on his shrinking dick, warm as a womb. She did not pussyfoot around—no fake refusals, attempts to give the money back. Her first husband was dead. She was on the hunt for Number Two, feeling desperate. Ackerman liked that, a needy woman filled with gratitude.

Ackerman was dropping off to sleep when she said, "You asked where Gerry met you, where he did the interview."

"In the morning, okay?"

"A small town in the Texas Panhandle," Marina said. "I remembered after I calmed down."

"Tell me tomorrow," Ackerman said.

"The town was called Amarillo."

Day Three

34

On Wednesday morning it was still dark when Karla rolled out of bed, her head alive with her budding mystery story for Helene's workshop. She wrote for half an hour, felt the surge of satisfaction, watching her words roll out. Five minutes in the shower, seven minutes in the kitchen. A handful of almonds, two prunes, half an apple.

Karla's apartment was on Fox Glen Circle, a cul-de-sac that led to Foxglove Lane. She came around a corner and saw the cop cars, three of them, nosed up to the big house at Number Ten.

The house with the Escalade, the Mercedes with the diplomatic plates.

A big black pickup with Arizona plates.

The white SUV was Coconino sheriff.

The black Crown Vic was Sedona police, a cop behind the wheel.

The black SUV looked Federal.

Portable sawhorses blocked the front entrance. Yellow crime scene ribbons shimmered in the early morning breeze. A media van was parked across the street, where a woman in a trench coat was talking to a camera, a portable light on a tripod, her face half in shadow.

Two cops came out of the house.

One in his uniform, pot belly, big head of white hair—Chief Larry Something, Sedona Police. The other cop was Steve Slattery, one of Karla's customers. The chief nodded at Karla, shook hands with Slattery, and headed for the Crown Vic.

"Hey, Steve."

"Hey, Karla, got any coffee on you? I am dying here."

"What happened? All these cops, even a TV crew."

"Tell you later, when I get clearance."

When she passed Fox Hollow, Karla turned her head. Mr. Cypher's house was on the cul-de-sac, number Three Fox Hollow. She pictured him in bed, alone. Then she pictured him with a woman. Blonde hair, tanned skin, a Purity Ring on a chain around her throat. The image made Karla sick to her stomach.

*****

THEY HAD BREAKFAST IN the Bell Rock Bistro. Helene ordered her special egg-beater omelet, dry toast, seven prunes. Murdock went to the breakfast bar. When he got back to the table, Helene was on her cellphone. She said okay, turned to Murdock.

"One of my students," she said, "about creating the killer."

"What advice did you give?"

"Trauma in the back story," she said. ""Followed by the Killer Interview. Here comes Axel."

Ackerman shook hands. His color looked good. He ordered the usual. The waitress nodded, walked away. Ackerman watched her go.

"The cat who ate the canary," Helene said.

"You talking to me?" Ackerman said.

Helene took a sip of coffee, then she stood up. Her omelet was half-eaten. Ackerman asked where she was going. Murdock kept eating. "The workshop," Helene said. She needed to get her head straight. Ackerman watched her walk off. Turned to Murdock.

"What was that bullshit about cats and canaries?"

"Girl code," Murdock said.

"Code for what?"

"She suspects you nailed Marina Ramsay."

"You should thank the Widow Ramsay." Ackerman said.

"Thank her for what?"

"For saying the magic word."

"What magic word?"

"Amarillo," Ackerman said. "The plane's getting serviced. Should be ready for a noon take-off."

"Thanks, boss."

Ackerman's food arrived. He took the first bite grinning, a billionaire with an appetite—he'd made it through Tuesday night without getting killed.

While Ackerman shoveled in the food, Murdock jotted a list for his trip to Amarillo. Before he was done with the list, his cellphone rang. Cypher wanted a meeting at Red Rock Coffee. He sounded lonely.

35

NINE O'CLOCK, WEDNESDAY MORNING, Helene stood at the door, greeting her workshop writers, wondering who would show—you always lost people after the first day. Karla Kurtz arrived early, dressed in black leggings, running shoes, and a vest over her red T-shirt. Helene had the feeling that Karla wanted to share something, but then the writers entered in ones and twos, and Karla found her seat, next to Giselle Roux. They were chatting like old friends.

Helene opened the Wednesday class with character and dialogue. She told them to connect the killer to a secondary character—a sleuth, a victim, a helper—and gave them the prompt, "Today I am writing about …." Time flew, hands moving. When the timer beeped, Helene asked for readers. Karla stood up, and her voice was shaky starting out:

> Today I am writing about the partnership in crime. I am older now, older and smarter. I need a young gal for bait. My job is waitressing at a Vegas casino. My work uniform is short shorts and a halter top. The high heels kill my feet. I meet this gal Sharleen in the casino. She works

the tables, roulette, Keno, blackjack. Sharleen is younger than me, sexy, with a terrific figure. She stays in shape by working out at the gym. She has dark skin and pale blue eyes. She makes fun of my Southern accent. Sharleen stirs my heart to love. She is a runner. Like me. I got this great route along the Strip, from Tropicana to Circus Circus. We run early, ahead of the swarm. I tell her about growing up in the South. My daddy was a preacher, my mom was a housewife. I want her to like me. I tell her about Uncle Lonnie sticking me, how I got pregnant. What did you do? she said. I killed him—I want her sympathy—I watched him drown. Sharleen does not turn away. Poor you, she says. Let me kiss you, I say. You hate men, Sharleen says. I can live with that. Sharleen likes the guys. I explain my theory—all any man wants with any girl is to stick it inside, get her pregnant. She tells me she's short of money. How bad do you want it? I say. We stake out a target at a convention hotel. He's old, his name is William. Call me Willy, he says. Can I buy you ladies a drink?

I hang out while she gets him drunk. I wait on Four. She brings him up in the elevator. We get him in the room, he grabs her, he wants to stick it inside. Goddamn, he says. Bet you gals didn't know I was wired for two-twenty. We lift his wallet, credit cards, fancy turquoise money clip. We walk him to the stairwell. Sharleen is jumpy. I want him dead. I push him, he goes down. Death by falling. Oh, shit, there's the timer ....

Nodding in the Yavapai Room, they could hear it too. Helene gave Karla the thumbs up, *good job, girl*. Karla's eyes were bright, her face looked flushed. *Writing can do that*, Helene thought, *but only if you let go*. Helene checked her watch, time for a break. Ackerman would be on the court. Where was Murdock? They had almost been a team last night, working Marina Ramsay. But this morning, the wall was back, thick as privacy glass, keeping them apart. In the hallway, Helene saw Karla on her cellphone, strain on her face.

Giselle Roux handed Helene a cup of coffee.

"How well do you know Karla?" Helene said.

"A few months. Since the massages started."

"Is she licensed?"

"In six states," Giselle said.

"Do you know where she's from?"

"Los Angeles, I think. But she's had some Army time."

"Like Mr. Cypher," Helene said. "And Murdock."

"Something going on with you two?" Giselle said.

"You're very observant."

"If you wanna talk," Giselle said. "I'm your girl."

Helene smiled. They touched coffee cups. She could be friends with this woman.

*****

KARLA'S PHONE CALL WAS from Charity Plum. She was lonely; she wanted to visit tomorrow. They could have some dinner, a couple drinks, no play-acting, no worries, just be themselves. Karla said no, she needed to be alone. She was busy, she had a new boyfriend—not her first fib.

"What's his name?"

"Josh," Karla said, plucking a name from the movies.

"Is he older than you?"

"None of your business," Karla said.

"You get off on making me jealous," Charity said.

"Where's the money, Charity?"

"All right. It came this morning."

"Any explanation ... for the delay, I mean?"

"He's a man, sweetie. All men are pricks."

"Send me the fucking money," Karla said.

"Doesn't it count that I love you?" Charity said.

"I've got to run, Charity. Customers waiting."

"You're not at work," Charity said. "I can tell."

"Goodbye, Charity."

"So where are you, sweetie?"

Karla hung up. Her hands were icy again, major stress from the phone call. Charity needed love, she hated men, that left Karla. Why did life have to be so messy? As she re-entered the Yavapai Room, Karla smiled. What would Charity do if she found out that she was the model for Faith Marie Hunsaker, the killer in Karla's fledgling crime story?

36

Murdock jogged to Red Rock Coffee. The sun was out, the sky empty of clouds, warm enough for shorts and a vest. The rhythm of running got his brain going on the Ackerman Case.

It was a shell game, Murdock against an unseen trickster, wearing a black tuxedo, white gloves, a top hat, a silken cloak.

There were three shells, red, white, and black. The trickster moved the shells around.

Murdock chose white.

The trickster lifted the white shell, empty.

Murdock touched the black shell.

It was empty too.

The trickster lifted the red shell and there was the clue, sitting there, but before Murdock could grab it, the trickster closed the cloak, a magical swirl of pricey black silk. Then he was gone.

Inside Red Rock Coffee, Murdock saw Cypher at the corner table, talking to Teri Breedlove. She wore the shorts, the knee sox, the barista uniform. She was leaning over the table. The neck chain dangled, and bright light winked off the little silver ring. As Murdock walked up, she held out her wrists. "Cuff me, please. Take me to your dungeon." Then she laughed.

"Ackerman's waiting," Murdock said.

"What are you bad boys up to ... or is it just coffee today?"

Breedlove walked away, her tight hips synched. Murdock shook hands with Cypher, then sat down.

Cypher's face was serious.

When he spoke, his voice was a whisper. "Did you hear about the shooting last night? It must have been quite frightening. It was close to my street. Yet I heard nothing; my neighbors heard nothing. One minute, it was a normal night in the Village. The next minute, police vehicles, no sirens, nothing. Did you ever wonder why they drive those Crown Vics?"

"Muscle car, I guess."

"Someone said you were there, you and Miss Steinbeck."

"Who was that?"

"A neighbor recognized her, I believe."

"We were scoping the place out."

"Find anything?" Cypher said.

"How far is your place from Number Ten?"

"I'm on Fox Hollow, maybe three blocks, why do you ask?"

"We were doing a recon for Ackerman," Murdock said. "He sent us to check on a guy named Ramsay. Maybe you know him—lives in Dallas, he runs Ramsbanc."

Cypher stared at Murdock. "There have been no names on the news. Are you certain?"

"That's what the cops say."

"This is crazy," Cypher said. "Ramsay is brokering the counter-offer, fronting for those Arab buyers. We had a meeting set for today."

"You ever have dealings with Ramsbanc before?" Murdock said.

"Well," Cypher said. "They did try to buy Vortex Bank."

When was that?"

"Last year. I took it to my board; they said no."

"Is the bank stock traded in New York?"

"The stock is privately held," Cypher said.

"Is there a majority stock-holder?"

Cypher nodded again. His face went blank. Then he glanced past Murdock, out the window. Something he saw in the parking lot made Cypher stand up. One minute he was seated, bent over his coffee, asking about the massacre. The next, he was out of the chair, eyes narrowed, red alert, Cypher the soldier in combat mode.

From their table to the front door was fifty feet, maybe sixty. To get to the door, you had to weave your way through tables. Some of the customers were hefty, the kind of people who took up extra space in a room, in an airplane seat, at a café table. No problem for Cypher, he was through the door in seconds. His exit was slick, smooth, flawless. The fast way to the bank was along Hummingbird Street. Murdock kept watch, no sign of Cypher, why would he take long way around?

37

CYPHER HATED LEAVING MURDOCK. He liked the man, felt a kinship growing.

Two old soldiers, jolted out of uniform, thrust back into civvies. A man needed a friend, someone to stand beside him. Someone to say, I've got your back, Buddy.

Cypher stood with his yellow bike behind a silver SUV, watching the senator and his CIA toady. When they went inside, Cypher headed back to the bank.

Wheeling along, hearing the hiss of bike tires on asphalt, Cypher retraced his life after Father died.

He remembered shooting in ROTC.

He shot Marksman in high school. Sharpshooter in college. Expert in the Army.

They sent him to sniper school, then to the Hindu Kush. He had orders to kill Bin Laden. He saw life, then death, through the cross-hairs, a trigger pull away.

He remembered Kabul. A cold day. He was on leave, drinking with Judson Jarvis, when the gunfire started, a fusillade.

Humvee under attack, VIP on board.

Cypher was armed. He wore a vest, regulations for off-base personnel. He cleared rooftops with his side-arm. Jarvis covered him while he pulled the VIP from the Humvee. More gunfire. Jarvis went down. The VIP needed help. Jarvis needed help. Cypher had a choice—save Jarvis, his best buddy, his only friend, or save the CIP. Jarvis was a soldier. He told Cypher to save the VIP, a really bad decision. Cypher hauled the VIP to safety, then he went back for Jarvis. The Humvee exploded. Cypher woke up in the hospital, bandages on his face. A nurse told him: After a couple more surgeries, Captain, you're gonna look like a movie star.

He remembered his voice breaking when he asked, "What about Jarvis?"

WHEN HE REACHED HIS bank, Cypher stared through the window of his glass-walled cage. Inside the cage, he saw his friend and benefactor, Mr. Norman Maddux. Cypher's heart leaped. Mr. Maddux was not dead after all. He was sitting across the desk from Judson Jarvis—he was not dead either. The man next to Jarvis was Murdock. They were drinking beer, waiting for Cypher. Murdock motioned to Cypher through the glass. Come on in. Three glasses raised by three good friends, waving Cypher inside. Tears blurred his vision. A man needed friends. The voice in his head told him he was seeing things. You're losing it, bro.

Cypher's hands fumbled with the bike lock. A tiny shard of metal nicked his finger, blood oozed out. He hurried inside. Time was short if you had a proper schedule. Before he died, he would raise a glass with his friends.

Inside the bank, Marta asked if he was okay. He stared at her. What was she talking about? Outside the glass door, he looked in again. No one there. No Maddux, no Jarvis, no Murdock—just Father's big oversize desk, the last remaining relic from the family business.

Marta arrived with a tissue.

"What?" he said.

"Your finger, Jeremy, it's bleeding."

38

Minutes after Cypher split, Murdock saw Monty Featherstone holding the door for a fat man in Arizona rancher garb—barn jacket, Levi shirt, sweat-stained Stetson—a politician trying to stand out. Murdock recognized Hiram Fish, Senior Senator from Texas.

Featherstone nodded at Murdock. A barista with red hair tried to seat them at a table up front. Fish shook her off and pointed at Murdock's table. Unlike Cypher, who moved through the tables like a dancer, Fish slammed into a guy who'd been headed for the men's room. The guy went down. Fish pivoted, his face red with anger, and collided with a barista carrying a tray. Cups and plates clattered when they hit the floor. Fish grunted, said he was sorry—*here's my business card, sweetheart, you call my office*—and stuck out his hand to Murdock.

Murdock was helping, squatted down, holding two porcelain cups and a broken saucer. The barista glared at Fish, pointed to coffee stains on her blouse, *thanks for ruining my day*.

As a politico, Fish was all grins and handshakes. Murdock opened his gooey hand—Fish stared at the goo. The barista arrived with a towel. Murdock wiped off the goo. Fish looked impatient, man with the tight schedule. Compulsory handshake over, Fish took Murdock's chair.

The room was watching, an audience waiting for the next sound-bite. Hey, welcome to YouTube. A guy across the room was aiming his cellphone; he had Fish digitized. Then Featherstone was there, flashing his Federal ID. A few words and the guy lowered the device and headed for the door. A woman two tables away tucked her phone away. The Senator's YouTube moment was squelched.

Fish stood 5'8", weighed maybe 240 pounds, a roly-poly testament to obesity in America. He leaned across the table, his eyes gleamed. At the coffee machine, Featherstone was grinning at Breedlove; her face was flushed. Fish jerked his head, indicating Featherstone.

"My man Monty there, he said you found them bodies last night."

"We called the cops," Murdock said. "They found the bodies."

"How'd you know to even call the cops?"

"There was blood on the kitchen wall," Murdock said. "Broken glass on the floor. There was a body. We saw the feet, a piece of trouser leg."

"Durn," Fish said. "Who'd that turn out to be?"

"The guy we saw was named Ramsay. A Texas banker."

Fish nodded, donned his sad face. "Me and Gerry, we were best buds. He was having money trouble, so I put him in touch with them Arabs, and that makes me feel like it was maybe … you know how big them Arabs were?"

"How big, Senator?" Murdock said.

"The young prince wanted a casino and since his daddy owns half the oil under that Saudi sandbox, there was no problem. So I brokered a deal with Ramsay, and now this shit …. Somebody's gotta tell his daddy. That somebody would be …. Whoa, here's my java, and, hello, sweetheart."

Fish was reacting to Teri Breedlove, carrying a breakfast

plate—muffins, Danish, bacon, toast, butter, a little pot of red jam. Fish grabbed a coffee, sipped, then beamed at Teri Breedlove. They shook hands.

"Pretty ring you got there," Fish said.

"Thank you, Senator."

"Mind if I took me a closer look?"

Teri was no dummy. She pulled the chain over her head, then dangled the Purity Ring in front of Fish. His fat hand, delivering a message, fondled the ring.

He quizzed her. Was she a good Christian? She said of course. Would she like to work for him? Campaign stuff. She said she already worked for Ackerman. Fish gave her a greasy smile, handed her a business card. Christians should work for Christians. How much was the old Jew paying her? Teri Breedlove gave Fish a dirty look, grabbed her ring, and hurried away. Fish watched her go. "Durn," he said, "that is one fine example of American womanhood."

At the coffee bar, Teri dropped Fish's business card into the trash.

"Fucking Axel Ackerman," Fish said. "That old Jew always has them bitches lined up, ready for …."

Murdock shoved his chair back, making extra noise. It was time to go, escape the stink of politics. Fish put a hand on Murdock's arm. "Stick around," Fish said. "I'll introduce you to our next President."

A handsome man came through the door of Red Rock Coffee. He was tanned, his face was craggy, and he wore a blue shirt, corduroys, and a leather jacket. Fish introduced Murdock. The tanned man was Senator James "Jimbo" Gypsum, a power-politician with two bodyguards. One was a thick Latino, who hovered by the door. The other was an Anglo, an ex-soldier like Murdock.

Jimbo did not look like a Jimbo. Instead, he looked like Gary Cooper in High Noon. His handshake was solid. His stance was presidential. He was pleased to meet Murdock and very disappointed that Murdock could not stay … for the pow-wow.

There was much to be gained in talking. Fish and Gypsum were experts at the art. Their words held a special emptiness. They talked service—they meant combat with the opposition, fighting to control the money-spigots.

MURDOCK WAS OUTSIDE, BREATHING the air, when Monty Featherstone caught up with him.

"The senator wants to set up a meeting."

"Why are you working for this guy, Monty?"

"I told you. It's my pension. When can you meet?"

"Next week."

"The senator wants a meeting later today, around five."

"I won't be in town," Murdock said.

"Where will you be?"

"In another town."

"Do you understand what you're doing here?" Featherstone said. "One phone call, he can have Homeland Security put you on the watch list, he can—"

"Get a grip, Monty."

MURDOCK JOGGED UP THE hill. His lungs felt better; the nighttime runs were working. He saw Ackerman on Court One, practicing his serve. Someone behind Murdock was calling his name. He saw Teri Breedlove on her bike; she wanted to rant about Fish.

"That fat derp claims to be a Christian, he's just a dirty little man. Why didn't you say something?"

"What's a derp?" Murdock said.

"Like it sounds," she said. "How does he know Axel?"

"Dallas boys," Murdock said. "How is Axel?"

"His game's been wacko ever since Monday," she said, "when he heard about poor old Walter. When are you gonna solve this thing?"

"Maybe today," Murdock said.

"Well, get a move on, dude. Yolo."

Before he could ask the meaning of *Yolo*, she was gone. Legs pumping, hair flying, aware of being watched.

Murdock's cellphone rang. It was Helene. The workshop was on a break. Her voice sounded flat. Ackerman's plane was ready for Amarillo. Murdock wanted her to go with him.

"Come with me," Murdock said.

"One of us needs to be here," Helene said.

"Bruno's here," Murdock said. "There are cops everywhere."

"I have a date," Helene said.

"Who with?" Murdock said.

"It's Axel," Helene said. "He's taking me to the gun range in Cottonwood. Why don't you ask Connie for a ride? She's been mooning around, asking about you."

"If you took me to the airport," Murdock said, "we could talk."

"Talk about what?"

"Talk about us," Murdock said.

"Our break is over," Helene said. "Gotta get back to my writers. Have fun digging."

The phone went dead. Murdock felt dead. On the tennis court, Teri Breedlove was across the net from Ackerman, feeding him balls, making it easy.

39

THE LUNCH TRAFFIC SLACKED off at two. It was Wednesday, and the valley buzzed with death. Who would die tonight? Was there a curse on Oak Creek Village? Teri Breedlove had a date with Olivia Olivera, to tour the crime scene. Teri finished clearing tables, consulted her cell. The time was 3:51. If she left now, she could buzz by Vortex Bank.

She checked with Karla, who was acting manager.

"Go with God," Karla said.

Teri rode her bike. The sun was diving toward the mountains. She parked her bike; she had left her lock at Sedona Landing.

She saw Jeremy in his office, on his red phone.

He held up a hand, stopping her.

Through the glass wall, she saw a yellow legal pad and an old lead pencil. Jeremy was very old school. There were all these drawing programs online. Why didn't he use one? Next to the yellow pad was Jeremy's copy of the *Odyssey*, that big deal journey of this Greek warrior war-hero guy trying to get home so he could murder this absolute crowd of creeps who wanted to nail the wife. Her name was Penelope. She was weaving this shroud-thing, stalling for time until her honey got back home.

Teri had been AP in high school and graduated a year early. Her class had read the *Odyssey;* Teri had gotten the plot from Google.

The phone call over, Jeremy waved her in. He looked tired. He asked what she wanted. She told him about her date with Olivera, one thirty on Foxglove Lane. He shook his head. He was doing that a lot lately. He wanted her gone, she could tell; she could read this guy like a smartphone. She tried some small talk.

"Whose idea was this fish-bowl office, dude?"

"It's a legacy," he said, "from Mr. Maddux."

"It makes me feel like everyone is watching. That's so weird."

"It represents transparency," he said. "What the world needs more of."

Teri picked up the *Odyssey.* There was a marker near the end. She opened the book, saw pencil marks, jottings, a circle, a square, two triangles. She could read the numbers but not the words—the handwriting was small and scrawly. The hero guy, Ulysses, had just whacked off the head of a suitor.

"You still reading this?"

"I'm a slow reader," he said.

"All these marks at the end," she said. "Like that massacre last night—Foxglove Lane is so close to our house. It's creepy."

"Don't you have somewhere to be? Doing your tennis thing?"

"My date with Olivia," she said. "And this goes into my piggy bank."

Teri pulled out the cash from Axel, nine hundred dollars—two weeks of tennis with Axel, less one hundred for essentials. She wanted the cash in her safe deposit box. Jeremy rang for Marta. Teri held up the yellow legal pad. Boxes, arrows, numbers.

"What's this, dude?"

"It's a floor plan of the CRMC, drawn from memory."

"You sick or something?"

"Going to visit a sick friend."

"When?"

"Friday, if things work out. Here's Marta; she'll take care of you."

When Jeremy acted weird, it was time to split. Teri headed for the glass door. Marta smiled, not a friendly smile, but the smile of a competitor, another chick with a crush on Jeremy. Marta went out. Teri was about to follow when Jeremy told her about the possible interview.

"Who am I interviewing?" she said.

"One of the suspects," he said.

"The usual suspects?"

"A suspect with one of two possible connections," he said.

"You missed my joke," she said. "*Usual*? As in Usual Suspects?"

"You'll need to scare up a nurse uniform," he said.

"I got it, for the CRMC."

"If you can't locate a nurse uniform by Thursday," he said, "please inform me. I'll make some calls."

"Swaggy," she said.

"Yolo," he said.

"Can I get a hug?"

"Not a good time," he said.

She left Vortex Bank wondering why Jeremy didn't catch her little joke. Last summer, he had told her to watch that old movie, *The Usual Suspects*. A cool flick, but majorly retro. She remembered the little frisson when Kevin Spacey turned from a cripple into an easy-walking guy. She remembered thinking, so this cool guy was hiding himself by walking funny; he made you think he was a cripple. How was Jeremy hiding himself?

She was still running with that idea—the masks of Jeremy Cypher—when she parked her bike at Ten Foxglove Lane, where Olivia Olivera, crime scene tech, waited in her van.

40

ACKERMAN'S PLANE LIFTED OFF the tarmac at Geronimo Airport. Murdock watched the shadow fade as they gained elevation. They flew east, away from the afternoon sun, into the coming dark. Across New Mexico and on into Texas, they fought strong headwinds. The wind was blowing hard when they touched down in Amarillo.

Ackerman had a car waiting—a giant Cadillac Escalade with Texas plates. The driver was cowboy sporty, a white Stetson, a Western-cut suit and green snakeskin boots. His name was Rowdy. He dropped Murdock off at the Marriott. Ackerman had reserved a corner suite complete with a Jacuzzi and a bidet. No need for a bidet when you traveled alone, when your woman stayed behind.

Murdock needed to move—plane rides made him feel like a mummy—so he walked from the hotel through the downtown. In a Walgreen's, he bought a little notebook, spiral bound. Then he walked to the library, buffeted by the North Texas wind. The library closed in one hour. He spent that hour digging and found a news story announcing that Wilson's Fine Furniture had been acquired by Arc-Angel Equity.

He lingered on the word, *acquired*—the noun was *acquisition*, a big poly-syllable that cloaked the buying process, made it seem okay. Like it was better to say "acquired a dozen slaves" and avoid using the word *buy*—"gonna buy me a dozen slaves."

First you acquired, then you sold. What was the accepted business lingo for *selling*? The word floated at him from the printed page—*divestiture*, a long word, four syllables worn like a mask. Helene would know the meaning. Maybe he should call her. Maybe she was taking a shower, naked, water streaming. The image stirred Murdock. No sex since Taos.

The dictionary sat atop a pedestal. An American Heritage product, it told you the roots of words. Murdock's fingers felt clumsy, flipping pages. *Divestiture* had three definitions. Murdock jotted them into his notebook:

One: *to strip off*, like getting out of your clothes.

Two: *to free yourself of*, the synonym was *rid*.

Three: *to sell off property*, the synonym was *dispose of*.

A front-page photo showed Ackerman's five-man Crew, thirty years younger, forming a half-circle around Joseph Woodrow Wilson, the founder of Wilson's Fine Furniture. The men identified in the photo, left to right, were Tyler, Coolidge, Findlay, and Delaplane—all dead. The man identified as George Hawthorne was on the end. He looked younger, blond hair tousled by the breeze, the classic facial features of a film-star.

The library was closing, ten minutes. A bearded guy in a thick jacket and battered boots headed for the men's room, last stop before he faced the sharp wind. And the night.

Murdock stopped at the information desk, where a woman with rose-colored glasses listened, her face a mask of impatience.

She pointed to the clock on the wall—seven minutes to closing—then led him to a distant shelf crammed with high school yearbooks dating back to 1901. Murdock wanted to see the other end of the acquisition—would the writer use words like *divestiture*? He found the article reference, "New York Firm Divests Itself Of Local Entrepreneurial Holdings." The author of the article was Gerald R. Ramsay. The name jumped out at Murdock, Gerry Ramsay in Amarillo, Gerry Ramsay and Honest Joe Wilson. Was the writer of this article the same fat-faced prick who had been in cahoots with that maniac in Taos? There was more story than Murdock could grab in four minutes.

At the desk, he asked the woman with the glasses if he could print an article. Sorry, he would need instruction, and the library was closing. Then he asked if there was any library staff member who had been around thirty years ago. There was a volunteer. Mrs. Dorothy Stanhope. She would be in at ten, sharp, tomorrow.

Day Four

41

ACKERMAN ROLLED OUT OF bed.

It look longer than usual because his legs felt weak, squishy muscles, ancient bones. His right knee made that popping sound. He braced himself, one hand on the wall, breathing hard, while he stretched. The bedside clock said 12:02—after midnight, a new day starting. Would they try to kill him today?

His feet found the Birkenstocks. He pulled on the gray robe, which smelled like old age and death. The wine glass was empty, needed a refill—wash your grief away on a sea of purple grape. In the bathroom, he peed. He swirled blue mouthwash, but the taste of wine lingered. He moved—right foot, left foot, bathroom to bed, bed to door, door to hallway. Voices came from down the hall.

Heat came from the living room. No one there, just a fake fire flickering. Voices from the kitchen, where Ackerman found Giselle Roux in jeans and a baggy sweater, her arms folded, talking to Bruno. In his shoulder holster and the inevitable white turtleneck, Bruno's face looked even blacker. Bruno was sixty and steadfast, like an ancient tree that grew in a sacred grove. Ackerman regarded Bruno as his brother, two outcasts who walked the razor's edge.

Bruno filled a coffee mug, added sugar and half-n-half. Giselle supplied water and twin Tylenols.

Giselle followed Ackerman back to the bedroom. Held the coffee mug while he got into bed. Stood there waiting. She wanted something. At that moment, she was worth every dollar of her contract, two million a year. At that moment, feeling his world collapsing, Giselle and Bruno were Ackerman's family. Would the killer kill them too?

He tugged on Giselle's hand. She sat on the edge of the bed. He tugged again, *come closer*. She shook her head. Giselle smelled sweet, like an exotic flower, and Ackerman was the honey bee. He sipped his coffee. She was thirty-one years old. She had been with Ackerman for a dozen years, twelve one-year contracts starting at eighty thousand. That first year, working for Credit Lyonnais, assigned as Ackerman's interpreter in Paris, nineteen years old, a slender gazelle of a girl from Montreal. He loved her body, the subtle slimness of her wrists and ankles, the surprising expanse of white girl bottom, presented for Ackerman's pleasure on the big bed in the Paris Ritz in exchange for his presentation of the necklace of emeralds that matched her eyes.

Her skin was so white, so sleek. The devilish laughter in the eyes, the low-voiced chuckle, the slender back arched, shoulder blades like bird wings, his fingers tracing the bones of her white spine. She had a dancer's body and the agile brain of a female raptor, good with numbers. Her red hair reminded him of Mama in her prime. Two high-priced shrinks had told Ackerman that he collected redheaded women because he wanted to fuck his mother. What bullshit.

"If I had had your child," Giselle said, "you'd be forced to keep me around, maybe even marry me."

"Two abortions," Ackerman said. "Getting rid of my babies. You could have kept one."

"I was afraid," she said.

"Afraid of what?"

He moved her hand toward his crotch, just like old times, a dozen years of signals and subtle codes. She shook her head, freed her wrist, and stood up.

"What is it?"

"I want a job change, Axel."

"From what to what?"

"I want to go back to school. Get a degree."

"In what field?"

"Architecture."

"You already went to school, four different times, on my nickel."

"You can hire someone to replace me. Helene would be perfect."

"When is this?"

"When the sale is done."

"You're breaking my heart, woman."

The phone rang. Giselle did not answer. He felt her pulling away, shielding herself. She stood there, arms crossed. The phone rang again, Ackerman picked up.

The caller was Daniel, Ackerman's eldest son, calling from Boston, confirming his arrival Thursday morning, with his girlfriend, who craved sun.

"Bad news about Walt Findlay," Daniel said.

"And Freddy Delaplane," Ackerman said.

"I didn't hear … what happened to Freddy?"

"Fell down the stairs in Santa Fe, so I was thinking maybe this might not be the best time—"

"Hey, Axel," Daniel said. "Nothing is gonna stop us. Iveta is dying for sun. We don't come, she'll kill me."

"Just so you're warned," Ackerman said.

"How's the hotel deal coming?"

"It's dragging. My goddamn banker wants to pull the plug."

"What for?"

"Some bullshit about blaming himself for Findlay falling."

"What's he like, your banker?"

"Fussy," Ackerman said. "Nervous, edgy about risk—a small timer."

"Axel," Daniel said, "you think everybody is small time. See you on Thursday."

As she was leaving, Giselle reminded Ackerman about the event at noon on Friday. Ackerman remembered. Two senators, Gypsum and Fish, were holding a press conference. Gypsum for President, Fish as veep. Ackerman had tried to stop it. He owned the penthouse, but the Maddux people, loyal Republicans, still owned the hotel.

*****

KARLA WOKE AT FIVE, touched her face, still smiling. She looked in the mirror, expecting to see the bait-girl mask. Her real face looked back at her, no mask. Today she was Karla. The kill jobs with Charity were fading. *Think of money, not death.*

She sat at the computer, checking her nest egg. She had half the money in brokerage accounts in Orange County. Four grand here, six grand there—low investments, don't trigger the Feds. The other half she kept in the Vortex Bank, her safe deposit box. The first kill had pulled in $50k. Then sixty for the second, seventy for the third. With the money from kill number four, her total nut would be $360k. With the money from kill number five …. When would that be? What would that bring in? She closed the computer, and the numbers went away. Today, she needed to check her safe deposit box, make sure of her tally. Thinking about the box made her think of Vortex Bank. Thinking about the bank made her think of Mr. Cypher, and that gave her a little tingle.

She went over her schedule. Work from seven to noon. Then her trip to Vortex Bank, open the account, launch her assault on Mr. Cypher. She kept waiting for him to remember her, from that time in L.A. She wanted to punch through his mask, whisk him back to the past, start right there, when he helped her out.

She ate a muffin, sipped hot tea, and wrote in her mystery journal. Her cellphone buzzed. It was Ackerman. He wanted a massage, early afternoon, 1:30 or two. Karla bartered for six. She had plans. She wanted a block of time in the afternoon.

Wearing only her knee sox, Karla checked her physical assets in the mirror. Just four pounds extra showed up in the mid-section, belly and hips. The legs were still good—all that outdoor exercise, hiking and biking. The hands and forearms stayed good because of the massage work. Her cheeks looked a little fuller—why did a weight gain show up there?—and her thighs needed more time on the bike.

Karla chose her new red hip-huggers. They were skimpy, fit real close, and made her feel like a sexy underwear model. Did Mr. Cypher care about women's underwear? Would she find out today?

42

BEFORE HE WENT DOWN to breakfast, Murdock phoned Helene. She was up, working on her book. She sounded sleepy, grouchy. Ackerman had phoned her at two a.m., told her about his nightmare of falling. He had not yet reached George Hawthorne, number five in the Crew.

Murdock told Helene about the Gerry Ramsay photos, about Mrs. Stanhope. Maybe she would remember something.

Helene told Murdock that Connie Fremont had asked about him. The silence hung in the air, making the distance longer—Sedona to Amarillo, a hundred thousand miles and growing.

In the hotel dining room, Murdock dug into a short stack, two eggs over-easy, and country ham. The maple syrup tasted real, not like chemical fakery. The library opened at ten. At 9:45, he zipped up his vest and headed into the wind. It swooped down from a cold blue sky, wind with an edge. At the first intersection, Ackerman's driver rolled up. Murdock shook his head; he needed to walk. The driver trailed him to the library.

The library doors were closed. Murdock counted seven homeless guys—dusty clothes, battered hats and scraggy beards—waiting for the public bathroom. A sign said, WE OPEN AT TEN.

The driver opened the door of the Escalade. Murdock sat in the passenger seat. The driver talked about college football; his team was Texas A&M. Murdock nodded, the words drifted past. He had played football in three high schools. He quit after the first injury. If you're going to get hurt, let it not be in a game.

At 10 a.m. sharp, the woman with the rose-colored glasses unlocked the door, and the homeless guys went in first, feet moving fast, heading for the men's room. Murdock double-checked cellphone numbers with the driver. When he opened the car door, he felt the wind.

In the library, Murdock narrowed his yearbook search to the late 1970s, then the early 1980s—and there the guy was, Gerald Martin Ramsay, class of 1982, looking geeky, a chubby-cheeked teen. He'd been photographed in the regulation jacket and tie, hair too long for the face, nasty eyes, a smug smile. Gerald was assistant editor of the newspaper, *The Golden Sandstorm*, and a member of the accounting club. He looked like nobody trying to be somebody, and now he was dead. For the price of three quarters, Murdock Xeroxed three photos of Gerry Ramsay.

At 10:02, an old woman came in. She was thin, gray, frail, and upright, with sharp blue eyes.

Like a schoolmarm from a black and white movie … before the days of the Internet.

She wore stylish glasses.

Her face had great cheekbones. Her lips wore pale lipstick. The woman's name was Mrs. Stanhope. They sat at a table next to the business books. Murdock asked about Joe Wilson.

Mrs. Stanhope said, "Joseph Wilson, yes. I knew him quite well; we were neighbors. I knew his lovely wife, and the boy. Joseph was creative, but without a head for business. Joseph was kind; he befriended his employees. When he couldn't make payroll, he went straight to his banker. You know how bankers are—they have this little club, men only, no females darkened their door—and soon after that came those people from New York, a firm called Arc-Angel Equity—who could forget a name like that? The company men got their photos on the front page, the angels who would rescue Wilson's Fine Furniture. Well, that was a fine day, and time passed. Joseph purchased a new car, his wife remodeled the kitchen, shiny new appliances, and then one day there was another photo, not front page, but way back there in Business News, a story by one of our high-school students, a story that told the world about Joseph's business going into Chapter Eleven, and that's what caused the fight, you see, though most people referred to it as a scuffle."

"What scuffle was that, Mrs. Stanhope?"

"I'm getting to that; there is order in my brain. Where was I?"

"Bankruptcy for the furniture factory," Murdock said.

"Yes, well, Joseph had his money, you see—that's one of the ironies of this whole ferment—because while he was wealthy, his employees went out on strike, fighting for their pension money. The Arc-Angel people had gone back to New York or wherever, except for the woman. I'm afraid I have her to blame for all of this. Even though she attended church, people said she was a seductress. She even hoodwinked Joseph's boy …. Oh dear, I do ramble on."

While Mrs. Stanhope talked, Murdock jotted notes on the back of an envelope.

"There were rumors, you see. For example, a bellman at the Amarillo Hotel saw Miss Diamond coming out of different rooms at two in the morning. This was before people from the church reported seeing her in Joe Wilson's pew. When things were going well, she was a frequent guest in their house, mostly for Sunday lunch. As the bankruptcy business was happening, the Wilsons went out of town, leaving young Joey behind, and guess who I saw leaving the Wilson house at dawn?"

"Miss Penny Diamond," Murdock said.

"Is my sad tale assisting you with your discoveries?"

Murdock said yes. Then he showed her the yearbook photo of Gerry Ramsay.

"Do you know this young man?"

"Why, that's young Gerald Ramsay. His father ran the High Plains Trust."

"What kind of kid was he?"

"Kind of kid? One look at that photo tells you everything. That boy was smug and smart-alecky. From the get-go, he was a bully and a trouble-maker."

Mrs. Stanhope had library skills. She knew how to extract a printed copy from a micro-fiche, along with a newspaper photo that showed workers holding picket signs. In the background was Wilson's Fine Furniture, with a tilted nameplate. Murdock asked again about the fight.

"Well," she said. "Some said it was a fight, some said it was a scuffle. It took place on a bleak winter afternoon in the playground at Wolflin School. Gerry was bigger; the Wilson boy was slight of build. People said the boy started the fight. Names were called, blows were exchanged, and bystanders let it go on too long. Young Joey boy spent time in the hospital. I took him a box of cookies, made them myself. In the hospital, with his jaw wired, that poor boy looked like death itself."

"What started the fight, Mrs. Stanhope?"

"Some people said it was the business, the nasty tone of this article you see before us. Others claimed it was a matter of honor. Joey Wilson was the white knight; Gerry Ramsay was the ogre."

"This is a wild guess," Murdock said. "But could the Wilson kid have been defending the honor of a female?"

"He did inquire about her in the hospital," Mrs. Stanhope said.

"Do you remember what he said?"

"He asked where she was. He said she had come to the hospital to tell him she was leaving. He couldn't say more because of Mildred."

"Mildred was Joey's mother?"

"Didn't I already say that? I could use a cup of tea, all this remembering. Do you have transportation, Mr. Murdock?"

THEY RODE IN THE Escalade to Furr's Cafeteria, where Mrs. Stanhope remarked on the high quality of the cherry pie, evidence of consistency in an otherwise topsy-turvy universe. Murdock bought two slices. Mrs. Stanhope halved her slice—for later, she said. She opened her purse, pulled out a plastic sandwich bag, inserted her half-slice.

She ate the pie with a knife and fork, European style. She talked about Europe. She liked England, the London library where she did research on Virginia Woolf. But she had fallen in love with Rome. She had been there seven times, wondering—was Rome a good place to die? If so, then one could come to rest in the heart of civilization. She quoted the opening lines from a poem.

> Midway upon the journey of our life
> I found myself within a forest dark,
> For the straightforward pathway had been lost.

"Is that the Italian guy who took the trip to Hell?" Murdock asked.

"That's our Dante Alighieri, Mr. Murdock. Good for you."

"That's where I am with this case," Murdock said. "Stumbling along a crooked pathway."

"I have been thinking about honor," Mrs. Stanhope said. "It would not describe Gerry, but it might have moved Young Joey Wilson … to take steps, I mean."

Murdock asked what happened to the Wilsons, that money they got from Ackerman. They remodeled, she said. They bought a new car. Joseph stopped going to church, Mildred was infatuated with the new preacher. After Joseph died, they moved to a new home closer to the church.

While Mrs. Stanhope chatted, filling in her picture of Amarillo 30 years ago, Murdock wished that Helene was here. This interview needed the woman's touch—all that mysterious linkage, the accuracy of intuition.

When tea-time was over, the Escalade drove them back to the library. They exchanged emails, phone numbers. Mrs. Stanhope promised to search for a photo of Penny Diamond from thirty years ago. Murdock climbed out, held the door, felt the bite of the wind.

"One last question, Mrs. Stanhope."

"Of course, and please call me Dorothy."

"Was Gerry Ramsay's dad ... was he Joe Wilson's banker?"

"He could have been. Great Plains Bank was always in the news, all that pilfering going on, wonderful words like *embezzlement*."

"So Ramsay Senior could have brought these Arc-Angel folks to town?"

"Bankers do run in the same circles," she said. "This wind is freezing. Would you walk me to the door?"

Murdock walked her to the door. A homeless guy tipped his hat as Mrs. Stanhope went past. Murdock gave the guy a five.

"How did Joe Wilson die?" Murdock said.

"He died from falling," she said. "It was Christmas. They found him below the fire escape at Wolflin School."

On the way to the Amarillo airport, Murdock phoned Helene. It was Thursday. Her voicemail told him to leave a message.

43

SHE CAME TO ARIZONA for the pool.

Prague to Paris.

Paris to Boston.

Boston to Phoenix.

Phoenix to Sedona.

Sedona to this village, the Oak Creek. How charming.

Iveta Macek stood with her nose to the curved view-window, looking down at the pool where children played a game. She felt grubby from travel. They had to wait three hours at the Logan airport, two hours in Phoenix. They had to wait for the rental car—Daniel had reserved a giant Range Rover—and then he had driven over the speed limit, passing cars, Iveta watching for the police. They made her nervous.

They were waiting now for a room.

Daniel had one of his lists. She could hear him behind her, talking to reception, a Latino named Raul. Last night, Daniel had proposed. Iveta had said yes. Her visa was good for two more months. She did not love Daniel. He emitted a body odor that was not pleasing.

Iveta watched a woman enter the pool area.

Dark hair, wearing a white hotel robe.

The woman came from a doorway that led outside.

Iveta twiddled her fingers at Daniel, pointed down at the pool, and made a modified paddling motion. She walked away from reception, through the Lobby to the outside door. A path curved toward the tennis courts.

She saw people playing tennis.

An old man in a red baseball cap and a pretty blonde girl with a ponytail.

The old man gave Iveta a look.

She shivered. The old eyes had to belong to Papa Ackerman.

Iveta turned left, went through a doorway that said Pool and smelled chlorine. The dark-haired woman was swimming laps. Mothers were herding their children to a doorway that said ELEVATORS. The old hotel had a lovely feel. Not so new, not so shiny.

Iveta shrugged out of her track suit. Underneath she wore a T-shirt and shorts. Her new bikini was packed away. The luggage was Daniel's problem. She kicked off her shoes—new Nike's—and ran for the water. She launched into a flat racing dive, hit the water and felt reborn, timing her stroke to the little blue float balls that held up the rope marking the lane. She lost herself in the glory of swimming.

Crawl, breast stroke, butterfly, backstroke.

She was out of shape. She had not told Daniel about her missed period. She was almost certain the baby was his. She was breathing hard when she climbed the ladder and left the pool.

The dark-haired woman introduced herself.

Her name was Steinbeck, like the American writer. Iveta had read *The Grapes of Wrath*. This Steinbeck woman worked for Papa Ackerman. Her face was brown from the sun.

Beside this woman, Iveta felt so pale. The Steinbeck woman waved at the pool boy. He brought a robe for Iveta.

"How about a coffee?"

"American coffee? It is not so good."

"They can make you an okay espresso."

Iveta sat at a glass-topped table with Steinbeck.

The coffee was better than okay. Iveta was living the American Dream. Sitting beside a pool, wrapped in a robe, no ice, no snow, no cold feet, no city streets with frantic drivers …. She felt bliss.

"So Helene, you are working for Papa Ackerman. What is your job, please?"

"Daniel didn't tell you?"

"From him I have heard nothing."

"Some bodyguarding, some detecting."

"Detecting what?"

"Someone is killing old friends. Mr. Ackerman thinks he's next."

"Daniel said nothing to me of this."

Steinbeck opened a spiral notebook to a page of circles and lines. She called it a mind-map.

"Here's where we are with the detecting," Steinbeck said. "It's a dance between past and present, something that happened thirty years ago."

Iveta saw a large box on the left; next to the box was a circle.

The box was labeled AMARILLO-THE PAST.

The circle was SEDONA-THE PRESENT.

There were many names she did not recognize, and then she saw Daniel's name in a box with Lottie and Arthur.

Iveta knew Lottie as Madame Belle, her friend and one-time employer. Seeing Madame Belle's name sent a shiver up Iveta's spine. She sipped her coffee, felt someone watching, looked up at the view-window where she had stood minutes ago. She went back to the mind-map. A curved red line connected Daniel's box to Papa Ackerman. Family.

"What is this mind-map doing, please?"

"Have you met Daniel's siblings yet?"

"Daniel says they are coming."

"So you only know Daniel."

"Yes."

"What's he like, anyway?"

"What do you mean?"

"Well," Steinbeck said, "Mr. Ackerman is very bright. Very generous with money. He has an eye for the ladies. Someone wants to kill him. I was wondering how he and Daniel were alike?"

Iveta shivered. What did this woman want? One minute she was friendly, the next minute she quizzed like a policeman.

"Daniel has the eye also," Iveta said. "He is tight with money, so tight we flew second class, the seats were small, he squirmed all the way. He likes me to shop at consignments. Killing? Who would want to kill Daniel?"

"How did you two meet anyway?"

The question hung in the air. It seemed innocent, girl-to-girl. But this woman Steinbeck, although she seemed casual and not interested, was very clever. So instead of telling the truth, Iveta evaded. "We met on the line."

"The Internet?"

"Yes."

"You were in Boston?"

"Paris," Iveta said.

"Were you modeling?"

"Why do you say modeling?"

"You're pretty," Steinbeck said. "You have a lovely figure."

Iveta said thank you. She felt quite warm. She looked into her coffee cup. It was empty. She looked around for the coffee boy, but Steinbeck had already waved at him for another.

"Sorry," Steinbeck said. "I didn't mean to probe."

"You were detecting, perhaps?"

The coffee arrived. Steinbeck grinned, touched her cup to Iveta's. What was this woman up to? Was she a friend? Was she an invader? The door to the tennis courts opened and the old man came through, followed by Daniel and the pretty blonde. Everyone knew everyone, except for Iveta.

"There you are," Daniel said. "I was starting to worry, baby."

The old man had a powerful handshake.

He had yellow eyes and a wide grin. The eyes ate her up.

She had met rich men before—most of them were Arabs—but Papa Ackerman was her first billionaire. The girl was named Teri … something American. She had a ring on a chain around her throat. She winked at Iveta; they were the youngest.

The coffee boy arrived with another table, followed by a waitress pushing a serving cart on wheels. Iveta saw pastries, a white teapot, bottles of water. There was an Americano for Papa, a fresh espresso for Iveta, iced tea for the blonde Teri. Daniel asked for a latte, nutmeg, and skim milk.

Papa Ackerman handed Iveta a keycard for the penthouse. "Visit anytime," he said. There was a twinkle in his eye.

Giselle Roux, who wanted to be Iveta's friend, arrived with keys for Nine, the suite with the best view, and Daniel's card for penthouse access. Iveta stood up, wanting to unpack. She shook hands with Ackerman and Helene. She spoke to Daniel, who was chewing a pastry. Daniel was fifty years old. With his father so close by, he seemed younger, a greedy little boy. Giselle offered to show Iveta their room. As she left the table, Iveta heard praise from Papa Ackerman.

"Danny," Papa said. "This one is a keeper."

"Thanks, Ack. When is Artie coming? "

"Tomorrow. He's flying in from Miami."

"What about Lottie?"

"The same, only from Paris," Ackerman said. "Would you excuse me? I need a word with Helene."

"Go, go. I see why you love it here."

*****

ACKERMAN WAITED FOR HELENE to gather up her student papers. He remembered his student days, books and paper, the never-ending quest for the perfect fountain pen for writing the best prose. He carried her rucksack. They walked to a table near the staircase. From here, Ackerman could see Danny's Czech chick and Giselle, waiting for the elevator. Ackerman asked Helene to sit down. He tapped on the table.

"What is it, Axel?"

"I want you to work for me."

"I already work for you."

"For a year. The pay is one million dollars—half now, half when you've worked six months. You'd be replacing Giselle Roux. She's going back to school. Think about it."

"What about Murdock?"

"Murdock's a good guy. When's he get back from grave-robbing?"

"This afternoon."

"When are you gonna see Dr. Ruth?"

"This afternoon."

"While you're confessing, think about my offer."

Ackerman left Helene alone. He strode across the room, to the table where Daniel Ackerman was stuffing food into his mouth while talking on his phone. Ackerman was thinking about Murdock. He liked the man, but did he want him around for a year?

44

THEIR ROOM ON NINE was a corner suite overlooking a jagged red mountain, identified by Giselle as Cathedral Rock. Iveta adored the view. The airy, spacious room had been rented by a man who died falling off Cathedral Rock.

"When was it?" Iveta said.

"Monday," Giselle said. "In the dark."

"Did you know this man?"

"He was Axel's old friend. The police think he was pushed. That woman, Helene Steinbeck, she's been hired to investigate. He was one of Axel's investors. I thought you should know."

"Does Daniel know this?"

"I'm so sorry," Giselle said. "It's your first visit. I hope I haven't spoiled—"

"Please, no," Iveta said. "I love it here. I am sorry about your friend. Is there more I should hear?"

Giselle said no. The woman seemed embarrassed by death. Iveta was 27. She had faced death many times. To her, the red rock seemed far away, and much smaller than Mont Blanc, which she had climbed in her Army days.

It was time for a swim. Iveta changed into a bikini. Checked herself in the mirror. Still no sign of the baby growing inside her. She left the pool robe in the bathroom and chose a fluffier robe from the closet. The monogram said Sedona Landing. She wondered what it meant. In English, *landing* meant a safe harbor at the edge of the sea. The brochure said this valley with the red rocks had once been underwater.

She found flip-flops in the closet. Outside in the hallway, she tested the room card. In America, everything worked. She entered the elevator, joining a family of three—father, mother, child. Two buttons were lit. The L for Lobby and the LL, for the pool and the outdoors. The child made Iveta think of her belly. When should she tell Daniel about her condition? She was pondering this matter of timing when the elevator stopped at L. The little family exited. The doors hung open. She was planning her exercise. If she swam for a half hour today, then tomorrow she could add fifteen minutes.

The door was closing when she heard the voice of the fat man.

Her heart raced; the voice was getting closer. Someone said, Hold the goddamn elevator!

Iveta's heart raced. The fat man sounded grouchy, whiny—that sharp voice, the Texas accent. The door closed. Iveta was frightened. The little bell went *bong*; the doors whispered open. She made a hood of the towel, scurried to the door that said TENNIS COURTS. She remembered the view window. If the fat man looked down, he could see her.

Outside, she stood behind some bushes, watching the tennis—a Latino boy hitting balls to a gray-haired woman. She counted to a hundred, took a deep breath, and walked up the path, opened the door to the pool. She saw the fat man looking down from the view window.

He had gained weight. His jowls shook when he talked. His companions were a woman with a clipboard and a tall man with gray hair who looked like an airline pilot. The gray hair was beautiful and abundant.

Iveta slipped through the door, hurried to the pool. No sign of Daniel or Papa Ackerman or the Steinbeck woman. With her back to the view-window, Iveta dropped her robe, grabbed a big red float ball, and went into the water. She put her chest on the ball, let her arms dangle in the water. When she saw people looking down from the view window, she hid behind the ball.

Iveta was here—America, Boston, Sedona—because of the fat man. His name was Hiram Fish. He and Madame Belle were enemies, something from the past—she must have been very young. Iveta was here with Daniel because she had done a favor for Madame Belle, who wanted photos that showed Fish having sex. The term in English was "compromising position."

Iveta had met Fish through a restaurant owner in Prague, a friend of Madame Belle. When Fish came to the restaurant to look her over, Iveta passed the test. He took her to dinner, tried to get her drunk, and then she took him to a perfect little *maison de passe*, made camera-ready by Madame Belle's technicians.

The hidden cameras caught Fish wearing a black rubber bra, a pink baby bow, and pink panties. Iveta wore a wig and a silver domino. "Let's pretend there's a party," she said.

The camera also caught Fish slapping Iveta, trying to tear off her mask. She was pushing him away, the girl who said no. She remembered getting angry when he broke her tooth. She punched him in the gut, he coughed. Then he called her a bitch. She broke his nose. There was blood.

She remembered the pain; it hounded her for weeks. But she had escaped Prague. She had thrived in Paris. She had found her man in Boston. She had counted on never seeing Fish again, and now here he was in this very hotel, looking smug and ugly and evil.

Iveta had a mission. She needed to warn Madame Belle. She was no longer in Prague, no longer in Paris, no longer working for Madame Belle. But the debt would last forever.

45

WHEN HER SHIFT ENDED, Karla rode her bike to Vortex Bank. The sun felt lovely on her legs. No word from Charity ... where was the effing money? She told herself to relax; Charity loved playing games. As she rolled into the parking lot, Karla could not suppress her excitement. She was smiling big-time as she parked her bike beside the yellow beauty of Mr. Cypher. He waved at her through his window, something he'd never done before today.

She was still smiling inside the bank, feeling the eyes of Larry and Joe, two old girl-watchers drinking free bank coffee and sitting in rent-free chairs along the west wall. Mr. Cypher was up out of his chair, holding the door for her. Inside his fish-bowl office, she asked him for help opening a new account.

His eyes followed Karla's legs as she crossed them. She saw what the girls were talking about. When a guy wanted you, and when he let you know it, and when he was a solid guy with a good job—then Mr. Darwin took control, not only of your body, but your survival reflexes.

She put Mr. Cypher through the Mr. Right Checklist—good genes, good resources, good behavior. His good genes showed up in the handshake, the slim build, his body heat. He had good resources—job, house, car, and he made steady money at the bank. His swell behavior back in Los Angeles had rescued Karla from a bad college loan. She was curious about his behavior if she could get him alone. The legs crossed again, testing, the eyes followed. For a moment she had control.

She mentioned her trouble in L.A. and that triggered his memory—of course he remembered helping Karla arrange a new payment plan on her student loan. Was he lying to make her feel good? Did he really remember or was it her bare just-shaved legs? His smile said he liked her, maybe even wanted her, and Karla could feel herself responding. She asked, did he also remember advising her to join the army? He said, Did I? But now they had a connection, soldier to soldier.

She kept waiting for him to bring up the subject of Benny Kelwin, the bastard who got her pregnant, deserted her. And she flashed on images from her pregnancy dream—the stolen pickup, the sturdy deer guard, the impact when she hit Kelwin coming out of the apartment of his new girlfriend. If Mr. Cypher knew something, he could send Karla to jail.

But all he said was, "I'm hungry. How about some lunch?"

THEY DROVE NORTH INTO Oak Creek Canyon. They ate outdoors, sitting side by side, shoulders touching, like two lovers in a fictional romance. The breeze came up and Mr. Cypher loaned Karla a parka from North Face that reminded her of Santa Fe, the cold stairwell, the falling body of Frederick Delaplane.

The wine was a Pinot Noir. One glass and Karla was tipsy, and then Mr. Cypher said how beautiful had been in Los Angeles, so young, so vulnerable. That was seven long years ago. The compliments flowed through her, fire in the blood, and voilà, she felt the sizzle of romance.

There was a motel next to the lunch place. The room was clean; the mattress did not squeak. There was a fake fireplace like the one in Ackerman's penthouse. Had Mr. Cypher been here with other women?

Everyone said Mr. Cypher was in shape. They were right on. From the doorway, Karla watched him strip down. Khaki suit, blue button-down shirt, boxer shorts. She had expected winter pale skin, but his skin had seen recent sun. Valley rumors claimed that Mr. Cypher was hung like a horse—those rumors did not lie.

Mr. Cypher asked permission to undress her, showing good behavior. His hands were clever—not his first time with a woman. He said how beautiful she was, how he had watched her from afar, from his office at the bank.

She was nervous, so she mentioned the mystery workshop with Miss Steinbeck and Mr. Cypher said he had a signed copy of the book, *Murder on Drake Island*. They stopped talking about Miss Steinbeck. He finished stripping away Karl's clothes. Naked, she moved close and there was his hand on her thigh. She turned, a slow pirouette, until his hand slid between her legs. She laughed, sounding like a girl in a movie. They moved to the bed. The sex was good; this guy knew about women, what they needed to feel comfortable. Karla was in love.

46

AFTER THE SUPERIOR SEX with Karla Kurtz, Cypher dropped into Zen Mode.

Had he found his perfect woman at last? She was attractive, hard-working; she knew what she wanted from life. A Latina Cinderella, climbing up from the ashes.

Her leg was thrown across his. Her lips nibbled his throat. She told him about her childhood in Los Angeles, the violence, stabbing a Latino guy because he got her sister pregnant, the cops were scary. Then she told him her hope of being a famous writer. Miss Steinbeck really liked her workshop writing and when she read, the whole room got hooked and ….

Cypher was not listening because Karla's memories shoved him back into the twisted tunnel of his own childhood.

Cypher remembered singing solos in the church choir, taking voice lessons. The teacher said, "You'll have a career in music." While Karla remembered violence, Cypher remembered drawing in art class, winning a state contest, where one judge said he was channeling Leonardo da Vinci. Leonardo became Cypher's first real hero—thinker, artist, inventor, man of the world.

Cypher remembered reading books about Leonardo's inventions, the parachute, the aerial screw-helicopter, the 33-barreled organ—the forerunner to the Gatling Gun. Cypher filled notebooks with hero stories, exotic weapons, adventures in foreign lands. He remembered burning the stories after Father died, after Mother was being courted by the preacher, Brother O'Brien, who had a fat face, like Senator Fish. He remembered the girl next door, Alyson the blonde cheerleader, he remembered her naked knees when she jumped, the sexy pleated skirt, *go team go* ….

"Hey," a voice said.

"What?" he said.

"Where did you go?"

"I'm sorry. You were telling me about the workshop, the Yavapai room, three days a week—taught by our local writer, Miss Steinbeck."

"And you drifted off."

"What's your gory tale about?" he said.

"A nasty uncle gets a girl pregnant," Karla said. "She loses the baby, then pushes the uncle off a bridge. He's drunk … no more uncle. The girl is named Faith Marie. She has red hair, a Southern accent, a killer body. She lusts for revenge. Her daddy is a preacher. She blames her parents, hates men. Flash forward, she's famous for pushing guys downstairs, and gets hired by this Mr. X guy, who has this list, see, but she needs help, so she recruits a newbie and—"

"You love the act of writing, don't you?"

"Writing is exciting," she said. "The words flowing, your heart beating."

"I'd be honored to view a sample," he said.

"It's on disc," she said. "Would you care to edit me?"

47

HELENE STEINBECK LAY ON the metal exam table. Her feet were cold. She shivered in the white gown. Her knees were open, her feet planted in the metal stirrups. The doctor wore a surgical headlamp. Her exam gloves were white latex. Helene could not stop trembling. Every time she felt a touch, she wanted to shriek.

"Sorry," she said.

"It's okay," the doctor said. "It's normal. Just one more peek, okay?"

Helene twitched at the touch. She was afraid. She kept seeing the eyes of the madman. The invasion of her body by the doctor triggered a flashback.

The doctor went away, leaving Helene on her back in the madman's office. On his bed with the ritualistic black silk sheets. He stood over her, grinning. Helen was pumped full of drugs. He swayed back and forth, fading, coming back into focus. Helene blinked. He went away. The doctor stepped back, stripped off her white gloves and dumped them into a little metal can.

"All good. You can get dressed now."

The doctor was named Ruth Gold. She still had the New York accent. Helene was here because Dr. Ruth was a friend of Axel Ackerman.

Dr. Ruth was a GP. She did minor surgery. She did gynecology and internal medicine. She did ears, noses, throats, but not eyes. She was a naturopath, a homeopath, an herbalist. She was a licensed pediatrician.

All that was on her office door. Squeezed onto her business card. Maybe she also did psychiatry. That's what Helene needed.

While Helene was dressing, the door opened and the madman strode through.

He was naked except for his uniform cap and pistol.

He aimed the pistol at Helene. She hunkered down behind the exam table.

"Everything okay?" the doctor said.

The madman frowned. He rolled his eyes. He vanished.

"I just saw my rapist," Helene said.

"That's normal," the doctor said.

"I'm going crazy," Helene said.

"Tell me about the rapist."

"He kidnapped young women. We went after him. We split up."

"Who's *we*?" the doctor said.

"Murdock and me," Helene said.

"Your significant other?"

"I think so."

"You're not sure?"

"I think so."

"How did you think about Murdock before the rape?"

"We were so good," Helene said. "It seemed fated. We were tight. Our brains were in sync."

"How was the sex?" the doctor said.

"The sex was amazing," Helene said. "Spontaneous, natural, loving."

"And after the rape … how's the sex now?"

"Zero sex," Helene said. "Nada, zip, nothing."

"Has he tried?"

"Not physically … but I can feel him. You know men."

"Have you tried?"

"I can't."

"Where do you sleep?"

"I have the bed. He has the sofa."

"Are you sleeping?"

"Not much."

"Taking any drugs?"

"No."

"Want some?" the doctor said.

"Sometimes."

"Tell me how you got locked in with the rapist."

Helene told her about the manhunt, how she and Murdock split up, how she ended up drugged, strapped to a bed, and raped.

"Whose idea was it to split up?" the doctor said.

"My idea."

"Why?"

"The man was attracted to me. I thought I could handle him."

"Were you right?"

"What do you mean?"

"Were you able to handle him?"

"I killed him," Helene said.

"How?"

"I drove a hat pin into his eye. And that's what I dream about, the close-up of his eye. And that's why I'm going crazy, and that's why I'm here!"

"You don't have to shout," the doctor said.

Helene shook her head. Had she been shouting? She looked around the room. She was in the doctor's office, sitting in a chair, sipping tea. She did not remember asking for tea. The cup was warm in her hands. Her face was hot. If the madman walked through the door, she would kill him again.

"So," the doctor said. "Was it morning? Afternoon? Night?"

"Afternoon," Helene said. "It was Indian summer on Angel Mountain. A lovely Sunday and that dirty, slimy bastard—"

"If you could replay that afternoon, would you make the same decision?"

"Yes."

"Knowing that the filthy bastard would rape you?"

"He would have killed Murdock," Helene said. "I knew I could handle him."

"Had you killed before?"

"Once," Helene said.

"How did it feel?"

"Necessary," Helene said.

"Because you are good killing evil?"

"It was clear to me at the time."

"So you feel justified?"

Helene nodded. The doctor handed over a small mirror. Helene stared at herself. Her face had the high color of anger, exasperation. Her eyes were narrow and fierce. Her lips were drawn back against her teeth. She exhaled. She was here, in a quiet office in Oak Creek Village, seven miles south of Sedona. She was alive. The madman was dead. Murdock was alive. She missed Murdock.

"What are you feeling right now?"

"Anger," Helene said. "I am pissed off."

"Are you angry about the rapist?"

"The code of honor," Helene said.

"Explain that," the doctor said.

"We knew this guy was bad. He was flaunting his evil, taunting us. He wanted to kill Murdock and have sex with me, then kill me too. There wasn't enough hard evidence, nothing we could take to court. Society has its rules. So we went after him."

"Were you doing it for Society?" the doctor said.

"We were doing it because he was evil."

"What are you feeling now?"

Helene grinned. She felt better. This doctor from New York knew her stuff. The doctor grinned back. Breathing was good.

"So what now, Doctor?"

"Have you talked to Murdock?"

"Not about this."

"Do you know why?"

"There's this wall," Helene said.

"Have you asked for a hug?"

"No."

"I can give you something to help you sleep," the doctor said. "It's herbs and homeopathy. The physical exam showed no internal damage. Think of the wall as a net across a tennis court."

"The ball is back in my court, correct?"

"Getting raped is terrible, and this thing is still big—larger than you or me—so don't downplay it. Come back and see me in a week."

Helene sat there, feeling heavy. Questions whirled in her brain. Why was she here? What did she hope to gain by coming here? Why was she eating so much?

"Something else?" the doctor said.

"I'm gaining weight," Helene said. "I feel really fat."

"Chocolate cravings?" the doctor said.

"And Danish. At the hotel. They are awesome."

"Eating gives you control," the doctor said. "Chocolate has caffeine; it gooses your endorphins, you feel good. You're tall, you can handle the weight. Are you exercising?"

"Not enough," Helene said.

"Has Murdock noticed?"

"He sees everything. He has a good eye for the female anatomy."

"Has he said anything?"

"No, but I can feel him thinking it."

"Anything else?"

"I'm jumpy," Helene said.

"Normal," the doctor said.

"Not for me," Helene said. "Before the rape I had nerves of steel. I was a cop, then a town marshal. I killed my friend and—"

"Why did you kill your friend?"

"To stop her from killing little girls," Helene said.

"Would you do it again?"

"Yes."

"So this rape snatched away your self-control. And the eating is further proof that you have lost control, and you're here to get it back."

"But I don't know how!"

"What does Murdock think?"

"Is that my assignment, professor?"

"Start with the hug," the doctor said.

THEY WALKED TOGETHER THROUGH the outer office. They stood on the sidewalk. The sun sagged toward the Hieroglyphs, southwest of Sedona. The doctor's office sat next door to Vortex Bank. Cypher's yellow bike was padlocked to the bike rack.

The doctor handed Helene a paper sack. Inside she found three bottles of pills. One said SLEEP. One said MEMORY. One said HUGS. Helene hugged the doctor, could they be friends? She said, "Thank you."

The doctor said, *"De Nada."*

On the way up the hill toward Sedona Landing, Helene phoned Geronimo Airport. Murdock's plane was due at four.

48

THROUGH THE WINDOW OF Ackerman's plane, Murdock saw the Humvee. It was parked beside the runway at Geronimo Airport. He thanked the pilot, grabbed his backpack. His heart did a little flip when Helene stepped down from the Humvee. She said hello, gave him a hug. He wanted to hang on; she broke away. The driver's door opened and she climbed inside. Murdock took the passenger seat. The wall between them was back.

"How was Amarillo?"

"Found a guy with a motive."

"Who?"

"Young Joey Wilson, son of Honest Joe Wilson, the owner of—"

"What's the motive?" Helene said.

"The Crew wrecked his family business. They also wrecked the family."

"How old was Joey?"

"Fourteen or fifteen."

"So he'd be like forty-five now?"

"I wish you had been there," Murdock said. "There was this old lady ... you could have gotten more info than I did."

Helene turned onto the road that crossed the Interstate. When she spoke, she did not look at Murdock. "Axel offered me a job," she said.

"Doing what? Firearms coach?"

"His aide-de-camp," she said.

"What about the lovely Miss Roux?"

"Giselle's going back to college, architecture. He offered me a million dollars."

"You need to barter with him," Murdock said.

"Barter about what?"

"About wages," Murdock said. "Job expectations."

"I'm confused," Helene said. "A million dollars and you want more?"

"Do the math," Murdock said. "You're pulling down five grand every twenty-four hours. Multiplied by three hundred and sixty-five days, that would mushroom into a million eight—"

Helene's voice was snappish. "I thought you would be happy for me."

"Check your speedometer," Steinbeck. "This old Humvee is jiggling like Jell-O."

"It's mine," Helene said.

"What's yours?"

"The Hummer. Axel gave it to me."

"I hope his job offer included gas."

*****

KARLA WAS IN THE Executive Spa, smoothing the sheet on Ackerman's massage table, still feeling the tingle from her afternoon with Mr. Cypher. Did she have a future with this guy?

Ackerman was in the bathroom; she heard the toilet flush. The door opened. He came out, his robe unbelted, sending a clear message—caveman ready for sex. When he grinned at her, she turned away.

"Don't blame me," he said. "It's those little blue man pills …."

"On the table," she said. "Face down, on your best behavior, or I'm leaving."

"We have a contract," Ackerman said.

"Face down, sir."

"Call me Axel," he said.

He lay face down. He had been after Karla for months. He was her only customer, five hundred dollars a pop, great tips. She oiled his back. Started with his left lat. Ackerman's spine was curved, forcing him to tilt to the right when he walked. For an old guy, he was in good shape.

Karla's phone beeped, text message incoming. Ackerman told her not to answer. The beep distracted her; maybe it was Mr. Cypher. Her fingers located a knot in the fascia, and she focused on making it go away. The phone beeped again. Karla wiped oil from one hand. The message was a text from Charity Plum.

"Got yr $$$. Job 5 happens 2-nite, the Xanadu, downtown Sedona, 9 PM, 100K. C ya."

Ackerman raised up on one elbow. "What is it?"

"Gotta go, sorry."

"I paid you in advance," Ackerman said. "Masseuse on call. Therefore …."

Karla wasn't listening. She felt hot, then clammy. Her stomach lurched. She ran to the bathroom, no time, sank to her knees. The vomit splashed yellow green and sour.

She was dizzy, her face burning. She wet a wash cloth, held it on her forehead. Returned to the spa, where Ackerman sat on the massage table. Thin shoulders, scrawny neck, a towel concealing his erection. At this moment, she hated all men.

"I apologize," he said.

"I gotta go," she said. "I feel like shit."

"We have a contract," he said.

"You smarmy old man!" she said.

As she ran out, she heard Ackerman yelling.

*****

Helene marched into Sedona Landing. She was furious, and she wanted Murdock to know it. She walked fast, almost at a trot. He did not choose to keep up, so she left him behind. *Take that, mister hotshot detective.* She blew through the front entrance and saw Karla Kurtz, her favorite writer from the mystery workshop, leaning over the reception desk talking to Raul, the concierge.

Karla had on white shorts. She was barefoot, her black hair tied in a ponytail, running shoes in one hand, a red rucksack over her shoulder. She looked distraught. When she turned to stare at Helene, Karla's eyes seemed out of focus. Her face was puffy; she had been crying. When she went by, Helene said hello and Karla said, "Oh, hi, gotta run." Murdock came through the doors. Karla dodged, cutting around him, her dark legs glimmering.

Helene called out: "See you tomorrow ... looking forward to the next installment!" But Karla was already out the door, into the night, moving fast.

"That's Karla, she's one of my writers—and doing some good work, on these two gals who team up like ..." she paused.

"Good legs," Murdock said. "Moves like a jock. What's she writing ... murder on a space ship headed for—?"

"Is that all you think about?" Helene said. "Tits and ass?"

"I said legs," Murdock said. "Let's find Ackerman, see what he remembers about Amarillo."

"You find him," Helene said. "I need a drink."

49

IT WAS THURSDAY EVENING and Axel Ackerman sat at his table in the Bell Rock Bistro answering questions from Murdock and Helene. Ackerman's shoulder ached. And his lower back, and his right knee. He had counted on the massage to keep him loose. Then came the phone call, and Karla had split, leaving him alone. Where the hell was she going?

Gripping the file folder, Ackerman confronted the evidence from Amarillo, from three decades ago. Images flickered across his memory, like an old sepia movie. He felt trapped.

He remembered those early years as exciting, make or break, moving fast, smell of money, smell of sex, fear of failure. He remembered having too many irons in the fire, too many projects, too many contractors, everyone needed teaching, coaching, mentoring. He remembered travel as a series of blurs—job to job, new faces, new forces. If he drove, he would barrel along, way over the speed limit, dusty towns, city fathers on the make, business owners who did not comprehend the power of Darwin, the survival of the fittest, buy low, sell high. He did not remember much about Amarillo, a dot on a map in the Texas Panhandle.

He looked at the evidence and remembered Penny Diamond and felt doom.

The first piece of evidence was a grainy Amarillo newspaper photo below the headline that said: NEW YORK CAPITAL INFUSION RESCUES LOCAL BUSINESS. The photo showed the five men of his old Crew—Tyler, Coolidge, Hawthorne, Findlay, and Delaplane. There was no photo of Penny Diamond.

As if she could read his mind, Helene Steinbeck said: "Anyone missing, Mr. A?"

"Me," he said.

"Anyone else?"

"Miss Penny Diamond."

"Was she part of the team?"

"The Crew didn't think so."

"Why not?"

"She was too smart, made them feel dumb. They got back at her by keeping her out of the picture."

"What did you think?"

"They were investors, had money in the pool. She did not invest; she took no risks."

"Did you like her?"

"I hired her, and the money was good."

"Did you have a personal relationship?"

"Jesus Christ, Steinbeck."

"So that's a yes?"

"We fooled around," Ackerman said. "She made the first move. She was so beautiful—they all are, at that age, like God's own angels."

"But you couldn't get your Crew to let her into the picture?"

"They were there, on the ground," Ackerman said.

"Five against one," Helene said.

The second piece of evidence was a photo from a high school yearbook. A shifty-eyed kid with a smug look, eyes you would never trust. The name under the photo was Gerald R. Ramsay.

"What's this?"

"Gerry Ramsay interviewed you for the school paper."

"It's coming back," Ackerman said. "Ramsay was a rat-faced little shit. He tried to wangle a summer job."

"What did you say?"

"I explained my process, contractors only. I told him to call the office in New York."

"So Mrs. Ramsay was right … about the job thing, Gerry traveling to New York, where you gave him the brush-off."

"I remember the interview," Ackerman said. "I remember no contact in New York. My so-called brush-off is pure bullshit. There is no way a sane man, grown-up man would worry about this after thirty years."

The third piece of evidence was a Xerox copy of a microfiched newspaper article with a headline that Ackerman had seen in other small-town papers—LOCAL BUSINESS TAKES SLIPPERY SLOPE INTO CHAPTER ELEVEN. Not a big deal. If you were a businessman, bankruptcy was a cog in the great wheel of profit and loss, the great cycle of economics. The sun coming up, the sun going down. If you were soft, you needed someone to blame. Blame the universe, blame Arc-Angel Equity, blame Ackerman.

He didn't care, because he understood the cycle. He lived by its laws, surrendered to its inevitability, made no move to resist. He gave Murdock a look, then he swung over to Helene Steinbeck. She blamed him—he saw it in her eyes.

The byline on the article identified the author, Gerry Ramsay, editor of the high school paper, the AHS Sandstorm. The writing was amateurish, snide, overdone. The photo of Wilson's Fine Furniture sucked Ackerman into the past. It was like watching an old newsreel in a theater that smelled of sweat, popcorn, and perfume. The photo showed Joseph Wilson and a teenage boy.

Father and son were standing in front of Wilson's Fine Furniture, facing a gaggle of employees holding protest signs. In one hand, Wilson held a sack. With the other hand, he offered cash money to his employees. They formed in a half-circle, staring at Wilson. Only a fool gave money away.

The fourth piece of evidence was a death notice from the same newspaper, *Amarillo Globe-News*. Joseph Wilson had died from falling, on Christmas Eve. An autopsy found alcohol in his blood.

Ackerman closed the folder. He glanced at Helene, then at Murdock, then he looked away, through the window. The patio was dark; the sun was down. That was a law of nature, sun-up, day, sundown, night. If you were a butterfly, you would be dead when the sun went down.

Joseph Wilson had been a butterfly.

Ackerman pushed out of his chair. His legs felt wobbly; he was no butterfly. He stood at the window, looking out. Who wanted him dead? Who wanted to torpedo this deal? There was a fist in his chest, pounding his ribcage. He saw a graveyard, a coffin, a handful of mourners. He stood at the grave's edge, looking down. The corpse had his face, his nose, his bald head. *Papa*, he said, *what do I do?*

Ackerman needed a drink. He needed to steady himself. Where was the waitress? Who was trying to kill him? He sat down in his chair. The room whirled around him. Maybe the nut-cases of Sedona were right about the power of the vortex.

"Okay," Ackerman said. "You're the sleuths. What's next?"

"Any contact with Hawthorne?" Murdock said.

"We spoke on the phone Sunday," Ackerman said. "He was in Buffalo, wrapping up a project. He had a date, no time to talk."

"How old is Hawthorne?"

"He's the youngest," Ackerman said, "and the prettiest. Women go crazy over his hair. It's like observing a movie-star in his favorite role."

"We also need to alert your son and his lady friend," Helene said.

"Be my guest," Ackerman said.

Daniel stood in the doorway, holding hands with Iveta Macek.

50

Murdock watched Daniel Ackerman take the steps down into the Bell Rock Bistro. He wore sandals with no socks, baggy Bermudas, a Waikiki shirt crazy with fronds. The woman with him was Iveta Macek, tall and blonde, a tough mouth, makeup over her pockmarks. Daniel was in his fifties, Macek edging toward thirty. A ring glinted on her engagement finger.

Ackerman's son had a businessman's handshake—honest, solid, perfect timing, just the right pressure. A handshake that said, *This is a good man, you can do business, no worries.* Iveta Macek was starving. She ordered a three-egg omelet with salmon, and a proper white wine. Daniel checked out the food bar and came back with a Sedona Burger, a huge patty, onion rings, fries in a hot sack, and a glass of the local red wine. Macek chatted with Helene. Between bites, Daniel asked Murdock if there was progress.

"Your dad's still alive," Murdock said. "I'd call that progress."

"He told me he's not buying your two female killer theory."

"It's all we've got," Murdock said.

"So it's just a theory, right?"

"All we've got."

"This blood-bath on Fox-something, did these two assumed female killers perpetrate that?"

"Foxglove Lane was someone else."

"How can you possibly know that?"

"Killers have styles," Murdock said. "Like signatures."

"What's their style then—knives? Poison darts? Strangulation à la garrote?"

"Death by falling," Murdock said.

"Isn't that how Will Tyler died ... by taking a fall?"

"You knew Tyler?" Murdock said.

"My little Fire Island bungalow is near his," Daniel said. "We hoisted some brewskis at the Blue Point in Patchogue. I was shocked when I heard."

"Did you know anyone else on your dad's Crew?"

"I did business with Freddy Delaplane a while back. I saw Walter through the years, but not Coolidge."

"Did you ever lay eyes on Penny Diamond?" Murdock said.

"Why would you ask that?"

"The small world of high finance," Murdock said. "She's about your age."

"I was older," Daniel said.

"Same generation," Murdock said.

*****

DANIEL TOOK A BITE of burger. He had a wide mouth and thick lips. He had his father's nose and eyes, but the bulky build came from his mother. Daniel was a businessman, maybe a shark in the boardroom. Before he answered, he swallowed his mouthful, took a slug of wine, and shook black pepper on the french fries. He offered the sack to Murdock. The guy made him nervous, the way he looked at you.

"We met in a class," he said. "Statistics. I was the TA."

"What school?"

"Wharton," Daniel said. "Miss Diamond was young and

brilliant. She could inhale the numbers from a spread sheet. Back then we had Lotus 1-2-3. The Excel spreadsheet was a whisper on the wind. We had Buddha—there was this joke about assuming the Lotus position when you wanted answers. Then along came Quattro, which was an advance on the 1-2-3 of Lotus. Then there was—"

"What did she look like?"

"What do you mean?"

"Was she pretty?" Murdock said. "Was she sexy? Did she date her professors? Did she date you?"

"Lunches, mostly," Daniel said. "Nothing serious. She wasn't really wife-material, if that's what you mean."

"Not high society?" Murdock said.

"It wasn't like that," Daniel said.

"What was it like?"

"Miss Diamond was ultra small-town. Her father was a stump preacher down south. She needed help with statistics; that was my forte."

"Do you have photo of her?" Murdock said.

"I told you; it wasn't like that."

"Here's a scenario," Murdock said. "What if Ackerman's Crew shut her out? What if she got pissed? What if she's still pissed after thirty years? What if she's losing her looks? What if she gets help from a second female?"

"Is this what you people refer to as sleuthing?"

"Watch your step," Murdock said. "Your fiancée too."

"Are you saying we might be in danger?"

"Don't talk to strangers," Murdock said.

"Have you seen our server?" Daniel said. "This is a serious red. I need a refill."

MAYBE IT WAS THE burger, maybe the fries. Daniel had gas. He farted, left the table. He burped. Where was the men's room? He felt Iveta's eyes tracking him. She was seated between Axel and the Steinbeck woman. He already knew from Axel that

Steinbeck was half Jewish. Daniel could tell from the old man's body language, the nose, the cant of his head, the hunter's gleaming eye, that sex with Steinbeck was on the agenda.

Thinking of sex made Daniel think of Penny Diamond, his first sight of her in the class on statistics. One look at her sinuous shape and his heart stood still. He took Penny Diamond for a Coke, then a drink, then lunch, then a candle-lit dinner. She said she would "lie with him in sin" if he helped her get the A in statistics. Her down-home argot, laced with Bible-talk, was pure charm. She got the A. She took Daniel to bed, he proposed, and she said she'd been praying for this moment. Yes-yes-yes, she would be his wife. He took her to meet Axel.

Axel gave her a contract, $20,000 for the summer—that was like $50K today—and shipped her to the Midwest, a church girl with a Southern accent. Penny sent picture postcards, *real busy, hon, wish you were here.* Daniel spent his summer playing the market, making serious money in puts and calls. He remembered the joy when he clocked his first hundred grand. Axel was worth ten million, on the road to becoming a bona fide billionaire. Daniel would devote his life to catching up.

In August, a postcard from Penny: "I am returning your ring."

In September, some crazy person burglarized the offices of Arc-Angel Equity. Axel blamed Penny Diamond. Daniel asked, "Something happen in the boonies?"

"The bitch burgled my office," Axel said. "The police won't take my word. I put the Crew on it."

So why had Daniel held back? Why hadn't he shared that precious Penny Diamond memory with Murdock? He'd been on the verge, but Daniel didn't trust Murdock. His warning about not talking to strangers was out of line. Daniel could buy and sell guys like Murdock. And besides, Daniel's investment brain was busy with the Sedona Landing thing. After so many years of being shut out, Daniel was gonna be partners with his dad.

Iveta met Daniel coming out of the men's room and they strolled around the grounds of Sedona Landing. Guys on the tennis court ogled Iveta. Daniel didn't mind; she was his lady. She loved it here, the warmth, the sun, the crisp air.

They rode the elevator to Nine. Their suite was next door to Findlay's, still draped in yellow ribbons. Inside their suite, Iveta pushed Daniel down on the bed. She ran her hand up under the shorts, took a grip on him, stuck her tongue in his ear. Christ, he loved this woman. She got him off sitting on top, her slim golden hands on his shoulders, using her weight to hold him down, gyrating her hips, her eyes narrowed and shrewd.

When he came, he whimpered, "It was so good."

Iveta whispered in his ear. "Invest with your Papa," she said.

51

GEORGE HAWTHORNE'S PLANE WAS late landing in Phoenix. The limo for Sedona was late picking him up. Phoenix traffic was thick, swarms of beetles crawling over a corpse. His cellphone gave him a message—no service. The limo had a little screen, where he watched *Vertigo*, an old Hitchcock movie with Jimmy Stewart and Kim Novak, where the acro-phobic gumshoe was afraid of falling.

The limo came into Sedona and he saw his hotel, the Sedona Xanadu, perched on a hill. His room was ready. The desk clerk was a brunette in a tight blouse. Hawthorne felt a stirring in the blood. He asked about night spots, and she told him Lemon Custard Bistro, just around the corner. A Mexican bell-boy showed him the room, a suite on Seven, with a balcony, a view south to Phoenix and Mexico. He tipped with a five, unpacked his casuals, headed for the bathroom. Time for a shower, wash off the filth of flying coach.

His cell rang. It was Senator Fish, his old shooting Buddy. He was downstairs, with a notary. "Well, come on up, Senator."

Hawthorne had met Fish on an elk hunt at Vermejo, Teddy Turner's hunter's paradise in northern New Mexico. There was shooting, good booze, men who thought alike around a campfire. They bonded over politics, the fate of a nation. A feisty foreign policy and a conservative social agenda—God, flag, the church of your choice. Females did not belong in government. A woman's place was in the home. Be a mother, be a wife, be a volunteer. Hawthorne had money back then. He'd pledged a hundred grand to Fish's re-election campaign.

The buzzer rang. Hawthorne opened the door. Fish had gained weight. His smile was still fake and his handshake was still sweaty. He was decked out like an Arizona rancher—baggy khakis, dusty boots, a Western-style shirt with pearl-snap buttons, a string necktie that looked silly. Fish introduced his notary, a nothing guy with a briefcase and a bland face. His name was Billy.

They sat at a polished table. Fish drank Scotch, Billy drank ice tea. He passed two documents to Hawthorne—one original, one copy. The document was a deed of trust transferring the fifth floor of Sedona Landing to Hiram Travis Fish for the sum of five million dollars. Hawthorne signed the original, passed the paper back to Billy, who stamped it with his little inker. Billy set an envelope on the table. As Hawthorne checked the envelope, his hands trembled. He saw five packets of hundreds, fifty thousand in cash. Fish scanned the transfer document, folded it, and tucked it into his pocket. Hawthorne was broke. He owed money in China, Thailand, Viet Nam. Fish chuckled, shook his head, and grinned.

"Always happy to help a fellow conservative," he said.

At the door they confirmed the next meeting, tomorrow at ten, Vortex Bank, Cypher's office.

"You take care, now."

"I'm a careful guy, Senator."

"You had any recent contact with our favorite Jew pinko liberal Democrat?"

"We chatted last week."

"You remember ... I'm gonna break the news—about the fifth floor?"

"I have the memory of an elephant, Senator."

The shower had power. Hawthorne used the massage feature. The word *massage* triggered an image of Saigon. They laid you face down and walked on your back. Magic toes of the women. He was eager to get back. He grinned at himself in the bathroom mirror. Pleased with his own film-star good looks, living proof of the power of the Fibonacci Paradigm.

The perfect size head, the perfect distance from chin to forehead, eyes to ears, mouth to nose. His teeth were pure white. His muscles flexed like they were thirty years younger. His hair was thick and blond—beach-boy forever. Hawthorne was grinning at his mirror image, girding for a hot night at the Lemon Custard Bistro, when he heard movement from the next room.

In the bedroom, he found a hotel maid.

She had a little chocolate in her hand, a mint wrapped in gold.

She was about to slip the chocolate onto his pillow. The maid turned, saw him, and looked startled.

She was dark, a Latina with cheekbones. She said something in Spanish, Madre-something. She looked like a bird caught by a cat.

A bird with a worm in its beak ... and a nice body.

The maid apologized.

Her face was red. She thought he was out for the evening. She had knocked; there was no answer. Once inside, she had called out, but no one answered.

Hawthorne stared at the maid. Under the robe, he was growing a boner. She was dark, with photogenic cheekbones, pale blue eyes, and hands with long fingers. She wore a perky little maid cap that he wanted to tear off. The skirt of the maid's uniform was short, bare knees, no stockings.

She looked scrumptious, she looked afraid, and he wanted her.

He told her to wait. He moved to the dresser—sleek black, chrome pulls. He extracted a twenty from his wallet. She was at the door, her hand on the knob. He handed her the twenty.

"Oh," she said, "I can't take your money. It's not allowed, the tipping."

He asked about her shift. When was it over?

"I love your music," she said.

Mozart was playing, an aria from *The Magic Flute*. The Xanadu had a Bose radio in every room; he always traveled first class. He was impressed by her comment—a maid who knew Mozart. Maybe the maid was a princess in disguise.

He asked again about her shift.

"One more room," she said, "one more chocolate."

She pronounced *chocolate* with a Latino lilt, adding an extra syllable at the end, cho-ko-la-tay.

"And then?" he said.

"And then a long drive in the dark, and miles to go before I sleep."

"Robert Frost," he said. "The poem about stopping to check out the snow."

"I was a college girl," she said, "before the money ran out."

"College where?" he said.

"Middlebury. I was on scholarship, studying literature. Are you related to Nathaniel Hawthorne?"

She was shivering. He poured her a brandy. She sniffed the glass, took a sip, nodded, sat on the bed, her back straight, the skirt rising up, showing exquisite thigh.

"Lovely," she said.

"Yes," he said. "You are."

"I was referring to the cognac."

Hawthorne had a philosophy: life is short, grab what you can. He wanted to grab the maid.

She wobbled as she stood up.

"Are you all right?"

"Cognac on an empty stomach," she said. "I should know better."

"When did you last eat?"

"Yesterday," she said. "It is not your problem."

He wanted her. He wanted to help her. He offered food. "Come back here after your shift. We'll order room service."

"Not allowed," she said. "I'm a maid, and I need this job."

He gave her another twenty. He had fifty grand from Senator Fish. Money made Hawthorne expansive. He could buy the world and all its pretty women.

She would think about it, she said. He didn't know her name. Merida, she said, going Latina on him. Her cheek brushed his, the flutter of butterfly wings, and his boner went rigid.

"If I come back," she whispered, "you must please put on some clothes."

He watched her slip through the door—a wraith, an unreal vision.

He shaved his face. Frowned at that droopy flesh under his jaw. Hawthorne hated wattles. He dressed in khakis from Abercrombie, the desert look, a two-pocket camping shirt from Brooks Brothers, sandals from Banana Republic. He had made money from United Fruit, had helped with the start-up of Chiquita Brands, and walked away with thirteen million, liquidity to invest in this Sedona Landing venture.

Hawthorne phoned Ackerman; he had been ordered to check in.

"Where the fuck are you?" Ackerman said.

"Thanks for the warm welcome, Axel," Hawthorne said.

"Did you hear?"

"Hear about what?"

"Freddy Delaplane, dead."

"Fell in the shower?"

"On some stairs. How come you're so calm, Georgie?"

"Simple statistics, Axel. One out of three old people fall

every year. Half of them break a bone, get a bruise. Last year falls killed one out of fifty who fell. Where was Freddy? Who was he shagging?"

"He was in Santa Fe," Ackerman said. "Are you snockered? You sound too happy."

"Willy Tyler died from falling; I read about it. So did Milt Coolidge, no surprise there, he was always clumsy. But I am not those birds, I've got a cane for outdoors, dogs, or marauders. I never make a left turn. How's my man Walt Findlay?"

"You didn't hear?"

There was a knock on the door.

Hawthorne was halfway there when the door opened. It was the maid, using her pass key. She saw the phone. Was she early? Was this a bad time? Should she come back later?

"Who the hell is that?" Ackerman said.

"The maid. She's turning down the bed."

"Listen to me, stiff dick. Get that female out of there, right fucking now."

"You were always jealous, Axel."

"Get your head out of your ass," Ackerman said. "And get the maid out—"

"I've come to a decision, old buddy."

"Is she out yet?"

"A decision about the current project," Hawthorne said. "When I came into this, I was feeling great, but a sudden turn of events has—"

"The maid! Throw her out!"

"I'm pulling my ante, old buddy. I've already spoken to your banker dude … he promised me a check for half a mil."

"Is she out yet?"

"See you tomorrow," Hawthorne said. "Buy you a beer, we'll catch up, then I got a plane to catch."

"Georgie!" Ackerman said. "Don't hang up. Walt Findlay is—"

Hawthorne hung up.

The maid was across the room, looking at a room service menu.

She asked again, "Should I go?"

He urged her to stay.

Room Service is a phone call away, he said. What would you like?

"I like you," she said. "Those are great-looking pantalones."

"How about roast beef?" he said. "Rare, and a red wine?"

"Let me call down," she said. "A guy like you needs something special."

She held out her hand for his cell. He handed it to her. She sat on the bed, the same pose as before, an actress rehearsing a role. He stared at her legs, shadowed muscles flexing. Her fingernails danced on the phone keys. So many beautiful women, so little time.

"Shouldn't you use the house phone for room service?"

"There's a secret number," she said. "I go for speed."

She spoke in rapid Spanish, pressed the end button, gave him back the phone. They had a drink—vodka martinis, mixed by her. His martini tasted funny, heavy on the bitters. Mozart still played. She pulled him close, and they danced. He smelled soap in her hair; heat came off her body. Her knee slid between his legs. She took his hands, they whirled, and she said something about the vortex. She pointed out the window. His room was on the tenth floor of the Sedona Xanadu. This hotel was ten years old, remodeled, rebuilt, reborn. Ackerman's hotel dated back to 1850.

He let her back him into a wall, unbutton his shirt, put her hand on his chest. She moved the hand down and pinched his belly; he could shed a couple inches down there. He grunted when her thigh eased between his legs, pressing against his boner. He danced her into the bedroom. There was a sound— the door buzzer. She gave him a squeeze, opened the door to a delivery boy with a pizza. He had forgotten the maid's name. His brain did a search, came up with Merida.

"Thirty-eight fifty for the pizza, okay?"

He went into his bedroom. The maid followed. She had something to say, a question—he might not like it. He handed her two twenties. Her question was something about a threesome. He looked past her, through the door. The delivery boy was a girl taking her shirt off. She had long hair and cute tits; the nipples were hot pink. Her upper body was lean. She was mid-forties and wore glasses, the tint hiding her eyes.

He felt a jolt of recognition. Did he know this broad from someplace? Impossible. "How much for a threesome?" he said.

"Couple hundred," the maid said. "But you gotta do me first. I am hot for you."

They danced in the big room, holding hands, like children in Ring-Around-the Rosy. He felt loose and wild. His last threesome had been in Saigon, a duo of child women in Saigon. He was sweating. The delivery person slid open the glass door. His second martini tasted better. He was ready for sex, he told the maid, Merida. First, she said, she wanted to see the view. They walked to the balcony, leaned over. The delivery person on his left, the maid on his right. Who can lean the farthest?

He felt them lifting him, a woman on each arm. They were strong; he was four pounds over his fighting weight.

"Okay, that's far enough."

"What do you see, Georgie?"

He knew that voice. It came swimming out of the past. He turned. The delivery boy had her glasses off. The eyes swallowed him.

He said her name, "Diamond," and then they dropped him off the edge.

52

THEY'D KILLED TARGET NUMBER five, their last job for Mr. X.

Another banker, this one was named George Hawthorne—a real ladies man, and not bad-looking for a guy in his sixties. Karla felt him wanting her. Three minutes on the massage table, she could get him off, make him grateful, turn him into a friend. A girl needed men-friends; they owned the world.

When they boosted him off the balcony at the Sedona Xanadu Hotel—a six story drop—Karla felt emotion. Regret, sadness, what a waste. She did not watch him connect with the rocks down below.

They wiped the room clean, suite 700.

They took cash from his wallet, then wiped the wallet.

Karla double-checked the clean-up work of Charity—no trust there. Charity ogled Karla changing clothes. That look of lovey-dovey, it made your skin crawl.

Karla put the maid's uniform into a backpack and took the stairs. Charity would take the elevator to Two, then the stairs to the parking garage.

They met in the parking garage. Karla asked for her money.

Charity wanted a drink—Oak Creek Village, south of Sedona, seven miles away—close to the onramp for Interstate 17, the road to Flagstaff.

"Don't be in such a rush, hon. I won't bite."

As they left the parking garage, Karla saw a small knot of people gathered near the hotel entrance. They were pointing down. Fear knifed Karla's stomach. Her last job. *Good*, she was tired of killing.

Charity drove her old Honda. Karla followed in her Subaru Forester, the nicest car she had ever owned. Older than Mr. Cypher's, but still good.

They sat at a table in the Half-Moon Bar, two blocks from Red Rock Coffee. Karla drank beer. Charity drank a martini. Guys hit on Karla. No one hit on Charity.

They had 20-odd years separating them, two women from different decades.

A whole generation, different moves, different priorities, different taste in clothes.

Karla asked again for her money.

Charity passed her the paper sack.

Karla told Charity she was light—again. Charity blamed Mr. X; he was holding out on them again.

Karla wanted to know who he was.

"No need to know," Charity said, her stock answer.

"You're fucking him, aren't you?"

"I could make you so happy," Charity said.

"You play games. You owe me thirty thousand."

"You have a place here, don't you?" Charity said. "In the village, I mean. You came right here from wherever, got a job, settled in. Whatever happened to that guy, Jonas?"

"The money, Charity."

"I am very tired. You have a place. Invite me to stay. I want to be your friend. I want to take care of you, show you just how nice I can be."

"These banker guys," Karla said. "Three out of five went for me. I could smell it, taste their need. I dig men. They dig me. You gave up on men. I've pieced together your story, Charity, all the man-hurt, your need for revenge. I earned that money and you are—"

"Just ask me to stay," Charity said. "Just for tonight. Don't make me drive that road in the dark."

Karla stood up. Her beer glass was half full, her sandwich half-eaten. The potato chips were gone. She looked down at Charity. Reminded her about the money. Asked her question again, Who was Mr. X? Charity shook her head.

53

D ANIEL LEFT IVETA READING in their suite. He had known
her for three months, and she always had three books
going, plus magazines or online information sites such as
Wikipedia. His bride-to-be was hooked on education.

He took the Sedona Landing blueprints to the penthouse,
where he sat with Axel at the big wood table at the end of the
great room. Daniel had been hot all day; now he was cold. The
fake fire helped. The glass of wine helped. Axel kept getting
off the topic, talking about the Crew, all gone except for
George Hawthorne. Daniel had met the man a couple times
and thought he emitted a phony vibe. He was handsome, great
teeth, a full head of hair. Women enjoyed his company; he'd
been married five times.

Axel talked about the past. Daniel building a sand castle on
the beach at Deauville. Daniel making all As in that school
in France. Daniel and Lottie, the only Christmas they spent
together, at the Negresco in Nice.

Lottie was on her way, Axel said. Paris to Phoenix, Phoenix
to Sedona. Maybe tonight, maybe tomorrow. Daniel did not
tell Axel that Lottie had introduced him to Iveta, for a fee.

Daniel switched the subject to Penny Diamond, Murdock's theory. Axel waved his hand. Goddamn detectives," he said. "They always have to have a theory."

"What do you think?"

"What do I think about what?"

"Is Penny Diamond capable of killing?"

"That young woman was one big surprise," Axel said. "You never were ready for what she did. Very inventive."

"How long since you heard from her?"

"Thirty years."

"You ever wonder what she looks like?"

"I like to keep the memory," Axel said, "when she was a knockout."

"She told me you proposed," Daniel said.

"A proposal," Axel said. "That's what they all want."

"So did you?"

"Tell you what," Axel said, "let's have Christmas in Paris. Lottie's there, and you can check with Arthur—see if he can wiggle loose from his boys in Miami. Plenty of room in the hotel. Bring your woman. She looks solid, real spunk. You propose yet?"

"Last weekend. She said yes."

"Arthur's flying in tomorrow," Axel said. "He's your brother, how long since you boys spoke, anyway?"

"Arthur is my half-brother," Daniel said.

"You were always a hair-splitter," Ackerman said, "even as a kid. What the fuck is that?"

"Blueprints," Daniel said. "If I'm dropping ten mil, I want to know what's the product here."

They finished the blueprints. Daniel liked what he saw; he liked being partners with Dad. Bruno asked if they wanted a drink. Ackerman ordered tea, Daniel asked for a Mexican beer. The TV in the Penthouse was on mute. Something happening on the screen—police vehicles, uniforms, a red and white ambulance, EMTs wheeling an empty gurney. A female reporter in a leather jacket was interviewing a witness.

Daniel punched the remote, and the sound came on.

The reporter's voice was excited, tense, on the edge of a scream.

She was talking about a jumper.

She made a half-turn, waved at the balcony.

"Sedona Xanadu," Axel said.

"That's the hotel I would buy," Daniel said.

"What the hell's going on?"

The camera panned to yellow crime-scene ribbons, then to a clutch of uniforms in a parking lot. One of the men wore a suit, a badge flickering from his lapel. Axel identified him as Steve Slattery, Sedona Police. He talked; the officers took notes. Daniel remembered seeing Slattery earlier, in the lobby at Sedona Landing. Slattery gestured at the building. The uniforms nodded, walked away.

The screen shifted back to the reporter in the leather jacket. She was talking to a female deputy—Daniel could tell from the jacket, the shield, the Stetson hat, the pressed uniform trousers. Axel identified her as Connie Fremont, Coconino Sheriff. Axel lectured Daniel on the dangers of split jurisdiction, turf. The cops sliced up the case—City, County, State, Federals. Too many chiefs, not enough Indians. Daniel was impressed; his father had always known stuff.

The screen became a wobbly sky view, shot from a helicopter. A man's voice, rising over the chop-chop of whirling blades: "This is the balcony where the deceased went over. There is no official report to confirm or deny the manner of death."

Daniel felt his stomach clutch. Axel stood up, walked to the TV, stood there staring at the screen. Ackerman said, "It can't be."

"Can't be what?"

"Can't be Georgie Hawthorne. I just talked to him."

Two people came out onto the balcony. One was Slattery, the other was Murdock, Daniel's dinner companion. Slattery waved for the helicopter to go away. A man had jumped to his death. Murdock still looked relaxed.

54

MURDOCK STOOD NEXT TO Slattery, buffeted by the wind from the whirling blades. The copter logo said Phoenix TV. How had they gotten here so fast?

Slattery waved his arms. "Fuck off!" he yelled. "This is my goddamn crime scene!"

They were close enough to see the pilot, wearing gloves and goggles. The machine banked, swooped away, a shot from a cop movie. Slattery moved to the balcony, looked over. From here, a moneyed guest at Sedona Xanadu could see halfway to Mexico. Eleven o'clock, a cold wind swirling.

Murdock took off his gloves. The metal railing was cold, with rough edges. The wind chilled his face. He gripped the railing, straightened his arms, boosted himself up, and looked down.

Down below, EMTs in blue wheeled the corpse away, a body bag on a gurney. The rocks where the guy had landed were too jagged for a chalk outline. A CSI agent sprayed white paint, marking the spot.

Murdock lowered himself, showed his hands to Slattery. Red spots, a tiny drop of blood from a rough place on the metal railing.

"You think he was pushed?"

"Check his hands," Murdock said. "He could have been assisted over."

"By two beefy females?"

"In the movies," Murdock said, "female killers are ever beautiful and seductive."

"We're at the scene," Slattery said. "Gathering data, playing by the rules. And you're hanging onto your dynamic Double-Broad Killer theory?"

"The killer has a plan," Murdock said. "And a timetable."

"By killer you mean the mysterious Mr. X?"

"It's like an opera," Murdock said. "Three acts and a climax."

"Oh sure," Slattery said. "And where are we now? Which fucking act?"

"I'm freezing," Murdock said. "Maybe there's coffee inside."

"Maybe they got donuts," Slattery said. "I skipped dinner."

Murdock was shivering. He pulled on his gloves as they walked off the balcony, followed by the wind. The suite had four rooms. A living room, a bedroom, a sumptuous bathroom, an office with a computer. All four rooms had lots of chrome and black marble—the opposite of Sedona Landing, which radiated a sense of history. Murdock saw two CSI people. Where was Olivera?

Slattery, man in charge, led the way across the living room floor and through the doorway, into the carpeted corridor. The suite was 717. The coffee cart, courtesy of the hotel, was at the end of the hall. Three burnished urns, three choices—French Roast, House Blend, Sumatra. Slattery chose House Blend, Murdock Sumatra. The donuts were flaky and warm. Slattery grabbed three. Murdock tried a bite. Too much grease, too much sugar.

Olivia Olivera exited the elevator, talking on her cellphone. They waited while she got coffee. For her first report, Olivera used the battered black notebook, pocket-sized, spiral bound. Her blue jumpsuit had a stain on the left sleeve. Her eyes looked weary.

"Our vic was helped over," she said, "helped by a strong guy. Or, if you ascribe to the current Murdock Murder Theory, two hefty females. They cleaned up before they left. No prints, no threads, no telltale pubic hairs. The bed was made. The vic's name is George P. Hawthorne, Florida driver's license, got an address in Boca Raton. The cops there are checking."

Murdock said, "Was George P. wearing pajamas?"

"Sport coat and slacks," Olivera said. "Before his demise, he used a razor with a blade. There's a Gillette Atra on the bathroom shelf, and a pricey shaving brush."

"Luggage?" Slattery said.

"Two bags, leather, made by J.W. Hulme—also, he had a ticket to Viet Nam, day after tomorrow."

Slattery said, "Fleshpots of Viet Nam, ripe with teeny-bopper whores?"

"Also on the list," Olivera said, "a good supply of condoms."

"Where did he hit when he fell?" Murdock said.

"On the rocks."

"Ouch," Murdock said. "What part of his body hit first?"

"The head," Olivera said. "The right shoulder looks like a bag of bones."

"Like Findlay," Murdock said.

Slattery said, "You got a theory about how he got boosted over?"

"Two person lift is my guess," Olivera said. "First the arms, lift him up, then one holds him steady. The other perp grabs the ankles—more leverage that way—and over he goes."

"So two perps," Slattery said. "They work together … like team coordination?"

"Yeah."

"What was his weight?" Murdock said. "Any idea how tall?"

"Height, maybe six feet. Weight, maybe one ninety-five."

"He was in shape?"

"For a guy his age."

"Mid-sixties?" Murdock said.

"You should have stayed a cop," Olivera said.

"Civilians have dinner," Murdock said. "Cops with major responsibilities gobble donuts at crime scenes."

"Why I get the big bucks," Slattery said. "What about maid service?"

"Not scheduled until ten," Olivera said. "That's when they turn down the sheets, plant a little chocolate kiss on the pillow."

"What's your read, Olivia?"

"I hate to admit it—maybe because I'm a girl, maybe because it's coming from the private sector of overpaid investigative professionals—but I'm starting to like Murdock's two-female killer theory."

55

CHARITY PLUM, FEELING FORLORN, watched the men watching Karla leave the bar—seven guys tracking Karla's ass, exchanging grins and knowing nods. Charity, left alone at the table, felt cold, lonely, destitute. And very jealous.

Through the window, she followed Karla striding, a knife through the parked cars.

Saw the headlights come on, bright shafts reaming the deep November dark.

What if she followed Karla home?

What if she dropped to her knees and begged?

Why did she have to fall in love with a bitch?

Charity looked around at the people talking at nearby tables. The ratio in the Half-Moon Bar was seven to one, men to women, and only one guy in the place had looked at Charity. Not like the old days, when she could walk into a room, feel the heat, good days when the eyes ate her up.

Her cellphone rang. It was Joey. He wanted a report.

"It was quick," she said. "Why are you calling, really?"

"There might be something else," he said.

"You said we were done. You promised."

"Where are you staying tonight?"

"What is this … an invitation?"

"Where are you staying?"

"Courtyard Marriott, in Flagstaff."

"Drive safe," he said. "There is snow on the way."

"If there's another job," Charity said, "I need a hundred grand. I gotta brief my partner … she's getting skitzy."

"Wait for my signal," Joey said.

Charity paid the bar bill. She used cash, no credit cards on the job.

The Honda was cold. She took 179, the closest onramp to the interstate.

Halfway to Flagstaff, the anger started. Life was shit, men were bastards, and she was a victim. Headlights zoomed at her. Today was Thursday. Tomorrow, she'd pack a couple bags. Her flight to the Caymans left at 7 p.m. A night of sleep and being pampered, then on to Saturday at noon. She had a date at the Ritz-Carlton with Harrison Strong—sixty, chubby, rich, a jolly man with a sweet smile. His wife had just died, and he was looking for a replacer. Maybe Charity wanted it too much. If she married money, that would cushion the fists of the world. Fists like hammer blows.

The road curved; the Honda whined. Snowflakes snapped her windshield. Georgie Hawthorne had called her Diamond. That was her real name. Now that she had money, maybe she could get it back. Georgie was dead. The Crew was dead. Payback for ruining her life. Men always tried that, ruining your life. Your only friends were women. Like Mrs. Annabelle Trice, back in Charleston.

She remembered when she was fourteen, when she was grouting the shower wall for Mrs. Annabelle Tryce, a widow supported by her men friends. Mrs. Tryce had groomed Penny for the real world.

"A lady always dresses well," said Mrs. Tryce.

"Always expects a gift. If no gift is forthcoming, give him the deep freeze."

"If you fall in love, don't let the bastard know it."

"Keep half your money in cash."

"Sex is real. Men need it for their sense of worth."

"When you marry, marry for money, not love."

"Love is fragile, like a plucked rose."

"With money, you have freedom."

At fifteen, in her other life before Ackerman, Penny had all As in math, English, Latin, and gym. She had a B in biology. She backed the teacher, Mr. Sweatman, into a closet, put her knee between his legs, and got him off. "How about a little old A-Minus?" she said.

Penny graduated at seventeen with honors and a scholarship to State. She aced her classes, lay with her first prof, trading fornication for knowledge, then wangled early admission to Wharton, where she met Daniel Ackerman, the TA who got her through statistics. Daniel was older, going for his doctorate.

She was lonely and they dated. She drank martinis—they were always her downfall—and then she met Axel Ackerman. He had money, a wily brain, and he understood a woman's need for foreplay. Axel got her hot, put her under contract, sent her on the road to Kansas, Oklahoma. "Find me a sick business," he said. "Give me a call."

The target town was Amarillo, and the sick business was Wilson's Fine Furniture, jumble of new construction and Quonset huts. The owner was an artist-artisan. He had created a sweet product line, but the business was bleeding red ink.

The owner knew nothing because the son was cooking the books. His name was Joey, and he turned the red ink to black.

Protecting his father from the truth.

Joseph Wilson made payroll, but he could not make a balloon payment to the bank.

Penny phoned New York. She was lonely, *they need you, I need you.* Ackerman sent the Wrecking Crew— five predatory

MBAs in suits and attaché cases—Tyler, Coolidge, Hardwick, Findlay, and Delaplane.

They were the Crew. They had the teamwork. They gave her flowers, candy, perfume, a bottle of British gin, promises, lies. When she refused to lie with them, they shut her out. She was saving herself for Ackerman. But he was in New York and Penny was in Texas, and on a lonely Saturday she found Joey sacking groceries at Furr Food—his real job, he called it.

His folks were in Childress, visiting relatives.

Penny cooked Joey's dinner, gave him his first taste of martini. They kissed. She felt him up. Joey had the face of an angel. He sang in the church choir. He was hung like a Brahman bull. She took him to bed out of loneliness.

Penny missed her period. She went to the hospital to be tested. She telephoned Axel. "It's your kid," she said. "You gotta make good."

Ackerman had said "Okay, no problem. Is September a good month for weddings?"

She was still in Amarillo when Freddy Delaplane told her that Ackerman had just married a society woman. There it was in the newspaper: FINANCIER WEDS SOCIALITE.

In her New York apartment, Penny had a baseball bat, a relic from her girlhood.

She broke the windows in the offices of Arc-Angel Equity.

She took money from the safe.

She found incriminating documents on the Wrecking Crew.

She made copies, mailed them to the papers.

The Crew tracked her. They invaded her town, interrogated her folks, her friends. Penny went to Mexico, changed her name, slept with a consular guy to get a fake passport. Her new name was Charity Plum, a churchy girl.

The road north seemed blacker. No clouds, headlights swallowed by the wild dark sky. Her GPS said she was going due north, but her brain said she was on the road to Hell. She rounded a long curve, saw the lights of Flagstaff. Saw the first signs for motels. ROAD-WEARY? THEN SLEEP WITH US. She followed the glaring signs to Luxury Suites. She did not take a room at the Marriott. With Joey—the new version with the new face, the spiffy wardrobe—you could never be too careful.

The room was ugly. The bed had a weird death smell. Charity did not care. The bar had three martini bottles. There was ice down the hall. She was tired. She said goodbye to Charity Plum.

As Penny Diamond, she drank herself to sleep.

*****

SAFE IN HER CONDO, Karla brushed her teeth, gargled, and rinsed her mouth three times. She could still feel the hesitation, still hear the order from Charity, "Now, bitch." She could still see the man going over, ten seconds to touchdown. Still see the mouth open, about to ask the final question.

Karla needed warmth, a hot male body next to hers, a body that smelled good. She phoned Mr. Cypher at home. His voice was slurry, a bedroom voice. She asked to come over, offered to bring her Mama's chili. There was a pause on her phone. Mr. Cypher went away, then he came back with an invitation to breakfast at Sedona Landing, the Bell Rock Bistro at eight. Karla said yes.

She was disappointed, shut out, a door closing in her face. Mr. Cypher was a loner, but tonight he was not alone. Who was he with? *Fuck him*. She would stand him up, not keep their breakfast date. She ended the call, turned on the TV, a dead man falling. She hit the button. There was a little bong, and the screen faded.

On the dead, dark screen, Karla saw Charity letting go of George Hawthorne, banker number five, reaching for Charity, his mouth working, calling her Diamond.

Day Five

56

THE PHONE WOKE DANIEL. The bedside clock said 4:50.

He was dreaming about Penny Diamond, nineteen years old, that macro-econ class, the tight skirts, flashing her legs. He remembered that she loved martinis. She never got drunk.

The caller identified himself as Lieutenant Steve Slattery, Sedona Police.

He apologized for calling so late, but he needed some information from Daniel about the jumper. Could Daniel meet him on the tennis courts?

"Now?" Daniel said. "It's four in the morning. I'm suffering from jet lag."

"You knew this guy, right? You knew Hawthorne?"

"Not well," Daniel said.

"We've got a lead," the voice said. "It concerns your dad—the Arab-Jew rivalry thing. Won't take but a couple minutes."

"Can't we meet in the lobby? It's freezing out there."

"Talking out of school here, but I got this jurisdictional thing—it's a turf war that destroys careers in law enforcement—

so I'd rather not be caught talking to you, because of your dad's involvement. You catch my drift?"

"What involvement?" Daniel said.

"That's why I wanted to see you, give you a heads-up. You can be my liaison with the old man."

"Ten minutes," Daniel said.

Daniel pulled on sweat pants, a hoodie. He stepped into his sandals, Mephistos. Fifty years old and already having trouble with his feet. Being able to help Axel, that was a big deal. Axel had never needed help.

Daniel yawned in the elevator. Yawned again on his way to the door that led outside.

He needed coffee, Arizona was keeping him awake.

It was cold outside, the desert at night.

A sign with an arrow, to the tennis courts.

He took the curved pathway. The tennis courts were empty, and the security lights cast sharp shadows.

When he was halfway to the courts, the cop walked out of shadow, into the light. He waved at Daniel.

Daniel called out, "Is that you?"

Daniel heard footsteps behind him, someone running.

He turned to see two figures taking up the walkway, coming at him fast.

No way they could be Murdock's two female killers. They moved like young guys.

He heard hard breathing. They were right behind him, not slowing down. He tried stepping out of the way. His foot left the paved pathway, and he felt the stab of pain in his ankle. He lost his balance. The two figures were on him, gripping his arms. He smelled tobacco, booze, strong Mexican chilis. A voice said, "Gringo, you are fucking *muerte*." The voice was male. So much for Murdock's theory of two female killers.

Daniel was falling. The world tilted, turned sideways. He grabbed a sleeve, heard a tearing sound. A hand gave him a shove. Where was that fucking cop, Slattery? He heard himself cry out. He felt stupid for coming out here. A pain roared through his head. The lights went out.

57

Karla's bike ride to Sedona Landing was wonderful. Brisk morning, images of sex with Mr. Cypher, deep deep feelings. Was it that easy to fall in love? Maybe she should start her new life by cancelling her massage with Ackerman. She had money now. Goodbye barista, goodbye massage oil, goodbye groping hands.

Mr. Cypher waited for her at a table in the Bell Rock Bistro, across the room from Helene Steinbeck, her teacher, and the guy named Murdock. Miss Steinbeck waved, and Karla waved back.

Mr. Cypher held Karla's chair. She wanted to ask who he was with last night when she called. Karla hated feeling jealous; it threw her off-balance.

Mr. Cypher ordered an omelet. Karla said, "Make that two." The coffee here was two steps down from Red Rock Coffee. He asked her about her mystery story, what happens next, how does the story end?

Mr. Cypher's questions gave her the shivers. They felt invasive, like they had little barbs attached. She told him she didn't know where the story was going. She was one of those writers who let the characters go. She followed behind, writing stuff down.

Mr. Cypher checked his watch, stood up, shook her hand, and asked her to lunch. Karla asked what time. He said twelve, on the button. She could do lunch at 1:30; she had a massage at noon. No problem, Mr. Cypher said. Find me at the bank when you're free.

At the top of the entry staircase, Mr. Cypher stopped. He was holding his smartphone with both hands. Karla saw his fingers moving.

Who was Mr. Cypher texting?

*****

PENNY HAD BREAKFAST AT the hotel coffee shop in Flagstaff. Her bags were packed. She had her ticket to the Caymans. Her Joey jobs were over. Tonight, she aimed to keep her hot date with a rich man. He was chubby, he was old, but she needed her name in his last will and testament.

Her smartphone bonged—message from Joey. "Red alert. Your compatriot in arms is enrolled in a writing workshop, exposing your recent exploits. The hotel construction boss needs a tile setter who works weekends. Get back to town. Ask at the desk for Elroy Pooler, builder."

The message was incomplete—no time, no place. He was making her wait for details. Joey loved keeping her hanging. What was Karla thinking, writing about Penny's life? Had she gone crazy?

Bleak anger drove Penny to Value Village. Anger made her efficient as she bought tools, overalls, boots. She had done tile setting for two years, working for a guy named Jeremiah from church, a guy who wanted to lie with her, get her with child.

Penny was on the interstate, approaching the 179 turnoff to Oak Creek Village when her phone beeped. Text from Joey: "Penthouse Spa. Sedona Landing. Noon. Weapons at the desk, under the name C. Plummer. Combination 01013."

*****

ACKERMAN SAT BESIDE DANIEL'S bed, Room 719, at the CRMC, watching his son breathe, chest rising, chest falling. Daniel was in a coma. He was bruised, some minor cuts. They were waiting for him to wake up. Iveta Macek sat next to Ackerman, not talking, no color in her face. He checked his watch, 10:30; he needed to be on the court, stroking the ball. He needed a massage. He phoned Karla Kurtz, no answer. Left a message: "If you've recovered your composure, how about finishing yesterday's massage?"

The door opened and Slattery entered.

Ackerman grabbed Slattery's arm, led him outside. Ackerman wanted to talk about the phone call. Slattery wanted to talk about George Hawthorne. Ackerman was pissed and frightened. Slattery was weary; his face sagged. They stopped bickering when Iveta came out, blotting the tears with a tissue.

Slattery went to check with Danny's docs. Iveta led Ackerman outside into the parking lot, the wind. She had a Massachusetts license; Ackerman let her drive. They drove back to the hotel in a new Prius. It was winter in Arizona. There was sun. The landscape was bleak. They passed the entrance to the Gypsum Ranch. A bunch of cars were at the big house. Not pickups, but shiny sedans and SUVs. Ackerman knew Gypsum, from working on committees. If he wanted to be president, why had he partnered with Fatso Fish?

58

HELENE SAT IN THE Yavapai Room, re-building her mind-map. She added Hawthorne's name, the last member of Ackerman's Crew, death by falling. She added Daniel, then the initials CRMC. She wrote "Slattery Impersonator?" boxed it, then ran an arrow headed for the center, and stopped. She was getting nowhere.

She printed the letters TFK, shorthand for Murdock's Two Female Killer theory, enclosed the letters in an ellipse, and ran an arrow to the center. Using her red pen, Helene connected the TFKs to Sedona Landing, then Ackerman, then Vortex Bank.

Nothing made sense. She needed Murdock's brain. Maybe later. Karla Kurtz entered the room, took a seat next to Helene. Her face looked older, her eyes were bleak. Helene slid the mind-map out of sight.

"Are you all right?"

"Having trouble sleeping," Karla said. "Could we talk later?"

"Of course. What time?"

"I've got a massage at noon, in Mr. A's Spa. How about after that?"

"We could do lunch," Helene said.

"I'd like that," Karla said.

THE WRITING FOR FRIDAY was creating the Killing Scene. Helene gave them ten minutes to do a Scene Profile: Time, place, furniture if inside, bushes if outside. Lighting, temperature, wardrobe, objects (murder weapon), characters, POV (killer or victim), action, dialogue, motive, Intruder, climax. Then she tossed out a writing prompt: *My latest kill takes place in….*

While they wrote, Helene started a fresh mind-map, a clean sheet of paper. A big circle for the past, a big rectangle for the present. She was filling in the past when the buzzer sounded, bringing her back to the Yavapai Room. Time for three readers. Karla read last:

> My latest kill takes place in Pebble Beach ... a name on a list, a target. The list comes from the past, along with hit money. If I do this job, I can retire, no more waitressing, no more hustling fat convention-goers. The Target on the list hangs out in Pebble Beach, a gated community. Me and Sharleen pose as house cleaners. Our van says Pebble Beach@Home.Com. Sharleen wears short shorts and a tight T-shirt. I watch her from the closet. The bedroom has a balcony. Down below, maybe twenty feet, there are hard, gray rocks. Target One comes out of the shower wearing a towel. He's got white hair and a deep, rich-man tan. He grins at Sharleen. Like all men, he's dying to stick Sharleen. He drops the towel, beckons Sharleen with a crooked finger. She bargains with him— her flesh, his money. He opens a drawer, pulls out a wad of bills. Sharleen counts the money and smiles. My heart hammers inside my chest. Sharleen strips down to her thong. You never saw anything so beautiful.
>
> She leads him to the deck. "Let's do it out here," she says. He drops the towel, a well-hung millionaire. The

sight of him hard as rebar triggers my rage. They're kissing when I come up. His hand is between her legs. I am so jealous. I've got this metal baseball bat. I pop his knee with the bat. He goes crazy, cursing us. The guy is heavier than he looks. We muscle him toward the railing, prop him up. She grabs an ankle. I grab an ankle. We give him a heave. I am sweating like back home in Charleston. He screams going down.

And there's the timer....

While Karla was reading, Helene had this creepy déjà vu feeling. The scene felt so real, the language so pure, no wasted words. The victim was rich. He lived in a gated community. Helene had forgotten—maybe Murdock would remember who had lived in Pebble Beach. It was time for a break. Where was Murdock? What was he doing? Who had said something about Charleston?

There was commotion outside—voices, shouts, laughter—and Helene remembered the press conference, two senators making an announcement, the grime of politics invading the hotel. Ackerman had some fancy contacts. When Helene opened the door, Helene saw Iveta Macek on her cellphone. Iveta's hair was wet. She must have been to the pool.

59

At ten o'clock, Hiram Fish showed up at Vortex Bank. He had an appointment with Mr. Cypher. A woman with a name badge made apologies. "Mr. Cypher's not feeling well. He called in sick."

Fish fumed. Hawthorne was dead. Fish wanted the bank to verify his signature. He brought out his transfer document. He stared at the woman; she was no one. Hawthorne had died last night, close to the time Fish had watched him sign the document. What the hell was going on? His cellphone rang. It was Jimbo Gypsum, asking where Fish was.

"Sorry," Fish said, "I had a personal matter to take care of."

"We've been waiting on you, Mr. Vice-President-To-Be. Too late to regroup now, so how about you join the party at the hotel?"

"Yes, Mr. President."

*****

Lottie Ackerman Bell answered her phone.

The caller was Iveta Macek.

The girl's voice was shaky. She had just seen Hiram Fish, the fat man from Prague. Danny Ackerman was in the hospital. Not a heart attack, but a concussion. Macek was frightened.

"What happened to Danny?"

"He was beaten by ruffians, then robbed."

"Let me handle Fish. You stay out of sight."

"Please hurry," Macek said.

Lottie pulled out her camera. She didn't trust her smartphone—not enough security. The camera was a gift from the Ack. It was old, it had been dropped, killed, mangled—and it always came back to life.

The photos showed Fish in a black rubber bra. He wore white diapers. A pink bathing cap.

He was wedging his fat self between the outflung legs of Iveta Macek.

Macek wore a mask.

Her body looked young, supple, shapely.

Her hands were on the chubby chest of Hiram Fish. She was trying to push him away.

The photos revealed Fish as a kinky sexual predator.

*****

COMING INTO OAK CREEK Village, Ackerman saw his hotel, the construction work on his penthouse. He had come here to die. Being here had brought him alive. A lot of others had died. Ackerman was still on his feet, feeling ten years younger. Iveta asked what he was thinking.

"I'm so glad about you and Danny," he said.

"Why do you call him that?"

"Always did, since the first day."

"I think Daniel, he prefers to be called, more than Danny."

"When he wakes up, we can talk about that."

She patted his hand. She parked the Prius beside the Humvee. The parking lot was filling up.

Ackerman remembered the upcoming press conference, Jimbo Gypsum and Fatso Fish, teaming up on the Far Right, talking like centrist compromisers, lying through their teeth.

On Court One, Ackerman saw Breedlove hitting with Javier Trujillo. Ackerman sighed. No tennis this morning, maybe this afternoon.

Ackerman was hungry. So was Iveta. She squeezed his arm. They found Murdock in the Bell Rock Bistro, sipping coffee, checking stuff from a folder. Murdock asked about Daniel. Iveta started crying, then rushed away toward the ladies. Ackerman briefed Murdock on the hospital. The noise from the lobby was louder now, the crowd chanting for Gypsum and Fish.

Ackerman turned to Murdock. "Helene tell you about my job offer?"

"Yes."

"You coming along?"

"You offering me a job, Ack?"

"One year," Ackerman said. "A million dollars."

"Make better money at five grand a day," Murdock said. "Plus a bonus if I stop a bullet headed for you."

Ackerman laughed. He liked Murdock. The guy was not a toady. He did not suck up. He did not kiss ass. Ackerman stood. Time for his massage. He took the stairs to the lobby, checking his leg strength. People with nothing else to do packed the lobby, holding signs—JIMBO FOR PRESIDENT. Someone grabbed his arm. It was Diana Trask, Phoenix TV. She wanted a quote. Ackerman hated sound bites, but she did look good. A little marijuana and she could fuck like a mink.

She waved the camera guy over. Her TV face was not like her bedroom face. "Hi," she said. "Diana Trask here at Sedona Landing chatting with Axel Ackerman, a well-known billionaire Democrat, and …."

Ackerman saw movement across the room. Jimbo Gypsum, surrounded by a phalanx of Secret Service guys. A booming voice called, "Hey, pool boy!" It was Hiram Fish, wearing a fake Stetson.

Diana Trask stared at Ackerman. She said, "Pool Boy … what's that about?"

Ackerman did not answer. He stepped into the elevator, used the penthouse keycard. Left Diana Trask standing in the lobby. It was time to put the hurt on Hiram Fish.

60

With the workshop done, Helene packed up her writing stuff. She felt frazzled. She needed coffee. She was disturbed by Karla's last read—the tone, the detail, the Pebble Beach setting. Didn't Freddy Delaplane have a home there? Was that just a coincidence? What did Delaplane look like? Did he have white hair and a good winter tan?

Outside the Yavapai Room, a crowd packed the corridor, a human stream moving toward the lobby—TV crews, people in Stetson hats waving handwritten banners that said GYPSUM FOR PREXY.

In the Bell Rock Bistro, Helene saw Murdock talking to Iveta Macek, Daniel's fiancée. They were sitting at Ackerman's table, and Iveta was using her hands as she talked. Murdock waved Helene over. Helene took a deep breath, stopped at the serving bar for a coffee. She hesitated because she craved cream and sugar. Shook her head and moved toward the table. There were tears on Iveta's cheeks.

Iveta was just back from visiting Daniel at the CRMC. She gave a teary-eyed report on his concussion, his bruises from the beating. His wallet was missing, and his Rolex. Helene listened while Iveta retold the story from last night. How Daniel had received a phone call from the policeman named Slattery. How excited Daniel had been, because he wanted to help his father. How the thieves stole his wallet, left him for dead. This was America. How could this be?

Helene sipped her coffee. Who would pose as Steve Slattery? Who wanted to hurt Daniel? Murdock needed more coffee. The waitress was busy. Murdock excused himself, walked to the serving table.

"I like your friend," Iveta said.

"Everyone does."

"How long have you been together?"

"A few months."

"I have started your book," Macek said. "It is quite good, you know—I actually saw the trees and bushes. Where is this Carolina?"

"On the East Coast," Helene said. "Could you answer a couple questions about last night?"

"Of course."

"What time was it when Daniel got the phone call?"

"It was quite dark," Iveta said. "Four-something. I was asleep."

"What did he tell you?"

"He was going to help his father. His face was, you know, bright with light."

"How did he know who Slattery was?"

"From the TV, that awful falling at ...."

Macek froze in mid-sentence. She had seen something ... or someone. She shook her head, *this cannot be happening*, and vaulted out of her chair. Quick-walking across the bistro carpet, she opened the door that led to the pool and the tennis courts and went out of sight. Murdock came back carrying three fresh coffees.

"Where's she going?" Murdock said.

"She was looking at the door—there's your jungle buddy. And a fat man."

"Senator Hiram Fish," Murdock said. "Ackerman's favorite politico."

Fish wore a fringed leather jacket and the symbolic badge of honor out West—the sweat-stained Stetson, tilted back. Fish made the telephone hand sign, thumb to ear, little finger to lips. Then he pointed at Murdock.

"How do you know him?"

"Monty introduced us at the coffee place. I told you."

"No, you didn't."

Murdock said, "Let's go up to the room. We can talk."

Helene said okay and stood up. She was worried about Iveta Macek.

61

THE PARKING LOT AT Sedona Landing was packed, forcing Penny Diamond to walk, lugging the canvas work bag. People were pushing through the main entrance of the big hotel. Penny joined them—good camouflage. She felt surreal, as if she was floating from kill to kill. A job, another job, then another, another, another … when would it end? She had to hurry, get to Phoenix, catch that flight to the Caymans, start her new life.

At the front desk, she asked for Elroy Pooler. The desk guy, a Mexican named Raul, dialed a number and handed the phone to Penny. The construction guy would be right down. Penny handed the phone back.

"You got a package for me? C. Plummer?"

"Sure do. You really a tile setter, lady?"

"Paid my way through school," she said. "Who brought this package in?"

"Some kid, works for a service."

"You didn't know him, a small town like this?"

"Sorry," Raul said. "Hey, here's your package."

The package from Joey was an attaché case—brand new,

weight maybe four pounds. The desk guy said, "Hey, here's Elroy. He's the man. Let me introduce you."

Elroy Pooler had a medium gut, a wide smile, the handshake of a working man gone soft. He took her tool bag; she kept the attaché. Elroy's tile guy, Francisco, had called in sick. Was there any way Miz Plummer could work overtime, set the tile by Saturday, leaving all day Sunday to cure? She nodded, no worries. She asked for double-time.

"No problem," Elroy said. "This guy we work for, Ackerman, there's no end to the money."

They rode the elevator. Elroy used his special keycard. The job was a big bathroom at the end of a corridor on Ten, the penthouse floor. She remembered the construction smell from her teenage years—sheetrock, dust, man-sweat, and glue. Before he left, Elroy gave her a keycard.

"If you need anything inside, just ring the bell."

*****

LOTTIE PHONED THE PENTHOUSE. Bruno welcomed her. Axel was having his massage, another fifty minutes, depending. Lottie was stiff from sitting—taxis, airplanes, limos—she could use a massage herself. Maybe take a run first, get acclimated to Arizona.

The penthouse was being remodeled, Bruno said. Lottie had a room on Eight, a commodious corner suite. Bruno said he would alert the desk.

Lottie grabbed the desk guy, handed him a twenty. His name badge said RAUL. He got her a cute helper named Javier. Raul apologized for the crowd, thanked her for the twenty. She wondered what Axel paid this guy.

Ramon and his luggage cart followed the crowd into the big lobby, and that's where Lottie saw Hiram Fish, fat as ever, behind a portable podium, wearing a Stetson and his oily smile.

Her old nemesis from the past was introducing the next President of the United States.

"This fellow is my closest friend," Hiram Fish said. "We joined forces in the Congress. Him and me, we been pals since those first early days on the Hill."

"You all know him. He's the Boy Next Door. He's Arizona's favorite son. Let's give it up for Senator Soon-To-Be President Jimbo Gypsum."

Applause rocked the lobby as a man in a suede jacket replaced Fish on the podium.

He was tall, with a lean film-star face and pale blue eyes. He wore a string tie.

He thanked Hiram Fish.

Lottie caught Fish's eye. She held up her cute little Nikon and watched Fish go pale. The men at the podium were surrounded by guys wearing ear buds. Lottie recognized them as Secret Service personnel.

The crowd blocked the elevators.

Lottie handed Javier a twenty. She would take the stairs. He could follow with the luggage. Her legs needed to move, to climb. As she went through the stairwell door, she could feel the eyes of Hiram Fish tracking her. Spooky.

She phoned Iveta Macek.

*****

HELENE WAS FEELING APPREHENSIVE about the upcoming talk with Murdock. What if it didn't work? What if they were not meant to be together? She felt tired. Maybe she'd take a nap, let Murdock stand watch over Ackerman.

They left the Bell Rock Bistro. A crowd blocked the way to the elevators, so they headed for the stairs. Helene spotted a woman who looked familiar, wearing a black pants suit, very stylish. She had red hair, worn in a French twist. Her face showed genes from Ackerman.

"I think I just saw Ack's daughter," Helene said. "She had glorious red hair."

"Where?"

"She was heading into the stairwell."

"Family reunion," Murdock said. "Just what the killer ordered."

"We should check on Arthur," Helene said.

"Have Connie do it, or Slattery."

"There's your jungle buddy," Helene said. "Where's he going?"

At the podium, Hiram Fish had turned away from Candidate Gypsum to say something to Monty Featherstone. Featherstone nodded, slipped past a guy with an earbud, and walked toward the stairwell.

He was a minute behind the woman with red hair.

The noise was loud in the room. As they went through the stairwell door, Helene felt someone at her side. It was Iveta Macek, gripping her cellphone.

"I can be with you, yes?"

"Of course."

"Do you know the fat man?"

"Murdock knows him. Why?"

"He frightens me. Please, might we go up?"

Helene said okay. Murdock was holding the door open.

The Ad-Hoc press conference was over. The new candidate for president, smooth Senator Gypsum, was being ushered out by the Secret Service. And Helene was about to sign a contract for a million dollars.

The world was a crazy place.

62

I N THE BATHROOM THAT needed work, Penny changed into her tile-setter costume, overalls, dusty work boots. Her phone beeped: a text from Joey with four numbers, 4117, the combination that unlocked the attaché. Inside she found two identical Sig Sauers, thirteen little bullets, bringing a cold chill. The attaché case plus the texted numbers meant Joey was close.

Thinking about Karla, Penny felt edgy and hurt and angry. Why was the woman she loved writing about her Charleston childhood? And how did Joey get his hands on the writing? Joey had to be here in this town. He had to know his way around. Karla was a very secretive gal. She would not show her writing to just anyone. Joey had always been persuasive; he could wangle stuff out of anyone.

Penny shook her head. Told herself to focus. This was the last job. No more Joey. No more Karla. Maybe it was the way Joey was leading her, step by step—he had to be close. Penny felt impelled, out of control, hands off the wheel, a vehicle on auto-pilot.

Text number two from Joey: "Target, check penthouse spa."

*****

LOTTIE ACKERMAN BELLE LIKED to keep in shape.

As a kid, she led her team in soccer scores.

She ran relay races. They wouldn't let her on the wrestling team.

She took boxing lessons to defend herself against Danny.

Her legs were happy to be climbing.

Even when she flew First Class, Lottie felt dead; the airplane was a coffin hurtling through space at 600 mph. In kilometers that was 965. The plane flew at 30,000 feet. In meters, that was 9144. She loved being a citizen of the world.

When she reached the second-floor landing, her legs were feeling better, more spring in her step. She could take the elevator or keep climbing. Her legs were strong because she walked in Paris. She was on the second-floor landing when she heard someone behind her. Lottie kept moving.

At the next turn, she caught a glimpse of a man in a leather jacket, climbing fast, two stairs at a time.

He wore a handkerchief, masking his face, but not the silver-gray hair. She had seen him before, in the lobby. Standing close to Fatso Fish. She tripped, moving too fast, and hit her shoulder. She had met him once, in Europe. The man's name was something-something. Her knees crumpled; the man was tugging at her shoulder bag. He wanted the camera. His name was ... she could not remember. He said "Goddamn!" Her eyes fluttered. She stopped moving. The man was into her shoulder bag. She knew she had made a mistake, warning Fatso Fish. Her world went black.

*****

THEY ENTERED THE STAIRWELL and Murdock heard someone up ahead.

Had to be Featherstone, moving fast.

"What does he want?" Helene said.

"Something for Fish," Murdock said.

"You and your old jungle buddies," Helene said.

Murdock was on the stairs between Two and Three when he heard a cry.

Sounds of a scuffle, grunting, slapping.

Sounds of a body coming down, bumping on the stairs, then stopping.

Murdock made the corner, saw the red hair, the black pants suit, blood.

He heard footsteps up above, light flashed off slick leather.

A door opened, then closed.

Murdock reached the woman. Still breathing. Blood still pumping, her eyes were closed.

Helene was calling for an ambulance. There was no service here, no little power bars, so she went into the hallway. Iveta Macek was on her knees, whispering to the woman.

Murdock found Helene on her cellphone.

"What?" she said.

"I'm going after Featherstone," he said. "Send help up, Six maybe, or Seven."

"Murdock, damn you. Don't go."

"Send me someone who's armed."

63

THE DOOR TO ACKERMAN's penthouse was black. It brought a smirk from Penny Diamond.

The door knocker was cast-iron, curved and thick, imitating a male sex organ, so ugly, so typical. Ackerman was a true denizen of Sodom. She pressed the button, a voice through the speaker, "Yes?"

"Got an eye injury here," Penny said. "Gotta flush the eye with clean water."

The door opened.

Framed in the doorway was a Penny Diamond lookalike.

A carbon copy of herself from twenty years ago, still young, still sassy.

Same build, same face, pale red hair on its way to white, a mirror-twin, another slave for Axel. Where did Axel find these bitches? The same place he found Penny—hungry girls, smart girls—they drove Axel crazy, so he bought their services, paid them top dollar, spread their legs, thinking he could fuck them and stay young forever.

She shot her younger self lookalike in the thigh. She wanted to kill her, a bullet in the heart, but the lookalike thing made

Penny weak, no resolve. Blood dribbled onto the area rug, a pricey Oriental. Axel collected carpets like he collected women, something soft to walk on.

A black guy came out of a doorway. He wore a white turtleneck, a shoulder holster with a pistol.

Penny aimed at the white turtleneck.

The gun made a spitting sound; the suppressor was first class. A red splotch splashed the white. The turtleneck guy went down, eyes fluttering.

Penny found keys, moved down the hall, thick carpet here. A sign over a door said Executive Spa. The key fit.

She left the moaners behind her. Life is tough.

*****

MURDOCK CHUGGED UP THE stairs, his mind locked on the past.

He had served with Monty Featherstone in the jungle.

Despite the grime and the humidity, Featherstone was always shaved, his shirt always ironed. He packed a Glock in a shiny shoulder rig.

Featherstone was an asset because he knew how to talk to generals and visiting congressmen, and he had a plausible explanation for this job with Senator Fish—to preserve his pension—but Murdock knew Featherstone was hiding something. He had arrived too fast at the Foxglove Lane crime scene. He was owned by Senator Fish. He would be armed. Murdock's weapon was in his room on Nine. He removed his belt, wrapped it around his right fist.

Murdock caught Featherstone on Seven, pressing the button to call the elevator.

His face was sweaty and red. Featherstone was out of shape, breathing hard. He trained his gun on Murdock. The woman's purse hung from his shoulder.

"Don't get into this, Foxy."

"What's in the purse?"

"My future," Featherstone said. "Orders from on high."

Murdock feinted to the left. Featherstone fired; the bullet whiffled past Murdock, dug into the wall beside his head. Murdock flicked his right hand. The belt unrolled, caught Featherstone on the ear. He fired again. Murdock felt a heavy weight slam his shoulder. Featherstone called Murdock a bastard patriot.

The elevator door opened and Connie Fremont stood there, holding her weapon in both hands. She yelled at Featherstone. He ran for the stairwell door. Murdock tripped him as he went by. Featherstone hit the floor, rolling, and took aim at Connie. She fired, Featherstone went down. Blood gushed from the wound. Connie's bullet had severed an artery. Featherstone gave Murdock a weak smile.

"It's only a hotel, Foxy."

"That's why you're here?"

"Fish wants a piece," Featherstone said. "The Arabs were his skirmishers, then you came along, Foxy Murdock, riding to the rescue. Now look what you've done."

"Soft target," Murdock said. "What do you want from Ackerman's daughter?"

Featherstone's eyes closed. No answer to Murdock's question.

Connie Fremont kicked the Glock away, going through the motions. She phoned for help. She knelt down, touched her finger to Featherstone's neck. She looked up at Murdock.

"Christ, Murdock," she said. "I had a date with this guy."

*****

THE PHONE CALL CAME to Raul at the front desk. The voice was muffled, like the person was talking through a wool sock. "Listen up," the voice said. "A woman in construction clothes is going to kill the old man in the penthouse."

"Who are you?" Raul said. "Who is this? What woman?"

"Get those two detectives," the caller said. "That babe who wrote the book. Hurry!"

*****

THE EMTs ROLLED ACKERMAN'S daughter into the elevator. They had been in the parking lot, three minutes away, on alert for the press conference.

Helene called Connie's cellphone—busy. Helene started for the stairwell. Her phone rang; it was Raul, the desk guy. A woman posing as a construction worker was going to kill *Señor* Axel. "Call Slattery," Helene said.

Helene's brain whirled.

Featherstone had gone up, but how far?

Helene rode the penthouse elevator to Six. No Murdock. She heard voices up above, took the stairs two at a time. She was out of shape, getting fat, time to regroup.

She found Murdock on Seven. He was on his back and bleeding. Connie Fremont had a tourniquet around his arm. His head was pillowed on Connie's thighs.

The two women exchanged looks. Monty Featherstone, the old jungle buddy, lay in the fetal position, hands between his knees, his eyes shut tight.

The elevator doors opened, two EMT guys with a gurney.

"Can you handle this?" Helene said.

"Yes," Connie said.

"Ackerman's in trouble," Helene said. "Send some help to the penthouse."

"You got it, girl."

Connie pointed to Murdock. "This one goes first."

Helene watched the gurney carrying Murdock enter the elevator. Before the doors closed, she was headed up to Ackerman's penthouse.

*****

PENNY DIAMOND ENTERED A room bursting with exercise machines, a forest of steel and rubber, pulleys and straps. The machines blocked her view of the massage table.

Penny eased between a leg press and a hamstring machine, saw Karla Kurtz, masseuse, writer, long-lost lover, a white tank top, bare shoulders shining with oil. Penny had longed to see Karla naked. Seeing her now, the skin smooth and dark, enhanced by the white halter, those exquisite muscles flexing, Penny felt crushed by love.

Ackerman lay on his belly, face turned to the side, eyes closed, the billionaire's Nirvana.

Penny felt clumpy in the work boots. They were new, obvious, clumsy, part of her disguise. Her heart pounded, a snare drum, maybe it was the room, the rubber floor, bouncing the sound.

Karla turned. Her eyes were wide, full of surprise. "Charity, what are you—?"

"Are you crazy, girl?" Penny said. "Writing about me? My life?"

"Writing about … how did you know … my God, oh, shit …."

Ackerman lay on the massage table, thin as a mummy.

He was bald; he looked dead.

The mummy turned his head, and his eyes opened. He gave her the famous money grin.

"Penny Diamond," he said. "I thought you were dead."

"You old bastard, you jilted me for another society whore."

*****

HELENE PRESSED THE PENTHOUSE doorbell. From behind the black door, she heard chimes. The door opened a crack. She saw Giselle's face just below the doorknob. Giselle was on her knees. Her face went away and Helene heard a thump.

Giselle's downed body was blocking the door. Helene pulled her aside. Blood leaked from Giselle's thigh. Helene fashioned a tourniquet on Giselle's thigh, halfway between knee and hip. The bleeding slowed. Helene found Bruno in the hallway. He was coughing. He'd taken a bullet in the shoulder. There was blood on his white turtleneck. His weapon, a Ruger Nine, was under his hip.

Helene said, "The woman?"

"In the Spa. Hurry."

⋈ ⋈ ⋈ ⋈

PENNY SHOT KARLA. *You always kill the one you love.* Karla fell, pulling Ackerman with her. They landed with a muffled thump. Penny walked over, her boots loud on the black floor. Ackerman's eyes were closed. The sheet had come loose. She let loose a stream of curses. She aimed at Ackerman's balls; no more babies from this monster.

There was noise behind her.

Penny stopped cursing and turned, saw a woman in the doorway holding a gun. The woman had dark hair, cop eyes that froze Penny's blood. She held the gun with both hands, a shooter in a cop movie.

Karla was down on the floor, trying to crawl, trapped under Ackerman.

Penny went into a crouch, started talking.

*****

HELENE STEINBECK PUSHED THROUGH the door to the Spa and heard voices, one of them Ackerman's. She held her Glock in both hands, the way she'd been taught to shoot—by her dad, by the flinty-eyed trainers at the police academy. She had not fired a weapon since that day in Taos, the crowded courtroom, all those spectators. The cops were frozen in place. Murdock created a diversion, giving the shot to Helene.

If you wanted to be a good shooter, you had to practice.

Twice a week, three times, or you lost the feel. Like swimming laps. Like practicing your serve in tennis.

Helene edged around the corner and saw exercise machines. At the other end of the room she saw a black massage table. She saw a woman in a baseball cap and gray overalls, squatting down. The woman was slender, with a narrow face. She held two weapons. Helene heard words spewing from her mouth— *society whore, jilted, altar, fornicating prick ....*

The woman in the overalls was half-turned away from Helene.

Then she was up, crouching, two weapons, no sound suppressors, aiming at Helene.

Helene was not a cop. She did not have to call out a warning.

This was not a TV show where an actor said Police-Freeze-Drop-Your-Weapon. This was real life, this moment, right now, and she was under contract to protect the body of Axel Ackerman. Helene trained her Glock on the woman. Lined her up in the Hex sights.

The woman fired. The bullet hit the wall with a splat.

Helene fired.

*****

PENNY GLANCED TO HER left, saw the woman with the pistol in the mirror. Saw the woman's eyes. Was she police? Police have to shout a warning. Police have to identify themselves as police. Who was this woman? Penny took cover behind the massage table and snapped a shot at the intruder.

Penny's brain was racing. She was set to fire more shots, shoot to kill, get away, keep her date in the Caymans .... Then her world went dark. A wet splash of black across her vision. One of her pistols went off. One minute, she was crouching over Ackerman and his whore, the love of Penny's tortured life. The next minute, Penny had lost her balance. She was falling; falling was her fate.

Her eyes fluttered, the tears clouding her vision. She crawled to the wall. She felt tired. Her eyes closed.

64

HELENE CHECKED THE SHOOTER. No pulse, no air from the nose. The shooter was dead. Her once-red hair was turning pale, on its way to white.

Ackerman was sprawled atop Karla Kurtz. His eyes were closed. His feet were tangled in a sheet. There was blood on the sheet. Helene put her ear to Ackerman's chest. The heart was beating, but not big time.

Karla Kurtz's eyes fluttered. She pointed to herself, to Ackerman.

"Who are you?"

"I'm Helene, your teacher. Where are you hit?"

"That son-of-a-bitch," Karla said. "He told her where I was. He's a snake. He—"

"Who told her what?" Helene said.

Ackerman was unconscious. Karla was talking crazy. Helene got on the phone. "Where are the gurneys? We need a body bag."

Karla was oozing blood. Helene opened a drawer, hunting for a clean towel, something to slow the bleeding, and saw Ackerman's pistol, shiny with chrome-plate. When Steve

Slattery arrived, he would confiscate weapons. Helene's Glock, Bruno's Ruger, whatever the shooter had used.

Helene took Ackerman's .45, dumped it into her shoulder bag. The bag was good, thick leather, a gift from her dad.

Karla groaned, opened her eyes. Opened her mouth, but no words came out. Helene flashed on Karla's writing, a story of two female killers, one named Sharleen. The other named Faith something. The door flew open and two EMTs entered, rolling a gurney. Helene moved to one side, watching the EMTs do triage. The lead guy made a phone call, nodding. They took Karla first. Helene looked at the dead shooter, slumped against the wall. This was no first-timer. The construction worker disguise had gotten her through the political crowd, past security, up the elevator. How had she known where to find Ackerman? What had Karla just said? A snake, a son-of-a-bitch—who was she talking about? Did the shooter know Karla?

Steve Slattery arrived, pushing a wheelchair. The gleam in his eye said he had questions that needed answers. Slattery said that Giselle was okay. Bruno had taken a bullet in the shoulder, close to an artery. Both of them were on the way to Cottonwood.

IN THE ELEVATOR GOING down, Helene briefed Slattery.

"Raul phoned with an alert," Helene said. "Some crazy woman was after Ackerman. When I got up to the penthouse, I found Giselle and Bruno, both wounded, both bleeding. Bruno was out. His wound looked serious … nothing I could do. Giselle told me the woman was armed. In the Spa, Ackerman was on the floor, tangled in a sheet. Karla was under him. There was a woman in overalls and work boots. She had a gun. She fired at me; I returned fire."

Slattery asked questions. Who was the woman shooter? Where did she come from? Did she say anything?

"She talked to Ackerman," Helene said.

"What did she say?"

"Not sure," Helene said, "but it sounded like they knew each other."

Helene handed over her Glock. Slattery hefted the weapon and nodded. Two cops—they knew the drill.

HELENE FOUND MURDOCK ON a gurney in the parking lot chatting with a pretty female EMT. There was a bandage on his shoulder. Helene touched his hand. The EMT walked off.

"Are you okay?"

"Needs more drugs," Murdock said.

"Featherstone?"

"Connie shot him."

"In the balls?" Helene said.

"Fish wants the hotel," Murdock said. "He was gonna buy it from the—"

Before he could finish, an ambulance arrived, and the EMTs loaded Murdock in with Karla Kurtz. She looked pale. Connie Fremont walked up, said hi. Helene gave Connie a quick hug. Thanked her for saving Murdock. Connie climbed into the ambulance. The doors closed.

Helene had that weightless feeling, as if there was no one behind her eyes. Maybe that came from killing another human being. They train you. They send you out there. You react faster because of the training. But there was no training for after. If you were a cop, they might send you to a shrink. You could talk it out, take your time getting your groove back. But Helene was not a cop. She was alone. She had Murdock, maybe, but he was packed in with Connie in the ambulance.

Helene looked around, saw no sign of Iveta Macek. Maybe she had gone with Ackerman's daughter. Helene saw ambulances, gurneys, cop cars, a fire engine, a big black limo. The limo's rear door was down. A cop leaned in. Explanation time at Sedona Landing. The man in the limo was Senator Fish.

Ackerman rolled by on a gurney powered by two EMTs in

blue jump suits. His eyes were still closed. A tube led from his arm to a plastic bottle hanging from a metal rod attached to the gurney. Slattery waved Helene over. He wanted her to ride in the ambulance with Ackerman.

Good. She needed orders. Someone to tell her what to do.

65

MURDOCK LAY ON THE gurney, feeling the ambulance rocking with the road. He estimated the speed at 52 mph. Eyes closed, he was listening to Connie Fremont question Karla Kurtz. His head felt fuzzy; that was the drugs working.

"How did you know the shooter?" Connie said.

"I didn't know her."

"She said something to you."

"She was yelling at Mr. Ackerman," Karla said, "not me."

"How long have you been his masseuse?"

"Since the summer."

"Are you licensed to do massages in Arizona?"

"Of course."

"Do you perform sexual acts during the session?"

"And lose my license?"

"The shooter tried to kill you … do you know why?"

"Ask her, why don't you."

"She's dead."

"Is there more painkiller? I really hurt bad."

Listening, his eyes closed, Murdock could appreciate both combatants. Connie was guiding Karla Kurtz toward a trap.

Karla was stonewalling the questions, dodging, feinting like a pro, making Connie work. When Karla asked for a lawyer, the questions stopped.

The ambulance went into a long curve. Murdock opened his eyes. Through the back window, he saw leafless trees planted along the road. They were approaching the Cottonwood Regional Medical Center. He counted up the wounded—Karla, Giselle, Bruno, Ackerman, himself, the shooter—a female in her late forties. Did she have red hair? Had she been with Ackerman and the Crew? No answers floated at him. He was too tired. As the ambulance slowed, he felt Connie's hand on his arm.

"How are you holding up, big guy?"

"I could sleep for a week. Did you really have a date with Featherstone?"

"Almost," Connie said.

*****

HELENE STEINBECK RODE IN Ackerman's ambulance. She kept seeing the woman in the Spa, disguised as a tile setter, a pistol in each hand, but not a trained shooter. Helene was a good shot. She always wondered about other shooters. Did they practice enough? The ambulance swerved, taking Helene's stomach sideways, then leveled off again. She tuned in on Steve Slattery's voice. He was asking questions, digging for motive.

"So, Mr. Ackerman, how are you feeling, sir?"

"Dead," Ackerman said. "Crushed. Bruised. Assaulted. Maimed. Betrayed."

"Tell me about the shooter," Slattery said. "Charity Plum is the name on her driver's license, issued by the state of Colorado, whereas she resides in Las Vegas. What alias did you know her by?"

"Penny Diamond," Ackerman said.

"Awhile back, was it?"

"Thirty years."

"What was the situation?"

"I had Miss Diamond under contract. She was brilliant. Her brain could hold a thousand spreadsheets. It was as if she inhaled rows of numbers. We had baby computers that filled rooms—remember QDOS, Quick and Dirty Operating System?"

"That was before my time, sir."

"Well, that young woman was a walking, talking computer."

"Was she easy on the eyes?" Slattery said.

Ackerman said, "If you're gonna be working close for days, weeks, months, they should be easy on the eyes."

"Did you bang her?" Slattery said.

"I'm the victim here," Ackerman said. "I'm the target and your tone of voice, you're treating me as a … suspect?"

Slattery said, "I got one corpse today, five people shot. This happened on my turf, on my watch, starting early Monday morning when I get this diver off Cathedral Rock, one of your Crew; then on Monday night we get a guy falling in Santa Fe—just happens to be one of your Crew. On Tuesday I get eight bodies piled up on Foxglove Lane, no connection to your Crew, I hope. Thursday we get the last Crew member dead at the Sedona Xanadu. Now it's Thank-God-Friday and we are hoping to connect this Penny Diamond to the earlier kills—three of them out of my jurisdiction—and where you could not remember before, now you admit she's really Penny Diamond, the numbers gal who looked real good back then, when you had her under contract. What I need from you is a reason for this Penny Diamond broad to wait thirty years to get even. What I need from you is how you got that massage gal to take a bullet meant for you. What I need … ah shit. Don't go to sleep on me, goddamn you!"

Helene watched Ackerman close his eyes. He did that a lot. One minute he'd be alert, eyes open—that sharp look when he thought about money and numbers and profit—the next minute the eyes would be closed, as if he was floating away. Cagey old bird.

Slattery sat back, looked at Helene, and shook his head.

*****

VOICES IN THE ROOM, two females.

Murdock smelled antiseptic.

His brain floated away from his body.

Wings sprouted from his shoulders. His arms went wide.

He landed on the ground with Cypher, looking through a scope mounted on a bipod. Murdock was the spotter; he had the target in the crosshairs. He turned his head. Cypher wore a boonie hat, and camouflage hid his face. Murdock heard the chop of helicopter blades.

Helene's voice: "Is our hero gonna live?"

"Your husband will be fine."

"He is not my husband."

Murdock looked around. They had him trapped in a cold white room with metal exam tables. Helene watched from a metal chair. A nurse pulled off the makeshift bandages. She hummed a Christmas carol. Murdock felt the sting of antiseptic.

"You got lucky," she said. "You clot really fast. The bullet sailed through. We got threads out, from your shirt. Don't want that stuff left inside. It could fester."

"How about some drugs for the pain?" Murdock said.

"They'll test your urine," the nurse said. "You'll lose your job, your position in the line-up."

"I like that oxycodone stuff—inhale and take yourself a secret trip."

The nurse turned to Helene. "Tell your husband he's riding for a fall."

"He never listens to me."

"You're that writer, aren't you? I saw your photo. You shot that guy in Taos."

"I'm trying to forget," Helene said. "Trying to unstick myself from that time and especially that place."

"Well," the nurse said. "It sure lit up the Internet."

The door opened and the doctor came in, a woman with black hair and a round face. Her name badge said DR. MENDOZA. She shook hands with Helene, grinned when the nurse mentioned drugs. She poked Murdock's wound, making him grunt.

"If you were really hurt," she said, "your reflexes would have shot you through the door like a cannonball."

"I was hit by a cannonball," Murdock said, "but not before I created a diversion, military-style, by the book. Let me tell you about—"

"Is he always this funny?" the doctor said.

"He's under the delusion that he's got hero genes," Helene said.

"I got one like that at home," the doctor said. "He wears the mask of male modesty."

"So," Murdock said. "In conclusion, no drugs are forthcoming to ease the hero's pain and suffering? I am correct, no?"

"I gotta go," Helene said. "Slattery's briefing the big boys."

66

IN THE DREAM, ACKERMAN stands on a fire escape in the dark wearing a white bathrobe, surrounded by Christmas lights winking from little windows in small-town houses.

The fire escape is three stories up. The wind is cold, cutting. The bathrobe is asylum-thin.

Ackerman is holding hands with Joe Wilson, artist, craftsman, husband, father, fool. It's Christmas Eve. Wilson wears a Santa Claus suit. Standing on the edge, wringing his hands. He grips Ackerman's wrists. It's confession time.

"Why did you bring that Diamond woman to my town?"

"To find the red ink," Ackerman said.

"She stole my boy, my business, my life."

"You wanted her too," Ackerman said.

"Did not," Wilson said.

"Every man wanted Penny Diamond," Ackerman said.

The fire escape looks down on a school playground. Wilson's grip is icy, fingers like cold claws.

Ackerman pries Wilson's fingers off, too late. Wilson jumps, pulling Ackerman along, the snowy playground rushing up.

*

ACKERMAN FELT A PAIN in his chest—fear, stress, guilt, his heart pounding. The death-smell assailed his nose.

The pain brought him awake.

He was in a white room with white walls.

No Joe Wilson here, no icy fire escape.

A tube ran from Ackerman's arm to a plastic sack hanging from a metal IV stand.

A toilet flushed, a door opened, and Iveta Macek emerged. She wore green scrubs. Her hair was a mess; her face looked burnished. He hoped she had looked better online, when Daniel first spotted her.

She sat on the edge of the bed.

"What are you doing here?"

"The ambulance," she said. "I am with your daughter."

"You know Lottie?" he said. "What the hell's going on?"

"She is down the corridor," she said. "I have something to tell you."

"How do you know Lottie?" he said.

"Daniel is still sleeping," she said. "We are to be married."

"Welcome to the family," Ackerman said.

She was standing close to the bed. She had something he needed to know, a little secret, she said. Her voice deepened, serious, a mature voice. How did a woman change so fast?

She raised the scrub shirt. Her skin was smooth, pale gold. The belly pooched out; he hadn't noticed before. Inside his head a little bell went *bong*. She guided Ackerman's hand to her belly. He smelled her scent, took a deep breath. What the hell? He felt life pulsing under his fingers. She was no longer the slinky girl-cat in the bikini, diving into the pool at Sedona Landing. She was a mother-to-be, Daniel's genes, her womb. Ackerman felt warmth, strength, youth. He felt an erection.

"I carry Daniel's baby," she said. "If something happens to him, the baby is yours to protect."

"Jesus Christ," Ackerman said. "Danny didn't say anything."

"Daniel does not know."

"Okay. You're here, you're safe, you're family. It's gonna be…."

67

In the Medical Center meeting room, Helene sat way in the back, working a mind-map, while Slattery made his rah-rah speech. Cops kept coming in late, interrupting Slattery. Cops from Prescott, deputies from Camp Verde, a cadre of state guys.

Slattery gave up the podium to his boss, the Sedona Chief, who gave it up to the Lieutenant Governor, who gave it up to Jimbo Gypsum, the Gary Cooper lookalike who would be president. Hiram Fish stood at Gypsum's elbow. Both men looked presidential. That was spooky.

The empty talk ballooned in the room, captured by the TV cameras. Gypsum and Fish left for their next appointment—a public appearance at City Hall in Cottonwood, fishing for voters.

Cops exited in twos and threes, discussing the big snow in Flagstaff—multi-vehicle collisions, two semis sprawled across I-17, a seven-mile backup, more officers needed.

The TV anchor, Diana Trask, asked Helene what she was doing. Helene covered her mind-map.

"Just notes," she said. "Armchair sleuthing."

"They say you shot the shooter, the one who tried to murder Axel?"

"How do you know Axel?" Helene said.

"From way back," the blonde said, "before the inevitable weight-gain."

"You don't look heavy to me," Helene said.

"Thanks. I'm Diana Trask, by the way."

"Helene Steinbeck. You're very good on TV."

"Thanks," Trask said. "I've got your book, and I've gotta run. Is there some time we could get together? I'd love your take on these killings."

Helene said of course. They exchanged numbers. Trask's phone buzzed, pulling her away. Helene watched her move off—nice figure, and Helene was always open to new friends. Was Diana Trask another Ackerman conquest?

Helene walked to the white board and started transcribing her mind-map. She drew a box for the Past, then put words inside: *Amarillo, Wilson Family, Ackerman's 5-man Crew, Ramsay, schoolyard scuffle, Penny Diamond, Wilson Family, Wilson's Fine Furniture, cooking the books, bankruptcy, romance, 30 years ago, photos of Joey and Penny, Joseph Wilson, falling.* Outside the circle, she wrote the word *Past.*

"What the fuck is that?" Slattery said.

"A mind-map," Helene said. " It gives us the Big Picture, connections, insights. You guys jump in any time."

"Like jumping into chaos," Slattery said, "of which we already got enough of."

"I like it," Connie said. "Keep going."

Helene drew a bubble, then printed words inside: *Sedona Landing, Oak Creek Village, Cathedral Rock, Findlay (Crew), Lemon Custard Bistro, Vortex Bank, glass-walled office, Ackerman, his family, tennis, Teri Breedlove, Executive Spa, Penny Diamond (Charity Plum) dead.*

She used a smaller circle to group the wounded: *Giselle, Bruno, Karla,* and *Murdock*. She added Ackerman, then the word *bruised*. She stepped back, her brain feeling jazzed, before writing WARNING PHONE CALL? in caps.

"Now we're cooking," Slattery said. "Ask your Ouija board who made that ever-so-coincidental phone call."

Helene kept working, tried to ignore the slurs from Slattery. She needed a chronology. She made separate boxes for days of the week.

Sunday, Findlay falls.

Monday, Delaplane falls.

Tuesday, Ten Foxglove Lane, 8 people dead.

Wednesday, no one dies.

Thursday, George Hawthorne falls.

Friday, Penny/Charity wounds two, kills one.

Helene drew circles around the word *falling*. She connected the five men who had died by falling. Then she ran an arc from the five men to Joseph Wilson. Printed the words DIED FROM FALLING in caps, and stepped away again.

Slattery yawned. "Translation, Steinbeck."

"Joseph Wilson," Helene said. "He jumped off a school fire escape."

"When was this? The Dark Ages?"

"Thirty years ago. In Amarillo."

"Ho fucking hum," Slattery said. "Who the hell is Joseph Wilson?"

"Father of Joey," Helene said. "Owner of Wilson's Fine Furniture—the last job for Ackerman's Crew."

"I don't get it," Slattery said.

Connie said, "Helene is digging up corpses from the past, Steve."

"Oh," Slattery said. "Cold Case City. I dig that angle. Why didn't you say so?"

Helene smiled as she enclosed the word *Catalyst* in a bubble. Connected Catalyst to Sedona Landing, Ackerman, the Crew—then she put Vortex Bank inside a bubble, connected it to glass-walled office. Slattery said "Fuck it, I need coffee" and left the room.

Connie stood beside Helene. She had heard of mind-maps; this one was very elaborate. Helene stepped away from the white board. She had forgotten Cypher. She added his name next to Vortex Bank, connected it to the glass-walled office.

Slattery came back with three coffees.

"Why is Jeremy's name up there?" Connie said.

"Cypher's the connector in the Sedona Landing deal," Helene said. "He sits in that office and …. How well do you guys know him, anyway?"

"He's a fucking fixture in this town," Slattery said. "Village Council, heads up committees, gets things done around here."

"You should query some of the gals in the valley," Connie said.

"I think he's banging the Breedlove chick," Slattery said.

"No way," Connie said. "Teri's a Virgin for Christ."

"Maybe that's her cover," Slattery said. "Maybe underneath, Breedlove is a Saudi. Works under cover for the Shah."

"The Shah was Iranian, Steve. Not Arab."

"Yo, Fremont. This is the US of A. In this country, a raghead is a raghead."

Helene sat down. Her brain had slowed—no more charged insights. She had left something out of her mind-map—she didn't know what. Slattery's negative vibe was stupid, and the coffee tasted bitter. She exhaled and went looking for Murdock. She liked him better when he went a little crazy. Like that oration in the exam room, his plea for drugs.

*****

WHEN HE WAS HURT, Murdock enjoyed drugs. They removed the pain, gave him a nice pair of rose-colored glasses. With those glasses, the world was a better place. The nurse left the room. Murdock stood up, and the room whirled. He sat on the bed. Helene came through the door. For a long hopeful minute, Murdock felt a hug coming his way. She touched his shoulder, asked how he was doing. He asked her how she liked the rose-colored glasses. She went out, came back with a wheelchair.

They were going to see Ackerman.

*****

ACKERMAN WAS PRESSING THE call button when his super-sleuths walked in. They looked tired. Murdock was in a wheelchair, his arm in a sling. Helene took a seat in a hospital chair. Ackerman was disappointed. Why didn't she sit on the edge of the bed? He was having second thoughts about hiring her. Watching Helene, Ackerman remembered Dallas, the big house of Dirksen Fish, the image of Daphne Houston Fish, bare tanned feet, the swimming pool, the trip up the stairs, his eyes fixed on her flexing calves, leading him into the master bedroom, tan lines across her smooth torso. *You naughty boy*, Daphne had said, *you caught me in my prime. After you, there is nothing.*

Ackerman shook his head, shooed the memories away.

"Give me a damage report," Ackerman said.

"Karla Kurtz is hurt but tough," Murdock said. "I was there when Slattery grilled her. He asked if she knew the shooter. She said, no way. Giselle Roux will need plastic surgery; Charity's bullet took out a chunk of thigh. Bruno took a hit in the shoulder; his wound is worse than mine."

"The penthouse?"

"What about it?"

"Is it livable?"

"It's a palace of yellow ribbons," Helene said. "They're guarding it twenty-four/seven."

"I haven't thanked you for rescuing me. You got there fast. Where were you, anyway?"

"We were on Seven," Helene said. "We had just found your daughter in the stairwell. Got her into an ambulance—"

"Lottie is here?"

"Right down the hall."

"Get her in here," Ackerman said.

"She was unconscious when we looked in," Helene said. "Daniel?"

"Still out, but the docs say he'll be okay. How are you?"

"I'm going ahead with the acquisition," Ackerman said. "So you people get Cypher lined up. Call him right now. We'll need a list …. Right now, okay?"

*****

HELENE'S FEET DRAGGED. HER face felt droopy. She shook off the wave of fatigue, moved to the big window alcove, phoned Cypher using her contacts list. Cypher's voicemail came on. Helene left a message. She was with Murdock in Ackerman's room and had questions for Cypher.

Room 700 had two beds, but it was big enough for two more. It had two bathrooms. The one with the open door showed a roll-in shower. *Get clean, never leave your wheelchair.* This room had the fire escape for this side of the building. The window was wide, like a French slider. Behind her, Murdock was quizzing Ackerman.

"How did you meet Karla?" Murdock said.

"You're off topic, Detective. I'm talking business here. I'm talking acquisition, maybe my last one on God's green earth, and you people—"

Murdock said it again, "Where did you meet Karla Kurtz?"

"Oh, for Christ's sake. I met her at that cute coffee place. She had a little card that said, Licensed Massage Person. She was so beautiful … those slick legs. I paid money for a trial massage. She was excellent, great hands, so I put her under contract. Haven't we been over this?"

"Okay," Helene said. "How did you connect with Cypher?"

"You people are trying my patience. Cypher knew the hotel owners; they had a banker in Tucson. Bud Tyler was working with the Tucson guy, something happened, and Cypher stepped in, as a favor."

"What happened?" Helene said.

"An accident, something with snow, skiing, snowboarding ... hell, why don't you ask Cypher?"

"What did you think when you saw Penny/Charity in your Spa?"

"Jumping around, are we? Trying to trick an old wounded man?"

"How quick did you recognize her?"

"When I saw those crazy eyes."

"What did she say?"

"She was babbling—altars, fathers, babies, who owed what to whom. I wanted to ask why she stole from me. Then she shot Karla."

"Who else knew you were getting a massage at noon?" Helene said.

"Giselle, Bruno, you people."

"How about Teri Breedlove?"

"Maybe. She's always checking schedules, filling up her day, but you don't really think—"

"Someone phoned Raul," Murdock said. "The voice was male, spoke with an accent."

"When?" Ackerman said.

"Helene took the call. She hustled up to the Spa."

"Pretty fucking close," Ackerman said.

"What do you think of Cypher?" Helene said.

"I think he should have known about the competing bid—Ramsay and those Arabs."

"So," Murdock said. "Let's run it again. Tyler got the ball rolling. Then he called you?"

"I was done with projects," Ackerman said. "Sedona was hectic, tourists fucking it up, but Oak Creek Village was paradise. Winter sun, no traffic—did I tell you I'm buying the airport? That runway is abominable. Did I tell you there's a man here, Dr. Timothy, a veritable shaman who keeps me active between the sheets? People are always doing that, coming in handy. Like you people when I needed sleuths. Like Cypher when I wanted to add the penthouse. From up there, you can see all the way to Mexico, not have to go there. My remodel? Cypher squared it with the owners, for an extra fifty grand. I was sick when I arrived—down on my uppers, my mama used to say—and this place healed me. Magic of the vortex, right? When can I see my daughter?"

68

L OTTIE ACKERMAN BELL WOKE up to find her stray cat, Iveta Macek, wearing hospital scrubs, her face splotchy from crying. Lottie held out her arms. "Hello, kitten." The two women hugged. The hug brought pain to Lottie's back. She asked what happened. Her brain rolled like surf off the French coast. From Iveta, she learned about her fall, the shooting in the Penthouse Spa. Lottie's father was next door. Her brother Daniel was down the hall, still in a coma. Iveta had not seen Senator Fish. But Lottie could feel him coming.

The mention of Fish triggered memories of the stairwell, a man wearing a handkerchief to hide his face, a baseball cap to hide his hair. Lottie asked about her purse, her wallet, her smartphone. She watched Iveta make a search. Fish had sent someone for those photos. Lottie had more on her laptop, which was in her room. She asked Iveta for help. But sitting up brought a headache, a knife slicing into her brain. She sagged back.

They chatted about the past, their first meeting in the dress shop in Prague. Lottie had seen something special in Iveta. They went for tea. It was a test, pouring tea from a china pot in a luxury hotel, with a clutch of men watching. Iveta was under thirty; she had served in the Czech Army. She knew how to read maps, move through the underbrush, handle weapons. Men found her attractive. Lottie needed her help, getting photos of an old enemy. Not just any photos, but the compromising kind. And today, Lottie had been attacked for the photos. She had duplicates in Paris. She had more duplicates on a flash drive in her luggage. She told Iveta to call Bruno. He was hurt. Giselle was hurt.

Lottie said, "Kitten, you've got to search my carry-on. That slimy bastard has to be stopped."

"But how?" Iveta said.

"Find a way," Lottie said. "Pretend you're back in the army."

*****

CYPHER CROSSED THE INTERSTATE, headed for Geronimo Airport. He checked his computer; the private jet carrying Arthur Ackerman was seven minutes late, time enough to set up with the sun over the left shoulder, perfect for the shot.

He laid the rifle in the bipod, adjusted the scope, and checked the crosshairs; they had a mind of their own. The crosshairs were alive. They stood at attention, waiting for orders. They tugged the gun muzzle to the right, just a tiny bit. The voice in his head said, *this way, yes, easy, now, there*, and then a tiny ching inside his head, like a wind chime from Tibet, and the voice—*shooter, we are on target.*

The plane landed. Arthur Ackerman emerged, the overcoat draped from his shoulders, sleeves empty, so cool. The cool vanished when the bullet tore into his leg. There were two bodyguards, one female, one male. When they turned, playing FBI agents on the TV, arms out, two hands on the gun, they looked straight into the afternoon sun. They each took a bullet. Three people down, ambulance needed.

Cypher telephoned Breedlove. She was heading for his house. She had the nurse uniform. What was it for? "Getting in," he said. "Getting out." Cypher loved the bank. He could have stayed there forever, grow old in Sedona, Golden Years for the old person, but now he had work to do. Payback for the family of Axel Ackerman.

He heard a voice, turned to see Joey in the death seat. Joey grinned, gave Cypher the thumbs up. He said one word, "Ulysses."

*****

HIRAM FISH HAD PLANS.

The two candidates for high office wound up the Cottonwood press conference and Fish said he was tired. He wanted to go back to the hotel. Featherstone was dead. Fish took his vehicle.

Fish wanted to drive himself. He had some thinking to do. He needed a disguise, something for a hospital visit.

In the consignment store on the edge of town, Fish located a section that said Medical.

He tried on white lab coats, each one troubled with a stain.

*****

CYPHER PARKED IN THE garage. He let himself into the house and turned off the alarm. Dumping the desert camos into the washer—trousers, blouse, Army-issue underwear, heavy khaki socks—he started the wash and entered the shower. The water cleared the cobwebs that always came with a mission—the brain in retreat, the synapses firing like little skyrockets. He shaved his face. Then he shaved under his arms, a trick he'd learned in the Hindu Kush. If you couldn't get a bath, you could still eliminate the armpit hair and cut down on the rancid smell of fear. He remembered the first time he had shaved. He was thirteen, using Father's razor, a major thrill. He was keeping the books; he was in love with Penny Diamond. She changed his life. She ruined his life.

Cypher stood in front of the mirror. Joey hovered over his right shoulder, waving the *Odyssey*, the blue-print for the ambush at the CRMC. Joey ranted on, blaming Ackerman for destroying his childhood. He blamed the Crew. He blamed Penny Diamond. She had caught Joey trying to save the business; she called it cooking the books.

The doorbell rang, and Joey faded. Cypher tugged on the EMT pants and a T-shirt. He opened the door to find Teri Breedlove, shivering in her nurse uniform and carrying a shopping bag. He smelled marijuana; she was high. Her face was soft against his cheek. She blew into his ear, led him to the bedroom, removed the uniform, and assumed the prone position, face on the pillow, arms like wings, butt in the air.

Cypher heard Joey's voice, *holy shit, bro, it's the girl next door*.

Cypher touched the Promise Ring; Breedlove touched his manhood. Her fingers were cool.

"Wow," she said, "my mom was right on."

"Right on about what?"

"About this," she said. "I am so juiced."

69

MURDOCK WAS YAWNING. HELENE took him straight to the exam room, helped him onto the table. Her lips were close to his cheek, *just turn your head and do it*. She stopped; Murdock looked sad. He took her hand. Asked her what she was going to do.

"Back to the mind-map," she said.

In the staff meeting room, Helene saw that someone had erased Cypher's name, but had left the connecting lines and part of the bubble. Slattery and Connie were on their phones. Helene took her time printing Cypher's name again. Connie finished her phone call and stood beside Helene. She asked about Murdock. Helene felt the heat; she was jealous.

"Did you take Cypher's name off my mind-map?"

"Yeah."

"Why?"

"Gave me the creeps," Connie said.

"My partner has the creeps," Slattery said. "Just what this fucking case needs."

"I dated him," Connie said.

"Dated whom?" Helene said.

"Jeremy," Connie said. "Okay?"

"Jesus Christ, Fremont," Slattery said.

"How did it end?" Helene said.

"We went out a couple times," Connie said. "He's single, good job, looks really safe. He was ultra-attentive to me, real clean guy. Shaves under his arms, what every man should do, in my humble opinion. He took me to some lovely restaurants. I got to wear clothes with him I would never have a chance to wear again."

"What about his house?" Helene said.

"Neat, clean. Everything looked new. The kitchen is immaculate. He cooked me a meal, coq-au-vin, yum, and he cleaned up, washed the dishes while I dried."

"Any guns?" Helene said.

"Not where you can see them. He's got a big closet, though. Big enough for a gun-safe."

"How did it end?" Helene said.

"There's no one inside Mr. Jeremy Cypher," Connie said. "It was like he made himself up. I asked him about his Army service. He'd seen a little combat, but most of his time he was a paymaster, a base budget guy."

Helene turned to Slattery. "Could you check on his military service, Steve?"

"Why would I want to do that?"

"See if he had sniper training."

"No need for that," Slattery said. "I took him elk-hunting last year—New Mexico, north of Taos, around Red River, they got this humongous herd. I nailed my animal, my buddies got one each, but old Jeremy couldn't kill an elk if it was tied to a tree and yelling for him to do it. The poor guy got down on himself. It's not a pretty thing to watch, a guy losing face."

Slattery's cellphone beeped. He walked toward the door and went out, leaving Helene alone with Connie. Helene wanted to tell Connie about her relationship with Murdock. She didn't have the right words. Should she say things were stalled out?

Should she say things were on hold? Should she tell Connie about ….

The door opened and Slattery was back, heels hard on the floor, gripping his cellphone, shaking his head.

"It's the youngest son, Arthur Ackerman. Shot in the leg; they're bringing him in. What does this guy want, the whole fucking family?"

*****

IN COTTONWOOD, AT A medical supply house near the hospital, Fish paid cash for a white lab jacket, the only one in the store that came close to fitting. He bought a second hand stethoscope. He bought a valise, leather, pricey, so he could carry the white coat. He drove to the hospital. The car was powerful, he was over the speed limit before he knew it. A white sheriff's SUV stopped him, Fish flashed his credentials, the deputy tipped his hat, told Fish to hold it down, sir.

From the highway, the CRMC had the appearance of a castle in a children's storybook.

It sat on a low hill that overlooked an arroyo.

Clouds blanked out the sun as Fish followed an ambulance into the curved driveway. The radio said *snow on the way.*

Fish parked in the lot. A dozen official-looking vehicles. There was one uniform, a cop from Prescott. He checked Fish's ID at the door. Who did the senator want to see? The director, he said.

A nurse with a knife-edge face took Fish to the director's office, to a chubby assistant in a sweater. The director was out, back in twenty. Fish sat down to wait. The nurse answered a call on her beeper, "Rivera here." She walked out talking.

Fish asked the assistant for help. "Which room for Mr. Ackerman? We're old friends," Fish said.

"Go on up," she said.

Fish used the men's room, put on the white coat. It felt tight.

He looked in the mirror, saw the sex scene that had destroyed his faith in family. His mother on her back, the pool boy between her legs. She was panting, cursing, enjoying herself. Fish remembered telling Father. He wanted revenge.

His mother went to visit her sister in Fort Worth. Father took Fish hunting, shooting in Arizona, where Fish nailed his first wetback. Always shoot righteous, his father said.

Fish draped the stethoscope around his neck, took the elevator to Six.

Huffed and puffed on the stairs, stopping to breathe.

When he reached Seven, Fish felt dizzy. He kept going. This was the chance of a lifetime—the pool boy in bed, weakened by drugs.

He passed a nurse's station, two women on computers.

He turned right. The room numbers went up—734, 735, wrong way.

Fish kept going, circling toward his target.

He did not want to pass the nurse's station again.

They would ask was he lost. They would remember he was there, a portly man masquerading as a doctor. *Make one mistake in politics, your career is over.*

Fish made another right turn, another, numbers going down.

Room 713. Room 710. Moving faster now, toward Room 700, where Axel Ackerman waited.

*****

TERI BREEDLOVE SAT NEXT to Jeremy in the Subaru.

Tried to hold his hand, but he needed both hands on the wheel.

Teri was in love; she had found Mr. Right. He looked amazing in his blue EMTs. He looked like a soldier.

They left the highway, followed signs to underground parking. She asked what was his assignment. He blocked her question. Teri's job was the interview. She should ask to read the manuscript. What manuscript, dude? Just ask, she'll know what you mean.

"Too much drama, dude."

"You have your orders, soldier."

Teri Breedlove watched Jeremy walk off, carrying a little medical bag.

Her body still tingled from his touch—call it expertise. Her fingers fondled the Promise Ring, dangling from a chain around her neck, where Jeremy had left bites. She closed her eyes and sent a text to God.

Dear God, I am still a virgin.

She added the word, *technically*.

The elevator door closed. She pushed the button for Five.

As she was lifted up, she sent another text.

Dear God, does a little Sodomy count? Her bottom was tingly with remembering, and excited— all those nerves down there. When God answered her, she hoped He used a text. She hoped it was in English.

The elevator doors opened, easing her into the corridor on Five.

Her interview subject was in Room 505. Jeremy called this person the key to everything, open all the doors, answer all questions. Jeremy was so cagey, always keeping secrets.

She needed to know this man. Maybe she could compare notes with her mother.

70

In the dream, Murdock climbs a curved glass staircase to a glass-walled room where Cypher is in bed with a redheaded woman who takes Murdock's hand, leads him to the edge. He looks down the twisting stairs.

Murdock wears his bear claws and his first Sunday suit and a wide orange necktie. The redheaded woman wears a Halloween mask. Murdock turns to the woman, shows her the newspaper photo of five guys in business suits. Murdock asks: "Where are you in this picture?"

The woman gives him a push, "There you go."

Murdock holds his arms out, like wings. He whirls inside a vortex. He crashes through a window, lands in a glass-walled room in front of a giant sheet of cardboard covered with words inside bubbles—Helene's mind-map, showing her road to the solution. Slattery and Connie are erasing the mind-map, wiping out the connections between past and present.

Murdock rolls away. He's safe in his wheelchair. *Keep moving.* His job is keeping it together.

The wheelchair rolls into the Amarillo library, doorway

to the past, where Mrs. Dorothy Stanhope turns over a photograph that shows Penny Diamond leaving the Wilson house, slim hips inside a tight pencil-skirt. A boy stands on the porch, waving goodbye.

Murdock hears voices, two women.

"What's he saying?"

"It's the meds, dear."

"Did he say something about wings?"

"Your husband will be fine, dear."

"He's not my husband, thank you very much."

*****

HELENE STOOD OVER MURDOCK's bed, watching him come back.

Helene's brain was on hold. She was an action person. She thought better when she kept busy.

Murdock was the thinker-planner, the guy with the sleuth's intuition. His eyelids fluttered. His face looked peaceful; his hands were folded across his stomach. Helene was jealous. Why did he get to rest while the world tilted into madness?

"Hey, Steinbeck. How about a siesta?"

"You are needed," she said. "It's two against one in the meeting room."

"Does that mean we're good again?"

"No," she said. "Yes, if you want … I don't know, I'm so tired. Just come with me, okay?"

"Who gets the wheelchair?"

"How can you be funny at a time like this?"

"Cosmic guffaw," Murdock said.

"It's Arthur Ackerman," Helene said. "Axel's youngest … he's been shot. They're bringing him in from the airport."

"Family reunion," Murdock said.

Wheeling Murdock along the corridor, Helene looked down at the top of his head and saw a little bare spot. Her heart did a thump. Murdock was taller; he always wore a hat or a cap.

Murdock was human. His hair was getting thin. *Oh, no.* She told him about Connie dating Cypher. Murdock nodded, like he was not surprised.

They pushed through the door into the staff meeting room. Slattery scowled, Connie Fremont looked lost. Slattery was at the white board, making a list, lifting names from Helene's mind-map. Axel Ackerman's name was number one. Arthur Ackerman was number 13, way down at the bottom.

"I gotta have order," Slattery said. "One-two-three, first things first."

"Good job, Steve," Murdock said.

"Thanks. Coming from you, that's an A-Plus."

"How many cops you got at the CRMC?"

"I got uniforms on the entrances," Slattery said. "Couple more on patrol."

"What did you get on Cypher's military service?" Helene said.

"Nothing yet. Maybe I don't know the right people."

"Did the airport shooter use a sound-suppressor?" Murdock said.

"They didn't hear anything," Slattery said. "They figured it out when he blew a tire on their transportation."

"Any others get shot?"

"Two security people. He left one unshot."

"No kills, right?"

"They got lucky," Slattery said. "Good questions, Sherlock. Maybe you should have stayed a cop."

"In combat," Murdock said, "if you shoot to wound, then you can shoot the rescuers."

"So he didn't mean to kill them?" Slattery said.

"He wants them all in one place."

"What then? He gonna blow up the hospital … with us in it?"

"Not his style," Murdock said.

"Oh, yeah. So how do you define his so-called style?"

"Clandestine," Murdock said. "Slice and dice, feint and withdraw, pick off the outliers, work your way closer to the target ... that would be this hospital, which is why I asked about manpower."

"Big traffic mess around Flagstaff," Slattery said.

"That profile does sound like Jeremy," Connie said.

"Any clues on the weapon?" Murdock said.

"I know what you're gonna say," Slattery said. "You want it to be a small-bore .223."

"We could check his house," Connie said. "Want me to call for a warrant?"

"I told you people," Slattery said. "Jeremy Cypher cannot fucking shoot!"

71

THE PROBLEMATIC PART OF the climactic plan was gathering the family into one room.

Cypher was human—two arms, two legs. He needed more arms; he needed to clone himself. Where was Joey when you needed him?

Cypher climbed the stairs from the parking garage. He used his smartphone to check the floor plan.

The surgery floor was Two.

Recovery was down the hallway from Surgery.

Cypher checked for police, saw a cop down the hall, chatting up a nurse. Cypher slipped into Recon mode, heard a chuckle from Joey. *Hand over the controls, Bro.* Stop calling me Bro.

A woman sat outside the door of Recovery.

Cypher recognized her from the tarmac—the two-handed shooting stance, the move you saw on TV. This was the woman Cypher had chosen not to shoot at Geronimo Airport. The woman security person looked up.

She asked his business.

Joey said, *Second chance, bro. Don't fuck it up.*

Cypher shot her in the leg, took her weapon and her

cellphone, and hauled her inside Recovery.

*****

ALONE IN ROOM 505, Karla dreamed of writing, her hand moving across the page, the ink forming words, sentences, paragraphs.

She dreamed of sitting at a table in a bookstore signing her name on the title page, smiling, *thank you so much*, the line of customers snaking through the bookshelves, out the door, curling onto the sidewalk, flowing onto the street, a flood of Karla Kurtz fans clutching copies of her debut novel, *Little Killer Girl*.

Her eyes opened. The door was opening. He had come to finish the job. Mr. Cypher was Mr. X, the man behind the scenes. Karla had sent him her writings from the workshop. He had sent them to Charity, aka Penny Diamond. Karla felt stupid.

She felt trapped. Her brain rocked from side to side; she saw a movie of her life. She was fifteen when she stabbed Chuy Medina in the *mercado* in South L.A. The cops handcuffed her to a metal table in an interview room. A red-faced cop felt her up. She learned to take care of herself, killing Benny Kelwin because he got her pregnant. She was doing real good until Charity showed her the police report; the Benny Kelwin case was still open, and the cops were hunting Karla. It was a lie and how could she get out of this hospital?

Someone outside her door.

*****

KILL THE NURSE, JOEY said.

The recovery room was a jungle of IVs, empty gurneys, a nurse wearing a face mask. Cypher shot her in the leg—another wounded non-combatant—took her beeper and cellphone.

Cypher stood over the bed of Arthur Ackerman, a handsome man with a lean tanned face and the bright fake-white smile of a film star. The eyes revealed a man on medication.

"And who might you be?"

"I am Transportation, *señor.*"

"Transportation for where?"

"To visit your father, *señor.*"

"What's the program, my man?"

"A family reunion, *señor.*"

"Where the fuck are we?"

"The elevator, *señor.*"

"Going up, going down," Arthur said. "Like it is with careers. You're lucky, you and your film star visage. I could agent you to six figures, then seven. Who are you calling?"

"*Mi esposa,*" Cypher said. "My beloved wife."

"What's your name, anyway?"

"I am called Death, *señor.*"

*****

TERI BREEDLOVE PAUSED IN the doorway to Room 505.

Her interview subject lay in bed; the room was dim. Teri saw bandages and black hair. Male or female, Teri could not see.

She put her smartphone on interview mode. *Record*, it said. A little red light flashed. Ready. A voice came from the bed: "Halt, who goes there?" Teri recognized Karla, from Red Rock Coffee, and felt better.

"It's Teri Breedlove, hon. Your fellow barista from the Red Rock."

"What's with the uniform, girl?"

"Jeremy sent me. He says you're writing a murder mystery— that's so fab—so I wanted to interview you … for my class."

"So this is a career move … interview with a victim?"

"Jeremy said you got shot. Mind if I ask where?"

"In the left butt cheek."

"Does it hurt?"

"Did you just have sex, girl?"

"Say what?"

"You're glowing like a girl scout bonfire."

"The person who shot you," Teri said, "was she a woman?"

"Nice evasion of subject. The shooter was a man."

"And why exactly did she shoot you?"

Karla hesitated. "Okay, a woman. I'll tell you if you roll me out of here."

"No way. You could die or something."

"You need money, I'll pay you big-time if—"

"Where is it?"

"Cypher's bank. I got a box."

"Why do you call him Cypher?"

"He was a captain, I was an NCO."

"You didn't answer me, hon, about the reason she shot you."

"Cypher shared with her, brought her into the loop."

"Shared what?"

"He shared my writings … from the mystery workshop."

"The manuscript?" Teri said.

"Yeah."

"You sure about that?"

"He set me up," Karla said. "He wanted her to shoot me."

"But how did she know?"

"The manuscript told the story of her life, girl. We got a love-triangle here, me and her and fucking Cypher. Now unhook these two tubes, unplug this little thing from the wall."

Teri's cell played a little tune. "Jesus loves me." The screen said Jeremy. His voice sounded tight, a tense whisper. He ordered Teri to roll the next suspect up to Room 719, two floors up. Her job was transportation, moving a so-called suspect to Room 700, at the end of the corridor. Suspected of what?

Teri tried protesting, her interview was going great—*lots of rapport, okay?* In a hard voice, Jeremy told her to move now, ASAP, no fucking around. Teri was stunned. She had never heard him swear. He didn't sound like himself. She said okay, turned back to the bed.

"Sorry, but I have to go."

"First he fucks you, then he kills you. Get me out of here, girl."

Teri stepped close. Karla reached out, grabbed her hair. Karla's eyes were angry. She said mean things about Jeremy. She accused Teri of having sex with Jeremy. She called Teri a Jezebel. Teri pried the hands away from her hair. Was everyone crazy?

*****

CYPHER HEARD A VOICE yelling in his ear. It was Joey, the crazy one. *Where the fuck are we going, bro?* Cypher told Joey to get lost. Joey wanted to control the op. It was his idea, his plan, borrowed from the *Odyssey*. *I'm the one who read the book, bro. Do what I say.* Cypher told him to back off. Arthur Ackerman opened his eyes.

"Who on earth are you talking to?" Arthur said.

"My alter ego, *señor*."

*****

KARLA TRIED TO SIT up. Her foot peeked out from under the hospital sheet. Teri saw a chain around Karla's ankle. The other end of the chain was locked onto the metal bar at the foot of the bed. Was Karla the suspect?

Teri left the room. Karla called, "Come back! We had a deal." Teri was confused, moving down the corridor, sliding into the elevator. Why was Karla chained to the bed? How had Jeremy known? She pressed the button for Seven.

No time to check with God. No time to process the new info. No time to separate fact from Karla's medicated craziness. No way to get back the innocent girl who laid on her belly in Jeremy's bed because she was competing with her mother, again and again. Was Teri excited by Sin? The elevator stopped. The doors opened at Room 733. Her brain felt clumsy. Where was Room 717?

*****

FISH ENTERED ACKERMAN'S ROOM. A big corner suite, two beds, but room for three. A big wide double-glass window leading to the fire escape. Fish imagined pushing Ackerman through that escape door, onto the platform, send him flying into space.

But there was a steel railing.

No way to boost him over.

Ackerman spoke from the bed.

"Fatso Fish," Ackerman said. "You gotta weigh three hundred pounds, boy."

"You look dead, Axel."

"Those Arabs," Ackerman said. "You sent them to fuck up my deal and look what happened."

"You can't prove that."

"And when did you decide you wanted my hotel?"

"When I heard you wanted it, Pool Boy."

"You are one sick fuck," Ackerman said.

Fish unfolded the agreement bearing the name of George Hawthorne. Ackerman shook his head. He was groggy, looped on drugs, so Fish seized his chance to gloat.

"On Monday when the banks open, I become the new owner of the fifth floor in Sedona Landing. If you should die—what a lovely thought—then my consortium will have first dibs on the whole goddamn building."

Fish felt rage, his cheeks on fire; that was the hate talking. He stood at the bedside, looking down. His fists kept clenching. He had hated Axel Ackerman since that hot summer day, catching the son-of-a-bitch in bed with his mama. Ackerman had ruined Fish's life; now he was going to pay.

Fish's eye traced the IV tube that ran from Ackerman's arm, down along the sheet, then up to a plastic bag that hung from an IV stand. He moved his hand to the little valve. If the valve lever was horizontal, it was closed. If it was vertical, aligned with the tube, it was open.

"It was just like you, revealing your total disrespect, showing up at mother's funeral," Fish said.

"Wanted to pay my respects. Despite giving birth to a moron, your mama was fine."

"What's this little tube do, anyway … this little valve?"

"Keep your fat political paws off the tubes," Ackerman said.

"You are going down, Pool Boy."

72

HELENE STEINBECK WAS RESTLESS—ENOUGH theory, enough talk. Murdock was too groggy to help. Slattery checked his messages. Nothing on Cypher's military record. No telling how long that would take, it being Friday and all.

Helene needed some air. Her brain was fuzzy. She had a hunch. She left Murdock with Connie and Slattery, walked down the corridor. Maybe there was coffee in the machine now. She met Nurse Rivera coming out of the elevator. She was agitated.

"Is there something wrong?" Helene said.

"Now I know why people don't trust their government," Rivera said.

"What's going down, girl?"

"At first," Rivera said, "I admit I felt honored. A U.S. congressman, friend of Senator Gypsum, taking a tour of our facility, so I left him with the director, but when I went back, he wasn't there."

"A fat man?" Helene said.

"With nasty eyes," Rivera said, "and a mean little smile."

Fish was in the building. Helene said thank you and

punched the button for Seven. The elevator seemed really slow; the doors took forever to close. The car stopped on Four, an orderly pushing a gurney. Helene watched the doors, heart beating fast. The elevator stopped again on Five, where two gurneys waited.

Helene left the elevator, ran to the stairs. Jerked the door open, took the stairs two at a time. Her legs were stronger now, but her knees sent pain signals as she made the turn. At the landing on Six, she phoned Murdock, back in the staff meeting room. One ring, two, she was wasting time.

*****

INSIDE ACKERMAN'S ROOM, HIRAM Fish was humming. This was his time, his moment for payback, *mine eyes have seen the glory*. He was on his feet, ambulatory. The enemy lay in bed, trussed by tubes.

Fish gripped the mattress, put his face close to the enemy. Ackerman's mouth emitted a sour odor, foul, gray as death.

No more words. Fish closed the valve. Ackerman turned his head, his eyes blazed, *for the last time*, Fish thought.

A bed rolled into the room, pushed by a blonde nurse wearing green scrubs. The patient in the bed was Lottie Ackerman Belle, her red hair hidden in bandages. The blonde in the scrubs looked familiar, a face from somewhere. She glared at Fish, told him to get away. She spoke with an accent. She was not American. Fish knew that voice. She was that hooker from Prague, the one who worked for Ackerman's daughter. The bitch from Prague had broken his nose, made it crooked for the cameras. They couldn't stop the bleeding, and Fish had flirted with death. This bitch was part of the daughter's blackmail scheme.

Out of the corner of his eye, Fish saw Ackerman's hand groping for the little metal clip that had closed off his IV drip. Scrub Girl's hand flew to the valve, made a quick turn, aligned with the tube, back to the "on" position.

Fish grabbed her wrist; this bitch owed him. He clubbed her with his fist. She grunted, fell sideways, onto Ackerman's bed.

In a groggy voice, the doped-up daughter asked what was going on.

Fish backed up to the wall. A door to his left—that was the bathroom—maybe there was a connecting door to the neighboring room.

Ackerman made a croaking noise.

Fish yanked open the door—another goddamn bathroom, no connecting door.

Movement, scuffling noises—that was Scrub-Girl charging him, brandishing a plastic tray. Holding the tray in both hands, she made a slicing motion. Fish dodged, felt a pain in his forehead, just over the eye. Fish went down, hitting hard, hurting his tailbone, hot and sharp.

He touched his head. The finger came back wet; he saw his own blood.

A voice asked what was going on.

Ackerman's bitch-daughter was up on one elbow, staring at Fish. She called him a fat bastard. Fish was out-numbered. Ackerman the Pool Boy was not dead. Fish saw his career going down the tubes.

Another bed rolled into the room, blocking the doorway— nowhere to run.

The man pushing the bed wore a blue EMT uniform, blousy trousers tucked into black boots, and a tan mountain-climber backpack.

The man looked familiar.

Fish blinked. The man was Captain Wilson, the soldier-hero from Kabul—same crazy eyes, different face.

The crazy eyes locked onto Fish. This man was insane; he was here to kill Fish.

*****

HELENE STEINBECK CAME OUT of the stairwell just in time to

see an EMT uniform wheel a gurney into Room 700.

The guy in the uniform was medium-height. He wore a blue cap and black jump boots. Helene checked her Glock. Nine rounds. Voices came from inside Room 700. Helene heard a woman mumbling.

She heard Cypher saying shut up.

Helene needed backup.

She phoned Murdock.

73

M URDOCK'S PHONE BONGED. 5.58 p.m. It was Mrs. Dorothy Stanhope, a short text message, "I found her, Mr. Detective."

Murdock's cellphone screen revealed a photo of Penny Diamond, black and white turning sepia—a photo from Amarillo, thirty years ago. Penny, looking young and pretty, was holding hands with a skinny kid, fourteen or fifteen, with the moony face of a guy in love. The kid had to be Joey Wilson. Murdock handed the phone to Connie. She loaded the photo onto her laptop. As the photo got bigger, Slattery said, "Jesus fucking Christ. Is that who I think it is?"

"It's Jeremy," Connie said. "Younger, with a different face."

*****

ACKERMAN SWAM BACK. THERE was magic juice in the IV bag; without it he was dead. If he got through the next couple of minutes, he would be happy to walk around with a goddamn IV in his vein forever.

Ackerman tried to remember the sequence of events.

He saw Fish moving toward the bed, wearing a long lab coat.

He saw Fish in a close-up, his pudgy fingers turning off the valve, sending Ackerman down the tunnel to Hell.

He saw the Czech girl wrestling with Fish, turning the valve back on, bringing Ackerman back from the dead.

He saw Lottie on the rolling bed, her voice weak, cursing Fish; they had a secret history.

He saw Cypher coming through the door, pushing a bed that held Arthur Ackerman, bloodstains on the sheets.

Ackerman got what was going on. Cypher was here to kill Ackerman's family, a staged execution, a death-ritual. Ackerman had to admit that Cypher looked good in battle dress. The fellow was a born soldier, holding a pistol with a sound suppressor, grinning down at Fatso Fish.

Cypher's laugh sounded hollow, insane, out of control. Ackerman watched as Cypher squatted down on his haunches, face to face with Fish. They were talking. "Kabul," Cypher said. "You took advantage, misused your power."

Fish said, "You murdered a Federal agent, Captain. His body has been found. You're a traitor. They'll dump you into that facility in Kansas with the crazies from Guantanamo. No one gets out of there, my fine feathered friend."

Ackerman was not tracking. What the fuck happened in Kabul? Some bad blood between Fish and Cypher, more secrets. Ackerman's brain was a slow train chugging uphill. He wanted to ask a question, but there was something wrong with his voice. The words swam in his head. Cypher knelt on the floor; his hand gripped Fish's throat.

The Czech girl held tight to Ackerman's hand.

Her nose oozed blood—that swat from Fatso Fish.

Ackerman saw movement, a flash of metal—that was Cypher hitting Fish with the pistol. A blow to the cheek, a second blow that bloodied Fish's nose. Fish crumpled, and his head flopped to the side. Cypher stood up.

Cypher's face had the woeful expression of a wounded teenager—a face that looked both hurt and hateful. He turned to Ackerman. The Czech girl moved closer, using herself as a shield between Ackerman and Cypher.

*****

CYPHER STEPPED CLOSE TO Ackerman's bed.

"Old man, you killed my dad."

"I made him rich," Ackerman said.

"He jumped three stories to his death," Cypher said. "I saw him after he landed. You and your greedy Crew destroyed my family."

"You're crazy," Ackerman said.

"Now," Cypher said. "You can say goodbye to your happy family."

Arthur spoke from his bed. "Oh, Papa, what have you gotten me into now?"

Grinning, Cypher shot Arthur in the leg.

The Czech girl grabbed Cypher's arm. He shook her off. He swiveled, shot without aiming, putting a bullet into Ackerman's daughter. She grunted, a woman on drugs.

"Two down," Cypher said. "One to go."

*****

TERI WAS THINKING THE guy on the rolling bed had eyes like Axel. He had the same nose. He was chubby; Axel was thin. The sheet did not hide the big belly. His patient tag said D. ACKERMAN. As she maneuvered the bed down the hallway toward Axel's room—*what was it, 700, the big room at the end of the hall on Seven*—Teri was feeling weird about the whole hospital deal. She looked good in the uniform; she was getting gonzo material for her class. The interview, even though unfinished, was A-Plus work, but she didn't like it that Jeremy had merked Karla Kurtz—one more lie from that dude. And he was acting really crazy. All that talking to himself, like he was out of control, like he was two people. Mama had said that Jeremy had a mean streak. Teri believed her now.

*****

BEFORE SHE ENTERED ROOM 700, Helene phoned Murdock again. He answered on the first ring.

"Where are you?"

"Headed for the great outdoors. Slattery is on board at last. Connie too. Where are you?"

"I'm outside Ackerman's room. Cypher's in there. Maybe the Czech girl. I don't know who else."

"You're going in, right?"

"I need a diversion, Murdock."

"Don't charge in like the movies, guns blazing."

"What about my diversion?"

"Where do you want it, coach?"

"The fire escape. It's right outside Axel's room."

"Okay, I remember. You went to the window and—"

"Gotta ring off, I'm moving."

*****

WITH CONNIE AND SLATTERY in the lead, Murdock rolled down a hallway toward the green Exit sign. His shoulder ached from Penny Diamond's bullet. His legs felt heavy. The sweat bloomed under his arms, felt thick on his chest.

Slattery was on his cellphone, demanding backup. Connie was checking her weapon. Murdock told them that Helene needed a diversion, maybe on the fire escape. Slattery stopped at the narrow door with a door that led outside.

The wind was cold, sharp as a knife made of bone. Connie was counting out loud, her voice quavery. "That's gotta be Room 107. We want 100, right under 700. Is this really happening?"

"That bastard fooled me," Slattery said. "Lady wants a diversion, I'll nail Cypher from the fire escape."

Connie was pushing his wheelchair. Murdock felt exhausted, trapped. Slattery used his mini-flash to locate the fire escape, a dim probing light skittering across the outside wall from

Room 100 up the outer wall to Room 700. *Perfect.*

The lower rung of the fire escape loomed ten feet above, out of reach. Connie spotted a truck with a ladder. Murdock watched as they leaned the ladder against the wall. Connie wanted to go up first. She had a history with Cypher, and she was not a woman who liked to be tricked. Slattery went first. He was the ranking officer.

Dizzy from the effort, cold from the wind, Murdock sat in his wheelchair feeling out of the action, watching Slattery climb, moving a little too fast. You never wanted to do that. *Always take your time, always keep your wits about you*, who wrote that? Some poet from Murdock's childhood, when he was reading Robert Service, those poems about the Klondike, and Rudyard Kipling, those poems about the Brits in India. Now, in the cold wind, the words slid away.

Slattery made it to the landing outside Four. Connie was on her cellphone again, "Where's the backup?"

She finished her call and started up the fire escape. Connie was young; she had strong legs. What was going on with Helene?

*****

HELENE ENTERED ROOM 700 in a sniper crawl, elbows and knees. The floor was hard. She smelled antiseptic, wounds, the fear of death. They bring you to a hospital, you never get out alive. Her head was just below the edge of the bed.

She saw green scrubs and green flip-flops; that was the Czech girl.

She saw Senator Fish, on the floor, grunting and sweating, pulling up his pant leg. The senator had fat little hands.

She saw three hospital beds, one close to the fire escape, one close to Ackerman. She saw blue trousers tucked into black paratrooper jump boots—the regulation uniform for cops and firemen and ambulance jockeys.

The boots had a high sheen; that had to be Cypher, neatness to the end.

Right hand on Axel's Colt 45., left hand supporting, Helene aimed at the nearest boot.

She squeezed the trigger, shooting through the forest of metal, bed legs, IV stands.

Her weapon did not have a sound suppressor.

The explosion filled the room.

The Czech girl screamed.

Helene saw a puff of blue from Cypher's uniform trousers.

The bed moved, exposing Helene. She was wide open to return fire.

She caught a glimpse of Cypher's face. He had used the EMT disguise to get inside. Why hadn't they thought of that?

Cypher shot at Helene. The bullet slammed into the wall. She smelled sheetrock dust.

Ackerman waved a hand, trying to say something.

On the floor, the fat senator was sitting up, using the wall to support his back. His trouser leg was up. He wore long black socks, like a CEO, regulation socks, the corporate look adopted by senators and congressmen. The little snap strap on his ankle holster was open.

In the holster was a small weapon.

Cypher said, "Senator Fish, you destroyed my Army career."

"Let me help you, son. It's not too late for—"

"I was on track to brigadier."

The Senator raised his weapon.

Cypher's gun whispered.

The senator looked surprised. *Wait a Minute! Why Me?*

A hole appeared in his forehead.

Helene heard someone coming through the door and swiveled around to see Teri Breedlove, pushing a bed. The guy on the bed was Daniel Ackerman—bandages, puffy face, his eyes closed.

Cypher turned. He was at the window, headed for the fire

escape. Grinning, he said, "You are late, soldier."

Helene fired at Cypher's torso. He took the round, rocked back, still alive—the guy had to be wearing a vest. He snapped a shot at Helene. The bullet went past; she felt that puff of wind. Had he missed on purpose? Was he that good under pressure? Teri Breedlove screamed at Cypher to stop. "Are you crazy, Jeremy?" she said. "Don't you care about anyone?"

Ackerman reached for Teri. She was already backing up. Cypher snapped a shot, and Teri squeaked, fell to the floor. A blood spot bloomed on her white nurse dress.

"Bitches," Cypher said, "all of you."

He was outside, on the fire escape.

His backpack was open; he was uncoiling a rope.

Helene was hunkered down behind Daniel Ackerman's bed. Teri Breedlove lay on the floor, blood staining her white uniform. Daniel's eyes were closed. Was he dead too? The room was thick with the smell of cordite. Helene leveled her weapon at Cypher. Teri Breedlove was crawling toward the big exit window, calling Cypher's name, blocking Helene's shot.

The rope was looped around the railing.

Cypher grinned at Helene. H looked insane; he looked in control. Helene fired again from the prone position. Her wrist was weak and wobbly. Cypher stood on the edge of the fire escape, both hands on the rope, then he pushed with his legs, launched out, away from the metal landing, and dropped out of sight.

Helene's hands shook; that was the adrenaline rush.

Ackerman was okay. The Czech girl was covering him with her body. They looked like mother and child—life was weird.

The senator lay against the wall, his fat face sagged to the side.

The gun was still in his hand.

Blood from his head leaked down his face onto his shirt and white lab coat.

Helene phoned Murdock.

"What?"

"Cypher," Helene said. "He's got a rope; he's rappelling."

*****

Murdock called out to warn Slattery, but he was too late because Cypher was already in the air, looping out from the seventh floor, looked like he was flying.

Cypher lofted himself over Slattery's head and hung there for a split second, just long enough to get off a shot. Slattery had stopped climbing. He was on the landing for the sixth floor, one hand going for the weapon, the other holding on. Cypher's weapon made a spitting sound. Slattery's knees buckled.

Connie Fremont reached the fourth floor of the fire-escape, using both hands to climb.

Cypher bounced off the wall like a professional rappeller.

The bounce put him level with Connie. His gun was out. She turned to face him, said something using his name. His pistol fired, sounded like someone coughing. Connie grabbed her leg—maybe he missed on purpose, for old times' sake. Connie had dated the guy. She dropped her Beretta, sagged to one knee.

"Jeremy," she said, "goddamn, you why did you …."

Connie's weapon bounced off the fire escape and landed with a crunch in the gravel under the windows. Dark under there. If Murdock could reach it, would the weapon still fire? Murdock left the chair in what felt like slow motion.

Cypher was one bounce away from the ground. He pushed off, soaring.

Murdock was huffing as he scrambled toward the Beretta. Cypher arced out from the wall, his left side to Murdock, no sign of his weapon.

Murdock had time—two seconds, maybe three.

Cypher's boots touched down.

His left leg crumpled under him. It was too dark to see his

face, but Murdock sensed something was off. The guy had lost some poise, maybe some balance.

Cypher's left hand gripped the rope. He was steady now.

Murdock stumbled, kept his head down. Where was Connie's gun?

Pale light came from the windows at ground level, making trapezoids against the dark. Connie's pistol was lost in shadow.

Murdock went to his knees, fumbled for the weapon. There. Cold steel, cold night wind.

A voice came from above—Helene calling Murdock's name, sounding concerned. And then a light beamed down, a cone of sudden brightness that located Cypher, holding his pistol in both hands, giving Murdock one last weary grin—two wounded warriors, a face-off at the end of the world, they should be working together, there was evil everywhere—but in that instant it was kill or be killed and the light was on Cypher, throwing half his face into shadow.

Murdock squeezed off his round.

There were three shots.

One came from Murdock—Connie's pistol worked.

One came from Cypher, that whispery sound.

One came from Helene Steinbeck, shooting down from the landing on Seven.

Cypher's shot tore out a jagged chunk of wall two feet from Murdock's nose. Did he do that on purpose?

Helene's shot missed Cypher's head, but broke his shoulder.

Murdock's shot hit Cypher in the throat.

Murdock sagged. He heard Helene's voice calling, "Are you all right, Murdock? Are you all right?"

74

A RECORD DAY FOR Helene Steinbeck and guns and confiscation.

First they confiscated her Glock Nine.

Then they confiscated Ackerman's Colt .45.

Helene had used her Glock to take out Penny Diamond, the mystery woman who rose up out of the past, a figure from a ghost story. Penny wanted revenge. How much had Cypher paid her? How well had Penny known Karla Kurtz?

Ackerman's .45, inherited from his father, put the first bullet hole into Cypher, slowing him down, forcing him to split before he completed *his* quest for revenge.

The cops took the Glock in the penthouse spa at noon.

They took the chrome-plated .45 outside the CRMC—a world lit by spotlights from the official police vehicles, where Helene had been twisting a tourniquet to slow the bleeding in Connie Fremont's leg wound, one more bullet from Cypher.

Connie was pissed off. "Goddamn Jeremy, anyway. That leg was my best feature."

Helene was thinking about cops and crime and confiscation when Slattery answered another phone call. Flagstaff had even more snow, more ice, more sleet, more traffic woes. All available units were helping out. Slattery was still in charge at the CRMC. Wounded and waiting in line for his turn in the OR, he worked the command post from his bed.

The four survivors were camped out in Exam Room number 2 at the CRMC, the same room where Murdock had spent the afternoon on his back, dozing, resting, mulling over his multiple crime theories—while Helene did the sleuth work.

Connie's metal bed was next to Slattery's. They were starting to look like a couple. Murdock was back in his wheelchair, downing his coffee.

Helene was still on her feet, playing gofer for the wounded, moving between the exam room and the coffee machine.

Slattery talked, Connie took notes. They were both on pain meds.

"So," Slattery said. "Here's what we got—correct me if I miss something. The guy from Miami, Arthur, he's dead—two gunshots. The guy from Boston, Daniel, he's dead, but not from a gunshot."

"What killed Daniel?" Murdock said.

"His ticker got him," Slattery said. "He was heavy, right?"

"Right on the edge of obesity," Helene said.

"We also got ourselves a dead senator," Slattery said. "I still don't get why he was here. He and Gypsum could have announced that running mate bullshit in Tucson or Phoenix or even Dallas and had more of a crowd."

"It's Gypsum's home base," Helene said, "and Fish was here to pester Ackerman. They had a fifty-year feud going, something that started with Fish's mother."

"Fish sent those Arabs," Murdock said. "He had no idea Cypher wanted payback from Ramsay. He wanted info on the Tuesday night massacre."

"I always voted Republican," Slattery said, "but this guy Fish turned my stomach. This time around, I'm going Independent."

"Be still, my heart," Connie said.

"Speaking of Republicans, did that Featherstone guy make it?"

"They've still got him in the ICU," Murdock said.

"I shot him," Connie said, "after he shot Murdock."

"Good job, Fremont," Slattery said. "Because of you, I'll be up to my ass in suits from Homeland Security."

"Featherstone worked for Fish," Connie said. "Fish hated Lottie. We still don't know why."

"There was also something going on with Fish and Iveta," Helene said. "Like they knew each other from before."

"Europe," Murdock said. "Good reason for a trip, checking on the Paris-Prague Connection."

"Back to my list," Slattery said. "We got the daughter in surgery. The Czech chick's gonna get a medal for saving our resident billionaire. We got the blonde tennis cutie in Recovery. Why the hell did Cypher shoot her?"

"Revenge," Connie said.

"Revenge for what?"

"Revenge on women," Connie said. "The entire female species."

"What's up with that?" Slattery said. "I heard he was hung like Tarzan, divorcées lined up for servicing."

"Maybe they'll find something at Jeremy's house," Connie said, "like who Jeremy really was."

"What happens to Karla Kurtz?" Helene said.

"Up in the air," Slattery said. "Why do you worry about her?"

"She's got talent," Helene said. "We bonded, two female writers in a world dominated by dead white guys."

"Confession time," Slattery said. "I asked her out a couple times. Both times she broke every goddamn date. What am I, chopped liver?"

"Karla only dates guys with money," Helene said. "She wrote about that in the workshop."

"As the ranking professional first-responder commander," Slattery said. "I am hereby commanding you to hand over every word she wrote."

"She took her manuscript back," Helene said. "You'll need a court order."

"Are you charging Karla?" Murdock said.

"I would," Slattery said, "only I got nothing on her. Cypher's dead, so is the redheaded tile-setter. But I do have a question—who made that call to Raul that sent Steinbeck to rescue Ackerman?"

Silence in the room, then Connie said, "Raul said it was Javier."

"Who the fuck is Javier?"

"Javier is Ackerman's ball boy," Helene said.

"How did he know?"

Murdock held up his hand, like a kid in school asking for permission to speak. "I got a theory, boss."

Slattery moaned, "Another fucking theory. I'm too tired for this."

"Let's hear it," Connie said. "Murdock did good on the TFK."

"If we don't nail Kurtz," Slattery said, "it's one-half of a TFK. Unless you count Penny/Charity as two females, which sounds okay at this time, in this place, at this moment in the history of—"

Murdock said, "Cypher made the call to Raul."

"No way."

"That makes sense," Helene said.

"No way," Slattery said.

"Cypher wanted both assassins dead," Murdock said. "He needed to clear the decks for his big finale. He knew Helene could shoot. He made the call, knowing that Penny/Charity was going after Karla. He sent Helene up there to execute Penny/Charity."

"No fucking way," Slattery said. "Cypher wanted Ackerman dead. No way he would … oh, shit, I didn't see it until now."

"Family reunion?" Connie said. "You said it earlier."

"I need a vacation," Slattery said.

Helene said, "Speaking of Grand Finales, did anyone notice that book in Cypher's office?"

No one said anything.

"It was a translation of the *Odyssey*," Helene said. "Odysseus takes ten years to get home from the Trojan War, leaving the little woman alone with a houseful of randy suitors. When Odysseus gets home, he executes the suitors."

"So Cypher used a goddamn book as a training manual?"

"Moral support from the classics," Helene said. "A warrior back from the wars cleans out the bad stuff."

"I can't believe I missed it," Slattery said. "That sucker Cypher has been here six or seven years, wearing khaki suits like a mask, ticking like a fucking time bomb."

"It took him that long to set things up," Murdock said.

Helene said, "Remember when Murdock laid out Cypher's profile? He said Cypher was precise, a slicer-dicer. He was a planner, a tactician. He used people and they didn't know they were being used."

"Like Teri Breedlove," Slattery said.

"Like me," Connie said.

"Like me," Murdock said.

"How did he use you?" Connie said.

"He wanted to be my pal," Murdock said. "We were both ex-military. We'd both seen combat. I liked the guy. A shrink could say we bonded."

"I wish you people had been on that elk hunt," Slattery said. "Out there in the bush, poor fucking Cypher couldn't find his ass with a rearview mirror. His hands were shaky; he dropped rounds into the dirt. I helped him pick them up, wipe off the pine needles. It was all a big fucking act."

"Maybe we'll know when the Army sends Cypher's records," Helene said.

"I hate to be the fool guy," Slattery said.

"Don't you mean Fall Guy?" Connie said.

The door opened to admit Iveta Macek, pushing Ackerman on a rolling bed. Ackerman's face was working, moving between sadness and relief. Two sons were dead; one daughter was alive. The docs were saying 70/30 on Lottie's chances.

"I wanted to say great work," Ackerman said. "I wanted to thank you all. The worst part for me was not being able to help my boys. The best part was watching my contract employee nail Cypher with my Papa's Colt .45. Who's got the weapon?"

"Forensics," Slattery said. "They'll send it to Tucson."

Ackerman said. "I'll pay good money to get it back."

"You trying to bribe law enforcement?" Slattery said.

"Hey, Steve, it's a fucking heirloom."

The door opened again and Nurse Rivera came in with an orderly. They had two ORs open—one for Connie, one for Slattery. Connie went first. As they rolled Slattery out, he passed his list to Helene.

"Finish up for me, Steinbeck."

"Yes, Lieutenant."

Ackerman said, "They're bumping you up to Captain, Steve. We'll have a party, my treat."

They congratulated Slattery on his promotion. He blushed. When the door closed, Ackerman turned to Helene and Murdock. He was eager to close the deal on Sedona Landing. Cypher was dead; he needed to be replaced. Life goes on. Business is business. Find another banker, get things moving.

Ackerman reminded Helene she had a contract to sign. Then he offered Murdock an identical contract—one year, one million dollars. Helene shook her head. She was tired; she needed to be with Murdock. But through the fuzz of fatigue, she noticed that Ackerman's tone was different. When he had first offered her a contract, the subtext was sex—he had come on to her like a suitor. Today, wheeled in by Iveta Macek, Ackerman was all business.

With Murdock, Ackerman's tone shifted from adversarial to paternal. He was counting on Murdock to replace two dead sons. With his business completed, Ackerman nodded at Iveta Macek. She wheeled him out. Murdock grinned at Helene.

"What?" she said.

"Macek's butt was wagging."

"Pregnant girl on the prowl," Helene said.

"She could do worse."

"Three decades apart," Helene said, "but their vibes are totally in synch."

The door opened. It was Nurse Rivera again. Mr. Ackerman had arranged a room for them on the sixth floor.

"Come along," she said. "It's kind of a bridal suite."

75

H ELENE LEFT THE BED.

She padded into the bathroom, carrying the flimsy hospital slippers.

She slipped off her vest and pulled off her shirt, splotches of Daniel Ackerman's blood.

She sat on the little shower stool and peeled off her socks, checked her feet.

She unbuckled, stepped out of her jeans.

Her face in the mirror looked like her mother's before she got sick. Before she turned gray and bony and old. Before she stopped wearing lipstick. There was a stubby lipstick in Helene's shoulder bag. The cops had taken the shoulder bag, along with Ackerman's heirloom weapon—evidence in a shooting.

She removed her brassiere, stepped out of her panties.

A sign on the shower reminded users to conserve water.

FIVE MINUTE SHOWERS, FOLKS. ARIZONA IS HIGH DESERT.

The spray was misty, comforting, cleansing.

Helene kept seeing Cypher leaping off the fire escape outside

Room 700. She kept seeing his eyes looking at her, the eyes of a lonely boy wanting to be understood.

There in the room Helene had shot at Cypher three times—leg, torso, foot—and a fourth shot from the balcony. His return fire had been warning shots—*stay down, you're not part of this.* Remembering those moments brought a sudden chill, Helene's brain running a list of Cypher's victims—five old guys from the Crew, four Arabs, two hookers, Ramsay and Latimer, Ackerman's sons, Senator Fish, kills in Afghanistan, maybe more. She felt lucky to be alive.

Helene rinsed her hair twice. She wanted to stay in the shower, but there was that five-minute limit, the sign on the door.

She turned off the water. Dried off, thought of Murdock.

The hair dryer was weak. She cleaned the lint off, the dryer hummed. The green scrubs sat on a shelf in the bathroom cabinet. They were worn from multiple washings.

They smelled clean, innocent, all the memories washed away. Sickness and death. She put on the scrubs. They felt soft on her skin, accepting. She pulled on the hospital robe. Stepped into the slippers. Opened the door to the room.

The TV was going, the sound off. Murdock lay propped by pillows, his eyes closed. Two wine bottles sat on the rollaway table. Two plastic glasses. The corkscrew came from Connie Fremont, Sedona party girl.

Helene stood beside the bed.

Murdock opened his eyes. His smile was a mixture of wary and alert.

"Lady needs serious mechanical assistance," she said.

"I was thinking about you," he said.

"You do the corkscrew," she said. "I'll hold on."

He used the foil cutter. When the foil was off, he positioned the corkscrew, did two twists, stopped. The tip of the screw was off-center, crooked from the start. He cranked it out.

"Crap," he said.

"Let me."

He handed over the corkscrew. Helene had been opening wine bottles since she was twelve. Her mother was French. There was always wine for dinner, wine for cooking. She popped the cork—that puffing sound, that grape smell. The wine was red, a Pinot Noir from Ackerman. He'd had a case delivered from his Sedona Landing wine-room.

They touched glasses. She missed the clinking sound of glass against glass. Were they going to be okay? Helene decided to go first.

"I have a confession," Helene said.

"It's about time," Murdock said.

"Karla was writing about two women killers. I didn't mention it because you and I were, well, you know. So then this morning—it seems like a long time ago—when she read to the class and her two killers pushed a guy over a railing, I had that sinking feeling, my world falling apart. But you and I weren't communicating—surely you remember that little rift between us?—so I couldn't share my suspicions with you. And then the class was over and Karla scooted out before I could grab her—she had a massage date with Ackerman. There was the political crowd and the senator's press conference, and Ackerman's daughter …. I'm not sure what good it would have done anyway, maybe fewer lives saved. I'm trying to sort it out now, so …."

"So you're saying it was my fault?"

"I didn't say that," Helene said. "What I said was, maybe if you and I had been communicating, then we could have talked it over … and if we had known, we could have been ready for Penny, who had another name in Karla's writing, and … so, yeah, maybe it is your fault."

"Whoa," Murdock said. "Hold up a minute, Steinbeck. You're blaming me for the fact that you missed a clue?"

"I'm only telling you what happened," Helene said. "We were talking, but not saying anything. You were busy sizing up Deputy Fremont."

"And you were busy with your favorite billionaire."

"I'd be happy with a simple acknowledgment of complicity," Helene said.

"Complicity about what?"

"The rending of our relationship." Helene took a sip of wine. They were talking now, and that was good, and she felt the atmosphere soften. Murdock was looking at her the same way he had looked at her in Taos, that first time in her SUV, sizing her up. "I confessed," she said. "Now it's your turn."

"My turn to what?"

"To confess," Helene said.

"Confess to what?"

"You know very well what, big guy."

"Okay," Murdock said. "I'm sorry too."

"Good start," she said.

"Well," Murdock said, "I'm glad that's over."

"You keep going," she said. "I want more from you."

"More of what?"

"More confession, more emotion, more feeling—I want you to dig deep, Murdock."

"Okay," he said. "I did not have sex with Connie Fremont."

"Good thinking," she said. "What else?"

"I'm sorry I bugged you about Ackerman's job offer."

"Yeah," she said. "What was that all about?"

"Alpha male," Murdock said. "I was jealous. Sorry for that. I was out-classed. I was—"

"We were together," Helene said. "We shared everything. I still owe you for that loan in Taos. What were you thinking?"

"I was playing big hero in Taos," he said. "I had you in my clutches."

"I remember liking that," she said, "being in your clutches."

"How are your feet?"

"Better every day."

There was silence while they sipped their wine—another dumb game show played on the TV. Helene turned it off. The dead screen watched her, like a giant eyeball. She covered it with a hospital towel, sat on the edge of her bed. Her hair was still damp from the shower.

"How are you doing with the Taos nightmares?"

"No nightmares since we got to Sedona," she said.

"I used to like Taos," he said.

"The summer was wonderful," she said.

"You sure about your feet being okay?"

"Are you asking about my body?" she said.

"Yes."

"Specific parts?"

"Yes."

"Can you say the words?"

"How are your specific body parts?"

She laughed. He laughed. She had forgotten his crazy sense of humor.

"Tell me why you care," she said.

"Aside from being greedy about a pleasure hitherto unbeknownst to man?"

Helene's cheeks got hot. Where did Murdock find language like that?

"Yes," she said, "aside from that."

"I couldn't protect you on the manhunt," he said. "I felt guilty."

"It was my idea," she said. "We had to split up."

"I hate to fail," Murdock said.

"He would have killed you, and forced me to watch."

"You could have been killed."

"I told you I could handle him. We were out-numbered—to divide his forces, we had to split up. It worked out okay."

"I still feel bad," he said.

She had been sitting on the edge of her bed, across from Murdock.

Now she moved to the edge of Murdock's bed and pressed her hip against his leg.

She held out her wine glass.

They touched, plastic to plastic. Helene pretended to hear the musical bong, glass against glass, candle-light flickering , a nice restaurant. She thought of Axel's million dollars, what money would buy. His eyes glistened.

She put her hand on Murdock's leg.

His eyes were wet, tears on both cheeks.

She had known him for three months. She had never seen him cry.

"What else?" she said.

"I wondered if we were finished," Murdock said. "All these signals—the book, the workshop, the million dollar offer. I knew you needed them, but it drove a wedge between us."

"The rape left me feeling ashamed," Helene said. "I needed reassurance, confirmation that I was okay. I was trying to wipe away the shame."

"Did it hurt?" Murdock said.

"Why didn't you ask me before?"

"I was afraid of losing you," he said.

"Move over," Helene said.

The bed was narrow. Murdock eased over. Helene swung her legs up. She turned onto her side, facing Murdock. She smelled the antiseptic; it wafted up from the arm dressing.

"So," she said, "what would you like to do now?"

"What are my options?"

"We could visit Axel," she said.

"He'll be surrounded by Iveta Macek."

"I could wheel you down to the staff meeting room. Take another look at our mind-map."

"I have it all up here." Murdock tapped his forehead.

"Or," she said, "we could stay here, lock the door, finish this wine …. You sleepy?"

"With you heating up the bed? No way."

Helene kissed his cheek. Her weight touched his wounded shoulder. He grunted.

She kissed his mouth, ran her tongue along his lips. He grunted again. She moved her hand to his belly. He was wearing a hospital gown. She pulled the gown up, moved her hand down, felt his reaction, Murdock back from the dead.

She was still wearing the green scrubs.

She told him to hold his horses.

The robe fell to the floor.

The green scrub blouse was a pullover. She left the blouse on, felt a chill as she stepped out of her floppy trousers. Keeping her hand on Murdock, she walked around the bed. Her fingers traced a line from his knee, down the shin, to his feet. She felt rough scars from that grisly Sunday manhunt. He was ready; her heart beat faster. She almost made a smart remark about going off half-cocked, but then stopped. Their best sex had been wordless. She climbed onto the bed, the right side, away from his wounded arm. She swung her leg over, straddling him, whispering. Am I hurting your shoulder? No, it's okay. Are you sure? Yes. Is this okay? Yes. Is this? Yes, it's okay.

There were more tears now. She licked them away. He nodded, wordless signal. She raised up, feeling ready. Feeling Murdock's love.

Photo by Jerry Jaz

ROBERT J. RAY IS the author of nine novels: *Cage of Mirrors,* *The Heart of the Game, Bloody Murdock, Murdock for Hire,* *Dial "M" for Murdock, Merry Christmas, Murdock, Murdock* *Cracks Ice, Murdock Tackles Taos,* and now, *Murdock Rocks* *Sedona.* Ray is also the author of a popular non-fiction series on writing, *The Weekend Novelist.* He shares techniques on writing at bobandjackswritingblog.com. A native of Texas, Ray holds a PhD from the University of Texas, Austin. Tuesdays and Fridays, he writes at Louisa's Bakery and Café in Seattle.

For more information, go to www.robertjrayauthor.com.

Made in the USA
Charleston, SC
25 November 2015